Bruce Arnold was born in England and educated at Kingham Hill School in Oxfordshire, and then in Ireland at Dublin University, where he read English and French. He is Literary Editor of *The Irish Independent*, and has been a journalist working in Ireland throughout his professional life. His books include *Orpen: Mirror to an Age*, the life of the painter, William Orpen, *Margaret Thatcher*, *A Study in Power*, and a book on modern Irish politics, *What Kind of Country*. His *Art Atlas of Britain and Ireland*, and a life of the Irish Abstract Cubist painter, Mainie Jellett, are to appear in 1991, as well as a book on James Joyce and *Ulysses*. His *Coppinger Chronicles*, a related group of four novels, will be followed by a further sequence, on which he is currently at work.

Praise for *The Coppinger Chronicle*:

'These are marvellous stories. No one writes better of the child's horror and humiliation at the careless hands of the passionate, unpredictable, imperfect father who doesn't measure up. What Arnold writes stays with you; long after the detail is forgotten the base not of anguish lingers to sound on in the reader's mind'

Grace Ingoldby

'The writing is confident, compelling, even beautiful. What counts is the quality of his voice, the finished style, the resonance of his language'

Financial Times

THE COPPINGER CHRONICLES

Running to Paradise

Bruce Arnold

An Abacus Book

First published in Great Britain in 1983 by Hamish Hamilton Ltd
This edition published in Abacus by Sphere Books Ltd 1991

Printed in Great Britain by
The Guernsey Press Co Ltd, Guernsey, Channel Islands

ISBN 0 349 10209 2

Sphere Books Ltd
A Division of
Macdonald and Co (Publishers) Ltd
Orbit House
1 New Fetter Lane
London EC4A 1AR

A member of Maxwell Macmillan Pergamon Publishing Corporation

For Mab

We have taken from the defeated
What they had to leave us—a symbol:
A symbol perfected in death.
And all shall be well and
All manner of things shall be well
By the purification of the motive
In the ground of our beseeching.

T.S.Eliot: Little Gidding
III 193–199

Chapter One

That is Betelgeuze, I thought. Dimly there came back to me words my father had used when I was a child, and with his drunken finger he had stabbed into the visage of the stars, prompting his uncertain memory: alpha, beta, gamma, delta, epsilon, wild gestures, uncertain recollection, awkward skeins, invisible, between the crystalline glowing spots of distant light; and from them he was asking me to imagine the figure of a man spread out in the heavens. But what was it about Betelgeuze? Shoulder of a giant. Angry, and incoherent, its power, its enormity, suppressed within that distant, dull red glow. What more serious aspect was there to be remembered about that single star, remembered because he had always said to me: how remarkable, how amazing? And again, from the obscure past of a forgotten roadway in the country at night, between pub and lodging, there came back to me the unreliable facts that had dropped with sonorous portent from his inebriated lips. Betelgeuze, he had said, was so large that if its centre occupied the place in the universe which was occupied by the centre of our sun, then we would be inside it, burnt to nothing at all. That was the main point, as he gave it to me, not once but many times, amazement slurred by inebriation. At first I believed him, with a thrilled excitement. Then I questioned it, and checked, and found he was right anyway. And now, years later, I was puzzled and in doubt all over again. Had I remembered correctly? Wasn't *our* sun, itself

1

a star in the firmament, 93 million miles away? 93 million miles! That meant that Betelgeuze had a diameter of more than 200 million miles! Was it possible?

On the balcony, in that city at night, sceptic as I was, I tried, as I had tried so many times before, to make the mind encompass once again certain undisputed, indisputable facts about this single star. It was not as if it was altogether the most important star in the heavens; nor was it the brightest, nor the most romantic. Facts about it were as extraordinary or as ordinary as the mind made them. The more astronomy intruded, the more we came to grips with its stranger aspects, the more we got scale and distance under control. Betelgeuze, being a red star, had a more lumpen quality about its light: solid, reliable, it did not flash and sparkle in the way that some did. It was not 'eloquently bright'; it was one of the 'patient' stars.

I knew it, remembered it, only through him. Coming home in the evening, as I have said, from country pubs, climbing the hillside of a southern town, preparing to part company once more, he would pause, the old navigator, retired naval man, and point up to the dark, star-studded skies, at Cassiopeiae, the Dog Stars, the Great Bear, the Little Bear, the Pleiades, and Orion. And, 'Canst thou bind the sweet influence of Pleiades?' he would ask me, his voice responding to the splendid quotation with perhaps a slightly exaggerated vibrato, and he would pause, and with even greater stress ask me: 'Or loose the bands of Orion?' And of course, before the rhetoric of paternal love, I would remain silent. And in the darkness he would look at me. Then he would say, 'Oh no, my son. It's not possible. And what does it matter? In a thousand years . . . in ten thousand years, what will be the odds? That is not the beginning, even, of enough time for the light itself to reach us. Hundreds of thousands of years. Millions of years. What does anything matter?' And I can see him frozen drunkenly in an attitude of disdainful astonishment, eyes wide, hands spread, dramatically dismissing the world and all its works.

Of all the constellations in the heavens Orion was his favourite. Though the names of stars and their formations in the sky tripped off his lips like poetry, there was something

2

about Orion that made him pause. It was as if the warrior was a challenge to him; or that he saw himself picked out and held fast between those points of fire. In me it had created also an instinctive response to the four outer stars, the three inner ones, girding the loins of that wild, free figure poised for some fearful, angry act.

Orion was faint, that night, as are all the stars over London; and it was low in the sky, making it more obscure. The firmament above contended poorly with the lights below. Giving thought to the stars at all was a tribute to him. But the very surge of thought itself, like a wave breaking on the shore, was fading back now, with a hiss and rustle of foam and debris, leaving me once again with the bare chamber of worry that had woken me up.

I listened, but no sound came from the room behind me. She was still asleep. I pulled tighter on the cord of my dressing gown, beginning to feel faintly cool in the night air, trying to make up my mind what to do, looking upon the stars for the answers which they never give. Why did he have this effect on me? Why did a letter from him prove to be both a pleasure and a burden, waking me up with worry, then filling my mind with sweet and sensitive memories? Why was I still obsessed with him?

Love mingled with fear: fear of humiliation? No, that was a thing of the past. Embarrassment, awkwardness, just the simple fact of his intrusion into what was now my adult life, was it that which weighed on me? What was my 'adult life'? I was approaching twenty-eight, had a reasonable job, a nice flat, was living with a girl who had at first attracted me, and was now beginning to seem a part almost of my inner life. So why should I fear his intrusion? All of that was in the past, surely? Those seemingly endless school-days at Coppinger, over which he had cast his shadow, all that was over. The humiliations of his drunkenness, of his poverty, of his growing decrepitude, the degradation of him being 'at the end of his tether': those were aspects of life from which I had long since walked away. Did I need to be haunted by them now?

Perhaps not, but I was. For me, the advent, in whatever form, of my father meant trouble. It had meant trouble

3

at school, when he had tumbled in on my life there with his misplaced concern, shrouded in the fumes of Dutch courage. It meant trouble now. His letters were like the distant bugle calls of a skirmishing party, heading into action. They threatened me, my life, the cosy superficiality of youthful, uncertain love. Instinct told me: keep him and Sarah apart, hold him at a distance, hope and pray that the old skirmisher will go elsewhere.

Yet at the same time I wanted him. I needed him for guidance. For judgment perhaps. In some vague, apologetic way, I wanted him to help me with my life. Something was wrong; I could not define what, but some prickly, creeping unease inspired my sense of need for his guiding hand. I was ashamed of him, but I was also ashamed of my shame. I wanted him for his approval, I also wanted to keep him away, in case his impact should do damage, in case his reaction might not be the one I wanted. The waves of conflicting thought nagged at me. The glow of the city right across the sky, the pinkish light rising on all sides, belittled Betelgeuze. Nothing made sense. A single candle, held close to the eyeball, would obscure all the candle-power of London. London made faint this star, so large that even to comprehend its size strained the capability of the mind.

One thought never crossed my mind. It was to be some years yet before the further possibility would come home to me, that perhaps he needed me. Perhaps his swiftly written, purposeful letters, letters so like the man himself, sudden, open, peremptory, were calls from a wilderness the true barrenness of which had always been concealed by the energy and determination with which he strode around within his own doomed territory. And it is only retrospectively that I see the faintest shreds of evidence that, beneath the surface of my self-centred nature, within the calculating framework of weighing up his pleas against my own interests, there was a faint subconscious response to his suppressed cry for – for what? Approval? Affection? Endorsement of his acts? I can only ponder on it, now, in a broad range of questions that will never be answered; and hope that my present bewilderment about him, and those meetings in my own early manhood, was matched then by a lack of awareness on his part over just how little his needs registered on my self-centred nature. I would not want him to know, even now, the full extent of this particular confession.

September had just come, and the fine, dry weather of late August that year, which otherwise had been unusually cool throughout the whole summer, seemed set to go on.

Up there in the heavens, I thought, goes Mariner Two. We, in the West, are answering the Russians. If they can put Gagarin up there, then we also must put our own man into space. Meanwhile, a closer look at Venus was what I vaguely realised was the objective of the invisible, man-made space traveller.

From behind me, in the room, I heard Sarah call my name. Then stillness.

'I'm on the balcony.'

Her voice was soft and sleepy. 'Why are you on the balcony?' Pause. 'I want you.'

I did not answer. In the darkness I smiled to myself, looking down at the lamplight shining up through the large plane tree in the garden. I stretched, a feeling of animal well-being running through me, a feeling too of desire.

She called again.

'If you want me. Then I'll come.'

'I do.' The wish was expressed with sleepy hesitation. I could imagine the way she was lying, across towards my side of the bed, on her front, her hands spread out as if stalking towards me to make a capture. She wore nothing in bed. During the summer she had gone to France, to the South, and she was very brown. Her long hair was bleached by the sun. It was long. I liked to hold it and brush it. Sometimes, when I was angry with her, I would hold her by her hair, tight in behind her head making it hurt, making the tears come into her eyes. Standing there on the balcony I thought about her, trying to make up my mind. Even after she had given sleepy expression to her own desire, triggering mine in turn, I went on standing there trying to decide what to do, trying to work out why it was that desire, at times, could put feelings to flight.

'What are you doing out there?'

'I'm looking at the stars.'

5

'But you can't see them in London. You've always said that. Too much light, you say.'

'I imagine where they are.'

'Do come,' she said.

She was moist. I loved it like that. But it was too quick. Later, it was better. Afterwards she said, 'What are we doing this weekend?'

'I'm going to see my father.'

'Am I to come?'

I didn't answer for a while. I liked the way she phrased the question.

'I don't think you would want to,' I said.

'Perhaps if you asked me you'd find out.'

She lay in the crook of my arm and I looked down at her shoulders. 'It will soon be too cold to lie like this.'

'Then we shall make love in front of the gas fire.'

'Or just under the covers. It's quite normal, you know.'

She laughed. 'You still haven't asked me.'

'I know.'

'Will you?'

'I'll decide tomorrow.'

'But it is tomorrow.'

'No. It's never tomorrow.'

'Have it your own way,' she said.

I pulled the counterpane over us both without answering, and thought, if only it was as easy as that, if only I knew what my own way was. On the one hand I was relieved at the slight nature of her persistence; on the other hand I felt that it was a reflection on us. Did it not matter, either way? Above all, I remembered her saying to me, at the beginning of it all, that it was no use, her art came first. And while I, also, at the time, had spoken words which echoed hers, I had doubted that she meant it in quite that ruthless fashion.

Her warm body close against mine kept me awake, staring up in the dim bedroom light at the corniced ceiling, remembering the strange intensity of that first meeting.

She had been with a man, a fellow student. It had been at a party given by my brother, Francis. Philpotts, with whom we had both been at school, at Coppinger, was back from the American university on the west coast where he taught. An

6

artist or two had seemed appropriate, and, among others, there were three girls in the flat below studying at the Royal College of Art.

My first preoccupation had been the man with her, another art student who had come uninvited with the three girls, to the intense annoyance of Francis. His name was Brian, and he was tall and good-looking, dressed in a loose-fitting, blue, smock-like jerkin, and with a scarf tied at his neck. He had studiously ignored my brother's flashing eyes, had smiled winningly, and had offered a bottle of Algerian wine. He stood close beside Sarah, when I met her first of all, staring at her in a completely possessive way. He seemed to me altogether too close, physically, as though he wanted to fall upon her and devour her. She talked about Metzinger and Gris, and asked why they and all the others had retreated from the reality of pure abstract. And her eyes were bright and intense as she spoke of the essential harmony of form and colour liberated from the object. I wanted to respond to that, but all I could think of was the size and closeness of Brian. He stood sideways on to her, and inspected her face, his eyes moving up and down, like a fly walking about on a window. Sarah was speaking to me, every word vital to the argument she was putting forward: speed in the age we lived in, and visual images in profusion, had swept away the contemplative stillness of representational art. It lay shattered all around us. And we were picking up the pieces. The most we could possess were pieces of it, fragments. I agreed, and watched Brian's eyes as they crawled over her clear profile inspecting possessively her animated features. All I wanted to do was brush him away, and have her to myself. *Then*, how I would discuss Metzinger and Gris, Braque and Léger, Picasso and Severini! Anyone she liked! It would be different without Brian, just the two of us; and art. And different it had been; wonderfully so, to begin with.

Brian was easily dispatched. A week or so, and he was gone. And we were more alone, then. There was art, of course. Lots of it. And it did obsess us both. She set it far above people, in her life. I was disposed to do the same, in mine. Agreement between us on this was readily reached. Yet somehow, though Brian had gone, a shadow remained

7

over the clear light of rational assessment. A point had been missed, in that first vivid flood of words, about the nature of art as she saw it. The point was not about art, but about her and me; about us. And each time afterwards, the raid upon inarticulate matter became more difficult. Metzinger and Gris, who had briefly featured as powerful commanders in vast territories of form and colour, became just names again, the ragged forces of their spent ideas slipping into the background again.

I was to be made ashamed, in time, of my very limited attempts to understand her. Instead of coming to terms with what she was trying to do, I came to terms only with myself as an increasingly preoccupied spectator. It took time, of course. And my negative judgments were lamentably wrong. But I must confess, at the outset, how little I sought to know about the clear intent of her mind as she put together shapes and patterns within an exact discipline of scale. I should have been more responsive to the authority of form to which she submitted herself with such suppressed enthusiasm. She almost revelled in its containing force; yet, increasingly, on the occasions when she tried to explain it to me, I was indifferent. Only when it did not matter any more, when it was lost, did I regret the neglect, the indifference.

That lay in the future, and we shall come to it. But lying there beside her, in the darkness, not sleeping, listening to her soft breathing, I recognised and tried to dispel the mirror-reflections of myself which the closeness of her flesh projected. Did the translation of this object of desire, brown, soft, sweet-smelling, lubricious, into a woman who thought and was ambitious, did it represent a challenge? Were Sarah's explanations of her work, her questions as to whether she should come with me to see my father, all evidence of layers of character, aspects of personality, elements of demand in her, which I perhaps would rather have ignored?

She had said, at the outset, that her art came first. And of course I had agreed. But had I, at the same time, erected similarly dismissive values setting artificial restraints upon the depth to which we could go on understanding one another?

8

I pushed her away. Gently. I could never sleep touching her. The only person I had ever slept touching was my father. Creeping into bed with him in the middle of the night, unable to contend with darkness or with dreams, I could still picture in my mind those very rooms in which our beds lay side by side, twenty years before, when I had been seven or eight. That was shortly after my mother's death. I had been sent to Coppinger. And the early holidays had brought together the two of us, in modest bedsitters, for a few weeks at Christmas, Easter, and longer in the summer. Was it to be expected, the waking in the dark, the awful loneliness? Then the comfort of snuggling in behind him, head down against his huge shoulder, knowing he would not send me away, just offer the reassurance of his murmured approval.

With her, the gentle disentangling was the prelude to sleep. Turning over, I thought again of that star, where it fixes the point of movement of Orion's right arm, the shoulder pivot for that Herculean club, grasped in savage hand. And it brought my mind away from her and back to my father. Our meetings were erratic now. Yet in the past month or so there had been a spate of letters, starting after a fairly long silence, running through the indicators of recovery until he met Isobel.

'Am feeling fit again,' he had written. 'My asthma is not too bad . . . I must get cracking again, get dug in somewhere as soon as possible, always hoping it will be permanent.' Then he took a job in a school, at the end of the summer, and it was from there the last two letters had come, one of them telling me how well it was working out, and inviting me down, the next mentioning Isobel for the first time. It was this letter that had woken me up, inducing vague thoughts of unease, thoughts that might seem to lack logic. Yet the long years of childhood and youth, lived out beneath the shadow of his life, had conditioned me. With catastrophe as inevitable as the rising of the sun, and with its source almost always as normal as that rising, the sudden passionate discovery of 'heaven on earth' once again, and the wish to involve me with it, seemed like a threat from the past we had inhabited together and which I really thought then was over.

'My dearest son, It is all wonderful, and you must come down. Isobel has made life a heaven on earth for me, an absolute heaven on earth. And of course the Wains and Miss Trevor have turned up trumps. They are a top-drawer sort, not your suburban, Broadshanks types. They're fairly new to it, and I help out in every way possible. Of course, I have vast experience of people, and I can guide them.

'I need have had no fears about taking the job. It was an embarrassment of riches, really, the response to my advertisement in *The Lady*. But I should have plumped for this from the start. I am much in demand because I know my job, and, more importantly, because *I do my job*.' (He had underscored the last few words heavily.) 'I would always keep *The Lady* in mind, if I were you. If things turn sour in Fleet Street you can turn to teaching or, indeed, working with your father. He's sought after, make no mistake.

'Anyway, come down if you possibly can. I am convinced this will go well, and that with Isobel I have at last found a happiness that will last. I am fit and strong, and young at heart. Of course there are creaks here and there—you can't get into your sixties and not feel it. But I try not to think about it, and just soldier on. And I don't tell Isobel. Can't talk to her about my asthma or my legs! Being young at heart, after all, that's the important thing. And I am full of hope for the future.

'Do come. Affectionately, G.'

When I did show it to Sarah my hesitations seemed absurd. It was the next morning, at breakfast. I pushed the letter across the table towards her. She looked at it, and then at me.

'Did this come this morning?' she said.

'No. A couple of days ago.'

'Am I to read it?'

'Yes.'

'Are you sure?'

I shrugged. 'You don't have to.'

She looked at me for a moment, then picked it up and glanced through it. If she read it all it was very swiftly. Then she gave it back to me. 'You go,' she said. 'Tell me about it afterwards.'

10

It seemed suddenly that we were in delicate territory, where her life and my life outside and beyond the realms of desire, away from the warmth of the crumpled sheets, the mindless comfort of love-making might actually collide. And the spectre of this came as something of a shock, since the context was the ferocious one of that tiger, my father.

'What will you do?' I asked. 'Will you go to the studio?'

'I shall paint, the whole weekend.'

'The big canvas?'

'I don't know. I shall have to see.'

'Colour?' I said, getting up. 'Line? It's all important.'

She suddenly flushed, and her eyes filled with tears. 'Sometimes,' she said, 'I hate you. You're so cruel. You've said that too many times. It's not a joke any more. It's over.' She stared at me, her fists clenched on the edge of the kitchen table. The tears did not fall. She blinked them away. Then she got up and went into the bedroom.

How different it had been at that first meeting, at the party Francis had given. The same words, but different. She had said that line was important, and I had searched fruitlessly in my own mind for an equivalent 'importance' in writing. Were *words* important? Was brevity important? Was a Saxon, as opposed to a Latin vocabulary important? But I had been captivated by her long hair and brown eyes; I had looked with desire upon the smooth brown skin of her neck and shoulders, agreeing readily enough that line was important, but only wanting to possess her.

And later, when she said 'I think colour is important', I looked at the blue silk of her blouse where it swelled over her breasts and could only agree. I asked if I could see her paintings. She laughed, and said of course not, she showed them to no one. But she had agreed we should meet again, and we had done very soon after the party. I was captivated from the start; it seemed so magical, to begin with; so balanced, and reciprocal, and at the same time surrounded by intense expressions of desire, readily and often fulfilled. It was headlong, and breakneck. And we were happy about that. In a short time her student friends accepted me into their group, though we drifted away to some extent, dividing our time between what we termed 'ordinary' work and 'creative' work, the rest at times obsessively expended on each other.

In a curious way I suppose it worked; for both of us, perhaps; but certainly for me. Bit by bit, with the passage of time, into that first real love affair, did the appropriate set of realities assert themselves: waking at night, as I so often did, and sitting up in the darkness, my knees drawn up and clasped by my hands, I would consider her vaguely defined form beside me in the bed. Her careless attitude was deliciously abandoned. She slept often on her belly, her arms above her head, and never with a pillow, so that her whole form was there beside me, unimpeded by the confusion of pillows into which I buried my own head. She slept deeply. I could pull away the covers from her naked body, and it would take time for the cold air to wake her. She did not mind that. She did not think it cruel. A tease, perhaps. But then she loved making love in the middle of the night; she loved being woken and taken quickly, then waiting and talking and making love again.

Yet increasingly, sitting up in the darkness beside her sleeping form, being just able, from the street lamps shining through the curtains, to define the outline of shoulder and hip and spread thighs, I thought more and more of the mind there, the spirit, cocooned against the world by the oblivion of sleep, yet ready to dream, and then wake, and then engage in the always desperate struggle to create. She was a woman, a partner, good after her fashion at some things, but bad at others; she was making her way, like me; she was fighting her corner, demanding affection, notice, attention, love, obedience, responses, just like me. She wasn't mine. She was her. My thoughts did not carry me quite that far. I was too young. But they carried me far enough to be disturbed by the spectre of complicated and real life to be lived, somewhere beyond the warm and scented stillness of that room with its balcony from which I often watched the patient stars.

I cleared things from the table in a perfunctory fashion, then picked up the letter and folded it. I was going to an eleven o'clock sale, at Christie's, and was in no hurry. The sun was shining on the backs of the houses opposite, and would be flooding the bedroom; yet I hesitated, uncertain about what I should say to Sarah to make up for the slight edge between us. I went into the bedroom. She had showered and was sitting naked on the bed, cross-legged. She had pulled the sheets around her, and propped the pillows behind her back, though she was not really leaning into them. And she was beginning to twist her hair and put it up, staring into a mirror which was propped in front of her. The position gave to her small breasts a fullness which was desirable, and I wanted once more to hold her. I sat near her, then reached over, preparing a superficial, conciliatory endearment. But she forestalled the lazy reaching for her flesh. 'No,' she said. 'Listen to me. You can't just be always making love, making love. What do you think we are? A Henry Miller saga? This isn't Clichy. There's more to it than that.'

She raised her arms above her head, gathering and twisting her hair. She was like a nymph after bathing, an artist's model, assured, self-consciously so, of a completeness of act and intent which I certainly did not feel.

Chastened, I said, 'You are lovely like that.'

Her face became troubled. 'What do you mean? Just what do you mean? It's so easy, isn't it? You're so good at it. You talk about loving, and we make love, and we talk after that about you. And you tell me what you want. And you go off, and do your own work, and I'm left to twine my hair. Where does it lead us?'

She was right. In everything she said. I felt ashamed. I felt the clumsiness of being selfish, of considering only my own purposes.

She had stopped doing her hair. She simply held the twisted braid of it on her head, with both hands, and looked at me. Had the form of her body, browned by summer sun, youthfully firm, small in stature and in the sweet honeyed features of her breasts, waist and belly, been otherwise, she might have seemed pitiful, even ridiculous in the face of her obvious question. But she was too lovely to be that; she controlled and exaggerated her vulnerability so that it operated as a weapon, and made me afraid. I loved her, surely, and did not wish to lose her. And to make something of this fact, which she knew was there enough to be worth testing, she said then: 'Go and get ready for work, and leave

13

me alone. Go away this weekend. Go and see your precious father with his wonderful Isobel. But leave me out of it. It's what you want, after all.'

[II]

He met me on the station platform. It had been an hour's run, south east out of London, towards Canterbury on the Ashford line. And in the mid-afternoon, after an uncrowded journey, it was the tense expectation in his figure that struck me. He seemed to stand out from the indifferent warmth and stillness of that day at the very beginning of September; he seemed to be deliberately at odds with the small number of people who alighted and swiftly vanished down the hill from the station building. He even eyed them with a certain stern reproof, almost as though they were unnecessary.

I saw him, of course, long before he saw me. Ignoring his advice about which carriage to get into in order to be opposite the exit when I arrived, I had walked the full length of the train, out of perversity you might say; and now looked back towards him from the front of the train as he scanned it with eager, stern curiosity.

He was in his early sixties, erect, forbidding, smartly turned out. His sparse hair was short and firmly brushed down against his scalp. He had, latterly, taken to wearing a beard, but it was limited to the point of his chin, a small, jutting goatee which he kept well trimmed as he did the bristly moustache above the stern straight line of his mouth. His eyes seemed to appraise me with a certain measure of disdain. It was not discomforting; yet I felt the challenge of it, the squaring up, his life against mine.

'I always find the fourth coach is the right one. Puts you down beside the entrance. Regular as Monday morning they are, these trains. It's what I like about this line.'

'It's a good service,' I said, indifferent to the detail.

He frowned, not willing to let the matter rest. 'I thought I told you. Fourth carriage. Didn't I?'

14

'You did.'

'Impertinence!'

I looked back at him. 'I like the walk,' I said. 'Relaxes me when I have to meet you!'

He laughed. 'Have it your own way. You always will anyway.'

He led me out to a shooting-brake, a Humber which had printed in perspective lettering across the back 'Brookhall School'.

'You drive this?' I asked, unnecessarily.

'I'm the cat's whiskers around here at the moment. Don't know how long it'll last. But it's "George this, and George that, and are you comfortable, and you *will* look after us?"' He laughed across the top of the car at me. 'And I do my job, sonny boy. That's why it is. I do my job. Do you?'

I nodded. 'I'm getting on all right,' I said. 'At least, I think so.'

'So long as you do your job.'

We got in. He squared up to the steering wheel, humming breathily to himself 'Silver Threads Among the Gold' and interrupting himself to name off, as a reassurance to us both it seemed, the sequence of tasks: 'ignition', 'no need for choke', 'neutral' and his hand took and shifted from side to side the long Humber gear lever. Then he reached for the 'starter' and pulled. The engine had a low sound, the large vehicle was comfortable, and there was an added and secret pleasure in watching the careful and methodical way in which he addressed himself to the task of driving away. Just before he did so, he turned to smile at me, a hint of triumph in his eyes, pride, self-confidence, conviction. 'When your hair is silver white, And your cheeks no longer bright. . . .' He turned back to the dashboard, went on humming, and as if steering a great ship at sea, put the car into gear with slow deliberation and we moved off majestically from the station forecourt.

I looked upon him with a kind of wonder, a stab of love mingled with admiration. How did he manage it, I thought; year after year, always more or less falling on his feet.

He drove carefully, and I kept quiet to begin with, listening contentedly to the deep and mellow resonance of

15

his humming. It was unrestrained and warming, the sweet compass of the notes. I felt as a child again, turning towards him in the comfortable leather seat, looking with careful and critical eyes upon the stern fixed profile.

'You'll love Isobel,' he said.

I almost laughed out loud. I was taken by surprise at his absolute assurance: he was demanding a reaction ahead of the encounter, as he always did. He was doing so with an unquestionable conviction. If I had laughed he would have flown into a rage, and the weekend would have been ruined, I could easily envisage all the problems that might then have arisen. Had not there been, over the years, countless 'Isobels' in his life? Had not I witnessed their comings and their goings as if they were part of the year's natural seasons? Worse still, was I not conscious when I looked back, of how enormously forgettable most of them had been—not to me, oh no, that would not have mattered at all—but to him? Forgettable, dismissed, forgotten. It was luck, good fortune, and the beginnings of judgement, perhaps wisdom even, that held in check my laughter.

'Tell me about her,' I said.

'She is the most wonderful woman in the world,' he said, staring ahead of him, as we creamed along the country roadway in the lush stillness of late summer. 'She has given me back my life. She has made me young again. With Isobel I will live forever!'

'But you were always young, father. You always said you would never grow old. You haven't.'

He glanced over. 'But I'm sixty-three! D'you realise that?'

'That's young. You look in tremendous form.'

'It's all her, sonny boy. It's all my darling Bella.'

I paused, wondering what he might say next about her. 'May I ask how old she is?'

He laughed. 'She's thirty-five, my son. A beautiful woman. We are deeply in love.'

I did not know what to say. I thought, with distaste, of Laurie. I remembered, with pity, Wendy. I considered, with distant affection at the time I must confess, the continuing plight of Alice. Before that there had been others, back and back through remembered childhood, an awful gallery of

16

lost and wasted opportunities, 'always hoping it will be permanent'. If the urge had not been there to laugh, it would most certainly have been there to cry.

'What does—er—your Isobel do, father?'

He frowned at the faint hint of patronage in my voice, and stared across. But my own expression of friendly inquiry must have reassured him. 'She's the school secretary.'

'That's convenient,' I said, a bit fatuously.

'Oh, we are invincible, Isobel and I. They rely on us completely. And in the night we lie together and make love. And I lose myself as I have never lost myself before.'

'You said she was married?'

'It's nothing. It's over. Poor man.'

'Children?'

He nodded, frowning. 'Yes,' he said. 'There are two children.' His face cleared. 'Wonderful. You'll love them as well. Yes, love them.'

I felt the warm tide of his certainty, and this comprehensive love, flowing over me. It absolved me from worry about my own circumstance. About Sarah. About my rather different interpretation of the boundaries of love, and how we defend them. For a few days I could allow myself to be engulfed in his version of the universal territory and enjoy, vicariously, pleasures and perceptions which eluded me in my own.

As if reading my mind, he said, 'Not married yet?'

'No, father.'

'The right girl not come along?'

'Not really.'

'Have you a girl friend at the moment?'

'Yes,' I said. 'Her name's Sarah.'

'Living together?'

'Sort of.'

He didn't pursue that. He seemed to accept the uncertainty, the coolness, the lack of conviction, as almost a compliment to his own quite total involvement with a woman half his age. Instead he broke into full song: '"Darling, I am growing, growing old, Silver threads among the gold. Shine upon my brow each day; Life is fading fast away."'

'Not exactly the most appropriate song, is it?'

'Memento mori!' he intoned. 'Memento mori.' His voice sank on the second word each time. He enjoyed saying it. 'We must all of us reflect on our mortality.'

'You seem to face the prospect of such reflection in high spirits,' I said, with a smile.

'She has given me back my youth. Inside, I'm young again.'

'And the rest of you?' I said lightly, wanting him to prolong the flow of words about himself.

'Wind and limb gone a bit, you might say.'

'Is it the asthma?'

He nodded. 'And my legs. Circulation's not what it was.' He suddenly glanced sharply across at me. 'But not a word to Isobel! You understand? Not a word.'

'Eternal youth?' I questioned.

'Invincible. That's me.' He slowed the car, changed down, and swung in through a gateway where a sign in similar lettering to that on the back of the car, gold and red perspective on a royal blue background, announced also that Brookhall School was a preparatory establishment for both boys and girls, and invited enquiries to the headmistress.

As we drove slowly up a winding drive, he turned and winked. 'The silver threads are there, my son. Nothing will take them away. But when the jack rabbit's roused, he doesn't think about the hairs on his head, does he?' And he lifted his right hand, his fist clenched, and made it quiver in the air, smiling to himself at the image of rampant desire.

'When do we see Isobel? Is she in the school now?'

'No. She'll have gone to collect her own children. We'll meet her after we've settled in here. Must show you everything. It's a good set-up. I'll show you the routine.' It was as if he wanted me to join him in the job. I would not have been altogether surprised if he had made me an offer.

He turned the car past a final clump of shrubbery and a group of buildings came into view. Then he swung it in a wide circle on the gravel forecourt of the house and stopped opposite a side door. He turned the engine off.

The house was long and low. It might once have been a vicarage. Now it was part of an untidy conglomeration of buildings, the later ones of a prefabricated style that made obvious their appendage status. Some attempt had been made to plant virginia creeper as a common camouflage, since the central building was heavily covered in it, but progress had been limited. The front was bathed in sunlight. A slight breeze moved among the wall of leaves; here and there an early hint of autumn was to be seen in a solitary red or brown leaf, but the general atmosphere was of summer, reinforced by the scent of mown grass coming from the playing fields. A motorised mower with a seat on it stood at the edge of the nearest lawn.

Uncertain, bemused, I looked round. Then I pulled out my bag. 'Do you do all that?' I asked. 'Cutting the grass, keeping the grounds?'

'I'll tell you the whole routine,' he said. 'Run the lot, I do.'

I felt strangely inhibited. There was no sound at all, beyond the song of birds, and the movement of the gravel under our feet made a defiant, sharp noise, so that I was transported back to Coppinger, absurdly conscious of all the inevitable restraints of a school.

'Is there nobody here?' I asked.

'Dr Wain and his wife. Her sister, Miss Trevor. That's all. The staff arrive after the weekend. The assistant master is around. But he lives in the village.' He stood beyond the car, observing my reactions. He seemed relaxed and easy; in control.

'Things are good, aren't they?' I said. I turned fully to look at him, frowning slightly as I did. 'Really good?'

He looked back at me, just as directly, a pugnacious expression in his eyes, his jaw set. 'I'm a swan here,' he said. 'Because I do my job.'

[III]

I retain in my mind that first image of him, so pregnant with information and so dismissive of everything and everybody around him. In the two days that followed I would catch myself looking at him in order to discover the same tense expectations, the pent-up impatience. It was an impatience to transmit his mood to others. Initially, it was just information about himself and about Isobel, about his work and his relationships with others around him. But even when that had been mostly done the tension still remained. There was a flood within him. He wanted *everything* within himself to be felt and understood by those around him. And it drove him wild that he could not achieve it. It was as if the great force of his nature was built up inside his passionate chest, inside his heart, pressing against a dam wall. The wall was his stoicism, the set of self-imposed restraints. Telling those things that he told me to begin with, like his love for Isobel, was like releasing, through a safety valve, an impetuous but controlled flow of water, only fractionally indicative of the huge force behind it. What was left incomplete was the transmission of his mortal soul. From time to time a breaching took place, triggered by, more than anything else, a sense of defeat. It was this that I feared: too great a pressure might build up and burst the dam. To use another image very much with us at that particular time, it was as if an aborted rocket, having blasted off from Cape Canaveral, and having passed the point of recall when its flames might be quenched, had still to go through the wasteful and pointless flight of a shortened arc before falling back into the ocean.

This fear about his impetuous nature, and the flooding force of his passion, was coupled with a persistent sense of the inequality between us. The more there pulsed around me the essence of his wilful nature, the more I was aware that it was his life that continually flowed over mine, an unequal contrast or conflict, not of wills, for I think in the end mine was stronger and more ruthless, but of passion, of feeling, of the very intensity with which everything was done. That I could not match. And it forced out, from within me, deep inside my being, a silent cry to him not to overwhelm my life with his. There was so much vitality; I could not match the self-assurance. And both then and later, just as it had been during my childhood, it was this forceful haste and urgency which deluded me into thinking that he shared equally in the common tide of happiness which I believed then ebbed and flowed over us all.

At one point I said to him, 'I'm thinking of buying a car.'

It stopped him in his tracks. He stared hard at me, as though I had materialised, there and then, into a human being not previously recognised. 'A car?' he said. 'You?'

'Yes.' It was in fact a very big decision; an exciting one as well.

Yet to him it seemed a means of defining me in some way. 'You doing well, then?' he asked. There was a stabbing quality in the question, stern and sharp. 'Everything going all right? Money? That sort of thing?'

'Well, yes, it is.' I was suddenly hesitant under the onslaught of his attention.

'I mean, new? Second hand? What make? I'd like to know, old son.'

'I'm still thinking about it, father.'

I felt subjected to a brief storm of concentration within his brain on my ability and the direction of my career. It was as if he had suddenly become aware of how little he knew me, really. How little he knew of what I did, each day, week by week. In the large and all-embracing manner that he used to encompass all those about him, yes, in that sense he knew me. But not in detail; friends, lovers, acquaintances, colleagues at work, those who held sway over the future, were all virtually unknown to him, so that we stood in the broad pasture of our abiding love oblivious to the details of each other's lives.

'Make sure it's one I can drive,' he said. 'Include me on the insurance. Could teach you a thing or two.'

'All right,' I said, with a laugh. 'But I haven't got it yet.'

We walked back towards the main building. He had been showing me round, proud of his responsibilities, but more generally displaying the whole operation of the school for my benefit, as though it would display him as well.

Across the cut grass and gravel a slightly stooped figure had emerged from the main entrance, at first peering round, then spotting us and taking a few uncertain steps in our direction. My father quickened his pace, and I followed suit.

'Dr Wain, I want you to meet my son. He's a writer. Fleet Street. Features Agency.' He said it all with enormous conviction, as though the force behind the words would explain what I did. I had the image of a music hall impresario introducing some very special act, and I reached forward

21

my hand with uncharacteristic force in order to fulfil the requirements of performance. It took Dr Wain by surprise, and he stared at it first before taking it, rather gingerly, and giving it an uncertain, vague shake. His own hand was moist and podgy. He was tall, and stooped, untidy in his dress, his hair white and curly, not really needing to be brushed or combed much, and in fact not attended to with any care. His chin was not all that well shaved, and on his lower lip there still adhered a crumb or two of cake from his tea. When he spoke it became apparent that his teeth protruded slightly: there was a faint indentation from them on his lower lip.

'Fleet Street?' he said. 'Men in my walk of life look upon you with a good deal of suspicion, you know. I trust you'll not be writing about Brookhall? Dogged by scandal, the teaching profession.'

'Surely not, Dr Wain?'

He smirked. 'I exaggerate, I exaggerate. But you can't be too careful. Down for long?'

'No. Not long.'

'You're not on, er . . . er, an 'investigation', are you? Is that what you call it?'

'That sounds more like the police, sir. With us it's a "story".'

He maintained the look of inquiry. When I didn't go on he said, 'And?'

I shook my head. 'I'm not on one,' I said. 'I'm not working. Taking a break.'

He looked relieved.

'I'm sure he'd do some teaching for you, Dr Wain,' my father said. 'He did teach before.'

He had been unusually restrained, standing back from us, and listening. It seemed now he wished to assert, on my behalf, some farm-horse willingness to play a part for the good of the school during my brief time there.

Dr Wain smiled wanly, and shook his head. 'We've all the teachers we can afford. We wouldn't be thanked if we gave them ideas about journalism. No offence, of course. Where did you go to school?'

I told him.

He looked at my father, then back at me. For one moment I thought he was going to ask more about Coppinger. From the faint expression of curiosity that flitted over his face, no more than a hesitation, I felt he knew of the school. I was tempted to ask him, but then decided against. An echo from childhood, of the embarrassment of always having to explain, held me back. Coppinger! Would any explanation of that strange institution in the Cotswolds suffice at all? Coppinger, which changed as the social pattern in England changed, was different itself from one decade to the next. What it had been to me, in wartime, when I had arrived there, was quite different from the place I left ten years later. And, uniquely for me perhaps, it had come to represent a charity for genteel derelicts like my father, not necessarily the way it was seen by others who had been drawn in and absorbed and cherished.

It was all too complicated to raise with Dr Wain, the crumbs of cake on his face making me doubt whether he would understand.

But he went on, 'And university?'

I told him that as well.

On safer ground, he talked for a moment or two about that, and then concluded by hoping I would have an enjoyable weekend.

'I hope so too, Dr Wain.'

'Good, good.' He turned from me. 'Now, George, a few things.' He raised from under his arm a battered clipboard and they discussed lime for marking pitches, water taps which leaked, and the roof of the scout shed. A list was handed over.

For an hour or so I helped him. Then we stopped. Walking back across the playing fields I said to him, 'It's very beautiful. It reminds me of the beginning of term, at Coppinger, the sadness, leaving home, that the summer was over. Then, getting back to school, and in a strange way the summer was still there. All different, but often days on end of sunshine and warmth. Just like this.'

'But it was colder there. This is more sheltered.'

'What do they think?' I asked. 'The Wains? About Isobel? About you and her?'

'They're absolutely delighted.'

23

I thought of the crumbs of cake around Dr Wain's mouth, and to myself I doubted whether absolute delight had ever penetrated his being. But I said, 'That must be a relief. Wouldn't do if they disapproved.'

'Oh, they're broadminded people. Open and above board. Of the world.'

'What about her husband? Isobel's?'

'He left her. Two years ago, just went off. Not a word. Nothing. Weak man, cowardly. It was very hard for her, with two young children.'

'Was she here then?'

'She was living in the village. After a while she took this job.'

'I'm looking forward to meeting her.'

'We'll go down there now.'

[IV]

In my childhood, his first encounters had always been of disproportionate importance, as if each new woman embodied in herself all of his hope for happiness. Yet at the same time the very repetition of the encounters mocked this perception, so that, while he seemed to have an infinite capacity for the renewal of belief in what was new, I had approached ever more warily the succession of women. It was not that they had failed him. The fault was his. But I was his also, a partisan spectator of arrivals and departures, hope engendered, hope dissipated, the memories building up and lengthening into the past, an ever-increasing succession of handicaps which threatened any prospect of eventual salvation.

Refreshed, however, by the long gap since last I had been directly involved with him, a gap filled with making my own way in both work and love, I now approached his new start with Isobel in a mood of optimism. To some extent I was infected by his manner. I simply yearned, on his behalf, for it to work this time as it had never worked before. And the prospects seemed good on that golden September evening

24

as we arrived at her house in the village. We walked round to the back. At a table outside the back door, bathed in slanting sunlight, yet still very warm in the sheltered space beside the house, were two children, playing. They greeted George rather gravely, by name, and stopped their playing to stare at me. He introduced us, and I absorbed slowly the calm features of Olivia, who was ten, and her six-year-old sister, Jessica. As they were explaining the elaborate relationships between a line of dolls and a golliwog who seemed at the time to have been doing unmentionable things, and was consequently in a state of disgrace, Isobel appeared in the doorway into the kitchen, shading her eyes against the sun, watching us, her shoulder against the door-jamb, her body and features relaxed. She seemed free of tension, almost laconic, vague in her welcome for us, certain of my father's for her. Simply dressed, in skirt and jumper and flattish shoes, she wore only the end-of-day traces of make-up, and yet the carefully-done dark hair framing her face gave to her overall appearance a firmness of effect that was striking and attractive. Something more than just contentment put fire and certainty into her eyes, the eyes of a happy woman. My father kissed her on the lips. It was a swift and decisive embrace, yet relaxed as well. Then he introduced us.

She forestalled any handshaking by the way she started speaking directly, not asking questions, but telling me, 'I've heard such a lot about you that it's made me quite nervous, meeting you; yet your father gives me very little real information. He goes on about you being all sorts of things. Yet when I ask him what you do, he can't tell me. He burbles on about journalism. What sort of journalism? He can't really say.'

'What does it matter, my love? In a thousand years the sort of journalism he does won't matter at all. But what he is, how he loves, how he succeeds in life, that always matters. And that's what I tell you about.' He raised his hands in the air, palms upward, in a gesture that suggested he had supplied all the answers that were required.

But she turned to me and said, 'Tell me. I'm curious. I'd like more details. Unlike George, I don't think a thousand years ahead. I think only of this year and next.' She paused.

With a shrug she added, 'Perhaps only this year,' and looked at her two daughters who had returned to the business of dealing with disaffection on a scale which had spread from the golliwog to a teddy bear and two of the dolls. 'I think of their time as well,' she added, wistfully.

'I work in Fleet Street,' I said. 'I write features for an agency. They're mainly about the fine arts.'

'You mean criticism? Theatre and exhibitions?'

'Not really. At least, not so much. It's more the practical side. I cover saleroom news and auctions. There's a lot of interest now. They say the market's rising and people are investing. I write about that.'

'It sounds wonderful. Just what I would like to do. Do you enjoy it?'

'Oh yes.'

'And where do you live?'

'Notting Hill Gate.'

'He lives in Chesterton territory, on Campden Hill, near the water tower and the tennis club.'

'I'm thinking of moving,' I said.

'You're not, are you?'

'Well, vaguely.'

'But it's a fine flat!' He seemed almost annoyed. It was as if I were wasting a perfectly satisfactory situation gratuitously.

'I want something a bit bigger.' As I said it I realised I was talking in a way that had no real meaning to him. Never in one place long enough or securely enough to be able to dictate the occasion of his going; never therefore in a position to decide to improve such everyday and ordinary things as physical amenities and location; he must have seen my decision as a simple disruption threatening him. While he always tried to avoid being a burden, there were times in those years when he would descend on me, briefly, in trouble, visits that were faintly pervaded by drink, by money worries, by the treachery of some woman or other, by the temporary neglect of Alice. They touched me, these visits, like the breath of wind on a still day, hinting at a possible state between us that never came to pass simply because of the unending succession of women in his life, responding to his needs with diverse needs of their own.

Did he feel I was edging away from him, becoming slightly more distant? That was in no sense what I had in mind. Yet I looked at Isobel, anticipating a question. Her calm eyes looked back at me without a single shadow of inquiry in them.

He, too, was silent. When she looked at him the expression in her eyes was of delight rather than admiration, a bemused wonder at whether or not he was real at all. Since he so obviously was, and by instinct responsive to every shift in feeling, there was added to Isobel's pleasure a hint of laughter; it affected the expression around her mouth, colouring her cheeks, for all the world as though she were a child again, and not the mother of two children, a woman in her mid-thirties.

I felt a twinge of jealousy. My own situation with Sarah should have been something like this. Yet it was not. It was different. In a host of ways it was just *less*. Here was my father, facing the great climacteric, the memories we shared of other women so numerous as no longer even to seem compromising, and he, now, in love like a teenager. I wanted to laugh, at them; but perhaps, deeper down, with them. I wanted to fit in, during the short time I had. And, if the affair lasted, to come again, becoming a part of their common joy.

The children had moved off down the garden on a short but involved expedition, and were under an apple tree whose yellowy fruits were thick on the branches. Notwithstanding past affairs, I felt I was in the presence of a love greater than I had witnessed before. Their message, transmitted by silence, pervading the warm air between the three of us, pushed forward, oh, so gently, by both of them, invited me to accept a state of affairs which would not be voiced. It was so totally, so dramatically unlike my father not to give verbal expression to his current state of mind and heart, that I could only hesitantly accept the reality of what I then felt. But accept it I did. It was quite palpable, deeply felt.

With a youthful formality I said, 'I would like to take you both out to dinner tonight, if Isobel can find a baby-sitter. Is that possible? Is there somewhere near where we can go?' I looked first at him, then at her.

He said, 'No, you mustn't think of it. Too expensive, old son. We can—'

But Isobel interrupted him. 'I would like that very much. It's most kind of you.' She paused. Then she said, 'I can usually get a babysitter from next door, over there.' She waved towards the roof of a cottage beyond a hedge of hawthorn. 'There's a place in the village. It's the pub, really, but they've started a restaurant. We sometimes go.' She added this tentatively, looking across at my father.

'An outing,' he said. 'We're honoured.'

I smiled back at him. 'And why not?' I said.

'Why not indeed! You're a good old sport, always good to your father, reliable, thoughtful—'

But I interrupted a flow of unction which would soon become sentimental—'It's for Isobel that I'm doing it.' I laughed to soften the check upon his flow of words. 'You weren't going to cook supper, were you?'

He raised his eyebrows and wagged his head from side to side. 'I stand corrected,' he said. 'I stand corrected by my son. A young Daniel.'

I did believe, that evening, it would work. I did not hurry into the belief, but let it come, a slow, pervasive conviction, different from previous experience. I wanted it to work, of course. I wanted all the usual platitudes about 'an even keel' and 'a sanctuary at last' to be real. I wanted that 'always hoping it will be permanent' finally to have come true. I sensed in her a patience with him which at that stage was unexplained except in the most obscure and instinctive way. He did not bully her, or demand things from her; he did not tell her what she thought, or what she felt; he imposed nothing on her. He was more relaxed with her than I had ever seen him, with any woman. Diffident, uncertain, almost boyish, his love was declared in every look and gesture. And when she looked at him it seemed secure. I waited, during those early encounters, that first afternoon, and on the two days that followed, for her to turn to me and question me about him. Other women had. And in their questioning I had always detected the fear, the uncertainty which, on previous occasions, had been the force destroying all the promise. But she asked nothing about him. Absolutely nothing. She

28

wanted to know no facts about his past life, his habits, his nature. No opinions, either. She wanted details from me; about my work, my leisure, my ambitions. But always she protected, as it were, the relationship between them which I had first felt in the silence, in the garden, in the September sunshine of the early evening of our first meeting.

The 'outing' was a success. The restaurant was simple, sincere in its cooking, and in those days amazingly cheap. We drank two bottles of burgundy between us, a soft 1953 Clos Vougeot, and both of them talked about the school and about Dr Wain and his female entourage.

'Is his wife a bit of a dragon?' I asked.

'Yes,' Isobel said.

'Rod of iron?'

'Yes.'

'Rules the roost, then?'

They both laughed.

'She said: 'You're so alike!'

'Can you get round her?'

My father put his hand gently on Isobel's, where it lay on the white tablecloth. 'I told you he'd get to the heart of the matter.'

'It is her, then?'

'They can't do without Isobel,' he said. He was just beginning to become expansive with the drink. 'She's a wonderful secretary. Does everything. And as for me, well, I've already told you, I'm a swan with all of them *because I do my job*!' Suddenly stern, emphasising the words, he looked round at other diners, who seemed mildly interested in what they rightly detected as surges of passion. 'And it must go on like that,' he said. 'We're happy here, aren't we?'

'There's no reason to worry, my dear,' Isobel said. 'It's the beginning of a new school year, a new beginning. I so love the autumn, picking fruit, storing things, looking forward to winter. They rely on you. Of course they do.'

'What are the teachers like?'

Again, they told me, in amusing detail. I listened, almost hungrily. In the choice of a life, a profession, I had, for a time, vacillated between teaching and journalism. At one stage, through Gabbitas and Thring, I had taken up employment in just such an establishment as the one run by the Wains, and I felt now slight stabs of regret as they recalled for me the eccentricities and feelings which swirled around them both in term time. He, of course, had only the experience of the summer term; yet his quickness of perception, and the economy with which he voiced his judgment, were more than sufficient for the large task of setting before me the full cast of the essentially *opéra bouffe* which dominated their lives.

'It's a pity you can't stay on and meet them all next week,' my father said. 'You'd like Dr Travers. He's a bit like your housemaster, the last one, not Forrest, the other one?'

'Patterson? The one who died?'

'Yes. That's right. Poor old bugger.'

I paid the bill, and we left. It was a clear night, without a moon, and the stars were bright in the heavens. The sharp intensity of their light matched the feeling I had of love and human response, of things being all right. We walked along, in silence. Isobel had her arm through his, and occasionally, without looking directly sideways at them both, I was conscious of her resting her head on his shoulder.

'I was looking at the stars last night,' I said.

'In London? It's not easy.'

'I know. But I was remembering when you used to do it. Trying to teach me which they were.'

'And how many do you remember?' His voice was soft and indulgent. 'Did I teach you well?'

'You always did that, father.'

'Can you tell me them now?'

'Well, there's the Pole, and the Great Bear. Castor and Pollux—'

'Good, good.'

'—the Dog star, and—'

'Orion.' He took my arm. 'Go on. Do you remember the other stars in the constellation? I taught you, once.'

'That's Betelgeuze, there,' I said, pointing towards its dull imagined immensity. 'But I don't remember the others.'

'Even I can't remember the names, now. Wait.' He paused. It was almost to himself he spoke, as he pointed again. 'The one in the middle of Orion's belt. That's Epsilon. And down a bit, Omega, the bunch of stars.'

Again he paused. 'Oh, dear,' he said. 'It's all so long ago that I needed to know them. It's gone from me.'

'Who was Orion?' Isobel asked.

'Orion the hunter,' he said slowly, as if to himself. 'That's all I know.' He paused. 'No. It's not true. I know more. Let me remember.' He paused again. 'We used to know, old son, didn't we? We must remember for Isobel, mustn't we, my love?'

He was drawing her back into the orbit of his concern, and I felt faintly jealous as I watched her move close to him again, taking his arm, resting her upturned head on his shoulder so that she could encompass both him and the stars within her gaze.

'He was a hunter, the child of Poseidon, God of the sea. He fell in love with one of the Pleiades. There,' he pointed up at the close group of glimmering stars, 'see, the Sweet Pleiades! And he was punished and blinded, and went to the rising sun to get back his sight. And in the end . . . what happened to him in the end? The Gods killed him, that's what happened. An arrow in the head while he was swimming in the sea. And he drowned.'

We walked on.

'I used to know them all,' he said. 'I prided myself on my knowledge of the stars. I used to memorise and check, during the night, in winter, in the Baltic. It was so clear, so necessary. Precision was everything then, my son. Everything.'

'And now?' I asked. I hoped for some guidance. Always, before, when I had not needed it so much, he had been full of advice and admonition and wisdom. But it seemed different now.

'If one is lucky,' he said. Then he paused. 'If one is very lucky—and I think I am, just now—life becomes softer, and richer. That's all.'

Chapter Two

[I]

'The routine,' he said, 'is as follows.' He paused long enough for our eyes to meet. Was he checking on my mood? Should I have laughed at him, then, and changed the direction of his mind? Would it have mattered?

I bent over the cup of morning tea which he had just brought in to my bedroom. 'The routine?' I said, and then sipped.

'Yes. Up at five. That's the first thing. And out. Go through the day's list, item by item.'

'Is it your list, or is it his?' He was sitting by the window of my bedroom. He looked at me over the top of his glasses. In the ten years or so since he had started wearing them he had gone through a number of different styles in a search that had never produced an entirely satisfactory answer. Latterly, he had come round to the idea of half-moon spectacles in what I supposed was mock tortoiseshell. They allowed him to read his perpetual lists of items, but did not impede his remarkably good sight for distant objects. On the other hand they gave him a distinctly donnish appearance. Coming to the school and not knowing, I would have taken him for a very senior member of staff if not the headmaster himself.

He chuckled. 'Lord love us,' he said. 'The lists are always mine. You know that. When has it been otherwise?'

'Go on,' I said. 'What next?'

'I deal with the routine work first, equipment, maintenance, breakages. Then, as soon as it's light, I like to get out to the playing fields, the gardens, the front drive. I like everything to be in order by the time the day pupils begin arriving.'

'When's that?'

'Between half past eight and nine. A few come earlier. I suppose their parents have to fit them in with other runs, catching trains, that sort of thing.'

'Are they rich, the parents?'

'Not particularly. They're all right. Good sorts. Trying to give their children a good education.'

'But it must cost quite a bit. I mean, Dr Wain doesn't do it for nothing.'

'It's not free, like Coppinger. But I don't suppose it's any better than the education you had. You did well there, my son. Gave you a lot, didn't it?' He looked at me with a sudden, pinched concern, as though realising, even as he spoke, how sharp the contrast was between the education these 'good sorts', who sent their children here, obtained for them, and that which, gratuitously as it were, had come my way, not because of his effort but through lack of it.

'When do we see Isobel?' I asked.

'Church,' he said.

I felt a mixture of wonder and pity. Later, I would probably laugh. Looked at objectively, discussed perhaps with my brother Francis, my father's presence at morning prayer in an English village church would seem eccentric, or at least would have about it that sense of it representing a brave, fresh departure at odds with the reality of his experience after more than sixty years in the world. And yet his yearning spirit, which had placed before me once again the essential target in his life—'always hoping it will be permanent'—this was not inconsistent with a certain deference he showed to those who, in his own earliest experiences, as a child in Folkestone, as a schoolboy at Canterbury, as a young naval midshipman in the first world war, had kindled certain simple Christian ideals. Towards 'men of the cloth', padres, priests, 'tub-thumpers', no matter how he would, in his different moods, characterise them, there was in the end an underlying respect, a feeling that, when it came to the point, they might be able to do something for his bruised and wounded soul.

'What time is the service?'

'Eleven.'

'And the parson? A good sort?'

'He's all right. Doesn't quite approve of me, of course.'

I frowned. 'Why ever not? What can he know about you to hold against you?'

'When they see us together, they know.' He nodded his head slowly, with resignation. Then he stood up, and turned towards the window.

'You mean . . . disapproval?'

'Well, it's a small village. The school is important to it. Relations have to be watched, appearances kept up.' Again, the rueful countenance, this time turned back towards me.

'But, Father! This is the sixties! And her husband's left her.'

He laughed, briefly. 'Don't worry, my son. Nothing on God's earth will hold us apart. We were made for each other. She is like an angel, descended from heaven.' He paused, staring directly at me. 'Do you remember, when you first went to Coppinger?' He seemed to address himself, physically towards me, legs apart, arms to his side, eyes fixed on mine.

I nodded, but frowned at him as well. 'You didn't come,' I said.

It was a statement, but a reproof as well, reminding him that it had been somebody else who had brought me on that first, lonely train journey to school.

'I came to see you. Afterwards. I came down several times. Don't you remember? Of course you were very small.'

I nodded, but said nothing. It was my turn to feel pinched by the recollection.

'The first time I came was in the spring. I was working somewhere in Surrey. Came up to London in the early morning, very early. It was wartime. It must have been the Easter of 1944. Came to Waterloo, and had to get over to Paddington. It was a long walk. I headed for Hyde Park Corner. Then I went through the Park. I didn't have a watch in those days. I was worried I would miss the train.' He stopped, staring in front of him.

34

'What time of day?' I asked.

'Oh, three o'clock in the morning.'

'Really? Early as that?'

He nodded, still staring.

'Was the park open?'

He nodded again.

'Well, what did you do?'

He looked up at me. 'I ran.'

'You ran? Just like that?' I tried to visualise him, twenty years younger, solemnly running through a deserted park before dawn. Odd enough then as an image in the mind, thirty years before jogging was heard of; it seemed odder still that he should be telling me.

'I ran through the park, between the trees, under the stars. It was absolutely still. There were no lights at all, of course. Blackout. Just the moon and the stars, showing the houses along Park Lane. And then Lancaster Gate coming up ahead of me.'

I waited. He seemed to be seeing it clearly enough in his mind's eye. It was not failing memory which made him delay, but some other reconstruction, of instinct, or feeling, as though concerned about why he was telling me, and what meaning it had. He went on staring at me. There was a solemnity about the narrative, recollection reinforced by his own simplicity in recounting the 'story' of that occasion. Yet I was still puzzled as to what his first visit to Coppinger, so many years ago, had to do with Isobel and going to church. I sat very still, my head propped against the pillow, gazing at his outline against the window, waiting for him to go on.

'I ran in and out through the trees. I knew I was in time, really. I wanted to run.' He clenched his fist in front of him. 'I loved the feeling of strength. I was lean and fit. I felt that everything was going to be all right. With you, with Francis, with Melanie. It was all going to be fine. I knew, then, that if I could get things to go right, if I could only get things right. . .'

'But you did,' I said. 'It was better than all right. Coppinger—' I stopped.

'It was Coppinger, not me.'

'No. It was you as well.'

His fists still clenched, he sat down again on the chair beside my bed.

'But the running,' I said. 'Go on about the running.'

'I remember it so well, the faint star light, the huge ghostly trees, plane trees, still without their leaves, and the morning mist. There was no one except me. No one. And I was sure, if we could only get things right, we would all be happy once again. I had you two boys at school. Melanie . . .' He paused. 'But the running made me feel invincible. I was absolutely sure of myself.' He shrugged, a look of doubt crossing his face. 'It didn't quite come off, did it?' His expression was one of appeal.

'We had good times, Father,' I said. I thought to myself, how disastrous it had all been; Francis, Melanie, me, all of us scrambling around trying to recover the things he had thrown away. My brother was still involved, both with me and with him; but my sister Melanie, adopted unsuccessfully after my mother's death, drawn back into our lives briefly and with the same lack of success years later, was a more shadowy figure, an unwilling participant in lives which no doubt she regarded with some scepticism. 'We had great times together,' I said. 'Those visits, they were—'

He raised his hand, stopping me. 'No,' he said. 'Listen. As I ran I cried out: 'George will live! George will live!' If anyone had heard me, they'd have thought me stark staring bonkers. Luckily, there were only the trees.' He chuckled to himself. Then he looked at me again. 'The thing is, I feel the same now. When I'm out there, the dawn light spreading over the pitches and the shrubs, I feel the same as I felt then. Invincible. And it's Isobel that's done it. I could move mountains.'

He took off his half moon glasses, and put them in the top pocket of his rather crumpled working jacket. He stood up slowly, with an effort, and turned then to the window, staring out. It faced the driveway, and the lawns leading to the playing fields; it was, in short, his domain.

'I think she's wonderful, too,' I said. 'And her children. Of course it's going to be all right. And I've always said you'll live for ever.'

'I'm sixty-three! Think of that!' He ordained that I thought of it only for a very short time, since his expression instantly changed, becoming peremptory. 'And now get up. And we'll have breakfast. And then, Onward Christian Soldiers. And you'll be expected to sing your best, your very best.' He turned, and crossed the room, and opened the door. 'I've told everyone, how you used to sing as a boy, soloist in the choir, singing at that wedding, performing in Gilbert and Sullivan.'

'But it'll only be a few hymns,' I said.

'We'll make the best of them.'

[II]

He sat between the children. I sat on the outside, beside Isobel. He found the hymns and psalm for Jessica. He sang, he knelt, he listened, he appeared to pray. Careful though I was not to stare at him, I could not resist doing so during one hymn; and as the words came from him, and floated out above the childrens' heads, I thought my sideways glance detected in his eye a faint reddening of compassion or regret:

> 'Time, like an ever-rolling stream
> Bears all its sons away.'

The small formalities of morning service, instead of flowing over him as they might have done, as I remembered them doing on any of the relatively few occasions when we had attended church or chapel together—mainly occasions at Coppinger—but also visiting friends, seemed to grip him and involve him. I could not believe that he had become religious. Nothing he had said or done suggested that. Yet I found it insufficient to see in the directness of his attention no more than a concession to the need to set a good example to the two children, or companionship of intent for Isobel herself. I hoped, even suspected, that it was more than that. I remembered, with some feeling, the phrase that had prefigured this little world, this safe haven, this paradise, 'always hoping it will be permanent'. What more it could be without becoming an embarrassment to my own spiritual doubts and prevarications I was not sure. To see him enter any realms of spirituality would hardly have made sense, and would have been difficult for me to treat seriously. What more could I wish for him beyond calmness and restraint, such moderation as had always been his goal but which had never been attained?

I had come with him for his sake, not my own. I had come in deference to the custom of the country, fully expecting to enjoy the hymns and canticles, the smells of an old church, the pretentions of a rural congregation, and to read upon the walls the frail echoes of sacrifice. I was still young enough and impatient enough to feel my heart sink with each step, as the vicar, an elderly man, climbed the pulpit, not daring to hope for the brevity that had made Coppinger sermons generally bearable.

He was not brief. He must have spoken for a full twenty minutes. And yet I would not have wished to surrender a single word, not even for the sakes of Olivia and Jessica, who wisely had brought books. He had chosen a line from the fifth chapter of Romans, 'We also joy in God through our Lord Jesus Christ, by whom we have now received the atonement', and he developed from it an idea of salvation peculiarly suited to the old, rather than to the young. The word, he said, was used just this once in the New Testament, and the meaning was different from those occasions in the Old Testament to which he also referred. He knew his Greek, but treated the knowledge with humility; it was merely to help us on our way towards understanding, and the Greek word was offered apologetically.

Surreptitiously, I glanced sideways along the pew, past Isobel, who was keeping a watchful eye on the two children, until I could see the expression on my father's face. It was, as always, inscrutable. The firm profile, turned upward, was fixed upon the preacher. The small, tidy beard jutted out. The eyes, grey, hooded, severe, gave away nothing at all.

From the given text I anticipated a disentangling of Christ as propitiator from the idea of repentance and amendment of life; to have, in short, the one without the other. But this was far from what the preacher had in mind.

His frail hands gripped the edge of the pulpit and he fixed his calm clear eyes on the back of the church. 'The idea of sacrifice, in order to bring about reconciliation with God, was lifted from us by Christ's death on the Cross. The process of divine punishment, which is at the heart of Old Testament teaching, that, also, has been replaced. Drought, famine, pestilence, earthquake, are what scientists tell us they are. Perhaps they always were. But in Christian teaching they no longer fulfil a role as God's retribution upon us for wrong-doing. That is what the death and resurrection of Christ has changed. But I come now to the difficulty with which this has left us all. Instead of atonement being achieved by undergoing a spell of punishment, or by priestly ritual, or by sacrifice, we have it now through Grace. Christ transcends the old law.'

He paused. The faraway look in his eyes seemed to be fixed on a distant point far behind and beyond the congregation. Then, without looking at the people in the congregation, his eyes fell to the ledge of wood on which his hands rested. 'We come to the difficulty of faith. Did God foresee the growth of disbelief? Did he anticipate the strains upon faith which would make it as difficult, or more difficult, to realise salvation after the sacrifice of Christ? For atonement is not automatic. It has not, I think, been deposited there as something we collect for ourselves irrespective of the degree of our faith. Christ did not suffer in order that we might deliberate whether or not he rose from the dead, whether he appeared to the disciples, whether it was really Jesus to whom Mary Magdalene spoke through her tears at the door of the sepulchre . . .'

I was moved by that image more than any other. That was faith, and I doubted my own possession of it, just then. But I felt that I had time on my side. For my father it was a different story. What was there that he could take up from these words? What possible reconciliation was open to him, within the stern prescriptions of faith now being offered? If nothing was easy, to me, how bleak did it seem to him? If I had set aside, for the time being, the stirrings of faith, the

39

commitments of a troubled youth, what could I hope for the gaunt, profiled figure along the pew from me, whose backward look towards an identical perception of salvation covered many decades?

'Well, what did you make of all that, then?' he asked afterwards. His face was still set in severe lines and I wondered how seriously he had taken it. I could not be sure that even the modest speculation I had had was anywhere near the truth. Truth tests truth, however, and I told him I thought the sermon was one of the best I had heard.

'Ever?' he asked.

For a moment I paused. 'Yes,' I said. 'Ever.'

His face softened into a smile. He was holding the hands of the two children and Isobel was standing beside me. 'You see,' he said to her, 'you are right. You are so right. A remarkable man, our vicar. That's what Isobel says. And I cannot fault her. I listen to him, and I am filled with sadness at all my wasted years.'

'George,' she said. 'Don't mock.'

'I'm not mocking! I mean it. It's gone. I don't know what I can rescue, but I can't rescue the past.'

'You don't need to,' she said. 'Just yourself.'

Whatever his mind had absorbed, his heart had been unable to accommodate. He was belittling the message, and yet instinct told me he was right. The alternative would have been a degree of terror which could not really be imagined. It seemed enough that he was there at all. Perhaps it was a small measure of faith. Perhaps something could be built from it. Perhaps a merciful God would look with compassion upon him, setting aside the sterner laws which had been implicit in the sermon. Yet in my heart I did not believe this, and my own feelings, out in the fresh air once again, were shadowed by a spiritual bleakness reflecting both my own self-doubt and my hesitations about him.

'You've a fearful sense of time,' I said. 'Why do you always look backwards over all of your life? Why can't you just consider the present?'

Jessica was swinging from his hand. 'Come on,' she said. 'I'm hungry.'

'So am I, Jessica,' I said. 'And I expect Olivia is, too.'

'Not specially,' she said. 'I can wait while you have some sherry and go on with your interesting discussion.' She looked calmly at her mother.

We walked through the village. There was some cloud, and the sunlight had become intermittent.

'I think it will rain this afternoon,' my father said. 'There are things that should be put away, so I'll call back first, and then come on down.'

'Shall I come?' I said.

'No. Go with Isobel. You can amuse the children.'

I did not amuse the children. They amused themselves. I stayed close to Isobel, helping her.

'What's the vicar's name?' I asked.

'Hanley,' she said.

'He's quite unusual for a country parish, isn't he?'

'He'd be unusual wherever he ended up. Just occasionally one comes across such men. There isn't any explanation of how they get lost, somewhere along the way. He pretends it's not so. But it is.'

'Do you feel sorry for him?'

'I never feel sorry for people. It's a kind of insult. George does. I tell him off, I can't agree with it.'

I felt hesitant about asking her about him, and yet my father, in his new mood, and in his love for Isobel, had given me insights which rendered any superficial chatter quite absurd. And yet, as was so usual in his life all along, time seemed short, emotion highly charged, the whole relationship brought to a pitch that required continuous exploration and assessment. Small talk, whatever that means, simply could not exist within the orbit of his intensely passionate nature.

Nevertheless, Isobel smiled at me when I asked her, in all seriousness, 'Does he think that he is atoning for something?'

'You're so like him!' she said, laughing. 'You want to gobble up life, all in one meal. And then have it again and again.'

'But is he?' I asked. 'Is he trying to make amends?'

She was suddenly grave. 'I don't think you should ask that. Just let each hour, each day, take its course. What

41

Mr Hanley was preaching about is all right, so long as you believe it. It does sound impressive, doesn't it? To seek atonement, to be reconciled with God. But if you don't believe it you spend a lot of time in the present making amends for the past, and that uses up time, present time.' She shrugged her shoulders and turned back to the stove, checking beneath the saucepan lids. 'I'm not good at explaining what I mean, am I? I just have a sense of fear when people start summarising their lives, talking about making a new start, putting the past behind them, turning over a new leaf.'

'Father does that all the time.'

She turned and nodded briefly, 'He shouldn't. It's bad.'

'Shall we stop talking about him?'

Through the window she looked up at the grey sky. Then she crossed to the door to see where the children were. Turning back at last she said: 'I want him to stop looking backwards over his life and assessing it all the time. I want him just to live it now, with me, with us.' She made a gesture towards the door. 'You see, he'll take something like that sermon this morning and treat it personally. Because he admires the man he'll actually think that the words are meant for him. I have nothing against atonement except the waste, if you're not serious. You waste the wonderful present regretting the past.'

'He's obsessed by the past,' I said. 'Loves it, hates it, doesn't know what to do about it, can't leave it alone.'

'I suspect you are like him in that, aren't you?'

'Maybe.'

'Perhaps you can afford it. Perhaps you have a sense of balance which makes it possible for you to indulge yourself.'

'And he doesn't?'

Gently, she shook her head. 'I don't know. I don't think so. I don't want to risk it. I can't share in it, you see. We can't be part of it.'

She began to lay the table. Obscurely I felt she was warning me off, quite gently, with sensitive appeal, but firmly as well. She did not want me not to be there, but she wanted me to avoid stimulating within him those echoes out of the past which would lead, first to nostalgia, then on

42

to regret, then possibly into anger, a sense of impotence, and finally shame. If she knew these later stages at all, she knew them only from what he had told her. And in this she was inferior to me in her knowledge of him. It was clear she did not want to know any more from me than she knew already. And this was right. But it placed between us a curious barrier, as if we were engaged in a mild dispute about our differing perceptions of him, but a dispute that could not be resolved because the only common ground was him, now; Isobel lacked experience of the flaws in his character which I could not forget.

I saw him in all the vigour of his desperation after my mother's death, running under the trees of Hyde Park, through the faint shreddings of morning mist, across the dew-laden grass, the marked sand of Rotten Row, the bare patches of April earth. Running to a given purpose, with unnecessary haste but driven along by the demon of his passionate nature. And I knew then that I should not have provoked the memory. It was twenty years on, he was slower now, weaker perhaps, and where had the running got him? Where had anything got him?

'I'm bad for him, I think. I remind him about the past. I shouldn't do that.'

'So long as you know what it is you're doing.' Even as she looked at me, a resigned expression in her eyes, I knew that her doubts on this were justified as were her very real fears about the ultimate impact on him. 'Have you ever considered when he is at his happiest?'

I thought for a moment or two, flicking through the different images of him, from the storehouse of recollected attitudes. 'When he's doing a job of work,' I said. 'When he's absorbed in some task.'

'Yes,' she said. 'And isn't that the time when he's most likely to have forgotten the past and the future? Isn't that the time when he's wholly in the present?'

I looked at her, and for a moment I contemplated making some blandishment about her concern for him, some verbal gesture that would have been more characteristic of his manner than mine. But I turned away from it, feeling a kind of shame. This woman loved him. No glib commentary upon her feelings was possible; no commentary at all, glib or serious. I felt, as I stood there, the value of silence, the positive, healing force of silence. Atonement? Redemption? Were they concepts to be applied to him at all? Ever? Surely he belonged to a different tribe of men, that of the wild and brutal hunter in the sky?

[III]

As soon as he appeared in the doorway I knew something was wrong. To begin with, he stood there arms akimbo. His attitude somehow conveyed more than the physical sense of him filling the doorway with his hands on his hips. There was a challenging expectation in his eyes as though he wanted us to give our full attention to some dark shadow that had crossed his horizon since last we had been together. The children, sensing from his return that lunch would soon be on the table, had come in on either side of him. But his fixed attitude, instead of a gentler gesture such as a hand on the head or shoulder, or an indulgent word, told them instinctively that something was wrong, and they paused also, drawing our attention more firmly in his direction.

'It's confounded cheek,' he said, staring at Isobel.

'What is, George?'

'Wain!' He said the name in a familiar but rare and unwelcome high-pitched voice, that of outrage at some lapse of behaviour.

From her eyes I could tell immediately that Isobel was already acquainted with the note.

'What has he done?'

'It's not what he's done! It's what he says I should have done! Confounded cheek of the man!' He still stood in the doorway, his hands still upon his hips.

Isobel said, 'Was it outrageous? Has he insulted you? Would you pour your son a glass of sherry? And one for me as well, George? We've been waiting for you to get back. I think the children could have some orange.'

He stepped in over the threshold. 'Don't you want to hear?'

'Of course, George. Was it about the mower?'

'How did you know?'

'Well, you were using it this morning early. You told me that. It was sunny then. It had clouded over by the time we came out of church. You know how touchy Dr Wain is about equipment.' She continued at the stove.

'But he told me—'

'The sherry's in that cupboard. The glasses are on the table.'

He frowned, still staring at her shoulder as she went on with her cooking. Then he looked at me, still frowning.

'What did he tell you?' I asked.

'It's not just what he told me! It's his manner!' The thread of high-pitched outrage was still in his voice, but forced now, the real strength of it dissipated by Isobel's apparent indifference and the knowledge he must have had that I was offering myself as an audience for him rather than caring what Dr Wain had said.

'Sherry, George,' Isobel said, without turning.

He reached for the bottle, then glasses. 'I mean, he said to me—'

'—things have to be put away immediately after use,' Isobel said, her voice intoning the injunction. 'He's always saying it to boys, girls, staff, everyone.' She laughed. 'You're no different.'

'But it's the way he does it! Something shifty about the man. Came up to me, looking sideways, a sort of grin on his face, hinting, you see. "Wouldn't do if it rained, George," he said. "Powerful expenditure went into this mower; can't be leaving it around." As if I ever leave things around!'

She turned and laughed and took up her sherry. 'But you did! You were in the wrong.'

'Swans are never in the wrong.'

'Even swans,' she said, 'must learn to put mowing machines away after they have used them.'

'Well, I think you're taking things very coolly. Very coolly indeed.'

He had ceased to dominate the room. The children milled

45

around him, mixing their own orange. He poured out more sherry, but for a time Isobel was too busy to turn back to the table, and I preferred just to stand, leaning in that irritating way large men have. I tried, at first, to avoid looking at him. Then our eyes met, and I detected in his the faintest of accusations. What he would have been able to demand from me, an acquiescence in his sense of outrage, was not forthcoming from Isobel; quite the reverse. My natural anticipation was for some kind of oblique counter-stroke, and it was in an effort to direct this that I was endeavouring to remain passive.

'Have some more sherry, then,' he said, an unnecessarily stern note in his voice. He held out the bottle, and I advanced my glass to meet it.

'Sherry,' he said. 'In moderation. That's what we must bear in mind, eh old son?'

The prospect of a homily on the evils of excess in drinking made me smile inwardly and raise the glass to sip again. 'You haven't really told me what they're like,' I said. 'You do get on, don't you? Basically?'

'With the Wains? Oh, yes.'

'You said they were "top drawer"?'

He looked up sharply into my face. I was staring steadily back at him, not a hint of mockery in my eyes.

'They are, they are! Absolutely. He's Winchester, and Cambridge. She and her sister were at Edinburgh. They've more degrees than they need. There's a bit of money there, too.'

'Really?'

'Well, it's hard to tell, but I suspect the reserves aren't bad. What do you think, Isobel?'

She turned and sat down, sliding her drink across the table until it stood in front of her. 'I'll tell you what I think, George dear. I think you're the most frightful snob in all the world. I've never been able to understand where it came from, since, at heart, you're really the greatest egalitarian of all. But the way you talk about "top drawer types" is really preposterous.'

He looked startled for a moment. 'I'm not a snob,' he said. 'A snob? It doesn't matter a hoot to me who people are!'

'But in your last letter,' I said, 'you made the same point about him being a "top drawer type". You said he wasn't a suburban, "Broadshanks type".'

'Well, he's not.' He spoke quite sharply and drank down about half his glass of sherry.

'What is a suburban, Broadshanks type?' Isobel asked.

My father looked keenly at me, first. 'Do you remember Broadshanks?'

'Vaguely,' I said. 'Not really, though.' I wanted to encourage a full explanation.

My father spread out his hands in an expansive gesture of appeal. 'I mean, we all know Broadshanks.' He paused, almost as if that was enough. The dismissive, brink-of-laughter suggestion of a universal 'type' teetering permanently on the edge of absurdity, was as good a prelude to an explanation as could be offered. I thought Isobel might spoil it by asking the obvious question; but she remained silent, and he looked back at me. 'You remember them, of course? When mother was alive? Always there, being friendly. Always telling us how they tried to do the right thing, and what that was. Being neighbourly, kind, helpful. And expecting us to be the same. Permanent commentators, they were, upon their own lives. We never came up to scratch, of course. And they were so persistent. Mother was the soul of tact. But I just couldn't stand them. Couldn't tolerate their unctuousness.'

'They sound harmless enough,' Isobel said.

'That's it! Nothing there! Nothing at all.'

'How can you ever be sure?'

'I just *know*.'

I think Isobel felt he had been a bit unconvincing. But perhaps some purpose had been served, since when we reverted to Dr Wain I could see in my father's eyes a renewed respect for him, as though he could now review the affair of the lawnmower in the light of a minor tiff.

'He does have a sense of where he's going with the school, George. He does look ahead. You do see that?'

'Of course. I've nothing against him. But he mustn't push me. I have my own way of doing things. It works. I am a worker. You know that.'

'But perhaps he only sees you as something quite modest in the scheme of things. You must try and remember. It isn't what "type" he is that matters. That is interesting, but not important. It's what he does.'

'Old Wain's all right,' my father said. 'So's the battle axe, "meat-cleaver type". That's a new one.' He paused. 'All all right, old son!' He emphasised the first word: '*All* all right.'

But I could tell, from the look in his eyes, that somewhere in the middle distance, obscured by mist or shadow, lay some kind of mine-field designed to test his tolerance of the fact that he was a very minor cog in the machinery of which he formed a part, and that one day, not being the centre of his universe, would provoke an explosion. How carefully, and for how long, he could be steered towards, and then through, the hazards was a problem that rested on Isobel's shoulders.

[IV]

Olivia said, 'Are you married?'

I shook my head.

Jessica looked approvingly at her sister, then at me.

We were sitting at a table in the window of a room inside the house, just the three of us. I had been reading to them. It was close to six o'clock. It had been cloudy all afternoon, but the rain had held off. The garden was very still. Isobel had been out in it with my father, first sitting under a tree, then helping him. Finally, they had strolled off together.

'So you don't have children?' Olivia asked.

'No,' I said.

'Do you want some?'

'Is that an offer? Can I have you two, and take you away with me?'

Jessica laughed.

Olivia said, 'You will have us, in a way.'

'That's good news. How do you mean? How will that happen?'

'Mummy says we're going to have a new family. With George. So you'll become a brother. Kind of.'

'And what do you think about that?'

'It would be all right.' Olivia looked at me, coolly. 'We could come and stay with you, in London.'

'You could certainly come and see me.'

'There's not much to do down here,' Olivia said. 'It's a dump, really.'

'When are we going to London?' Jessica asked. 'Will it be soon?'

'When is your Mummy going to marry George? Will that be soon?'

'Oh yes. Probably.'

'Can we come next week?' Jessica asked.

'That might be a bit premature.'

'What's premature?'

'A bit early.'

'But if they got married they'd want to have a honeymoon. So what would we do? We'd have to take a bit of a holiday.'

'I think, with work and everything, it wouldn't be possible to go on honeymoon; not just now, anyway. We should save up your visit.'

'We'd have to come together,' Jessica said. 'We always do things together.'

Olivia frowned. 'If we came, what would you do with us?'

'Well, let me see. I'd take you both to the Tower of London. We'd go on the river in a boat. We might go down to Greenwich. We'd look at Buckingham Palace and the changing of the guard.'

'Would we go to a den of vice?'

I must have looked faintly startled.

'There are lots, aren't there, in London, now?'

'Yes,' I said, 'there are rather a lot.'

'Perhaps we could go to a few.'

'I don't think your mother would be too keen on that.'

'Oh, Mummy wouldn't mind. I'm sure they're over-rated. But it would be interesting just to see.'

Outside the windows the first full drops of rain fell. They seemed individually premeditated: plop, plop. The wind stirred in the leaves on the apple trees.

'Yes, let's go and see,' Jessica said.

I laughed. 'I think you'd need to be at least sixteen years old to get into a den of vice. These days, anyway.'

'Why, "these days"? Was it different once?' Olivia asked.

'Well, they used to like young girls in dens of vice. But the law has stopped that.'

'What a pity,' Jessica said.

Olivia asked, 'Are dens of vice found in Streets of Shame? There was an article called Street of Shame in the newspaper.'

'Which one?'

'*The News of the World.*'

'Did you read it?'

'I just glanced at it.'

'Do you think young girls will get into dens of vice again?' Jessica asked.

I looked from one serious, persistent face to the other. 'It seems that anything might happen, these days. I can't really answer.'

'It seems, then, you're not well informed,' said Olivia, looking directly at me. And in her eyes I saw her mother's simplicity of challenge.

'Not about dens of vice,' I said.

'Have you ever been in one?'

'When you get inside,' I said, 'they generally turn out to be very tame. When you're both older, I'll take you. But I think you'll be disappointed.'

The rain had become a patter. Through the house I heard the back door closing. They had got back in time.

Jessica said, 'We could have two places, then. Here and in London.'

'But suppose I was married, as well?'

'Are you thinking of it?' Olivia said.

'It had crossed my mind.'

'Who will you marry?'

'Well, that's the question. It takes time to find the right person.'

'It didn't take Mummy long to find George. After Daddy left.'

'That's different. A bit, anyway. They're older than me.'

'Are you thinking of getting married?' Isobel was standing in the doorway. From the ground outside the window there rose the sweetish smell of wet, warm earth.

'Well . . .' I said, hesitantly.

I looked from her to the two children. The flow of conversation, checked by her question, which was no more nor less serious than theirs, but different in attitude, came to a stop. It was time, anyway, for them to get ready for bed. Isobel said so, and they got up obediently enough.

Later, we had supper. We talked of marriage, and of the future. Bit by bit it became more real. Seeing them together fixed them together, in my mind. And to myself I kept saying, everything's going to be all right.

It was late when we left. The rain had stopped. We needed a torch going through the school grounds, and for most of the time we walked in silence. I told him how much I had enjoyed the visit. He said I must come again, and I agreed that I would. Soon. He said it would take time, waiting for the divorce. And I replied that it did not matter, that Isobel was as wonderful as he had said, and that I could see they were going to be happy. Were happy, I hastily added.

The night smell of pine resin was pungent at one point, near the turn in the drive. Then, as the buildings came into view, lit by an outside light, he switched off the torch.

'You must go on being a swan,' I said.

He laughed. 'Don't worry about that.'

I guessed he was referring to the trouble over the lawnmower, but I felt it would be a mistake to issue any kind of homily.

'When you're not a swan,' I said, 'what are you?'

He paused. 'If I am not a swan, then I am nothing.'

And I thought to myself, no, it isn't so, though you might wish it. You are never nothing. When you are not a swan, gliding, much approved of, and dignified, then you are a tiger, savage, instinctive, and dangerous. 'Best,' I said, 'you stay as you are.'

Chapter Three

[I]

Tiger or swan, doing his job, he survived. Whether I had grown wiser or more gentle, whether it is just that we are more attracted by stability in those we love rather than instability, I kept more in touch with him during that autumn and winter than I had done for several years. Part of the reason for this was Alice; always there in the background, a shadowy presence.

Oh yes, in all of this there was, indeed, Alice: woven between my father and herself, her advent uncertainly recalled from the shadowy period that followed my mother's death, so that she was first a guardian angel, and too often afterwards forced back into that role, one that she did not want: always, there was Alice.

She loved him from the harsh standpoint of not being loved in return. She waited for him, permanently, patiently, against the odds, never giving up because there was nothing else in her world to give up except him. Dumpy, slow in her movements, slow in all her reactions to the point of being ponderous, with her thick legs and carefully manicured, plump hands, she seemed never to change. The almost imperceptible spread of grey hairs among the brown, under the disguising restraint of careful and regular attention by the hairdresser, had preserved Alice in a kind of mummy-like state of ageing perfection. She had been there during my days at Coppinger, always there. And now she remained on, as a partner of mine more than of his, monitoring his progress as I did, performing the least attractive function of the unwanted, rejected partner: the role of the voyeur. Yes, it is true, when everything else deserts us, curiosity remains.

She pretended otherwise. It was habitual for us to meet at certain times during the year, a custom we had kept up since my days at school, even retaining a memento of those days in the timing of our encounters which corresponded with school holiday occasions. There was always an 'outing' at Easter time. There was a ritual exchange of presents at Christmas time. And in the new year we managed a regular visit to the theatre together. No longer was it the ballet, at Covent Garden, to which I had been taken so often as a child. It was now to the Royal Court we would go, close to her own flat, and, as entertainment, a lively centre in those days. There were other opportunities as well. Though never demanding, Alice's presence made itself felt in little isolated acts of thoughtful kindness; working as she did in a well-run office, there were occasional 'perks' (and she used the word, in inverted commas, in her notes to me) which came her way, tickets to theatres or concerts, invitations not taken up by her boss, which she either passed on to me with 'no strings attached' (another of her phrases) or which she offered to share with me, a device that afforded 'an exchange of views'. Carefully, deliberately, she would embark upon an unvarying catechism, concealing from me as best she could her overwhelming curiosity about himself, his welfare, his state of mind and heart, his whereabouts, his 'companion' of the moment. And I would generally pre-empt the rising tide of questions—a tide which she tried hard to stem behind a weakly-built wall of indifference—by volunteering what I knew.

With the advent of Isobel the feigned indifference had become more real. Seeing Alice in early October I could only report what I conceived of as happiness surrounding them, and my feeling that it would last. Meeting again, in the second half of December I reported the same conviction. I had been down, for a second visit, and found things as before. Alice had not heard from him at all since the one letter in the late summer which my father had told me about, and her resignation in the face of a measure of defeat, never accepted totally, actually made for a more enjoyable evening.

Sarah and I spent Christmas alone that year. It was not a happy time. We struggle too much, I suppose, with our own lives, independent of each other, and too little with what existed between us. It was a relationship compounding desire and convenience, both of us pursuing our not very profound exploration of art's possibilities, which were not producing a great return, and falling back into each other's arms as a temporary respite from a struggle the seriousness of which we maintained was absolute. It kept us apart; it kept us together; but at the end of what was then a couple of years of being uneasily yoked in a strangely web-like set of obligations—'I think line is important'; 'I think colour is important'; 'I think words are important'—we had established a situation that was static without being stable.

In recalling it, I am being less than fair to her. She had greater singleness of purpose than I had. Swifter, and more direct, her ruthlessness as an artist justified the demands she made as a woman, demands I was not generous enough to fulfil. It came out in the perspective on her character thrown by her friends. While I had few, and the few I had mainly associated with work, Sarah had many, and kept up with them. I remember particularly, among the parties that Christmas, meeting with Jane and Avril, the two girls who had originally shared the flat with her at the time we first met. They were both working in textile design, and their enthusiasm about it was infectious.

Suddenly, Jane turned to me and said, 'Has Sarah finished working on that spectrum cycle? You know, the seven paintings on the theme of random dominance. She was going to develop it to fifteen, taking intermediate colours as well.'

I must have looked slightly blank, just for a moment. Then I said, perhaps too quickly, 'They're coming on.' And then, remembering, but hesitating about whether or not I had it right, I added, 'It is going to be fifteen.'

'I'm glad she expanded it,' Avril said. 'She was easily the best. She'll do something quite original.'

And I agreed she would, but looking into Jane's eyes I perceived there a shadow of doubt as to whether I really understood Sarah.

'She's working very hard,' I said.

'And what about you? Do you help?'

'I don't think I am much help,' I said. 'I'm busy with my own writing. I find it hard to understand at times.'

'But she's so witty!' Avril said. 'Visually witty. She had a marvellous sense of colour, vivid and pure and strong. She always had answers. Try this, she would say. And then she introduced us all to Löhse's work. We had all stuck in front of Vasarely, metaphorically speaking. And Sarah came along and just shrugged her shoulders, and said it was all a bit like wallpaper, and told us to be serious, and then laughed when we found she was right. She was *so* right!'

'You must help her find a gallery,' Jane said. 'Don't you write about galleries? Or fine art, at least. Surely you can do something.'

What a strange appeal it seemed to be to me, afterwards. It should have been the very least I could do. In reality, it was like an indictment. Instead of asking myself, did I really love Sarah, I was constrained to reduce the question to a much lower level: did I really know Sarah? What did I want of her, or she of me? Were we conforming to current custom? Recruiting each other as bed-fellows, because that was the fashionable thing to do?

Her friends had made me conscious, more sharply than I wished, of the fact that I knew nothing of her real ambition, and of the distinct possibility that it was a great deal more serious than either she would admit or I could envisage. We had, it seemed—and it came as something of a shock—agreed to be agreeable to one another, and yet to remain strangers. It was almost as if the self that laid bare to friends, like Avril and Jane, the essential purpose of work, was refusing to do the same to me. And I wondered why. She could cry out in my arms, and close her mind, and the reason behind that had to have something to do with my lack of response or of understanding. Though I was troubled by this, I was somehow inhibited from doing much about it. If anything, it encouraged greater

55

indulgence in the physical side of our relationship. We enjoyed that; more at some times than at others, that is inevitable. But part of the purpose, I found, was to by-pass or frustrate those questions I did not wish to answer, such as, 'Who are you loving?' and, 'What do you want of this girl, and how will you achieve it, who does not grudge you her wildest embraces, yet refuses any more than the most transitory glimpses into her mind or her heart?'

Through all of this, heightening the contrasts, there came evidence of fulfilled love from my father, as he marked the pitches, mowed the lawns, skirmished with Dr Wain, and loved Isobel. I have the sweetest memories of that time, as far as it concerned him. From the calmness of his temporarily satisfied heart he sent forth messages of inquiry and encouragement, homily and homespun philosphy, ad-vice and affection. At one point I told him I was going on holiday in South Wales; back came the reply, 'I know it well. Take no risks. Only go sailing if you have to. There have been a lot of drownings recently, and your responsibilities are growing as you go forward in the world, making a career for yourself and hopefully, one day, a permanent home with children.' His logic was flawed; self-centred as well. There was word at the time from Melanie, who had gone from job to job. 'I don't think she will hold this one long,' he wrote. 'But then her father didn't either—drifted from job to job, from place to place until I found Isobel—and as long as she keeps going I don't think it matters very much.' Sometimes, I would tell him of setbacks or frustrations simply to provoke a reaction; it would have the effect of concentrating and making more vivid his essential goodness of heart, so plainly stated in his letters. 'My advice to you,' he would write, 'in the circumstance is not to bear resentment towards anyone. Just go forward with your work and forget it, doing your best, my son, doing your job.' And I would not take the advice, generally because it was always too complicated for that. But I would laugh at the simplicity of it, and love him for his vital capacity for bringing things down to essentials. In his own contentment his intrusive expressions of guidance for life flowered like daisies in summer, pricking up in abundance from the pages of his frequent letters.

In the new year I bought a car. It was a second-hand MG. It cost £120. I took Sarah down to meet him. As a visit, it was long overdue. Doubtful about it, I was surprised at how well it went.

My father got off to what was, for him, a good start. Within ten minutes he had fixed upon Sarah his stern gaze, and was asking her, 'Is he a good lover? Is he affectionate? Are things all right between you?'

She laughed at him. 'Which question will I answer first?'

'I shouldn't answer any of them,' Isobel said. 'I don't think he knows you well enough yet.'

'That's never stopped my father.'

'That's never been a good reason for not answering questions,' Sarah said to Isobel. Then she looked at him. 'It's yes to all of them, anyway.'

He seemed pleased with that. Then his stern gaze switched to me. 'And why didn't you tell me she had beautiful feet?' he demanded. 'You know I like to know that above all else.'

'It's why I hesitated to bring her down at all,' I said.

'But they are lovely,' he said to her, as though referring to jewellery or clothing. 'Show them to me.'

She slipped off her shoes, and held out her left foot, slim and elegant and small. He reached out his great hand, and cradled the foot in it for a moment. 'Yes,' he said. 'Beautiful. Like Isobel's feet, perfection.'

She withdrew, putting her shoes on again. He sighed. Then he turned towards me. 'And work? Fleet Street? All under control?' The broad sweep of canvas embraced by his questions was typical of him, and I had the urge to laugh. Fleet Street was, for him, simply there, like the City, an entity responsible for all news and comment, and since I worked in it I must have some share in control over it, able to answer for it in the way he expected Alice to speak up for Fenchurch Street or St Swithin's Lane.

I nodded. 'Everything under control. No, better than that. It's going well.'

It did not matter that I was telling him lies. He was simply setting the stage, anyway; fixing those around him in relationship to himself but ensuring that he would hold whatever centre there was. It was a commentary on life, his questioning: how things should be. And if they were not, it did not matter to be answering yes. It simply mattered inside oneself.

'And how is Dr Wain? Behaving?'

'He's all right.'

'And his women?'

'Bit of trouble,' he said. He glanced at Isobel. 'They're a pair of old trouts, really. Need careful handling.'

She sighed. 'They're all right.' She began to get up. 'Must see about lunch. And the children. They're very quiet.'

But he put his hand on her arm. 'You stay where you are,' he said. 'Don't move. Relax and talk and drink your sherry. I'll take charge.' He got up as he spoke. He looked at us, as if noting for himself the impact of his concern.

'All right,' she said. 'There's not much to do, anyway. But the children could lay the table, couldn't they?'

After he had gone out, trailing, I thought, the assertion of a new role rather too obviously, Isobel turned back towards us both and said, 'I'm changing my name. By deed poll.' She looked down at her hands.

Rather gravely, I said, 'But they'll know you here as you are.'

She looked directly at me. 'I'm not sure that we will stay indefinitely. 'The trouts', as he calls them are a bit tense about us. It's understandable. It is a school, after all. Parents, teachers, there's always gossip.'

'But it's a lovely cottage,' Sarah said. 'Wouldn't you miss it?'

She nodded. 'It's going to be difficult. But we'll find somewhere. It's fitting it all together; a job for George, a job for me, and somewhere that agrees to children. They're the problem.'

'Will it be soon?' I asked

'It won't be before the autumn.'

I did not ask Isobel why she was changing her name. But later, out walking, and being with my father some way ahead, I said to him, 'Is there some difficulty over Isobel's divorce? Is that why she's changing her name?'

58

'Yes,' he said. 'That's it. It's going to take time. And we've got to be prepared for any eventuality.'

'But there's no immediate problem, is there?'

He stared ahead of him. 'You never can tell,' he said.

I sensed in Isobel, on this occasion, a difference in attitude, softer towards him, more resigned, not in any sense recriminatory, but faintly tinged by sadness. I could not put my finger on what it meant, but Sarah did, later.

We were only there for the day and we left quite early to avoid Sunday night traffic. I was the second half of March, which that year had been very wet, but not too cold. Yet that weekend, from about Thursday, temperatures had fallen, and there had been fog drifting in over the east coast. We drove through it: not thick enough to delay us, but nevertheless casting a yellowish filter over the deserted streets of Chislehurst and Sidcup.

We talked about them in order not to talk about ourselves. And I tried to explain the difference I had detected in Isobel.

'Could it be she's pregnant?' Sarah asked.

I thought of the implications of that on top of what had been said about moving from the school. 'That'd be bad. What makes you—'

'Why else would you change your name by deed poll? Why not just wait for the divorce?'

I nodded, watching the blurred edges of the lights through the thin screening of the fog.

'And he did things for her. Is he usually like that?'

I thought of previous visits, my father being expansive, Isobel at the stove, or dealing with the children. 'No,' I said. 'I can't say he is.'

'That's what it is, then.'

We were silent. Through Sarah's eyes I saw my father and Isobel quite differently.

'Do you know how old he is?' I asked.

'I'd have thought he was in his fifties.'

'He's as old as the century.'

'Sixty-three? He's worn well. I wouldn't have thought it.'

'And now a child.'

She didn't answer that, just looked out of the car window in the other direction, as if giving expression to some kind of collection, female reproach: at men, who penetrate women, generating with their seed whole sheaves of problems, peopling the earth. And in her indifferent silence I felt a slight reverberation from the shock which the news if true must have delivered to my father. Inescapable as a logical outcome of their lovemaking, despite the usual precautions, though welcome in its way to his fundamentally natural and affectionate disposition—welcome also I would guess to her, bathed in this new and passionate love affair—this complication must, in sober judgement, be adding enormously to the difficulties already existing for them in their lives.

[II]

Alice's voice, on the telephone, was calm; but her message had an ominous ring. 'I must see you,' she said, 'as soon as possible. Tonight, if you can manage it.' It was the end of the week, Friday afternoon.

'What is it?' I asked.

'I can't talk on the telephone.'

'It's him, I suppose?'

'Yes.'

'What time will you be home?'

'By six.'

'I'll come round.'

'Would you like me to make you some supper?'

'No thanks.'

It was April. I had not seen him since the day's visit with Sarah. Easter had been wet, and the days after it uncertain, with cold winds in the street, flurries of driving rain, and a longing for summer on everyone's lips. Alice led me into her sitting room, an expression of the utmost gravity on her face. She asked me to sit down at the table, facing her across it, and I noticed that she had put down on it a small sheaf of papers and letters.

She asked me a few perfunctory questions, about my work, about Sarah, about Easter itself. I had been away, but alone, and my replies were equally non-committal. I was impatient to know the reason for her summons.

When she had stopped asking questions she moved the pages about, uncertain how to go on.

'You've heard from him?' I asked.

She nodded.

'Something's wrong?'

She nodded again. She looked up at me. Her eyes were clear. 'This woman,' she hesitated before the hurdle of her name; 'this woman . . . Isobel . . .' It sounded darkly in my ears, as though we were discussing the heroine of a play by Webster or Tourneur. 'She has had a miscarriage.'

I looked at Alice, trying to think what I should say. 'Oh,' I said. 'That's bad. When?'

'On Monday. She went into hospital. I don't know whether she's out yet or still there. I don't know how serious it was.'

Ignorant of such matters, I did not know then how serious it could be. I felt only, a long way off, the tumult shifting under him. How serious was it for him?

'How did you hear?' I asked.

She picked up a blue envelope. She held it in her podgy hands. She tapped the edge down on the table, all the time looking at me with an apparent calmness that made me think of her as opaque. She was opaque as a piece of china, still dressed in her office outfit, immaculately winding down from taking letters and answering the telephone. 'He wrote to me,' she said. 'He wants help. He needs money. He's afraid he'll be thrown out. And he probably will. His letter is confused. Would you like to read it?'

I reached out across the table. I half realised, then, how much of a shield Alice had been to me, and that now, as the letter was passed over, it was like a military order, my own marching papers to some front line where I would take over from her responsibility for a battle that had been going on for many years. I opened the letter.

'My dearest Alice: Isobel has had a miscarriage, and is in hospital. It has smashed up everything. I feel that I will have to leave. The Wains know, and I have the feeling that it's the final curtain. I shall come to London. You must

61

help me. I'm just about at the end of my tether. Love, George.'

I read it through a second, and a third time. Unlike his usual letters, which were dated, day, month and year, this one, scrawled in large untidy writing which quickly filled a single sheet of blue paper, had no address on the top, simply 'Tuesday, 9 a.m.'.

'I'd better go down,' I said.

'Will it do any good?'

'They can't sack him for this! Only he may have gone on the beer.'

'I'm sure he has done.'

'Isn't that pre-judging things?'

Alice said, 'I can't help him any more.'

'It's as if he's had the miscarriage, not her.'

'It's not unlike him.'

'What isn't?'

'To collapse in the face of crisis.'

I nodded, gravely. She had almost talked me into an inner admission of defeat on his behalf.

'But he hasn't come to London?'

'He will. You can be sure of that.' It was so much a matter of fact.

I thought to myself, it is what she wants. For the first time, in Alice, I saw what I can only describe as a predatory streak. She was more threatened by this than she had ever been.

'And will you help him?' I asked. I was going to add, 'if he comes'; but instead I went on, 'when he comes?'

'I couldn't have it on my conscience that I didn't help, at such an unhappy time.'

'So you will?'

She stared at me. 'People can't help it if they fall in love,' she said. There was a catch in her voice. I thought she might cry.

There was a pause. I wasn't sure whether she meant herself and him, or Isobel. I concluded that she meant all of them. There was nothing non-committal that I could say in answer to a platitude that contained more of the world's agony than any other ever uttered.

She went on, 'If your father wants to make his life from now on with Isobel, well and good. It is their choice, his and hers. He can't really expect me to help in holding them together.'

There was no note of interrogation in her voice. She appeared to be stating fact. Yet literally moments before she had said she would help.

'Is this the only communication you have had from him?' I asked, pushing the letter back across the table.

She looked down at her hands, neatly folded. 'He telephoned me last night.'

I waited for her to go on.

'He needed money. She's in hospital at least five miles away. He has to take a taxi. Dr Wain won't let him use the school shooting-brake.'

'And did you send money?'

'I wired some to him this morning.'

'And what did you say to him?'

She looked up at me and said in her calm, deliberate voice, 'I have written to say how furious I am with him, and I absolutely refuse to do anything more. Giving him the money, so that I don't have any of the present unhappiness laid at my door in the future, has also given me the chance to say things to him, in black and white. There will be no more money. He is her affair now.'

The flaw in her case was plainly detectable, yet how could I comment on it? The best I could do, in the circumstances, was get down to him and make sure he did not precipitate things beyond rescue.

'He's nothing if not dramatic,' I said, getting up. 'It's lucky it's the weekend. And I have the car. I may even go down tonight.'

'Will you be sure and tell me what the situation is? Will you ring me? Monday?'

'I will,' I said. 'As soon as I know how things are I'll tell you.'

There was relief, then gratitude in her eyes, lifting her spirits as it were. But it was only after I had left that I began to puzzle over this, and to see in it the true expression of her determination. Over so many years she had been hurt so much; hurt by that laconic indifference so cruel to women, and to men, in the arena of love. There should have been greater recrimination, much more bitterness. A real and final dismissal would not have surprised me, since I, at that point in my life, had no real grasp of the force or reality of love. Instead, what was I witnessing? The unwavering hand held out to help him, just as I had been, over the years, an instrument of conciliation between them. It would never change. I was the closest witness of the true nature of this stubborn woman.

[III]

As soon as I rounded the shrubbery at the end of the driveway, I saw him: alone, working at some self-appointed task with a broom or a hoe on the gravel of the forecourt, he had already paused and was looking up when I came into view. Dressed in white painter's overalls, and with a dark blue shirt and a cloth cap, he was very inch the working man; only on drawing close, and seeing certain details—the stern gaze, the hard lines of his face, the carefully clipped goatee partially covering the silk scarf carelessly tied at his neck—did the stereotype begin to reveal something different.

We imagine that when we talk of the unforgettable in a person that we are thinking of the memorable word or gesture, the striking verbal image, the tilt of the head, some characteristic stance or movement of hand or arm. Of course, it may be all of these. But when we are considering those for whom we feel deeply, love reinforces memory. It is our love that translates the trivial phrases into poetry; it is our love which imprints upon the mind's eyes, for all the years of our own lives, some recollected position in which the object of that love stood or sat or turned, not just at a particular time, but regularly, over and over, investing words and gestures with a relevance invisible to those with less concern. So that when I say that the image of him as he stood there with the hoe in his hand, staring towards

64

me in his overalls and cap, is firmly fixed, I am really saying something quite different; that at that moment it was the wave of my compassionate love for him in his need, so clearly visible in his eyes, that fixed the occasion, turning it into one of the permanent images by which I recall him.

I was diffident about *my* car in front of *their* school, given the doubtful circumstances, and I drove it cautiously and slowly towards a parking place not far from where he stood, staring expectantly at me. I got out and waited as he came over.

'Glad you've got the car,' he said. 'We may need it.'

'A quick getaway?'

He laughed. 'Things aren't too good.'

'Not a swan any more?'

'It's hard to say. I do my job. But they no longer smile at me.'

'It's not always possible. Has Dr Wain—'

'You know George, sonny boy. You know your father. Can't work if there's an atmosphere. It's just no good.'

The note of deep dismay seemed alarmingly exaggerated, as if his perspective on everything had gone completely awry. 'But how is Isobel?' I asked. 'What about her? And the children?'

'It's all under control. Don't worry.' He stood still, not a yard from me, his left hand resting on the top of what had turned out to be a large rake for the gravel. He treated it like a beadle's staff, a badge of office giving character and depth to the attitude he had assumed.

'But is she still in hospital?'

'Comes out this afternoon. We'll collect her.'

I looked round at my small car; then at him. 'Shall I bring my bag?'

'No,' he said. 'Leave it. I don't have the extra room any more. New member of staff. You'll have to stay in the village.' He paused. 'You'll stay with Isobel.' It was said peremptorily. Perhaps I should have left it at that.

'She'll hardly feel up to it,' I said.

He looked sharply back into my eyes. 'It'll be a help,' he said. 'She'll welcome the company.'

We went inside. He led the way up to his room. There was a savage determination in his stride, as though he were forcing himself on, quite careless of whether or not I kept at his heels. His room was different. The fundamentally strict tidiness of life, when all was going well, had been dissipated. Imperceptibly at first, there grew in me a sombre conviction that things were very wrong. The objects in his room were more or less the same, but the atmosphere and the detail had altered. Through the bedroom door I could see clothes on the floor. On the desk blotter were two crumpled pound notes and a heap of change. His jacket hung over a chair, not squarely, the shoulders filled by the chair back, but dangling carelessly from one side, the pockets touching the ground. A paper lay across the armchair, its racing columns marked in biro.

We looked at each other across the room. I knew he was drinking, and I waited for the obvious proposal, thinking desperately of something to say that would put it off. Perhaps because he knew that I knew he paused, and looked round, and then picked the jacket off the chairback and felt through the pockets, putting things out on the desk beside his money.

'Why did you contact Alice?' I asked.

He stood still, his hands together holding the neck of the jacket somewhere level with the front flap of his white overalls. They were loose on him—he loved his working clothes to be loose—and he looked somehow crumpled and defeated.

'She's my lifeline, old son.'

'Not any more, father.'

'I was desperate,' he said. 'I thought the balloon would go up.'

'Were you at the end of your tether?' I used the phrase from his letter as an intentional, if minor cruelty, thinking it might jog his mind.

But it was an over-subtle device; he swept it up and used it back at me. 'Of course I was! Don't be a fool! Absolutely at the end of my tether!'

'Why didn't you contact me? Did you think Alice would?'

'You've your own life to lead.'

66

'Hasn't she?'

He looked away. He could not bring himself to answer in the negative. Yet that was what his silence meant. And he expressed it in his faint smile as he looked back at me. 'I needed a lifeline,' he said.

'You mustn't talk of lifelines,' I said. 'You're not drowning. You're not even in the sea, yet. The ship's not going down. You've got to think of Isobel. You've got to think of the children. It's *got* to be all right.'

'You never can tell, sonny boy. I knew Alice would stand by me.'

'Did you know she would contact me?'

'No. I never thought that.' He spoke sharply, his eyes looking sternly into mine. 'I didn't want to drag you in.'

'But father, I'm glad. I want to be here. I want to help.'

Suddenly we reached the moment I had been trying to fend off.

'I need a drink,' he said. 'What time is it?'

I told him.

'Let's go,' he said. 'Let's get out. Let's get right away.'

As luck would have it, Dr Wain was standing out in front of the school building talking with a member of staff, and he turned and beckoned my father, and then started crossing towards us. I couldn't decide whether he wanted to speak privately with him, but the rather toothy smile at me suggested a social encounter, and I followed a yard or so behind my father, who had, of course, divested himself of overalls and put on his jacket.

'I see your son is down again,' he said, nodding at me. 'On to a good story? Sleuthing around?'

It seemed so singularly inappropriate that I replied, I suppose with some daring, 'My father's the best story, Dr Wain. I need go no further.'

'We can't do without him, and that's the truth.' He spoke the last word forcibly, and drops of spit flew from his lips, glinting in the April sunshine as they fell. 'Minor upheavals, eh, George? Nothing for the newspapers in that.'

I was reassured. But I was less certain about my father, who stood squarely in front of Dr Wain. I felt he could easily lose his temper, punch his employer on the chin, and

67

the 'balloon' certainly would have gone up. Equally well, he could just ignore the inane exercise in staff relations which was going on.

He did the latter. 'I'm going to the hospital with my son,' he said. 'We are going to collect my future wife. She comes out today.'

'I'm so glad to hear that,' Dr Wain said. 'We can't do without her either, you know. Not even for a day.'

I saw my father clench his teeth. The ridge of muscle at the corner of his jawbone pulsed.

'She's a wonderful person,' I said. 'I hope she's fully recovered.'

He moved off then. 'I hope so, too,' he said as he went.

'Slavedriver!' my father said, under his breath.

We got into the car. He looked round at its confined space. 'It'll be a tight fit. Should we get a taxi?'

'I can put the hood up. How will she be?'

'All right.' He paused. 'We'll have to see.'

We drove off.

Looking ahead at the road he asked me, 'What did Alice say? How was it? Did you go round? Did she give you supper? Were you bored to tears?' He turned. 'I didn't mean you to be involved.'

'But I am, anyway,' I said. 'I'm glad.' I paused. 'You can't expect Alice—'

'I know. You're right. We're not in the sea yet. But I was afraid, my son. I don't want to go back to the Broadshanks type. This has to work. If only I was a younger man. If only I was forty again, if only; or even forty-five. Strong, in my prime, able for anyone.'

'You are what you are.'

The pub was virtually deserted. The owner said 'Here's the Commander!'

His wife came into the bar. 'Hello, George,' she said.

He downed his scotch like water. It seemed not even to touch his throat. Just flowed away.

'Steady,' I said. I bought him another.

'I must atone for my life.' He stared at the bottles. 'And yet,' he paused. 'There is something illogical about atonement. If you spend the present going over the past, in order to make it right, aren't you neglecting the present? Some of the time I think you must just live out every day.' He was echoing words I had heard before. This was Isobel's advice. Had it also been Isobel who had identified this fault in him, this failure to live wholly in the present? He glared ahead of him. The drink was unregarded on the counter. The owner and his wife could be heard, but were out of sight. 'For better or worse,' he said, 'it's there, what you do. Once you start making amends, or putting things right, you lose the momentum of life. The present becomes compromised by the past.'

'But you love the past,' I said.

He lifted the drink, but took only a modest sip. 'Too much,' he said. 'I am driven by it too much. It is too vivid. I see myself as a young man, and it's all too vivid. What I might have been, that cannot be redeemed.'

We drank for more than an hour. I was careful not to keep pace with him; yet I indulged him, recognising within him certain crying needs, and encouraging his examination of himself, though in retrospect I sensed it was all wrong. Others were in the bar when his growing expansiveness began to show a concern for me.

'What about Sarah, then?' he asked, his voice penetrating the hum of sounds.

'What about her? She's well.'

'You make love together?'

I looked at him.

'Why aren't you married, then? What's the problem? Are you just messing about? Trial basis? Usual thing with the young these days.'

I did not know how to answer. 'We're getting on well enough as it is,' I said.

His own desperate set of needs, multiple, pressing, never to be wholly satisfied, were put aside in favour of this almost jocular approach to my relationship with Sarah. For, in the worst sense really, the 'modern' sense, that is what it had become: a 'relationship'. Unlike him, I never considered need, where Sarah was concerned. I had come to a point, in the face of lack of commitment, in the face of having failed to live up to the modest expectations friends of Sarah's, like

Jane and Avril, had of me, of believing instead that I was respecting her independence of spirit, whereas, in reality, I was ignoring that creative companionship, that essential commentary on what she might be doing in her art—even without having full access to it—which is the infuriating demand artists make upon those with whom they endeavour to share, always partially, their lives.

He gave a short laugh. 'Mustn't pry. None of my business. You've your own life to lead, sonny boy.' He drank, this time, it seemed to me, with distaste. 'You decide, you decide. But keep me informed.'

[IV]

'Why don't you let me collect Isobel?' I said. 'There just isn't room for the three of us.'

'Then we should get a taxi.'

'Do you want a taxi driver listening to you?'

He stood in the middle of the room, looking cross, his hair on end, his braces down.

'You're sure I can't drive your car?'

'No.' I think at the time I would have said it was more precious to me than he was.

'Then you go,' he said.

'It's better.' I meant it as a reflection on the state he was in. He had slept for more than an hour; when he awoke the benign muzziness of our relatively innocuous drinking had been dispersed, so that he was at odds with everyone.

'I've made a mess of things,' he said. 'Again.' His voice was deep and tremulous. He raised his hands on either side of his body, the palms upward, in a gesture that was meant to be an appeal. He stood in a patch of afternoon sunlight. He wore only a vest on the upper part of his body. With his braccs hanging down by his thighs, his trousers, unsupported, were low on his hips and crumpled into folds at his stockinged feet. His now sparse hair stood up in weirdly bent tufts and points.

'Don't think like that,' I said. 'You only make it worse.'

'But it is worse. It's always worse. At the bottom of my heart I always know—'

'Don't say it,' I said, interrupting him. 'Look at yourself. Pull your braces up. Do your hair. Get ready to meet her when I bring her back.'

'It's too late, sonny boy.' He broke into song. '"When skies are grey, dear, I don't mind the grey skies . . ."' It petered out.

'Don't bring on catastrophe,' I said. 'Don't invite dramatic climax where none is intended, except in your own mind. You've got to go on. Isobel needs you.'

It was a shot in the dark. I did not really know, at that stage, whether it was all over or not. The logic of it required that he should try again, and logic was all I could rely on. I wanted to steer him away from adopting attitudes, since attitudes seemed to define for him, in a peculiar but indelible way, the direction his life should take.

He slipped one side of his braces over his shoulder. Then the other. He looked round for his shoes. One hand came up to his head and began smoothing down the rumpled hair. 'You go on,' he said. 'You'll be late. I'll smarten up. It'll be all right,' he said. 'Don't you worry. We'll win in the end.'

On the way back from the hospital I said nothing at all about him. It was she who had suffered not him. She asked me about Sarah, and I was evasive. It was almost as a defence that I said to her: 'Did you want the child?'

'I didn't want to lose it.'

'If you don't want to talk about it . . .?' My eyes were fixed on the road, and I was driving quite slowly.

'We didn't intend to have children. You must realise that. Yet for both of us, once it was there, it seemed, I don't know, right is such a silly way of describing it. But it *was* right.'

'Would it have been difficult?'

'It would have been bloody impossible!'

'But worth it?'

'Oh, yes.'

71

I waited. But she didn't say any more. I told her that he had had a few drinks, and a rest, and seemed all right now.

She said, 'That's good.'

'Have you . . .? Has he . . .?' I found the question difficult to phrase. 'Do you know about his drinking bouts?'

'I know what he's like when he's drunk. When men get drunk they need handling.'

'But a bout of it?'

She sighed. 'You'd have to explain. And I don't want you to, if you don't mind. Let's see how things will be. He got drunk the day I went into hospital. That frightened me. You see, there were the children. Suppose there had been no one else?'

My father seemed transformed when we got back. He had collected the children, and they ran out to the car. He appeared behind them, so smart and upright, both his hair and beard brushed; and shy as well, waiting for her embrace, longing for it, but diffident and cautious and passive. How important she was to him, and how frail were the tendrils holding up the plant, not so much of their love, but of their life together. I felt nervous of being a witness. What could I say, to myself, to them, but 'Go on!' What else was there? And yet, how delicately balanced it all was! Young as I was, I had been conditioned, at that stage, by a lifetime's speculation as to whether relationships between people, situations affecting lives (with my own always one of them), and future prospects, would in fact 'go on', or founder. And I measured off my father's prospects then, as I had always done in the past, in just those terms. Of course Isobel came under the same judgment. But because *they* did not consider it in those terms, because, that afternoon, I had deflected him away from the melodramatic course of setting his own life firmly on a downhill route to destruction, I felt confident that it would survive.

I became a party to their debate, that night. They would leave. It would be difficult, but together they would find a job, as man and wife, she changing her name as had been decided anyway. In time the divorce would come through. The children would be a handicap, but they would manage.

They could not rely on Dr Wain. He was too close to what was now in the past. They had to make a fresh start. My father used the phrase with such passion. He was like Caesar in his tent: 'That civilisation may not sink, its great battle lost.' And I believed in him, I believed in them.

Chapter Four

[I]

It was November, and very mild; in fact, the mildest November in Worthing since records began. It was, for me, a special month, that year, and I keep, in mind and heart, firm recollections of certain days on which the precise tone of light, the softness in the air, even the smell, all of which, in ways, derive from temperature, can be summoned up from the past with what seems like effortless immediacy. It was the month in which that beloved constellation of Orion was thought by the Greeks to bring on late Autumn storms. It was my father's great climacteric; the exact occasion on which he reached out, one last time, for something of his own fashioning. It was a climacteric also for me; but so trivial by comparison that I hardly care to recount the details or the events.

He had made me aware, so consistently, of my own emotional shortcomings. He had not done it consciously. He had probably not been aware that he was doing it at all. And yet, even in the curious reticence he observed in the occasional cross-examination to which he submitted me, in a good-natured fashion, about why I was not getting married, and what I was doing with my life, he managed to leave hanging over me a cloud of guilt and self-doubt.

Was it deserved? Each in his own heart makes a final judgment about 'the meannesses of the mind' of which Hopkins tells; each in his own heart selects some standard by which he measures; each person is swayed in that judgment by the intrusion of love. And it may be that in attributing to him a fineness of feeling, a quality in the totality of his passion, that my judgment was distorted by that love. It was of a helpless kind. I witnessed the events without being able to direct them, without being able to give assistance of any kind. I did so from the emotionally shabby comfort of my unfulfilled liaison with Sarah, the source of his probing, the base against which I measured his love for Isobel.

'So you're going down to Kent again this weekend?'

'It's not Kent. They've moved. I told you.'

'Sorry.'

'Yes. I'm going to see them.'

'And I can't come?'

'You said you wanted to work.'

'If I changed my mind?'

I didn't answer, but got up from the breakfast table and went to the window. There was light fog, but the sky above, tinged with the blushing colours of ripening peaches, promised to dispel it. Line is important. Colour is important.

'You don't want me, do you?' She was wearing a full and loosely woven woollen skirt and a polo-necked ribbed jersey which fitted closely to her slim body. She had done up her long hair. Objectively, she was very pretty.

'If you want to come, then come. We'll drive down together. I've said that.'

'Where will we stay?'

'With them, if there's room. Or somewhere else. It's not a problem. It is winter, after all.'

'But you don't really want me.'

Again, I didn't answer. I should have worked that morning, and hadn't. It had been days, even weeks. I was conscious, more than anything else, that she was painting each day, calmly, deliberately, coldly even, and I was doing nothing. We can't go on, I thought, looking at her. Yet I could not bring myself to say anything; all I could do was gnaw at the bone of contention between us, feeding my own jealousy, feeding hers.

'It's up to you,' I said. It was as good as telling her not to come.

'I'll come, then,' she said.

'All right.'

'If you do want me—?'

'Oh, Sarah!'

She started to cry. 'You don't love me, do you? Not really.'

I crossed to the table where she was sitting and resumed my place, putting my hand out to cover hers where it lay beside her coffee cup.

She pulled it away. 'You don't answer,' she said.

'I do love you,' I said.

'You'll need to. I'm pregnant.' She stared balefully at me through her tears. I felt panic rise within me.

'You're pregnant?'

She nodded, not taking her eyes from me for a moment.

'Oh, God! How did it—?'

'You may well ask!' Her laugh was brief and bitter.

'Have you seen a doctor?'

She nodded. 'It's confirmed.'

I frowned. 'Why didn't you tell me before?'

'I didn't know till yesterday.'

'But last night?'

She shrugged her shoulders and looked away from me towards the window. 'I was afraid to.'

'Afraid?'

'Yes. We're not ready for it, are we? It isn't right for us. We . . . we're . . .'

She tailed off. I wondered if she were contemplating some examination of the strength or otherwise of our love for each other, and was relieved at her inability to put words on it. I felt the same. Within me there was panic, despair, anger, a feeling of being trapped. I could only consider myself. We had been playing in an emotional minefield, and had sprung one of the oldest snares of all. It seemed unfair; yet it wasn't. It was an exact retribution.

Sarah, who had not really wanted a man, who had wanted her work, and its fulfilment instead, carried within her body the inimitable, growing, determined evidence of my involvement in her life just when that involvement was dissipating itself in indifference. This, in her womb, was reality, and not the effete toying with existence which constituted our cohabitation. And I could not give expression to any feeling.

I am ashamed to say that, when it came to it, I drove down to my father and Isobel alone. I remained indifferent as to what she would do. I was engaged in my own form of escape.

[II]

They had survived. My delight and relief at this was immense. It had blinded me as well. The remarkable fact that together they had come through the 'balloon going up' against the odds, against Alice's justifiably jaundiced expectation, blinded me to the parallel fact that the circle had narrowed. They had left for employment together. An encounter between my father and Dr Wain, as foolish as the one which concerned the mowing machine and this time to do with the scouts' and girl guides' shed in the school grounds, had brought about the abrupt if anticipated conclusion of his job at Brookhall School.

But the inevitable had not happened. The flailing around, which on innumerable occasions in the past had created a vortex of destruction and recrimination affecting everyone, like the unconvincng climax of a minor Elizabethan tragedy where the stage is littered with casualties all discovering the absurdities which have brought them to perdition, had, on this occasion, left himself and Isobel, with the two children, intact.

It was to my immense relief that this was the case. Alice saw it differently. When there had been the cry for help she had given help. In her exact and careful fashion, perhaps a little balefully, she had arrested the characteristic lurch towards disaster. She had thought that it would end things with Isobel. Now that she was shown to have been wrong she affected indifference.

I could not see it from Alice's point of view. I never did. She was, to me, another dimension of him. This did not make her any less real as an individual. It probably intensified her character, since what was important for me in her emotions was to her the very lifeblood of all that she did. She had little else; and that little else did not greatly matter to her. It must therefore have been a grey period for her, the time of their survival from that spring into November.

'I have done all I am going to do,' she told me, the evening of Sarah's announcement.

'Is he looking for help again?' Preoccupied with thoughts of my own, the question was fairly perfunctory.

Without answering she handed me a letter which I unfolded.

'My dear Alice: It's going to be alright. They're very kind to us here. We have a cottage. It's not well paid, but there is security. It is so difficult getting anywhere, with children. Altogether, we answered 46 advertisements. Seven replies, three of them negative, four interviews, and only one that turned up trumps. So there you are. I thought I'd let you know how things stand. It has been expensive settling in, and we're broke. If you could help, with a loan, which of course I'd pay back, we would be so grateful. But of course I will understand if you feel you can't do this. I shall always be grateful for what you have done. George.'

I stood, foolishly looking down at the blue paper, not knowing what to say. Eventually, I said, 'You can't do any more.'

'It's so unfair to ask,' she said.

'It's so like him.'

'Do you think Isobel knows about this?' she asked, taking back the letter from my hand.

I think she hoped that I would say no. 'Oh, yes,' I said. 'He would have talked to her about writing.'

'He's so like a child,' she said.

I nodded. 'What will you do? Nothing?'

She paused, collecting her thoughts. 'I can't leave them, in trouble, just like that. I would have it on my conscience.'

'It's so wrong.' I said it automatically. What was wrong with me, that I could see their tangled lives more seriously, as the substance of a kind of unending tragedy, while I could not address Sarah's problem—and my own, of course—with the same degree of maturity? Their lives—not just my father's and Isobel's, but Alice's as well—were more real than my own.

'But I do love him, my dear.' She broke in on my thoughts. 'I shall always love him. I cannot bear to think of his unhappiness, and it would weigh on my mind so much if I did nothing.'

'But he's not unhappy,' I said. 'He's just broke.'

'Still, with all the difficulties they have . . .' She looked up into my eyes, a kind of blank, pugnacious expression on her face. Then she said, 'Deep down he's unhappy.' And I knew it reassured her to believe that. She was clearly not to be deflected from whatever course of action she had chosen. And, in purely human terms, I was by no means unwilling to see her respond positively to his appeal. After all, I thought, there were no emotional constraints on *me* giving him help. Just financial ones. Running my little sports car was not cheap. Living with Sarah exacted certain costs. If Alice failed him, would he not turn to his son?

'I have decided,' she said, 'to give him fifteen pounds. It is here, and I want you to take it down when you go. I have written him a letter, rather formal, I'm afraid, saying that it is the last he will hear of me. I don't want any more letters or phone calls. I just want him to leave me alone.'

It seemed the worst possible way of persuading him that she was serious. And I debated telling her so. But on reflection I just took the envelope and put it in my pocket.

All of this had taken place quite calmly. I wondered very much if Alice saw through her own self-delusion, and anticipated the next round, deriving from this her calm acceptance of temporary defeat. If so, it explained an almost casual complacency.

Afterwards, we had supper together, carefully prepared and served, and accompanied by a well-modulated litany about my work and hers, about my friends and hers, about my leisure pursuits and those which filled up her solitary evenings. I only half-listened. I left at about nine o'clock, cash for my father in a sealed envelope in my pocket with the accompanying note of hollow valediction.

79

[III]

'Yours the sports car, is it?'

'The MG? Yes.'

'Very nice, I say. Very nice indeed. So this is your son, eh, George?'

'He's a writer,' my father said. 'Works for a Fleet Street agency. Down for a day or two to see his father.'

'No pretty girl to go with the car?' The man, who was in his late thirties, looked round the uncrowded bar of the White House Country Club. Then back to me.

'I didn't catch your name,' I said. 'Was it Billy?'

He looked a bit sharply at me, as though I were pulling his leg. 'Willie,' he said. 'Short for William. That's how I'm known around here, isn't it, George?'

My father nodded.

'No girl goes with the car,' I said, in response to his inane remark. 'What do you drive?'

'I have a Jaguar,' he said. 'But I pranged it. Using mother's at the moment. She was in last night, wasn't she, George?'

Again, my father nodded.

'And what do you do with yourself, Willie?' I asked.

He looked at me again rather sharply. 'I have a business in Godalming. Keeps me busy during the week, bringing in the shekels. Try to let my hair down at the weekend. Pour me another one, George, there's a good chap.'

'Don't you work today? It's only Friday.'

'Closed. Funeral of the works manager.'

'Aren't you . . .?'

'Been.'

My father went behind the deserted bar, and took Willie's glass with him. Willie said to me, 'Sure you won't have something?' He spoke quietly, as if fearful that the two elderly men at a table nearby, who were silently staring at their empty glasses, might hear something that would give Willie a bad name in the club.

'It's a bit early,' I said. 'But perhaps I'll take a sherry. Thanks.'

One of the men looked up.

'Your son's cracking,' Willie said to my father. 'He'll take a sherry. What kind do you like?'

I told him a Bristol Milk would do. Others came into the bar. My father gave us our drinks, but was then preoccupied with more orders. He seemed distinctly ill at ease in his role as barman, and I watched the uneasy exchange of pleasantries while at the same time coping with Willie.

Willie was unusually interested in feature writing, and wanted to know all about it. I told him some facts about the agency and tried to make it sound interesting.

'Is this a good club?' I said.

'It's all right.'

'I know nothing about such establishments,' I said. 'Do women come?'

Willie chuckled. 'Oh, yes. It's good in that way.'

I wondered what way he meant. I felt incurious, and resentful towards him. He would not make the mistake of getting a girl pregnant. Or if he did he would handle it differently. Either way, it would not hang over him like a shadow, poisoning present and future. It would just be different with Willie. His mother would intervene and take over, just as she had done with her motor car.

'And it's busy on a Friday?' I asked.

'Fairly. Warming up for the weekend.'

When I did occasionally intercept my father's glance, he would wink, his right eye closing and opening very rapidly; but the rest of his face remained quite expressionless, hard as well, so that I felt insecure about him. What was he telling me, except that I was there? He seemed tired, and a bit old behind the harsh line of nose and cheek, the small close-clipped beard. At noon two girls took over behind the bar. Willie and I had completely exhausted every conversational avenue, and he now turned his attention to one of the girls whose name was Mildred. Mildred laughed a good deal at Willie's references to a man called Stephen who had been telling stories at the bar the previous night. I took the opportunity to walk across the room to a window. I felt awkward and standoffish, but could not help it. Whether or not my father minded was of little account. But it could not really matter, not even in the mild way it had with Dr Wain.

It was a raw, still November day, one on which only the slow changes in the light made any movement. Even that was slight. The tall, bare elm trees stretched away across about twenty acres of flat parkland into a mist that shrouded the edges of distant woods. A watery sun was visible in the sky, weak and easy to look into behind the heavy gauze of persistent white that gradually deepened above into a bluish wintry sky. A bonfire of leaves, I thought, and the epitome of autumn would be complete.

I felt the envelope of money in my pocket, and wondered how he would spend the fifteen pounds. The cold-blooded relief I had felt in Alice's company, ridding me of responsibility, turned now to sadness. The stillness outside was like a prison, a wall of endless fields, woods, houses, people, towns, countries, continents, the world itself, with him pinned here by unfair circumstances serving unnecessary drinks to unnecessary people. I felt that the vitality normal in his relationship with those around him was ill-suited to a world of Willies and Stephens and Mildreds. Yet, I couldn't fail to realise that all his life he had been part of it. It was just ironic that, with Isobel and the remarkable survival of their love, they should have ended up here.

I heard him coming across the room to the window where I stood, but did not turn.

'We'll go,' he said.

Outside, I took his arm, and he looked at me, not so much startled as challenging me to criticise. Instinct had told him what to expect; in part he was resigned, in part defensive.

'It's a bit, "Broadshanks type", isn't it?' I asked.

'You mean Willie?'

'I mean the whole thing.'

'It's a job.'

'Are you a swan here then?'

He looked back into my eyes, gently biting his lip. It's not like that,' he said. 'It's not that sort of job.'

'But it's all right?' I forced into my voice a note of concern.

'Yes. It's all right,' he said, slowly. 'Don't worry. We both work hard. Isobel's been an absolute brick. Guides me through all the shoals. Wonderful woman.'

The cold air carried the sharp scent of late autumn into nose and throat. After the stuffiness of the bar I breathed deeply. 'It's lovely,' I said. 'The countryside here.'

He turned his rather gaunt expression from me to look ahead across the discoloured grassland into the faint pockets of mist. 'A bit flat. We have a nice cottage. Small, but we manage.'

'Do you have many Willies in the club?'

He laughed. 'They're not as awful as you think. Willie's all right. They're all all right, really. What does it matter?' He made a little, angry, shaking gesture with his fist in the air in front of him. 'Oh, God!' he said. 'If it weren't for Isobel's restraining hand and calm judgment—if it weren't for that—I'd have gone off the handle completely.'

'Have you come near it?'

Anger flared in his eyes, then was suppressed, leaving them watery. 'I'm like a spring, old son. Wound up tight. Something has to give. Yet I just can't let it. Isobel, the children, she's tried so hard.' He paused. 'All the same, it just isn't right. Not for us. It can't last.' He held out both hands, tight-fisted, in front of him, and shook with tension. 'We'll have to get out.' Having made this apparent decision he began to relax.

'But has anything happened?'

'No. It's just everything.'

I stared at him, puzzled. I thought of the lines from Blake—

> 'And when the stars threw down their spears
> And watered heaven with their tears. . . .

What possible plan could he have which could offer an alternative to this? There was no alternative. Change, possibly; one country club is much like another, and all need men and women to run them. One school is much like another, but the Dr Wains of this world are concerned with making the business of education work, not with throwing lifelines to inevitable and irredeemable casualties. There was no likely perfection to be sought.

'So you're a tiger, not a swan,' I said.

He didn't answer.

I took out the envelope and handed it to him. 'That's from Alice,' I said. 'It's the fifteen pounds you asked for. I went to see her last night. We had supper, and she told me.'

He took it quickly and stuffed it into his pocket, almost as if he were ashamed. Then he turned towards the car. I could see he did not want to talk about her. Nor did I. I felt suddenly as I had felt years before, as a child, stopping him in a London street and asking him, 'Why don't you marry Alice?' And him being completely dismissive, 'Marry Alice? Never!' Now, a net of guilt spread over the dismissal.

I followed him to the car.

'Did she tell you why I wanted it?' he asked. 'The money?'

'She said you had written. That things were difficult, you were broke.' I thought of saying that she had shown me the letter, but then felt it might stop him telling me how things really were.

He turned back at the car, and again looked out over the grass towards the trees, so still and stately in the faint afternoon mist.

'They're not difficult,' he said. 'They're impossible.'

'What do you mean?'

'You've seen it all. Willie, Mildred, the whole shooting match.' He gripped his fists tightly, staring ahead of him. His jaw was clenched, his eyes cold as ice.

'It's a job,' I said. 'For both of you. It's something. Relax, father. Unclench your fists.'

He laughed. He opened his hands and looked down into them. Big, careworn, capable, how little in fact they had changed over the years. 'You realise I'm sixty-three,' he said. 'She's in her thirties.' He looked up. It was so still. Far, far away I could hear the sound of a train travelling fast on the main line through Haslemere. 'It's no use. If I were the same age, my son. If I were in my thirties, too. I could manage it. I could change.'

'If you were in your thirties I wouldn't exist.'

He stared at me. For a moment there was a flash of anger in his eyes. I supposed it to be at my intrusion into his collapsing dream. Then his look softened.

'It's too late,' he said. 'It's too late.'

[IV]

'The children liked you reading to them.'

'They're very good.'

'I'm glad you came.'

'I never realised you were on your own at the weekends. From tonight, through Saturday and Sunday, he's up at the club, then?'

Isobel added a log to the fire. 'A country club like this comes to life at the weekend. The secretarial work is done during the other days. But his job is now. It works well, on the whole. Our being free at different times makes looking after the children much easier.'

She spoke with quiet resignation. I could not get out of my mind the feeling that she shared the knowledge of the despair in him that I had witnessed earlier. We had eaten supper, all of us together, the children as well, then he had gone off. I had read to Olivia and Jessica, separate stories, each in turn, while Isobel had cleared up. Now we were sitting together.

'I missed the six o'clock news,' she said. 'We must listen at ten.'

'It's got warmer. It'll rain.'

We sat on either side of the fire in the stillness. 'He has to start at seven, does he?'

'About seven. They're not all that concerned about time-keeping, up at the club. Not in that way. It's him, really.'

'He was always a stickler for that,' I said. 'I suppose he sets his own timetable, and it's more dedicated than anything they might expect.'

She laughed. 'Well, that's the way with him, as you know.'

She got up and turned the radio on.

'He doesn't really like it much, does he? It's not like Brookhall.'

She looked sadly at me from where she stood beside the fire. I looked back at her, half-listening to the voice on the radio, with its emphatic tones of social concern: '. . . *People get lonely and feel they don't have enough occupation to justify life . . .*' I wondered why we were listening, and remembered we had heard no news. But it seemed not to matter.

In one of those illogical exercises of the mind I considered the irrelevant fact that she was the same age, now, as Ursula had been, all those years before, when I had become so convinced my father and I were on the brink of that 'something permanent'; the time we had enjoyed, through one Christmas which still, so many years later, stood out in my mind as the happiest I had ever known, indeed the very epitome of happiness to me. And it had been lost. Now, once again, all of it threatened to go wrong. I had begun to feel happiness again, not for myself, as it had been on the earlier occasion, but for him, with her. Yet there rang ominously in my ears his words: 'It's too late, it's too late.'

'Nothing will ever be like Brookhall,' she said. 'It's not so much this place—that's not important; it's the feelings we have, the stage we've reached.'

Her last words produced in me a numbing sensation of fear. Clutching at a rapidly vanishing hope, I murmured, 'I don't understand.'

She seemed to deliberate over whether she would explain, or just turn the issue aside. I listened to the disembodied voice: it had a tone of calm practicality: '. . . *there are surveys going on in various parts of the country to establish just how many old people there are struggling by themselves against increasing frailty . . .*' He was sixty-three; I appealed, silently, 'George, live for ever!' Had statistics already numbered him in their survey?

'He still thinks we will be getting married,' Isobel said. She paused and shook her head. 'We won't. I've changed my name, by deed poll.' She glanced at my troubled face. 'Don't worry, *I* won't desert *him*. But I fear it can't last. I must think of the children.'

I thought she was going to cry. But she just looked steadily down at me. 'You've written to him,' she said, 'trying to advise him about this crisis or that, impending or past. You're very stern with him.'

'Am I?'

'Yes. It's as though you are always expecting the worst.'

'How should I be?'

'Don't be too hard on him. I know you've lived with him much longer than I have, and that you've seen it happen again and again. I know it seems silly to say it, but you have to believe that it won't happen again.'

'It's very hard,' I said. 'It's happened so many times. All of my life has been lived under the shadow of one crisis or another. All of it, really, until now.'

'I want to say something to you,' she said. She spoke with slow deliberation. 'The good side of him has given me more real happiness than anyone else I have ever known. His love for me has made me see life in a completely different way. I did not know the meaning of happiness until he taught me.'

I stared up at her, unable to say anything. The tone of voice from the radio had taken on that gathering together, that dying fall, of conclusion. I caught a few phrases: '. . . *the cult of youth . . . gone too far . . . change of attitude . . . ready to acknowledge the qualities of age . . . our own involvement in it . . .*' But I was really listening to Isobel. She was speaking about him in a way that I had not heard her use before, as though, in her mind, it was over. She was relinquishing the command she had over him; and echoing exactly his own sad statement: 'It's too late.'

The programme had ended. It had been called 'The Dispossessed'. There was a pause. Then the sound of Big Ben. I checked my watch. I was going to ask her, 'Is it really over then?' But I felt afraid of doing so, unable to reconcile that it was over—with the things she had said about him giving her so much happiness.

'Isobel?' I said.

The voice on the radio said: 'Ten o'clock.' Then there was a single chime. '*This is the BBC Home Service with the ten o'clock programme of news and current affairs. First the news . . .*' Though this was the moment for which we had been waiting, I felt almost impatient with the interruption; hoped, almost, that she would turn it off.

'. . . *With deep regret we report the assassination of President Kennedy. He was shot as he was driving through the city of Dallas in Texas. We are going over to Washington for a full account from our correspondent, Leonard Parkin . . .*'

In the hallway the telephone rang. We left it ringing as we stared at each other in disbelief. Then she went out. The full drama—in sombre tones—was unfolded from halfway across the world. It was a world, just at that moment, in which everything seemed to have gone dreadfully wrong.

Isobel returned and stood in the doorway, her hand across her mouth, listening. There were tears in her eyes. I had stood up and was staring across the room at her. I did not know whether her tears were for Kennedy or for something else. I couldn't think of anything to say.

'He's not there,' she said. 'I can't think where's he's got to.'

I was confused. 'Who's not where?'

'Your father,' she said. 'He's not at the club. They've rung, looking for him. It's getting busy.'

I paused, looking at her. 'But it's more than three hours, isn't it? He left before seven.' We stared at each other. 'The crisis is with us again, I'm afraid.' With an uncomfortable certainty I added, 'He's gone to drown his sorrows.'

'But he's got no money. Nothing. He doesn't get paid until he finishes tonight.'

'He has money, Isobel. He has fifteen pounds in his pocket now. I brought it, from Alice. He had written to ask her. I thought you knew.'

She shook her head. Her expression was one of disbelief, not at what I was saying, but about everything. 'He can't,' she said. 'He can't do this to me, to us.'

'He can,' I said. I paused. 'I'll go and find him.'

'What's the use? You can leave him, wherever he is. It doesn't matter. Oh, George, why? Why?'

It was a cry of hurt and anger. In that moment she seemed very young. She was not of his generation. She was more of mine. She was close enough in years to draw me forward also in understanding towards her, making me realise that I was part of the disintegrating fabric of their two years together. I was trying to tell myself that John F. Kennedy was dead and what a waste it was. But it would not sink in. It was too awful.

'I'll go,' I said. 'Where should I look?'

She told me two or three places. Her directions were carefully deliberate, but uncaring. I put my coat on and went out into the night. It was raining, not too hard, but the wind was carrying the drops in gusts against my face. I got into the car. As I was settling into my seat I saw that a scarf of Sarah's had fallen out on to the gravel. I retrieved it and shook off the drops of water. The movement released from it a faint breath of her scent, and I recorded it passively as something from the past, now irretrievable. Starting the engine was, for the first time, a mechanical gesture bereft of the excitement I so innocently but automatically felt over my first car. Driving carefully away from the halo of light from the lamp over the porch into the stormy darkness, the windscreen wipers humming precariously, I knew, with careless indifference that, somewhere, I would find him; I knew he would be drunk, Alice's money spent; I knew it was over. Beyond the rain clouds which had gathered during the evening, with all its doleful news, the constellation of Orion was fulfilling its late autumn destiny, shrouded in the storm clouds and desolation for which once it was held accountable.

Chapter Five

[I]

'He suffers from nostalgia, you know.'

She said it almost in passing, as though it were chilblains.

'Oh?' I said. 'Has he got it badly?'

'Badly enough,' she said. 'Can't get him out of it at times.'

'Is it catching?'

She frowned then, and I realised she was being serious. 'You don't have to live with it,' she said. 'Coming on visits from abroad like this, what do you know about how difficult he can be?'

'I do know,' I said. 'I know just how difficult he is.'

'Day in, day out,' she said. 'It's not fair, really.'

'It's not just nostalgia, surely? There's no real harm in that, is there?'

'I'm not one to complain,' she said. 'But he's a difficult old man. Very difficult. And I know. I've had experience.'

'Drink?' I said.

'Not in this house, he doesn't. I tell you, and he knows it too, he'd be out. And Alice feels the same about it.'

'But does he? Ever?'

She stared at me, unwilling to answer. I was asking for an instant analysis of the ups and downs, as expressed in terms of drinking bouts. Yet with his growing old the pattern had changed, and could not be so easily explained. 'He's a difficult man,' she said. 'He get's bored easily. You know that.'

'He was always impatient.'

90

'Now that it's warm he goes into the garden at night. Stargazing. He can't sleep, you see.' She seemed to recollect that I had just asked her a question. 'No. He doesn't drink so much now. Just sometimes. But it's not popular, not with her, nor with me. I wouldn't stay, you see. I wouldn't.' She shook her head deliberately. 'He has to watch his behaviour, he knows that.'

'And his health?' My catechism was a careful one, but at heart based in self-interest. I did not believe Gladys's threats about leaving him. After all, it was nine years now, and in spite of the capitulation he had made both to her and to Alice, there must have been many lurches into wild drunkenness in that time. But I could not be entirely certain. And she was my best insurance.

'He's old,' she said. 'He's an old man. And a great deal is wrong with him. Most of it can't be put right. He's punished himself, over and over, for years. It's a miracle we still have him.'

He suddenly took on the dimensions of a great animal that should have become extinct, but had not. Having him still was a precarious privilege which involved special safety precautions which fortunately for me Gladys undertook. Yet I found it very difficult to express gratitude. After all, she had married him.

My father was her fourth husband, a faintly demeaning statistic which, on occasion, she had endeavoured to improve by telling me about the others; yet without any great interest on my part. She, in her turn, was his fourth wife. Years before, after the sad but inevitable parting with Isobel, he had moved into the west country to work, and had read in the matrimonial column of the newspaper an advertisement: 'widow in her early sixties seeks companion with a view to marriage'. He had shown it to me; picking it carefully out of a pocket in his wallet one afternoon when I had asked him how he had met Gladys, he had watched me quite seriously as I read the faded bit of newsprint. Then, as I handed it back, he had murmured, 'It's for the best, old son.' I had doubts as to whether this was true. Life for both Gladys and my father had been turbulent to begin with; and it was only when Alice retired that a change came.

Like so many other changes in his life it was provoked by crisis. Her experience of men had been sufficient to see Gladys through the first few drinking bouts, the moves from cottage to flat, from live-in employment to odd-job dependence. But then she had issued an ultimatum: her advertisement had not anticipated so strained an old age, and she was calling him to order. His response was to turn to Alice, and with some reluctance from both women they had all come together in this divided cottage on the outskirts of a Somerset market town. It took on an atmosphere of permanence at last. It became home to him; more, in fact, than to either of them. This manifested itself in a curious detail: he detested all of Gladys's relatives and never allowed her to put up any photographs of her family. She herself appeared in several snaps with him. But that was the extent of it. Photographs, to him, were evidence of permanence; and they multiplied in number around the room, to the ones of my mother, myself, Francis and Melanie, being added those of Gladys and him.

Alice was confined firmly to her part of the house. And she must have been lonely. The west of England was not her part of the world. The arrangement between them all had been dominated by one condition from Gladys: that they should live in the county of her birth and upbringing.

'There seem many more photographs,' I said, looking round.

'Not of *my* family, you'll notice.' Her tone was bitter.

'He never used to like photographs of himself. Not photogenic, he used to say.'

'He's all right, the old dear,' she said.

The more I looked at them, however, the less 'all right' he seemed to be. Though he loved, in life, the attitude, the gesture, in photographs taken in his old age there was a rigid, self-conscious, even fearful quality, as he stared out in unhappy condemnation of this fixed record of himself. What in life seemed natural, if flamboyantly so, the hand gesture, or the sharp expression of inquiry, was turned by the eye of the camera into an awkward parody of those aspects of him that I held dear. Angry old man, I thought to myself; that's what he looks like, an angry and a frightened old man.

But Gladys would not wish to discuss that.

'How's your son?' she asked.

'Peter? He's well. He was ten last week. I took him out for the day. Birthday treat. Farewell, you could say.'

'Why is that?'

'Sarah is marrying the chap she's been living with, and they're moving abroad.'

'George will be sorry not to see the boy again.'

'They got on well, didn't they?'

She was silent, and I reflected with resignation and not without a faint hint of bitterness on the swift demise of my relationship with Sarah. In reality, this concealed my sense of guilt about Peter, to whom I had been so unsatisfactory a father, and the relief I now felt that Sarah was getting married and going away, taking him with her. I had always regarded him as more her child than mine, and because she could offer him the stability which had been so lacking from my own childhood I had deliberately distanced myself from him, seeing him only at intervals. But Gladys's recollection of my father with him, the last time they had been together, provoked a twinge of jealousy. They had always got on so well.

Of the infrequent occasions on which I had brought Peter and my father together, I remembered particularly an earlier one when the child had been young and excitable and my father playful and indulgent. And there had stuck in my mind the image of his huge hands plucking up the shrieking, running figure of the child, tickling him, tossing him in the air, admonishing him about safety and caution and self-preservation. Both then and later my father had accepted, not without regret, that a reconciliation with Sarah was not possible. Yet it had not stopped him from voicing his own conviction that happiness in life lay in marriage and in children, urging me to seek and establish for myself those essentials.

'Sarah's becoming quite a successful artist,' I said. 'She's had a couple of exhibitions, one in New York.'

'What sort of things does she paint?' Gladys said. 'Would I understand them?'

The simple answer to that was a swift negative. I said: 'Abstracts. A bit scientific. They wouldn't suit this house.'

She watched me as I stared at a print of a field of tulips with a windmill in the background. 'He gave me that,' she said.

I said that I liked the carved frame.

'He's lonely,' Gladys said, still industriously clicking away with her needles. 'With you abroad.' She was appealing to me, on his behalf. 'You mean such a lot to him, you know. But he's proud. He wouldn't say it.'

She stirred within me a faint anguish, derived from shame. All those years, being with him, childhood, youth. And now, in manhood, a translucent curtain of indifference. It did not cut us off from one another. But we stared through it at each other, partial strangers, keeping our distance.

'Tell me about the nostalgia. I never thought of it as something you could suffer from.'

'Oh, yes. When I started nursing in the twenties it was accepted as a complaint. I don't know whether you'd call it a disease, exactly, though that's how it used to be regarded.'

'What is it, really? Nostalgia?'

Gladys stared back at me. 'It's homesickness. That's what it is.'

She picked up her knitting again and the needles began their rapid plunging into the edges of thick, beige wool.

'But he's not homesick.'

She stopped again, her placid round face displaying no great emotion about him or his nostalgia. 'You can be homesick for the past,' she said. 'It's part of nostalgia, the idealisation of the past. He thinks that, once, it was all all right. You've heard him say it, about "it's going to be all right". You've heard that?'

I nodded.

'He bases all his future hopes on the past. He gets the present wrong.' She said it in a dismissive way, as if that was all there was to be said about nostalgia.

'Do you want shopping done?' I asked. 'I thought I'd go into town.'

'We do need some things. Can you wait while I go and see? In a minute now, when I've finished this row.'

'Of course.' I paused, then got up and looked through the window at the garden. 'He keeps it well, doesn't he?'

'He does it for Alice.'

'No,' I said. 'For himself.'

'She thinks it's for her.'

'She has to have something,' I said.

Gladys was silent. Even if she told me what she felt about Alice, I would not *understand* it, not in the real sense, not inside myself, not as a comprehension of passion, only as a capitulation to the convenience of Alice being there and doing what she did. What Gladys thought was only relevant in that light, and therefore not really relevant at all. Alice made their lives more bearable with comfort and security, and she was tolerated because of that. But the undertow of real feeling: how much of it was benign? What scrutiny would it bear? Looking out at the garden, thinking of her, seated behind me, made me conscious of how unbearable this last, and presumably final state for the three of them must be to Alice. I did not then see my father's life as inescapably intolerable; that came later, and I therefore did not direct towards him, just then, the same beam of pity. As for Gladys, with phlegmatic dismissal she had told me of three earlier and elderly husbands all now gone to meet their maker, and it was therefore with the same cheerful approach that I saw her as keeper, cook, nurse, companion, commentator and gossip, perhaps with the view 'as well him as another', knitting away, waiting for the fourth tumbril to come by. Not that she did not have feelings. I had seen tears brought to her eyes by cruel words. I simply did not see much depth to them.

'Are you going to get married?' Gladys asked. 'Your father keeps going on about it.'

I had expected the question, but as a reflection of his curiosity, not hers. It was an accident that she got in first with it. 'I hope so,' I said. 'One day.'

'Only "one day"?' Gladys said.

'I'm afraid I can't be more definite than that.'

'Your father wants to see you settled. All of you. But especially you. You know that.'

95

'I wish I could help him,' I said. I had often voiced the same feeling before, to him rather than to others.

'You're a rum lot,' she said. 'Secretive.'

'Maybe we are,' I said, without looking round. I would tell him more, when the opportunity presented itself; but I felt no desire to say anything else to Gladys.

'I wonder if Alice wants anything in town.' I waited to see if she would comment, either way, but she remained silent. 'It's nice and secluded,' I said.

'The garden?'

'Everything.'

'We're very lucky.'

Was there a note of defiance in her voice? I looked round. 'Is he safe when he uses the bicycle?' I asked.

'I prefer to see him on the bus. After all, it passes the door. You can't ask for better than that. His legs, you know.'

'It's all very convenient.'

'Just a short run.' She had come to the end of a row. 'We need some margarine. I know that. I'll go and see if there's anything else.' She stuck the needles through the big ball of beige double-knit, and wrapped the already sizeable woollen garment around them. Then she put it all into a big soft bag.

'You're very fast,' I said. 'At knitting. You could run something up for me while I'm here. The time it takes you.'

'You should come more often, and stay longer with him. Seeing you has bucked him up no end. He gets down in himself.'

'Nostalgia?'

'You could call it that.'

She got up and went out. There was still a relaxed, fluid quality about her movements, though she was somewhat shapeless now with age. For a woman in her early seventies there was an appealing presence, a consciousness of self hard to define in sexual terms, and yet only definable in that way. She must have been attractive, in her time, to many men. There had been plenty of them, filling sections of her life, among them the husbands. It was a background which she did not let my father forget.

On one occasion, as I stood beside her in the kitchen, helping with some task like washing up, she said to me,

96

rather in the way she had spoken of the nostalgia, 'Of course, he can't do it any more.'

I paused, and allowed a faint look of inquiry to come into my eyes, without comment, however.

'No,' she went on. 'He get's out of breath, poor old man.'

Would it be worthwhile, I thought to myself. But only said, 'He tries, does he?'

'He can get it up all right,' she said. 'It's just he can't go through with it. It's the asthma, you see, and his chest.'

With anyone else in the world the observations would have been interesting, a detail satisfying one's endless curiosity about other people's lives. With him, I had envious feelings of pity and dismay. This was the great engine of his physique she was referring to, falling into desuetude, and being commented upon in terms that were somehow gross, while at the same time implying a physical relationship between himself and Gladys that was welcome and admirable. Years before, with Isobel, the talk had been of love and of passion, of her coming to life in his arms, and never thereafter being the same. Gladys, like the good nurse I imagined she was, reduced the whole thing to functional terms; his being able to 'get it up' was comparable to the working of his appetite, or of his bowels. And what he was losing was bodily integrity: the parts in service of each other, the whole working as one.

Of her husbands Gladys did not have nostalgic feelings. They were the past, and the past was kept in its place by her. I imagined it would be the same with him when the more serious disintegrations took place, and the malfunctions spread until the machine stopped.

I had come to stay for a few days. Always, with him, it was a few days. He pretended resentment, but when they were up it was usually time to go anyway, with relief on either side. I had not been, in fact, for about three years. And this was the first time at their cottage, shared with Alice, who owned it all.

When Gladys came back she had a small scrap of paper and a pound note in her hand. 'There are a few things,' she said.

'OK.'

'You'll take the bicycle?'

'Is that all right?'

She nodded. 'He won't be needing it.'

'I thought of hiring a car. But it seemed an unnecessary expense. I mean, we can always get a taxi if we're going out.'

'You have one, in Paris?'

'Yes, I do. Of course it's second-hand.'

'If you lived nearer you could come more often, couldn't you?'

She addressed herself to the problem of his life and hers being folded together in a fashion that was surprisingly vigorous and positive. She complained, but the style of her complaining was only very rarely edged with despair. In other words, she valued him and the problems he brought with him, far more than the lonely peace or the boring alternative there might have been. This is hardly a prescription for love; yet viewing dispassionately all that she had done for me, in taking him on, I was reassured by this quality almost of enthusiasm which she brought to the task of caring for him. He seemed a more or less incalculable burden. He seemed, looking back, always to have been that. And here was this practical woman, at different times in her life a nurse, with her knitting and her cooking, experienced with men, affectionate in her own way, a bit earthy, a bit aggressive, persevering with what had always been impossible.

'I may move to London,' I said. 'That's really why I'm over here. A job has come up, in the agency. Head of art features. If I could get it I'd be coming back.'

'You didn't tell him that. You know how he wants to know everything. He'd be thrilled if he thought you might move back.'

'I don't really mind him knowing. Do you want to tell him?'

Her face was animated. 'Oh, yes. He'd be pleased, anyway, that you wanted to come back to England. He'd think it was partly for him. You wouldn't mind him thinking that?'

'It *would* be partly for him.'

'You're a funny lot, I must say. Francis is the same. So's Melanie. One minute you're worried about him, the next minute you don't give a damn. And each of you lurches from one state to the other. Your father's the same. I wish I could understand it.'

'I'd better go,' I said. 'Will I ask Alice?'

The animation faded from her face, the light in her eyes glazed over with an expression of calculated indifference. 'It's up to you.'

[II]

Alice moved more slowly now, and with a stick. She was deliberate and careful, pausing, on her way through the rooms which constituted her half of the cottage, at certain well-appointed places, where she would stand, often for a minute or more, gathering strength for the onward advance. Her speech had been affected by a stroke, sustained shortly after the time when my father had left Isobel, and it had thickened her voice, slurring it at certain times, particularly if she were moved or angry. She stood, with one hand resting on the table, the other holding the walking stick, and she said to me, 'Of course I had to insist that the dogs went after that. It was just too dangerous. It doesn't do to fall at my age.'

'Were they put down?' I asked.

'One was. The other went to a sister.'

'They must miss them.'

'George was always in two minds about them. They messed up the garden, and that's what he really cares about. You see, the garden is mine.'

'Not shared?'

'Everyone *uses* it.'

'But father *does* it.'

'Well, he's the *worker*, of course.' A glittering of sudden pride enlivened her eyes. 'I try and get out a bit myself. Dead-heading the roses for him, pulling away dead leaves from the clematis. But he isn't the easiest man to help, you know.'

I nodded. 'Do you pay him? For the work?'

'I pay for plants. And for the things we need, like fertiliser. It's only right that I should.' She did not answer the other part of the question.

Inwardly, it made me smile to think of money, in modest amounts, still passing between them.

'It's very peaceful. What you have,' I said. 'He must be very grateful.'

'Things are never altogether what they seem.' She stared back up at me. 'Will you be able to spare some time for me while you are here? I want so much to talk to you.'

'Of course,' I said. I paused, waiting for some indication of the direction such a discussion might take, not sure whether she had something specific on her mind, or whether 'wanting so much to talk to you' meant just the usual conversation, bringing us both up to date.

'I thought of getting him up to London,' I said. 'For a break.'

She frowned. 'When did you think of doing that? Soon?'

'If and when I move back,' I said. 'It's a possibility, you see. Promotion.'

Her face lighted up. 'That's good news. You must be pleased.' But then she frowned. 'I'm not sure about him, though. I wouldn't be in favour of trips any more, he's not really strong enough. Better for you just to come here. You can stay with me if they don't have room.'

'But it would take him out of himself,' I said. I was conscious of using her kind of language, and wondered what my father behind her back might make of me aiding and abetting him.

'That's exactly what I have in mind,' she said, with a firm, abrupt little chuckle deep in her throat. 'It's just better for all of us if he isn't taken out of himself.'

I remained non-committal, thinking I would still try out the idea with him, as a test, if nothing else, of how much he felt himself to be a prisoner among his women.

'And you want nothing in the town?'

'No, my dear, nothing at all. My needs are very simple.'

I cycled in along the deserted country road in the June sunshine. The smells of farmyard and hedgerow were, in their sweet and pungent mixture, strong and clear and simple. And, against the diverse mechanisms by which the memory is activated, I was transported back by the sound of the bicycle machinery under me, the waves of scent-laden air, to the country laneways of childhood and the invasive echoes of Coppinger.

They were seductive recollections, all the sweetness of youth drained of its heartache and tension. First love, and then the subsequent experimentation with love; the unenduring friendships we suppose will last for ever; the unforgettable first experiences in which we test mind, flesh and spirit; and beyond it, behind it, like a protective wall surrounding everything, my father: it was a deceptive, unreal world into which I allowed my mind to journey as I cycled along the roadway in the still afternoon sunshine. I had done it so often, revelling in the easy sweetness with which the past can be used to disown the present and allow one to escape from it. I had been taught by a master practitioner. It needed so little, with him, to set the machinery in motion. Yet, rather than seeing it as some kind of skill, some gift, there now intruded a different perception altogether, one towards which Gladys had given irreversible direction by her classification of nostalgia as a disease. Seeing it now in this new guise, threatening, though not in any way fatal, hardly serious even, nevertheless pervasive and demoralising, had a strangely disturbing impact. I began to feel, I think for the first time, at odds with those seductive memories that could so easily be summoned up to crowd the mind. Were they not like a thick mist, coming in off the sea, obscuring what was real, and by creating a false and deceptive resonance, undermining our physical reliance on our senses? Was that not the reality?

This was certainly his trouble, memory. Was it to become mine also? Why did I encourage him in his emotional journeys back into the past? Why did I likewise go back in time? Was I trying to escape as well? If so, from what? The answer must lie in the present, and in its unresolved perplexities.

I was in my mid-thirties then. I was reasonably successful in my job. I had published a book. I had periodically deliberated over the choice between inevitable, modest promotion and a new start in something different, and each time had come down in favour of staying with fine art journalism since it gave me the time and opportunity for the more serious study of what I loved best. I had the modest, father's responsibility for a son whose mother, Sarah, was marrying, and who had given me sufficient participation in the boy's life to leave me dissatisfied with my own. For I had not married. There had been other women, periods of inconclusive happiness, but nothing like that 'permanence' which my father had always sought after, and which now he possessed in a form that would make many run from it. From its hollow safety he sought to guide me into the haven of marriage and security; and I was disposed to be guided. Yet so far it had not worked out.

Perhaps it was because of this that Gladys's strange words about nostalgia struck a chord within me, sounding a warning before it was too late. Perhaps it was other things as well. In a curiously muted way I was, at that time, approaching a watershed of my own.

[III]

I went into the garden when I got back. He was standing by the roses, staring at the cottage. He was perfectly still as I walked towards him. In his loose-limbed way he seemed much younger than his mid-seventies. He was wearing white overalls and a yellowing straw hat with a black band, and in the bright sunlight it threw the upper part of his face into a deep shadow in which his eyes glittered. He had one hand on his hip, though with the palm turned outward; in the other he held a pair of secateurs. It was an 'attitude', statuesque, familiar, challenging.

'Why didn't you tell me? About this new job?'
'It isn't certain.'
'But it's on the cards, isn't it?'
'Better than that, probably.'
'Better than that? Well, I do think I should have been the first to know.'

102

I smiled at him. 'Does it matter who knows first? I thought if I told Gladys . . .' My voice tailed away rather lamely.

'You're quite right,' he said, suddenly. 'Quite right.' Then he stared into my eyes keenly, leaning forward. 'Have you told Alice?'

I shook my head.

'Good.'

I raised my eyebrows at him.

He looked towards the cottage. He seemed, over my shoulder, to be scrutinising it from end to end. 'It's difficult,' he said. 'Things have to be done in a certain way.' He paused. 'She's a grand old scout really. It's just . . . it's just . . . Well, it is a prison, isn't it? You can see that? Anyone could see it.'

'It's one of the "open" variety,' I said. 'You can walk away if you want to.'

He sighed. 'Not any longer,' he said. 'I can't escape any more. I shall die here.' He shifted his feet and clicked the secateurs in his hand. The harsh metallic sound was at variance with the softness of our voices which had modulated from the first sharp question into a key of confidences and secrecy.

'It's quite a comfortable prison,' I said. 'Are you not content?'

'I am resigned.'

'I'm sorry I didn't tell you,' I said. 'About the job. I'm pretty sure I'll get it. Probably move in the late autumn. It's just what I want, writing all the time about art. It's what I've always wanted, *faute de mieux*.' The phrase was an afterthought. He didn't take it up.

'I wrote to Ursula,' he said.

I stared at him. 'You did *what*?'

He smiled, secretively. Then he winked at me. 'I write a lot of letters now,' he said. 'Getting in touch with people. Keeping in touch. It gives me something to do.'

'But *Ursula*,' I said, 'that's *years* ago!'

'We had good times together.'

'And has she replied?'

He nodded.

I didn't know whether to ask him if Gladys knew. It seemed an impertinence. Instead, I asked him, 'Have you contacted Isobel?'

His eyes lighted up. 'I've written to her as well.'

'And you've heard?'

He looked down. 'No reply.'

'Who else, father?' I felt as if I were hearing his confession.

'Others,' he said. 'Mine are letters from prison. Want to recover the past. It's all that matters.'

'It's not as bad as that, surely?'

'I sometimes think I'll go off my chump.' He made a half turn away from me towards the rose beds. It was an uncertain movement, slow, fearful. 'Not steady any more, old son. Can't rely on 'em.' He shuffled forward.

'They're looking lovely,' I said.

'Brave show, isn't it?'

'Alice is very proud of the way you have it. Does she help?'

He snorted. 'Fusses round me, fusses round. Doesn't know her arse from her elbow. But she's a good sort. Don't look now, but she's probably watching us. She's always peering at me out the window. Likes to keep an eye on things.' He leaned forward and with his secateurs trimmed down a short spur of brown wood to where it was green again. The cut left an oval of white over which he rubbed his thumb, discolouring it.

'And when you're not writing letters, do you look at the stars?'

He glanced up at me, suspiciously, thinking perhaps that I was mocking him. But my question was quite serious.

'I can't sleep, you see. I wake up in the middle of the night, my mind filled with thoughts.'

'Are you in pain?'

He shook his head. 'Just a jumble of thoughts. Everything. You children, your lives. My own. It's restful, staring up at the stars. It's like reading an old, familiar book. Of course I want to talk about it, but there's no one to talk to.'

'Isn't it always the same? Boring? Or does it change?'

'Lord, no! Different all the time. Wonderful clear nights just now. No moon. Full extent of the milky way right across the heavens!' His eyes were lit up. But the excitement of

104

thinking about the panoply of the night sky brought on a sudden fit of coughing. He was not smoking, nor did he have a cold. Yet the watery, phlegmy sound seemed to come from deep within the great barrel of his chest. And it went on, his face going red. When it subsided he pulled a red cotton handkerchief from his pocket and wiped his mouth.

'All right?'

'Yes.'

'What does it make you think of? The stars.'

He laughed. 'It makes me think how futile it all is.' His voice was wheezy and faint. He cleared his throat, and I thought he would start off again. 'A little prick of light in the sky which has taken nine hundred thousand years to reach the earth. How can we contend with that? We are just nothing.'

'Doesn't it make you depressed?'

He shook his head. 'No. What makes me depressed is being a prisoner here. The stars should make me feel free! That it doesn't matter. But they don't. That's what's so stupid. We are nothing. We deserve to be nothing. We cannot rise above our basest instincts.'

'When I move back you must come up and stay.'

'I'd like that,' he said, his voice eager. 'It'd be good to get away from time to time.' He seemed to reflect on the prospect of parole, perhaps disappointed that it lay, at its earliest, in the autumn. He took off his hat and scratched his head. Then he smoothed down his thin grey hair, but kept the hat off, letting it hang in his hand. In a low voice he quoted at me, "*The fault, dear Brutus, is not in our stars, But in ourselves, that we are underlings.*"

'Call yourself an exile,' I said. 'Not a prisoner. Will Ursula come down?'

He laughed. 'Set the cat among the pigeons, eh? Put 'em on their mettle. Nothing like a bit of competition.'

'But what will come of it?' I said. 'How will they take it if it really happens? Do you expect to hear from Isobel?' It seemed altogether too absurd.

'I've asked her to come and stay.'

'Who?'

'Ursula,' he said.

'Not Isobel?'

He shook his head. He seemed confused at my mention of them together. In my mind, though they existed in two widely distinguished pasts, one recent, one distant, they were joined closely in the quite different sense that both had been special objects of his love as far as I could judge, and in both instances I had been involved enough to be a judge.

'What does Gladys think?' I said.

He raised his eyebrows. 'Thinks it's a good idea.'

I thought her wise for so thinking, but wondered how faithfully he was reporting her state of mind, indeed, if he understood it.

'And Alice?' I said. 'What about her?'

He frowned at that. 'Not so good,' he said. 'Not so good at all.'

'You mean she's against it?'

'Haven't asked her, old son. Mentioned I was writing. Frosty reception to that.'

'Did you tell her you'd written to Isobel as well?'

He shook his head. 'Least said soonest mended. She doesn't have to meet them, you know.'

'But a bit difficult?' I looked round myself at the cottage. At their end there was no one. But through a window at the other end, occupied by Alice, I could see her in profile. She was quite still, as though having paused on her way through the particular room for one of her respites. I had the sense that she had been watching us, and that even now, as she stood stock still, ostensibly not looking at all, nevertheless, out of the corner of her eye she was waiting for, hoping for, anticipating, movement of some kind from the object of her abiding love.

He followed my gaze. 'Yes,' he said. 'It's difficult.'

[IV]

Gladys cooked, well, and my father ate prodigiously. In all the years of our wandering, together and then separately, he had remained lean and muscled; now he was growing sleekly

106

fat. His spare, big-boned frame carried the additional weight well enough, and the essential gauntness of his face, the lines in it, the austere look given to it by the carefully clipped and confined beard, above all, the cold sternness of his steely grey eyes, did something to counteract the effect of corpulence. But I felt he had capitulated to something, and creature comfort was part of it.

To all outward appearances we constituted a rural idyll. Anyone looking through the window of that Somerset cottage at supper time that evening would have seen the slanting rays of the late June sunlight falling upon the table at which the three of us sat. In one dish were new potatoes, small and prematurely dug from the garden to celebrate my visit and his endeavour; fresh young peas from the same source; a roast of lamb; butter, water, country bread. His roses were in vases round the room. The strawberries he had grown were in a bowl on the sideboard. Even the things we said to each other could be construed as expressions of a simple, unalloyed relationship, timeless, primal, inspired by contentment.

'So what would this new job involve?' My father said.

I told them both what I would be writing, and where it would appear.

'Would you travel?' Gladys asked.

'A bit,' I said. 'Mainly in England. Sometimes abroad.'

'So your father would see something of you?'

'It would be better than it has been,' I said.

'It would need to be,' he said. 'Never see you at all. You don't even write much.'

'I know. I'm sorry.'

'It doesn't matter. We have our own life, don't we, duckie?' He looked across at Gladys with an expression of forced affection. He put his hand out, tapped hers twice, gently, where it lay on the table, and then withdrew it again.

'I don't know how much I share it with your other women,' Gladys said. 'Now that you've started writing to them.' She paused, looking at me. 'Just pen pals. That's what he tells me. But I'm not so sure.'

'That's all they are, my love. Never fear. You will always be first in my heart.'

She laughed and shook her head. 'Hurry up and finish your dinner.'

'I'm too old,' he said, looking down, clearing his plate with some vigour. 'It's all memory, really.' He paused and was silent for a moment. 'That was very good. That is reality. There are times,' he said, pushing the plate away, 'when I'd just like a cigarette.'

She frowned. 'You know your chest, George. Don't.'

'What about you?' he said, turning questioning eyes on me. 'And girls? What about all that? Why aren't you married? Still waiting for the right one to come along?'

I looked back at him. I had feared he would come back to the topic, but though I was no longer intimidated by the strange force of his direct interrogation, I was not quite ready then.

'Something like that,' I said.

'Don't want to talk about it?'

'There's nothing to talk about.'

He shrugged his shoulders. 'There can't be nothing if you're your father's son. You always go your own way, you never tell him anything.'

Through the window I could see Alice, moving with cautious steps along the flagged path beside the roses. All her movements were slow and almost self-consciously deliberate, so that the pacing of the point of her walking stick between the stones on the ground looked as though it responded to a preordained pattern in her mind. Not that she looked down. In a strangely awkward gesture of the head she held her nose in the air, as if scenting something. As the hunted beast might raise its muzzle to the wind seeking evidence of a threatening enemy, so Alice raised hers to the roses, seeking evidence of him and his labours on her behalf. The scent of the rose is a secret thing. Only a few, among them Crimson Glory, his own favourite for all its undisciplined characteristics, have a smell pervasive enough to be caught on the evening air; and I doubted, as I watched her, if that was really what filled her nostrils.

'She's out, sniffing about,' Gladys said.

'Alice takes her constitutional at this time,' said my father. He swung in his chair to look out at her. 'Up to the end, three pirouettes, back in again.'

He laughed at the ludicrous image of her dumpy figure, like a Hoffnung cartoon, responding to the joys of nature. It fitted his and my own periodic joking at Alice's expense. But when I looked at Gladys there was no smile in her eyes.

'She's nosing about. That's what she's doing. She's not smelling the roses. She's smelling you.'

I was surprised how exactly she echoed my own suspicion.

'Alice is all right. Doesn't do us any harm. Where'd we be without her?'

'I don't know where you'd be.' Gladys took plates from the table and went out. I looked across at my father.

He winked. Then he raised his hand from the table and, very quietly, said, 'Least said, old son, least said.' When Gladys appeared in the doorway he put the hand out to touch my shoulder, and pointed to the sideboard. 'Strawberries. There's a good lad.'

I fetched the bowl of strawberries and the dish of thick, yellowy cream, and we sat together again, continuing the meal.

I could not prevent myself staring out through the window at the slow, protracted 'constitutional.' Her movements were really quite restricted, and the idea of her helping him, even with his own limitations, was ludicrous. But it was not just that. It was when she stood, as she was doing now on her way back towards the cottage, her head raised in the air, her eyes fixed unseeingly on some boring, empty patch of evening sky, her nose like a badger's snout, twitching at certain unseen, subtle evidence, that I felt most powerfully the sombre force of her presence on the whole household. It was a statement, the perambulation; a territorial claim as deliberate and automatic as the songs of birds, the squirts of dogs.

Later, when night had fallen, my father and I went out into the garden, taking the same route but moving more swiftly down the first bit of garden to a point beyond that at which Alice had ended her own short walk. Between the roses and the apple trees there was a hedge, broken by a gap.

The flagged path ended there, and the rest was mown grass. But along the hedge, a little out from it, there was a bed and he had planted night scented stock which now filled the air with its heavy perfume. It was late, but being June there were still threads of light, reddish mixed with cream, along the horizon to the west. Above our heads the sky was clear and filled with stars.

'I like this time best,' he said. 'It's too dark to do anything. In the daylight I'm always looking for things to do. Now, there is just the scent, and the feel of the air around you.'

'It's warm, isn't it?'

'It's only got warm recently.'

We were underneath the apple trees. It was very still. I put my hand through his arm, and said, 'It's not really too bad living here, is it? Could be worse?'

'It's all right,' he said. 'I'm all right.'

I remembered his use of the phrase about other people. 'Robert's all right,' Ursula's all right.' It never meant that. It meant the opposite. 'No better than that?' I asked.

He was silent.

'I'll come more often,' I said. 'When I move back. I've been abroad too long. When I was in town this afternoon I really felt how much I missed it all. It's awful, really. Provincial smugness. All those pots of honey and chutney and relish and marmalade. Conservative women buying more than their families can eat.'

He laughed. 'It's not so bad. But don't leave it too long. You'd best hurry back. I'm on the way out, old son. Not long to go now.'

I squeezed his arm. 'Don't be ridiculous! You've years in you yet.'

He hummed and laughed at the same time. It was a strange ribbony noise in his throat. Then he sang to himself, softly: 'When skies are grey, dear, I don't mind the grey skies . . .' He left it at that, and we turned.

Through the gap in the hedge the lights of the cottage were visible, the window at Alice's end curtained, that at Gladys's end open to our disinterested gaze.

I held him for a moment beside the roses, and looked up at the stars. The constellation of Orion was clear in the heavens above us. The milky concentration of the Great Nebula in Andromeda shone against the blackness, as did the other drifts of stars across the unchanging heavens. 'How do you navigate?' I said.

He stood beside me, looking up. 'How can I begin to tell you all that I once knew? The principles of navigation are—' He stopped. 'The belt of Orion.' He pointed, then swung his arm slightly. 'Cassiopeia, Andromeda, the Great Bear.' He let his hand drop. 'The principles of navigation.' He paused again. 'I have forgotten. It's all gone, what I once knew.' His finger indicated a point low in the sky. 'See there, Aquarius, the constellation of my birth. But how to navigate? I'd have to think it all out again.'

'Will Ursula come?' I asked, with a hint of mocking laughter in my voice.

'Hard to say. Gladys thinks it's a good idea. She's quite curious. Wants to meet one of my women, she says. But Alice'll have a fit. I don't think we could have her staying in the house.' He spoke quietly and chuckled to himself at the end. Then, almost in a whisper, he said, 'It'll have to be handled rather carefully.' He pointed at Alice's lighted window. 'She doesn't miss too many tricks.'

'And Babette?' I said. 'Any news of her? Does Ursula still see her? And what about Madge?'

'I must ask,' he said. 'Unlike you she got married. Family. Got on with things. But that'll change now.'

'I feel like an exile,' I said. 'Coming home again and finding everything changed. I need to piece it all together. But it'll be more settled from now on.'

Chapter Six

[I]

I slept badly, waking to mixed and at times bizarre confusions about the three of them. Alice kept appearing in my mind's eye in this new and somehow more threatening posture, sniffing the air; it had a sinister connotation. And Gladys, to whom in reality I owe so much, and who seemed to do and to have done her many kindnesses in such a flat, even unattractive manner, had struck discordant notes the previous evening that echoed adversely now in those night hours. As for him, to what had the tiger of past years been reduced? Toothless gums, clawless pads, fumbling in the Somerset earth and growing fat on clotted cream and the indulgence of two jealous women, had he really been brought so low?

The ceaseless night time roundabout of thought did not end there. I dozed, and at about four o'clock in the morning I had what I can only describe as a waking nightmare, a sequence of conscious thoughts, provoked gratuitously, leading to an intense feeling of dread, about myself. Lying on the pillow, knowing with unhappy certainty that I would not go back to sleep, watching the faint outline of the dawn light pick up the frame of the window, the edge of the curtain, I was drawn back in time a great distance, twenty years. It was not towards a precise point in time, but towards an imprecise, general, but no less vivid perception of myself as I might have been in my fourteenth or fifteenth year. No particular event presented itself, and yet, if the detail was imprecise, I was aware that the emotional atmosphere generated within me was intensely of my untried youth. Lying there, I was confronted with myself twenty years earlier, challenging myself as I now was. And it made me afraid.

Provoked by his growing old, perhaps; or perhaps by the persistent presence of Alice among what he presented as the dying embers of his life; or possibly, most likely reason of all, by Gladys's rational voice sounding a determined death-knell over nostalgia as a solution to anything; some, or all, of this had forced me, was forcing me, into a corner about myself. Gladys imposed new perceptions about him, new and almost frightening ones about Alice; and in turn these became questions for me.

It was this realisation which gave the nightmare quality to my confrontation with that self which had started out, so many years ago, surrounded by the memories and anecdotes, the attitudes and physical gestures, the angry glances and the fearful eyes, of this man sleeping somewhere in the same house, having settled on the final circumstances in which he would end his days.

The child, or youth, brought thus before my eyes across so great a passage of time, as though seen through a telescope that had been turned round, seemed to be mocking me with what I might have been, while I sought to persuade him to accept me as I was. Reality demanded that I reconcile the two selves. It is the illusions created by nostalgia that keep these selves apart. And the force, the instinct, the atmosphere, are pernicious.

I needed to change this, although I hardly understood what 'this' was. It had come to me in the form of a waking nightmare, a sudden, instinctive perception of two selves, crying out to be reconciled with each other, not in the past, as my father was perpetually trying to do, hunting through his childhood, his youth, his early and triumphant manhood, for something which time had long since wasted away, but in the present, so that all the past selves as we perceive them could be gathered up and contained in the human being we have become. A muddled recognition of this began to dispel the fear. And the image, the experience, which at

113

first had frightened me, began to fade. Almost, I regretted its departure; tried to hold on to the vision it offered, tried to recover and go over in my mind the strange lessons the dawn brought.

The birds were singing, emphasising the silence of the dawn. Then, from the room below my small bedroom, which led out into the garden, I heard a sound followed by the door opening and closing. I slipped out of bed and crossed to the window. Drawing back the curtains I saw the white overalled figure of my father walking towards the rosebeds. His movements were slow and deliberate. Twice he stopped and looked carefully from left to right, checking, it seemed to me, that plants and other objects were in place. I imagined he would be holding secateurs, but when his hands dropped to his side and were visible from behind, he was holding in one of them a sheaf of papers, and in the other a pencil.

There was a faint dawn mist along the hedge and among the apple trees. But the sky above was already blue, and the brightening glow of sunlight in the east was making it lighter every moment.

I leaned on the window sill, the curtains falling against my shoulders on either side, watching him, sure for some reason that he would not look round at the sleeping cottage. He stopped beside the large bush of Peace, and reached his hand out towards it to pick something off. In order to do so he had clenched the pencil in his teeth. Whatever it was—probably an offending greenfly—he brushed to nothingness between his fingers and took back the pencil. But he was not really interested in his garden that morning. It was the sheaf of papers in his hand that occupied his attention.

I watched as he wrote, crossed out, and then read. Then, as if aware that he was being watched, he swung round and stared up at my window. Stock still, we looked at each other. His face was expressionless, except for a faintly haughty light in the eyes. But no movement. For a long moment we maintained the mutual stare.

Then, quite abruptly, he lifted the hand with the papers in it, beckoned me down, sharply, just once, and turning away

114

again moved at his slow, careful pace along the flagged path towards the gap in the hedge that led into the orchard.

I pulled on socks, trousers, a jersey over my pyjamas, took my shoes, and went down. It took only a minute or two; a few moments more to tie my shoelaces, and then, with the same careful deliberation as he had shown I opened the door, went out, closed it quietly, and followed him through the dewy morning mist.

'Father?'

He turned under the apple trees looking at me with some concern. 'Couldn't sleep?'

'No. I had a strange night. Seemed to be awake all the time.'

'At your age?'

'What are you doing? Writing your will?' I laughed.

He looked resigned. 'In a manner of speaking,' he said, 'I am.'

'I didn't mean that,' I said. 'I was only joking.'

'No,' he said. 'It's . . . its . . .' he paused and tapped the papers with the back of his other hand. 'I'm no use at writing things down, you know.'

'What did you want to write down?'

'Just wanted to get something straight.' He clenched his fist. 'Sort it out, in my own mind, before I go.'

'Go? But you're not going anywhere.'

He laughed, and it was a soft, deep sound. 'Oh yes I am, my son. Where one day you'll follow me, and we'll all be blokes together.' As an encouraging afterthought he added, 'Not for many years yet, as far as you're concerned.'

'Nor you,' I said. 'You've a long way to go.'

He shrugged. 'Who knows?' He looked at the sheet of paper in his hand, then let the hand drop to his side, as though he wished no longer to go on considering whatever points were listed there, for I assumed, knowing him, that it was a list.

'What is it?' I asked

He looked up, but without answering.

'The paper,' I said. 'One of your lists? Jobs for the day?'

'I suppose you could say that. Not jobs for the day, exactly. A bit more permanent perhaps.'

I waited for him to explain, but he turned away from me and began to fold up the sheet. His evasive answers made me curious. 'Tell me more,' I said. 'What is it?'

'Trifling matter, really. I wrote out these precepts. Heard the word in "The Pallisers". Trollope. Excellent production, you know. When they do a thing like that they do it well.'

'What precepts are these?'

He shook his head. 'Nothing, really. Just . . . just some ideas about life. It's futile. Yet we try, we must try, it's the need to understand. I wish I could put it on paper, old son. Like you or Francis.'

We stood silent. Then I reached out my hand. 'Let me see, old man.' He did not like to be called that, and frowned. 'You must wait,' he said.

I still had my hand out. 'No. Let me see.'

'It's nothing. I haven't got it right.' He looked up at the curtained windows of the house. 'They own me. You realise that.'

I stared back at him, making no response.

'I can't give you this.' He pointed round with a vague movement of his right arm, the pencil held in his hand like a conductor's baton. 'It's not mine. It's hers.' He gestured towards the hedge. 'The roses. Everything.'

'You don't have to *give* me anything,' I said.

'But I *want* to! Don't you see?' I noticed a faint moisture in his eyes. 'When you asked me, last night, to tell you how to navigate, I realised I had forgotten all that. It's all gone. That was me. That was my life. That was my ambition and my achievement, when I was much younger than you are now. And it's just gone!' He raised his hand and snapped his fingers. He seemed amazed and bewildered, as if the knowledge could and should have survived for the half-century that had elapsed since it was so well acquired, and so efficiently deployed.

Very quietly I said to him, 'But you've taught me, father. You have.'

He frowned. His eyes seemed to blaze for a moment with anger. 'What have I taught you?'

'Everything.'

116

'Nothing,' he said. 'I've taught you nothing.'

I stared back at him. 'What I am . . .' But I could not go on. His perpetual pride in what I was, in the little things I did and then showed him or recounted to him, served only to emphasise the doubt and uncertainty that pervaded me at that period. I recalled the telescope, and with the intense feeling of need about understanding myself I once more asked him to show me the paper.

'These precepts,' I said. 'What are they? Some sort of advice?'

'For me, really,' he said. 'It's futile. But when I wake up in the early morning I sometimes sit for an hour and more in the window, staring out, trying to make sense of things. The only way I can express myself, it seems, is in lists. So I make lists. About life.'

We stood and stared at each other. He nodded, his eyes those of a rheumy old man. The sun was up, its rays striking the leaves of the apple trees and falling upon us in a dappled frieze of shadow and brightness. The light caught and reflected in the moisture above the lower lids. 'It's going to be a lovely day,' I said.

'That's all they are, really. Just phrases. Sometimes I think there is wisdom there. Not in the writing, but here, in my head.' He tapped his skull with all the fingers of his right hand held stiffly together, so that it made a thumping noise. 'But then it seems ridiculous. All the advice boils down to childishness.' He spoke the last word through gritted teeth, and struck his fist in the air like a hammer, bringing it down through the sunlit emptiness between us.

'May I?' I reached out my hand towards him.

'Seven Precepts,' he said. He handed me the top sheet of paper.

The usual flood of familiar feelings of being at one with him whenever I looked at his open, upright, aggressive handwriting, with its big bold loops, ran through me, coupled now with a sense of occasion bounded by humility. 'Don't talk unnecessarily,' I read, the injunction preceded by a 'one' carefully circled. 'Don't reminisce,' I read; or, rather, 'Don't reminiscence,' for that was how he

117

spelt the second commandment. Then the third: 'Don't become nostalgic.' I glanced up at him. He had turned away and stood in profile, the intense, slanting sunlight on his jagged, expressionless features. 'Don't philosophise.' All the things he did, the things I wanted from him, the past, the memories, the wisdom. I felt that my own eyes would blur with tears and steeled myself, looking down, to absorb this strangely moving ordinance. 'Don't say "why don't you do this or that"' was the fifth, and I could hear him checking himself, but too late. 'Don't air your troubles.' He had underlined the sixth precept with deep inscription, twice, and I paused over the words, thinking of the odd equation which brings together in a particular kind of person that pre-disposition to nostalgia, stoicism and sentimentality, mixed. The seventh and last seemed to mock him where he stood: 'Don't boast of what you've done.'

'May I keep this?' I asked. I held the paper up, looking at him over the top of it, so that I could remind myself of the brief prescription between us.

He shrugged; then he nodded. 'You might as well. I won't have anything to add.'

'It's a dispensation,' I said. 'It might even work!'

He laughed at that. 'You should go back to bed. You'll be tired.'

'What are you going to do?'

He started to move slowly up the garden towards the gap in the hedge. 'Give me your arm,' he said. 'My legs are weak now. Like matchsticks. I'd garden. If I could do anything. But I can't. It's futile, fiddling at the branches of the roses with my secateurs trying to pretend it's work.'

I yawned. 'I'll have to see Alice today,' I said. 'Must have a chat with her.'

'You do that,' he said. 'It's only right. Cross the battle line. Be a peacemaker. Won't do any good, though.'

'Bad as that?'

'They can't stand the sight of each other.'

I 'crossed the battle line' in the middle of the morning, stepping over the threshold of her half of the cottage from the flagged passage which once had been the entrance hall for labourers' boots coming in from the fields. Alice treated my arrival as if it were from some distant citadel of the empire rather than from a room across the way. 'It's good of you to come,' she said. 'It's good of you to spare the time for an old lady.'

'You're the least old of anyone I'm visiting here,' I said.

'Well, that's very true.' The expression of comfort on her face did not quite reach the point of being a smile, but it certainly indicated satisfaction. 'We're all growing older, my dear. I'm not as sprightly as I used to be. Can't hop up and down any more.'

'Well, you don't exactly need to.'

She laughed, briefly. It was not the kind of joke she liked. 'Well, now, tell me all your news,' she said.

I told her most of what I was doing, including the proposed move back to London. She welcomed this, and said it would be nice to see more of me. The hesitation and the silence were not unrelated to the view I had that, whatever the degrees and kinds of love that existed between my father and Gladys—and they were of an order that did not rise much above mutual affection and material tolerance—little if any spilled over in the direction of Alice. Close as she was, she was alone.

'He misses you, you know. He's caged in a bit here. She has to be strict with him.'

'And you?'

'I'm not his keeper.'

'But Alice, it was you made this possible.' I spread out my hand and made a gesture which was meant to embrace cottage and garden. 'You always said you couldn't live in the country. You used to tell me you were a city girl. And then you move to the depths of Somerset, surrounded by fields, an orchard, all the flowers. Why did you do it?'

'It was at his request,' she said. She stared with level gaze across the table at me.

119

'He asked you?'

She nodded. 'There was no alternative. They were thrown out twice because he drank. She would have left him. He appealed to me. Would I help them.' She paused. There was a certain measured pride in the way she spoke. 'Of course, I made it crystal clear that I was helping *him*. But, my dear, I looked upon the prospect with pleasure—no, with more than pleasure—the idea of sharing my roof with him.'

'And her?'

I thought she might say 'one can't have everything'; it would have been appropriate enough. But she just looked back at me, the triumph fading in her eyes to a certain limited satisfaction. Across the battle lines she was eyeing friend and foe ranged side by side in front of her, and endeavouring to make sense out of the conjunction.

'Gladys is a good nurse,' she said. 'A capable woman to look after him.'

'They seem to get along,' I said, rather tentatively.

She stared out into the garden, not willing to concede that.

'You always told me,' I said, 'that the countryside was not really for you. You must find it strange, now that you've planted yourself down here. Don't you miss the city?'

There was a faintly baleful glint in her eyes as she looked back at me. 'You mean the hustle and the bustle? The tube into the office? Falling into the train, all of a fluster. Trotting out to lunch? Jumping on and off buses? And then home in the rush hour?'

'And all your friends,' I said. 'The things you used to do. Weren't there people in Virginia Water you used to go down and stay with? And I remember a school friend in Bournemouth you used to talk of, and go and see.'

She laughed in brief acknowledgement of my dutiful persistence. 'How well you remember! Yes, I miss all that. But I have a lot here to keep me going. I go to a course on gardening in the town hall every Thursday. There are concerts some weeks, with occasional recitals as well, and not all that bad in quality. Then I have my friends here as well, you know.'

'You mean friends coming here to the cottage?'

Again, the look of faintly severe reserve came into her eyes as though I had touched once more upon an embarrassment.

'We prefer to meet in town,' she said.

'Does he go with you sometimes?'

She answered softly, 'I'm afraid not.'

'He's a bit wobbly,' I said.

'Do you think so?' There was a sudden keenness in her curiosity.

'Unsteady on his legs. He says they're like matchsticks. Says it's circulation. I noticed it this morning; he leaned on my arm, very heavily, in the garden.'

'He tries to do too much,' she said. 'And I'm really not all the help I should be.'

'What about Gladys?'

'In the garden?' she said.

I nodded.

'Glady's doesn't go into the garden.'

I looked out through the window at the sun, on the grass, on the flowers, on the trees. It was a breathless day, warm and still, and beyond the tops of the apple trees, all intensely green, the sky was clear of any cloud.

'It's very beautiful,' I said. 'I wish he were more able for it, in himself. He seems quite frustrated, not being able to work.'

'Oh, he does well enough, my dear. He does keep going.'

'He thinks he's not getting down to it properly,' I said.

We talked on about him. For her, it was an inexhaustible topic. Flowing and swirling, the words were a hymn of love. And it was only with the occasional indiscretion, a misjudgment of the fine balance of things, that just occasionally I checked this benign flow, jarring her sensibilities.

At one point I asked her, 'Is he afraid?'

'Of what, my dear?'

'Of death.'

'Why do you ask?'

'It's the photographs,' I said. 'He seems to have more of them. Photographs of himself.'

'Yes?' Her polite look invited me to go on.

'Well, it's the look on his face. In all of them. He seems afraid.'

'I think it's your imagination,' she said. 'That's all. He's in good heart, your father. But we must be careful not to excite him.'

[III]

He got at me again. About marriage. And it served to hammer home the lessons of the dawn nightmare. Exactly what was I, and where was I going? He seemed to pose the question in our discussions together without actually voicing it. Merely by reference to my career, my intention to return to England, my general expectation of promotion, he made me consider central questions which I would have preferred to leave aside. Even he had reason to think again after he had raised them. Yet he had this curious ability to turn his failures to his own advantage.

On one occasion, quite unpremeditated I was sure, and certainly unprovoked by anything said before, he adopted one of his more challenging attitudes and said, 'You'll have to make up your mind one day.'

'Oh? About what?'

'About marriage, of course.'

We were standing outside the kitchen door, quite close together. Gladys had gone into town. I thought he would take up a hectoring line, with the usual run of personal questions, most of which I managed to deflect. But on this occasion he chose to be more philosophic. 'The unity of all life,' he said, 'is to be found in a happy married life.'

'I'm sure that's so,' I said.

'All the happiness I have ever known has come from . . .' He faltered, and then was silent. He was speaking with the one person who knew most of the facts in the case, and I suppose he realised that his argument needed qualification. 'I'm speaking,' he said, 'of what might have been. I have always told you to learn from my mistakes. But you can also learn from my wisdom, old son. Don't get me wrong. I'm no example for you. And I don't mean this—' He waved his arm towards the building behind him, not

122

even bothering to glance over his shoulder. 'Once or twice in my life I have held within my grasp the possibility of that happiness to which I refer. Your mother. I ruined that. Isobel. I ruined that. Ursula. I threw that away. The chances for it are so rare. You just don't realise, my son.'

'And if it—?'

'By the time I was your age—' He stopped himself and looked at me.

'Go on,' I said.

He shook his head. 'A happy married life,' he said. 'It's the sole human condition that gives unity.'

'And if it's married life,' I said, 'and it's not happy?'

He turned away without answering.

We had other conversations during that brief holiday I spent with them. It was as if, by tacit agreement, we reverted to the generalisations about happiness implicit in his seven precepts which had served to draw us closer together. It was better for both of us not to be engaged in a form of detailed interrogation. For me, this side-stepped the factual situation. For him, it inevitably provoked an almost angry impatience with my evasiveness. For my part, what I sought to draw from him was his wisdom, in which I had great faith. And though, viewed harshly, his seven precepts were hardly profound enough to form the foundation for a philosophy of life, in their odd way they represented something truly fundamental. In addition, while I was there and able to talk with him, I could test them against all the exact experience which lay behind them, the anecdote, the recollection, the erratic detail of his life, adding to the images I already had of him: powerfully running, in his prime, through the trees of Hyde Park, at dawn, on his way to Coppinger; swimming after the cutter as it drifted in the Baltic wind, faster than he could swim, and his ship a mile off; him turning in the garden, the greenfly's wings just visible between his thumb and finger before he twitched it away into eternity. Yes, these images, and now many more, with his objective judgments upon marriage and its place in life, added up to the secret of life itself, to be drawn forth like honey from the flowers.

As well his precepts as those of any other. But there was more that I needed to know.

'Tell me,' I said to him, 'about that day you nearly drowned.'

[IV]

'It was still the war, you know. Nothing was easy. I was going from job to job. You were away at Coppinger. So was Francis. It all seemed to be breaking apart.' He paused, and looked at me across the room. We had finished supper, and Gladys was 'at things' in the kitchen, deliberately, perhaps delightedly, clattering away. 'I felt then that I was at the end of things. All of it was so futile. My wife gone, my children gone, the work I was doing quite meaningless. I think, if I'd had the courage . . .' He shook his head at me.

'You shouldn't talk like that,' I said. 'Even now.'

'I was desperate. I even . . .' Again he stopped, and I wondered what path, beyond suicide, he had contemplated, or taken.

'You even . . . what?' I asked.

He shook his head. 'It was then that I came up to Coppinger for the first time.'

'How long had you waited?'

'I suppose it must have been nine months.'

'Nine months?'

'About that.'

'Wasn't it a long time to leave us alone? How old was I? Seven? Eight? And Francis? Twelve?'

He ignored the questions. 'You see,' he said, 'I was ashamed.'

Instinct told me to reach out to him in some way. It was as if, in the stillness of the room, bathed in the evening sunlight which flooded through the window, suffused by the scent of flowers, that he was making confession; and that, like some freshly ordained priest turning, for want of both experience and human frailty to practise on, to his parents first of all to offer blessing, I needed to grant him some kind of unction, voice some expression of forgiveness: not in my own name, but in the name of that secular god who ruled most totally his life; I mean, of course, the past. But reason told me otherwise: break not the thread of his recollection, but augment it.

'Ashamed?'

'Yes,' he said. 'Ashamed.' Even thirty years later his voice betrayed the emotion of that time. 'You had been taken from me. Do you understand? I was beholden to Coppinger, and to the people who ran it. I had failed. It was their turn.'

'You never failed me,' I said. 'You never did.'

'Oh, yes, my son. You don't know the half of it.'

'But you did come, didn't you?'

'I'd been off the rails completely. All that winter. It was the first Christmas apart.'

'Why did you do nothing about that?'

'I couldn't. I just couldn't.'

'So what was it made you come to see Francis and me?'

I could see, in the look he gave me, that he was not really considering my questions. They were, as I intended, a form of therapy, designed more to keep him going than anything else.

'I ran, old son. That spring morning I ran through Hyde Park. Once I'd decided, then it had to be done—swiftly.' He clenched his fist above the arm of the chair. He was filled with certain untapped reserves of strength, nothing to do with his physique, but drawn from memory. 'I was so strong in those days. I ran with great strides, my knees coming up and my arms pumping away. And the stars were bright above the trees. And even now, when I see the metal slatted seats in a park, tipped over, and lying on their side, they always remind me of that morning, the first time I came to Coppinger. The only time I came that way, through the park.'

Don't let him drift off, I thought. He will be reminiscing about reminiscences. Keep him to the point.

'And what happened? That first time? How did you find us?'

He stared at me, his eyes softening. 'You came running to meet me, down the hill. You must have been waiting. I

125

suppose,' he paused, 'a bit uncertain as to whether I would come or not. And there was Francis, out ahead of you, so much faster, and you racing along behind as fast as your legs would carry you. And I was afraid you would fall on the tarry road and graze yourself. But you didn't. And then you were both with me, and those few days had begun, the two first days at Coppinger.'

'Did you still feel ashamed?' I asked.

Gently, he shook his head. 'No,' he said. 'It was all right. I should have known it would be all right. You were loyal, you see. Once I saw the two of you running towards me, racing against each other, I knew it was all right.'

'What did we do?'

'I don't know,' he said. 'I forget the details. I have a diary somewhere. Of each of the visits. But what we did doesn't matter so much. It's how we felt. You were always so cheerful.'

Gladys came into the room with a tray of tea things. 'Here we are, then,' she said. 'Time for your father's medicine.'

'Medicine?' I said.

'For his nostalgia. A nice cup of tea and the telly. Put him right soon enough. I've been listening to the pair of you.'

'And how was it, my ducky-doo? Did you feel shut out? Did you feel you'd have to intervene?'

Gladys laughed dismissively. 'I wouldn't dream of spoiling your fun. But it's me has to nurse you if you have a bad go.'

'A bad go?' I said. 'Do you mean of nostalgia?'

'Gets him down. I don't have to tell him that. He always says so, himself. One of his so-called precepts. Then he never takes any notice.'

I had forgotten the precepts in the flood of remembering through his eyes. I now looked at him, and he winked.

'Turn that machine on,' he said, pointing at the television. 'And hand me those papers there. I'll see what therapy there is tonight.'

I did as he said.

Gladys poured out the tea.

'I'll need him when I come back, Gladys,' I said.

She looked up at me over the tea things.

'Finding a place in London, settling in. It would help, if he came up for a day or two. Borrow him, you might say.' I looked over at him as he checked programmes. The television set was on, too loud. He had not heard, or did not notice.

'Borrow him?' she said. 'You could have him and keep him, if he'd go. Glad to be rid of him.'

'It would only be temporary,' I said. 'Just a bit of his advice. It's always good. He's so practical.'

She looked at me for a moment. Then she said, more quietly, as if consciously not wishing him to overhear, 'Don't you realise he's not up to it anymore?'

'Do you mean even a day or two in London would be too much?'

Her voice sank even lower. 'If he drank it would.'

'What are you pair talking about?' he said, staring hard at us both. 'You know I can't stand whispering.'

'We're talking about you,' I said, 'and your nostalgia.'

'Well speak up, so that we can all join in.'

'I was just saying to Gladys that it would be a help, when I find a place in London, if you came up and stayed for a day or two. You could advise me.'

His eyes lit up. 'Would you want me?'

'If you could spare the time I would.'

'Spare the time? Come like a shot out of a gun, old son. What'd you think, duckie? You wouldn't mind, would you? Well, that's settled, then. When would it be?'

'You'd have to be careful,' Gladys said. 'No drinking.'

'Drinking?' he said, his voice vibrating with moral outrage. 'Of course there'd be no drinking.'

'I haven't found a place yet. But I have a few flats in mind, to look at this week. They sound promising.'

'You tip me the wink, I'll be up. It'll be just the ticket, a break from here. Do me good. Won't it, duckie?'

'Duckie' looked distinctly dubious, and resumed her knitting, not looking at him. For a moment or two my father fixed her with his steely grey eyes. It appeared to me that he was contemplating further pressure in an attempt to force a more positive answer from her. Instead, and in a low voice, as if to himself, he said, 'Drinking? Drinking? Of course there won't be any drinking.'

'Will your legs stand up to it?' I asked.

He nodded. '*Pas de problème*,' he said, waving his hand in the air.

'And your chest?'

'*Pas de problème*.' His gesture was even more dismissive.

'That's good, then.'

'It's Harry Worth in ten minutes. Excellent.' He adjusted his glasses and stared at the screen. Gladys's knitting needles clicked away above the noisy hum of the set. They expressed her faint disapproval, and it added to the claustrophobia of the closed circle of our conversation. Outside, the sun had set, but only just, leaving residual gold to lighten the reds and mauves in the sky.

'I think I'll take a walk,' I said. 'Before it gets dark.'

'And miss Harry Worth? You must be out of your mind. Best laugh on the box.'

'I'm not really in the mood.'

I walked out, in the opposite direction from the town, past a couple more cottages, and then between hedgerows and trees. The air was still, and smelt sweetly of dogrose and honeysuckle, and the heavy mixed scents of grasses along the edges of the road, their stems curving under the pollen-laden and ripened seed. In my mind I could still see that stooping figure making its laborious progress along the garden path towards the gap in the hedge. I tried to think of him running. His figure, set in violent motion through the trees of Hyde Park against the enormous, ink-black curtain of star-studded sky, could only be fleetingly sustained. I saw him, for some reason, in naval uniform. It was decidedly at odds with the factual position; and yet, somehow, it was emblematic of that lost time. Dressing him up as once he must have been, as indeed I had seen him in photographs, helped for a while to give greater permanence to the invented image. But then the fact of it not being so, of it never having been so, fractured the brief and unsustainable sequence of rapid action, so that, instead of the gasping, vigorous figure, racing through my waking dream, the sequence of frames, as of a film, came to a stop, and like some personal, poignant

128

version of a strip of studies by Eadweard Muybridge, which in their very emphasis on movement seemed to epitomise stillness, he was brought down to a series of jagged stills which cruelly locked him like an insect inside the amber of my mind.

Then I thought of myself, running to meet him, and Francis out ahead of me. That was easier. Time's telescope, reversed, caught for a moment the eagerness, the rivalry, the passion that drove those fleet and youthful feet across gravel and grass. And it was a more conscious and deliberate act, transferring from his memory into my own that small fragment of feeling seen as energy.

Even so, the question was there: did the force of passion, driving him, driving me, make sense over all the years that lay between? Could I, looking back, more than three-quarters of my life, and picking up the image of that child running, feel that it had all been worthwhile? That it all made sense? And could he, doing the same, in his case looking back only thirty of his seventy and more years—another climacteric—do the same?

I had stepped out briskly, away from the cottage. Now I turned. There were stars overhead. A full and pinkish moon was visible above the trees of a wood that began a field or so from the road. From it there came the hooting of an owl.

When I got back I went first into the garden, and was not really surprised to see him there, in the diffused light from several windows, standing beside the roses.

'I shall miss the smell,' I said. 'It's very beautiful.'

'Unique,' he said.

'I have the stars, of course.'

'Nobody has the stars. Inscrutable and unchanging, they are completely impervious to all of man's endeavour.'

'So you'll come to London?'

'Like a shot, old son. I've got to get away. It's driving me crazy.'

Chapter Seven

[I]

I sought at this time for an image that might capture and explain both my state and his. I sought it consciously, within writing; ranging through poetry, drama or fiction, the way I had been conditioned to do in youth; and continuing the search visually, in paintings and drawings as well. But without result. The states of innocence and experience, in growing up, when the years are green, seem so much more amenable to some specific, parallel human statement from the deep well of creative imagery, than when we have moved on into more barren, more bewildering years. Even the stars failed to yield for me that welcome, night-time provocation that brings to one's lips the familiar lines of poetry remembered from youth.

It was, perhaps, this frustration that made me turn towards the creative treasure house of literature and art for an ill-defined symbol that might explain the search on which I vaguely felt a desire to embark, not fully understanding what it was I sought.

But there was another reason. In leaving him, that time in June, I had a curious sense of us reversing roles. He was now as I had been in childhood, a prisoner of circumstance. I was now as he had once been, the man of action and of independence. He was looking out, from the strict confinement of unwanted care and unsought for concern, at my freedom and self-determination; I, in my turn, had taken over that responsibility for myself, that liberation which in childhood and youth we look forward to with such pleasurable anticipation, not realising the checks and balances which always qualify each state to which progress leads. And, true enough, I felt no certitude: where there should have been assurance there was self-doubt. Between the simple clarity of youth and the confined and spartan wisdom of age there lurks a shadowy territory of the middle years, and it was that territory in which I moved then, the clarity of my vision blurred by the impact of his personality, which no longer held over me the controls exercised in my childhood.

He had come to the gate of the cottage on his own to say goodbye. His legs were hurting him so that he was not even able to take the short stroll down to the bus stop. I had said goodbye to Alice and Gladys earlier. Only he had come out. He was dressed, as usual, in his gardening overalls. He had left off his hat. A summer storm was brewing in the banks of grey cloud at his back. Yet the sun was still shining and he was caught in it, staring at me against its rays.

'Come again,' he said. 'Soon.'

'I'll try.'

'I don't know if I'll make it to London.'

'You must. It's important.'

'You'll keep me informed, won't you?'

'Perhaps they won't want you to come away.'

He made a face. 'I must do as I'm told now, old son. You see that.'

I nodded.

As if aware of his own precepts, the need to avoid self-pity, the obligation to assume a stoic disposition hardened his features. Sadness at my departure had temporarily softened them but now I saw what I had seen so vividly in the small framed photograph in the house: fear. There was no precept for that. Momentarily I was disposed to check my departure, to reach out to him, to lighten, in some way that was quite unclear to me, the burden which was descending there and then upon his statuesque form. But I realised, just as immediately, that there was no point. Nothing I could do would change by the smallest degree those fetters which,

131

like Marley's, had been forged through life and now held him in this strange and peaceful prison in the depths of the Somerset countryside. He had been given his chance; he had made of it certain things, as all of us do; and it had come to this.

His large hands gripped the top of the garden gate. 'Remember: don't talk unnecessarily!' He winked and nodded his head.

'Don't worry. I won't.'

Hard, in my own way, I lifted my hand in salutation, then turned from him. I looked back once only to see that he had not moved at all. Then, as I pressed on to the bus stop which was further down the road, at a turning in my route he passed from sight.

It was only out of his presence, in the slow sequence of ordinary events, wondering if the rain would start before the bus arrived, and then seeing in the faces of the other passengers and their casual indifference a further weakening in the links between myself and the strange situation I had left behind me, that I began to have second thoughts about him and his precepts. What were they but rather muddled clichés, all negatives, scraped together to no particular purpose by this foolish, irascible old man? What had he really done for me? What had he really taught? Where had he left me? An angry, frightened old failure, whose every nuance of voice, whose every gesture, was burnt and engraved in my heart and soul, where had he left me but in a state of doubt and unfulfilment? Things that I sought to do were overshadowed by him. I felt crowded in by the past. Ghosts needed to be laid.

The bus journey, which carried me to the railway station, and then the wait for the train, were productive of almost bitter thoughts directed against him and what I saw as his fumblings for truth. The single sheet of paper I had taken from his hand in the garden was in my pocket now. I did not need to take it out to be able to visualise the layout on the page, the handwriting, the grammatical mistake, the clearly circled numbers. The words came back to me, both the words we had exchanged, and the words written down. And slowly, from a mood of scorn and dismissal, itself the reverse of having been deeply moved on the occasion itself, I came round to being wistfully amused by my father's attempt to offer me, and the world at large, a testament which certainly the world, and probably I, would reject. But then, what of that? Did not the world, daily, reject and scorn far greater precepts.

The storm was some time in coming. Leaving the town by train eventually, out along the river valley, the scene had that curiously frozen quality, as common to summer as to winter, of reluctant hesitation before the climax of disturbance by the wind, to be followed by the first heavy drops of rain. The vigorous movement of leaves in that gusting wind came as the train gathered speed eastward. First, the leaves of the willow trees, narrow and flexible, turned their silvery undersides against the banked grey cloud. And then others followed: even a sycamore joined in the mounting fury, its large, ornate leaves twisting and flapping to reveal the pale, liverish green in an ugly shimmer of light. Then came large drops of rain, on the compartment window, followed by a sudden hissing downpour in conflict with the sombre, monotonous throb of the train's movement.

Journeying, journeying; the physical movement being so small a part of it one is tempted to take, all the time, from memory, from the imagination, robbing and looting the past. Deliberately, cold-bloodedly, in order to lay certain ghosts, I had caught his disease. And, infected by nostalgia, temporarily imprisoned in the railway system of England—*mal de pays* in more senses than one—I thought of Ursula, Madge, Babette, and of that Christmas long ago; I thought of Coppinger, and of how, for so many years, it had been my own form of confinement—unwanted care, unsought-for concern; I thought of Francis, and of his inviolable determination; I thought of Mr Porphyry, shaping, arranging, but losing in the end. I determined on going back. It was not just back, physically, to certain places, or to encounters with people not seen for many years; it was back in time as well, the conscious act of will designed to recover and to test feelings, perceptions, beliefs. I believed that if I met them, then, in their eyes, in gesture, in words, in recollection, possibly in place as well, I would release some blockage in myself.

We are all flawed, but in different fashion. In my own case the shadow of my father, who had given me life, who had made me happy, who had taught me with relentless passion so many of the things I should not do, had also perhaps cast a shadow, fulfilling a natural law about the inveiglement of death with life, of sickness with health, of failure with success. How I was to find out, I did not know. I believed that something of innocent, childhood love would still have survived, over the years, between Babette and myself, and that it might release understanding. I believe that Ursula, in her wisdom, would have things to teach that had been impossible when she and my father had been lovers. I believe that the roadways and hedgerows of Coppinger might release, along with the scent of honeysuckle, answers. I was as simplistic about it as that. I wanted answers! Do not we all want answers? Could I blame myself if, like Irina, listening to the band, knowing that it was all hopeless, I should assert future knowledge, the possibility of future knowledge, about what all this is for, why there is this misery, and why it is so unevenly distributed? To live, to work, to let time pass; that is the message. But to understand it all, that is the gift.

[II]

I tried Francis first. It is perhaps a measure of the extent to which I did not understand him, while at the same time placing so much trust in him, that I discussed my 'disease' as though he were a fellow-sufferer. He was not. 'Don't reminisce,' was what he told me. Of a practical turn of mind, living very much in the present, engaged at the time in research work for the political party which now employed him, it was remarkable I suppose that he even listened to all that I had to say.

I told him first about my visit.

'I must go down, I really must.'

From the expression on his face I did not judge the intention as entirely serious. 'You know he's invited Ursula to go down?'

'Ursula?'

I reminded him of Ursula's identity. I had to explain a bit about her.

'Doesn't Glady's object?'

I shook my head. 'Alice does.'

'I'm not surprised.'

'I was going to look up Ursula myself. She's still in the same flat.'

'What age would she be?'

I hazarded a guess on that, too.

'Remarkable, how he's come through, isn't it?'

'Has he?' I asked.

'Well, it's quite a time since I last saw him, but when I was in the west country—it must be three years ago—I spent a day with him, and I certainly thought he'd landed on his feet. A comfortable cottage—no owner's responsibilities—a garden which he reigns over absolutely, a wife who is also a nurse, and Alice, as benign as ever, presiding over it all and finding so little wrong in him.'

I smiled at Francis. 'Maybe you're right,' I said. 'I can't argue. It adds up well on paper. You make it sound idyllic. Yet he is afraid.'

'Afraid?'

I told him of the photographs and of my feelings.

'I suppose there must be a price he has to pay.'

I nodded. 'I feel sorry for him, though.'

He ignored that. 'So you've found somewhere to live?'

'I think it will be all right.'

'And when will you move?'

'Some time in the early autumn.'

'So you've time on your hands?' He looked at me, I thought, a little nervously, as though I might be contemplating impositions upon him which might impede his work.

'Well, I didn't expect confirmation of the job to come through so quickly. I was reasonably certain, but it still meant that I was dithering a bit over the flat. Now I can make a decision.'

'Puzzles me how you work,' Francis said. 'Is there a market for all this stuff you write?'

'It pays me,' I said.

'Evidently. Expanding as well.'

'It's a growth market,' I said. 'And I enjoy it.'

'I can't fathom journalists,' Francis said. 'When you want good coverage they're hard to find. When you have problems, there they are, probing away.'

I had no wish to get into a philosophic discussion about our respective professions. I was faintly irritated by his obliqueness. He had veered away from the detail of my work into generalities, and evinced no real desire to understand what I would be coming back to. He was incurious about my life. Perhaps I was the same about his, tolerating only a thin measure of comment which in any case was surrounded by various security restraints. He was still the elder brother, ahead in experience and knowledge, holding back on details.

'I thought I'd call on Ursula.' He didn't seem greatly interested.

'I was going to go back to Coppinger, Francis. Would you like to come?'

His stare was expressionless. As a bachelor I guessed his weekend, like my own, might be free. He said, 'I wouldn't mind. When had you thought of going?'

'I've only this weekend. I have to be back in Paris on Tuesday.'

'All right. I'll come with you.' He said it guardedly. At best, I suppose, he was fulfilling a certain curiosity about a place which had been important to him, yet in a much more neutral way than it had for me.

'I'll hire a car,' I said. 'We'll drive.'

[III]

I had anticipated some kind of capitulation by Ursula to the fortunes of time and destiny: the bohemian woman who had decked out moments of my childhood with a special kind of colouring and excitement, both in her relationship with my father and also in the time and interest she had so generously expended on me; but now brought to heel, as it were.

I could not have been more wrong. All those years before, the house she lived in had been one of a terrace condemned. It had been for this reason that the electrical wiring of the house had not been done, and it had then been mysteriously gaslit, quaint to the point of being sinister. Now, on my return, I found the same houses standing there, only restored and wired and occupied fully by people whose taste was reflected in unusual colours and austere, self-conscious expressions of design. Amid all this, Ursula's flat, not greatly changed from the way it had been so many years before, seemed just as spare and virginal and impressive as it had been when first I visited her. She had made no concessions to Chelsea 'chic'. She had been sophisticated when the streets had been the haunt of real people; she was still sophisticated as she stood smiling in the doorway, telling me it was a kindness to call.

I wonder if it was. I wonder what she detected in my presence there, on her doorstep, more than twenty years after our last encounter.

'Come in,' she said. 'You'll have tea?'

'That's very kind.'

'It was good of you to ring. I don't see many people.'

'Are you still teaching in the same schools?'

'The schools have changed. And the pupils, of course. I hope the teaching's improved.'

'Father's looking forward to you going down,' I said, later. 'He's quite excited about it.'

She laughed shyly. 'I didn't know whether it was the right thing to do. His letter came as such a surprise. Dear George. He's so impetuous. I thought at first, better not. But he was very insistent.'

'And you don't mind?'

'Of course not.'

I told her about myself. It took some time. She was intrigued that I had moved to Paris, a city she loved, and quite dismayed that I should now be leaving it to return to London.

'It's lonely,' I said.

'Paris? Lonely? But there's so much to do!'

'But when you've done all the things, it's still rather lonely. At least, I find it so.' I crossed over to the window and stared out at the soot-grimed façade of the church on the other side of the street. It was made benign by the clear sharp June sunlight. Below, in the courtyard which surrounded it, and in playgrounds beyond, children were playing.

'I was rather frightened of you when I first came here, all those years ago.' I turned from the window and looked at her where she sat in a small button-back chair. 'But then you weren't frightening, not at all. You were the opposite. You made me feel at home, from the first moment . . .' I paused, held back by a reserve over that emotional involvement of so many years before. 'You were the first person that I knew him to be in love with. My mother died years before that. And there must have been other women, and I must have met them, since I was always with him. But you were the first I knew about. Knowledge was switched on as sharply as if it had been an electric light. Click, and there it was.' Again I paused. 'You don't mind me telling you this?'

She shook her head. 'No. Go on. I never realised. I don't remember it very well, your first visit. Was it winter?'

'It was before the Christmas,' I said; 'you know, when we came down.' I almost felt anger that she could forget.

'Oh, yes. Of course. Of course.'

I stared at her for a while, deliberating whether to go on. 'The logic of children is very simple. They add things up, and come quickly to a final reckoning. It's never like that. But we only discover the fact years later. If my father loved you and you loved him then you would marry. It was as simple as that. Babette and I would be drawn together. As he used to say, everything would be all right. And the unhappiness that came after my mother's death would come to an end.'

'It wasn't as simple as that.' She spoke without a hint of sadness; almost the reverse. If anything, I detected a glow of pleasure at her being made to recall what I was recalling, and yet obviously in a quite different mould of memory.

'Of course not,' I said, laughing. 'I was foolish to think it. That a whole lot of lives could be organised, or reorganised, around a single kiss, an embrace. So foolish. Yet children do that. I did it.' I looked straight at her, smiling still. 'Am I being nostalgic?'

She shook her head. 'I don't think so. Don't become nostalgic.' She paused. 'Remembering is different.'

'I was so disappointed you didn't marry,' I said.

'It wouldn't have worked. I wasn't strong enough for him.'

'Of course I wasn't thinking only of you two; there was Babette,' I said.

'Babette?'

'She was part of my reason for wanting you and father to marry.'

'Oh, well.' She frowned. 'You haven't seen her since then, I suppose.'

I shook my head.

'She's due back. She works in Brussels. Goes to Paris as well. I think she's been there recently.'

'Married?'

'She has been. Not any more. It didn't work out. You should ring her mother.'

When I was leaving I asked her: 'Do you still go to exhibitions?'

Her face became animated. 'Oh, yes. I went recently to Apsley House. No one ever goes to it. There are such good paintings there. He had a wonderful—'

I interrupted her. 'It was you first taught me that paintings 'spoke', Ursula; like fiction or poetry.'

'I?' she said, exaggerating the disbelief.

'Oh, yes,' I said. 'Don't you remember the exhibitions you took me to? Don't you remember? Don't you remember taking me to see the Leonardo drawings? There was one there, a terrible face, and you said that it made you understand how it feels to be ugly. The picture had a language, you said, about how people feel. And that was what the artist wanted you to understand.'

139

'I said that?'

'I've always remembered it. I never thought of pictures as decoration after that. It was different, though of course many *are* just that. I used to stare earnestly at paintings, remembering what you had said. I suppose I was very deliberate about it. Perhaps boring.' I smiled in recollection of that callow, serious youth I had been, hungrily absorbing painted surfaces, and trying to see beneath them. Then I smiled at her. 'I must go, Ursula. You've a lot to answer for.'

She laughed. 'Then do one thing for me, will you? Go to Apsley House. It's well worth it. Particularly for the work you do.'

And as I descended the stair which I had climbed in nervous expectation at my father's heels so many years before, she called after me: 'And ring Madge.'

[IV]

It was almost accidental, in the end. Following Ursula's assurance that Madge would like to see me, I rang up. I am sure Ursula did not mean me to do it the next day. Probably, she had intended to talk with her sister, and explain other things, including the unexpected return, after a long time, of my father into her life, issuing an equally unexpected invitation for her to go and stay. All of which, in retrospect, would then have made more sense of things to Madge. But I was in a hurry. Quite unjustifiably, I was not only determined upon a resurrection course which covered a particularly narrow field of vision, but on completing it in a period of days before hurrying back to Paris, rather than giving to it the measured planning and care which it deserved. When I should have seen what I was doing in the perspective of all the people involved, when I should have measured my actions against the impact they might have had upon lives other than my own, all I did in reality was to act selfishly. I had before me a quest to fulfil, urgent and finite. My father's perpetual surrender to the ethos of the past, to those powerful sights and sounds and smells which he evoked with a passion which could quite literally fill his eyes with tears or set his nostrils quivering and his lips trembling, was clearly derived from forces to which I too could easily succumb. If I were not to become more and more heavily infected myself then I must discover, quickly, some cure. The course I had to pursue was a classic of medicine, not unlike that which saved James Phipps and turned the course of medical history. Like Jenner, I recognised that vaccination might well offer the proper prophylactic.

Thinking about Madge induced in me the silent recreation of her voice, musical, low, backed by fluency and originality of perception. Without actually recalling all the details of the first occasion of our meeting, at the wedding years before when I had sung a solo, or even of the last time I had been with her, not so long afterwards, at the end of a Christmas holiday, I simply extracted out of the past enough of her character to be able to anticipate, not without pleasure, even excitement, the sound of her voice. To me, a child, she had said so definitely, and yet sweetly as well, 'Call me Madge; I won't answer to Mrs Springer,' that I almost said, to the low voice announcing the number in reply to my phone call, 'Is that Madge?' But instead began immediately to tell her of Ursula and seeing her again. I was well launched on what I had to say before the voice interrupted me.

'It's not Mrs Springer speaking. It's her daughter.'

'Babette?'

There was a pause; and then, the tone faintly questioning, 'Yes. This is Babette. Who are you?'

I told her.

There was a longer pause. I was about to speak again when she said, 'How extraordinary! I didn't know you were in touch with Mummy.'

'I wasn't. At least, not until now. And I'm not now, yet.' I laughed a bit nervously. 'How silly it is to meet on the telephone, as it were. I should have written, or something. I've been to see Ursula. She gave me the number. I was hoping I might to able to see your mother.'

'Well, she's away.'

It was the tone in which she said this that I tried to measure, as I absorbed the slight rebuff.

141

'Oh,' I said.

'I'm using her flat.'

'Could we meet?' I blurted it out. 'I mean, I was only looking up old friends. I'm back from abroad.'

'Abroad?'

'I work in Paris.'

'Paris! I've just been there. On my way from Brussels. I work as an interpreter.'

'Ursula told me. How extraordinary! All the more reason we should see each other. Are you free? Can we meet?'

Again, there was a pause. I heard, as it were, the thoughts and recollections trickling through her mind as through an hour-glass. All the time that had gone past, together with the present knowledge that she knew I must have, from talking with Ursula.

'Come and have lunch. Come now. Nothing elaborate.' She laughed. 'We'll feed on memory.' And she gave the address, and hung up, so quickly. All I could think of was how she had been just like that, before, giving me orders, taking charge, oh yes, so definitely she had been in charge, that Christmas morning so many years before. Nor was there much, beside memory, defective memory, on which to feed when we did meet, an hour or so later.

Babette continued to be in charge. Her mother's flat was frugal in its furnishings, the walls and curtains white, the floor carpeted in grey, no pictures, but several works of sculpture including at least three masks from New Guinea, one of considerable size. Such furniture as there was, apart from a large sofa along one wall, and two Victorian button-back chairs upholstered in a plum-red velvet, was made of oak and seemed to be eighteenth-century or earlier. It was all very different from the brocades and patterns which I remembered from the house I had visited as a child.

'What happened?' I asked, looking at Babette, as she poured glasses of sherry. 'To Robert?'

'He found somebody else.' She turned and handed me the drink.

'And your mother? Was it . . . was she very unhappy?' I faltered over the question, knowing that behind it lay the much closer issue of her own situation.

'It took her time to get over it. It's never easy.'

'And how is she now?'

'All right.'

I looked round. 'The flat's so different,' I said. 'You never had anything like this. Not when you lived in Sloane Street.'

'Did you know us then?'

'Yes.'

'That's so long ago.' She said it without regret.

I nodded. To me it seemed quite recent. There was no effort of will remembering. I could see before me the comfortable, even complacent opulence of their main drawing-room, with lamps and paintings and the large, ornate mirror above the mantelpiece, through which I had watched the distorted image of my father's face on one occasion, and thought to myself that he did not quite belong there. I felt certain I could describe it well, even remind her of episodes that were, in their way, amusing. And I wanted to do so, if only to demonstrate the fact of my familiarity and of my occasional presence. But it seemed futile. What was I trying to do?

'I don't remember you coming,' she said. There was a smile on her face of faint apology, polite, distant.

'I only came a couple of times,' I said. 'Certainly, with my father, I came. And he had an argument with yours. But I can't remember what it was about. Then there was the time we went out, you and I.'

'Did we?' She looked across the room at me. 'Where did we go?'

Almost nothing of the face I had known then was left in the face that I looked on now. Hedged round with all the caution of experience, carefully made up, and in a sophisticated way quite beautiful, I had to search for the mocking innocence of the child upon whom I had once fixed the totality of love and expectation. It was there. I could just see it. But it was not forthcoming. None of the feeling I once had known was now available.

With a precision that was really quite frightening, I realised that I could, if I so wished, recapitulate for her what we had done together on that afternoon. They were scored in my memory, each of the deliberate acts, down to the last and most important, the pledge we had made, and never kept, to meet again.

I thought to myself: If we were to become lovers, then I could tell you. Together, in each other's arms, we could restore that little fragment of the past which at the time had meant so much to me that it had become quite indelibly permanent. But time had robbed it of any significance for her. Instead, I said to her: 'I don't remember. We probably went out with Ursula. An exhibition. A film at the Classic, in the King's Road. It's a very long time ago.'

'That flat was really rather awful, wasn't it?'

'I don't know. At the time . . .' I tailed off, not wishing to emphasise the clarity with which I could recall its details.

'Oh, yes. We were keeping up appearances.'

'This is certainly very nice. How often do you come and stay with Ma-, with your mother?'

'Let's go and have some lunch. It's nothing very elaborate.'

We talked about the present, not the past. We talked about Paris, which she often visited, fusing together our quite different experiences of the city. If anything, it emphasised the gulf that lay between our lives. The fact that I was moving back to London did not in any way put her out, and this made more definite the transience of our fresh encounter. Yet in what seemed to be a curious exercise in objectivity, in the absorption of factual reality, I found myself in possession of a rounded and composite view of Babette that seemed to mock at my comprehension of other women I had known. In the midst of the structured artificiality of our meeting, perhaps because of it, I was made aware of myself as I might appear—as perhaps I did appear—in the eyes of those who knew me. And I did not like what I perceived—it was incomplete and ungenerous. It was an unflattering self that I reconstructed, in love with Sarah, with Olivia, with Margaret. I say 'in love'. What exactly do I mean? Sitting there with Babette, the bottle of white wine almost empty between us, sunlight dazzling on one portion of the white wall, and the possibilities of our conversation virtually exhausted, I was increasingly aware that I had once loved her with a greater passion than I had ever felt since. She had been life, and hope, and purpose, for me. She had been my future. She was now unquestionably part of the past. I could tell her none of this. It would have been absurd. Yet I felt the urge to tell someone. It was important. Something was there. Something had happened.

'So your father's settled down?' There was in her eyes a hint of mockery which I hesitate to claim as familiar. Yet it was just that. Remembered over the span of years as the most persistent of all her expressions, and the one which, more than compassion, more than interest or curiosity, had held me so firmly under her spell so many years before.

'You could call it that,' I said.

'In a country cottage? With a garden to mind? And two women to watch over him? I think that's settled enough, isn't it? There are times when all of us could envy it.'

'I don't envy him. It gets explosive at times, Babette, I sometimes think he will turn against what he has and throw it all away.'

'Why would he do that?'

I paused before answering, looking at her, and realising that, whatever she had once known, was now forgotten, and that to explain to her my fears and expectations would serve little or no purpose. 'He always has,' I said. 'You understood him very well. You were very good with him.'

'Was I? I don't remember.'

'Oh, yes! There were times when you—' I looked across at her. 'But I'm boring you.'

'We all loved George.'

[V]

We drove to Coppinger the Saturday morning before I returned to Paris. Francis showed no great enthusiasm for the trip. His initial willingness to go with me was now qualified by his brief, clipped remark about having to be back in London for a dinner engagement. He was in one of his non-committal moods, oppressed not so much by work as by the many veils of secrecy which seemed to envelop the particular position he occupied. I had no wish to intrude; so long as he was disposed to listen, I was willing to talk about myself and my various encounters of that week in London. By his polite replies he gave me sufficient encouragement to do this during the hour's drive to Oxford. Yet he hardly knew Ursula, had never met Madge or Babette, and may even have felt, in addition to a natural indifference, a certain resentment at the extent to which these people and the remembered events which I recalled for him, represented a period of alienation, which he did not necessarily want displayed in front of him, at least, not by me.

Bypassing Oxford, we took the Banbury road and followed the valley of the Cherwell as far as the Astons and the Bartons, where the first long, flattish wolds entice one over what seems to be an edge, and yet is too subtle for that; a rise in the ground, yes; a lip of different earth, and yet so gradual and so muted in its impact.

'Do you ever come up here on your own?' I asked.

'No.'

'Did you ever?'

'Once or twice. A long time ago.'

'And you just stopped?'

'I couldn't see the point. To begin with, there were people I knew. At the very beginning you were still here. But after that it was just there, the place.' He paused, then looked across at me. 'It was so *indifferent*.'

He meant me to laugh, and I did. It was a dutiful response, whereby I let his interpretation of why we go back prevail. It is a form of exorcism; we cure ourselves by surfeit. Yet behind the laughter I was not agreeing with him. As we came closer, and recognised more of our surroundings, I did not care that so many of the people, indeed almost all of them, had departed.

'Should we not be turning down this way?' Francis pointed left at a junction at which I was turning right to cross the oncoming traffic. The signpost said 'Great Rollright'.

'We should. Yes. I just want to go down into West Aston, the village. It won't take long.'

'Are we calling on someone?'

'No.'

146

He stared ahead, frowning. I think Francis did not altogether like me to share control over what I did with him.

I drove into the village and stopped beside the church. In spite of it being late morning, and a Saturday, the centre of the small village was virtually deserted. In the graveyard two women were tending flowers in front of a newly erected tombstone. I got out. Francis followed me, reluctantly.

'A bit off our track, isn't it?'

'I came here once,' I said. 'To a wedding. The choir came. I sang a solo. It was after you had left. It has always stuck in my mind.'

We went through the wooden gate together. I wasn't sure whether I wanted to go into the church even. And the low hum of women's voices, which had stopped for a moment or two as we passed by, now sounded again on top of the summer noise of birds and insects.

I wanted to tell Francis about the occasion and by doing so make up my mind about whether to go into the church and whether, afterwards, to go and look at the manor house in which the reception had been held. But he was already stalking away from me, his hands clasped behind his back, his head up in a determined and inscrutable confrontation with the stocky tower and the squat, ancient building. And as I followed him, hoping he would pause, he disappeared into the porch and on into the church itself.

It was my turn to feel reluctance. There are moments when pace and timing are everything. A sudden impulse had made me turn down towards the village. It had been quite unplanned until we reached the turning. But now that we had come I wanted to recapture something of that winter wedding when first I had encountered Babette. It was difficult; for the time and the season of the year combined to destroy a frail recollection, and Francis was rushing me through.

Inside, the coolness and the rays of sunlight created an atmosphere quite different from the one I vaguely recalled, in the depth of winter, in the frosty darkness, with glittering lights and the sharp sound of expectant guests. Had we processed up the aisle? I could not remember. Francis

147

had already reached the far end, and stood at the altar rail, his hands still grasped firmly behind his back, his eyes inspecting, with a stony precision, his surroundings. I joined him, and turned to face the empty pews. '"For all flesh is grass",' I said, '"and all the glory of man as the flower of grass; the grass withereth, and the flower thereof falleth away; but the word of the Lord endureth forever."'

'Who are these Fishers?' Francis said, looking up at the plaques on the wall beyond the pulpit. 'Wasn't there a Fisher on the board of trustees?'

'Sir Joseph. It was his daughter's wedding. They live in the manor house here. He's retired. May even be dead.'

'Should we go and see it?'

'We might get a glimpse of it, through the trees.'

'He was an MP then. Certainly active in the Conservative Party. But that ceased quite a few years ago. Didn't quite make the grade.'

'Wasn't all that good as a trustee, either. Philpotts didn't think much of him.'

'Philpotts?'

'There was an episode at the wedding, some kind of row in which everyone got worked up. He was involved; so was I. It all ended in nothing, the way these things do, but at the time it was very tense. Fisher handled it rather badly. At least, that's what Philpotts thought.'

'The opposite is often the case,' Francis said. 'After all, if it came to nothing, wasn't that good?'

We drove to the manor house gates. There was a notice indicating that it was private: a calm, smug negative. I was unwilling to drive in. We got out, and walked part of the way down the drive. It seemed wholly different from anything I could remember. The road dipped and there was a small bridge over a stream; coming up from that, the house came into view, and I remembered then the last view I had had of it, across the snow, the lights gleaming, people setting out, at the end of the wedding reception, the sky sprinkled with stars, and the moon shedding a ghostly light on the frozen snow.

148

But if I anticipated anything more than the formal recognition of a tiny portion of geography which fitted into time's landscape in that chilly and exact way which defies our emotions, I was mistaken. The well-kept house, the fenced meadow with two or three horses cropping the grass, the deserted driveway, and the tall trees, with everything bathed in midsummer sun, held no special appeal for me, just then. Perhaps it was the season of the year; perhaps it was Francis's presence; perhaps it was the fact of my deliberate decision to stop in the village; perhaps, over it all, it derived from the curious and cold-blooded exercises in exploration on which I had been engaged during that week in London. Precisely because I was looking for some kind of expiation, it would not come. And I felt mocked by the hard, bright sun.

We leaned for a while on the fence, looking at the house. Then I said, 'We'd better go. We really came to see Coppinger.'

Francis did not answer, and I looked sideways at him. He was staring at the house. I could see no reason for his interest. He had not known it, and Sir Joseph Fisher had been little more than a name, representative of higher powers at Coppinger. It occured to me that he was displeased in some way with something I had said or done, and I considered carefully the day's events, but nothing seemed to suggest itself as a tangible offence. I waited beside him, not speaking. Suddenly he turned and walked off, back in the direction we had come, his hands clasped behind his back as usual, but the effect this time more rigid and austere. He walked jerkily, rising on the balls of his feet, and his arms, stiff behind his back, seemed to push his shoulders up, making him look bony and angular, almost, I felt, physically *impoverished*, so that I had the urge to soften him, to relax him, to *warm* him in some way.

I walked after him, wanting to talk; but his pace was too rigid, and we were back at the car before I had the chance. By then, the opportunity had passed. The faint yet clear hint of some kind of antagonism faded away as swiftly as it had come, leaving a curious neutrality behind, as difficult to cope with, if not more difficult.

'Do you have remembered scenes in your mind which are permanently there?' I asked. 'Not places that you know, but just scenes, bits of landscape?'

He sat beside me, looking ahead of us as we drove along, and did not answer straight away. Then he said, 'I don't know what you mean.'

I paused. I wondered to myself: what am I trying to do? Am I trying to win him round? I said, 'I can close my eyes—'

'Not now, I hope!'

'No. But let me tell you. I can, at will, recall a roadway rising towards a gently sloping horizon that drops from left to right across my line of vision. It is unremarkable, and treeless. The road is thick with snow, but it is packed and frozen. The fields on either side are also white with snow, but the sense I have, in my recollection, is that it has lain on the ground for days. The sky is leaden grey, the air cold, and it surely will snow soon. The road simply runs ahead, goes over the hill, and disappears.'

'Do you dream this, or is it real?'

'That's the odd thing about it. All the places I can remember, and reconstruct, and link up to other places, all of them are somehow less vivid than this tiny fragment of landscape. With these two fields, the hedges, the road and the sky, I can do absolutely nothing. I don't know where they are. I don't know what was over the top of the hill. I don't know what lay behind. Yet it was a real place. I haven't dreamt it. I was coming back from somewhere. It was cold, and we—whoever I was with, and it might have been you, even—were tired and hungry. It was at Coppinger, somewhere around here, I suppose, and whenever it occurs the scene is accompanied by the most vivid inner sense of despair. Whenever that fixed scene, which never changes, in which I am perpetually toiling upward towards the line of the horizon, presents itself, I feel utterly forlorn.'

'Does it last long?'

I wanted to say to him that that was not the point, but I felt it might offend him. Instead, I answered, 'It passes. But what's odd about it is the intensity of the feeling of being lost. I am convinced it happened, on a particular day, in a particular place, that my feelings were so strong, about

150

myself, about Coppinger, perhaps about us, I just don't know, that they fixed the scene for ever.'

I told him all this as I drove, and my preoccupation, mechanical though it was, with the turns and twists in the narrow roads as we neared the school, prevented me from making any assessment of his reaction. Out of the corner of my eye I could see him, but his expression was inscrutable. I think, in reality, he was indifferent.

'Are you going to philosophise about it?' he asked.

'I don't think so,' I said.

'Good.'

'Why are you so cool about such experiences?'

'I can't explain. They do one no good.'

He offered no comparable experience. He posed no further questions. And the emergence, as we topped a rise in the road, of the outline of familiar buildings, brought to an end any further consideration of an experience which, for all its intensity, was really imponderable. I had never mentioned it before. And, though it is still as vivid as ever when it recurs, or when it is recalled, I have never touched on it again, either with him or with anyone else. All that it did for me, on that summer afternoon, was to point me more firmly still down the pathway I had been travelling all that week, into, and away from, recollection of the past for its own sake.

[VI]

We drove on to Coppinger. We didn't talk much. The narrow roads were deserted: it was not a sightseer's portion of the Cotswolds. The frequency of familiar places grew, and I felt the urge to stop; I wanted to say to Francis, 'there was where I came with Philpotts the day after I heard of father's marriage,' or, more marginally, 'there Pritchett and Lytton and I decided on our underground invasion of a staff meeting;' but, though the essence of recollected reality resided strongly enough in the places as we passed them—a road junction, a gateway overlooking a steep fall

151

of grassland towards a plantation's edge—the motive that might have brought them forth, at least with my brother, had evaporated. And if this were so with him, then who was left? Could I summon up Philpotts? Would Lytton or Pritchett be interested? Did they ever come back? Would they remember? Did it matter? Did any of it matter at all?

We parked in front of the main building. 'Should we make known our presence?' I asked. 'Will they give us lunch?'

'Do we want to stay for lunch?'

'Oh, surely. Isn't it the form, with old boys?'

'I think there's some kind of visitors' book which we sign.'

The difference I felt was aggravated by the need to reach some kind of tacit agreement with Francis. I could see we would not be staying too long into the afternoon. Nevertheless, even for a few short hours, it was going to be a problem getting things right.

'Shall we sign the book first? Or go into the Chapel?'

Though there was no one about, the buildings to be seen in different directions, and the cars parked beside or in front of them, created an atmosphere of expectation which itself had echoes from the past. Someone, somewhere, would ring a bell, and Coppinger would spring into life. Staff, pupils, obedient to strict timetables, would pour forth from the main buildings; wives would gather near to where we were standing; we ourselves would be gathered into the throng. Just for a moment or two I wondered, was this what I wanted? Did I come here seeking company or solitude? Then I saw Francis, without answering my question, turn and enter the main door. He met someone inside, and I heard voices. Still I did not follow, but waited until he came back.

'That's arranged,' he said. 'Lunch. At a quarter to one. They seemed *pleased*!' He expressed an almost disdainful surprise.

'Why wouldn't they? Honoured guests.'

'I would have said awkward guests.' He looked at me, the residue of disdain still in his faintly challenging expression. Somehow, in the tiny initiative of 'signing us in', he had gained over me an advantage. Nor was he finished. 'We'll have company at lunch.'

'Company?'

'Someone called Hannay.'

'Hannay? Who told you?'

He shrugged towards the closed door behind him. 'Some member of staff. I didn't catch his name.'

We walked away, out of the shadow of the building into sunlight, and set off across the cropped grass towards the chapel on a ritual tour of inspection which began with the place of worship in a faint but automatic imitation of the way things had been ordered in the past when we had been there. Stepping out side by side I was aware of an uneasy, prickly conjunction. We looked at things around us with different eyes and diverse memories, and the more we looked the less we had to say to each other.

At first, I thought this might be dispelled by the presence of Hannay, whom we would see at lunch, if not before. I half expected that Francis would inquire about him, and hoped for it. But he remained silent.

After a while I said, 'I wonder what's brought Hannay down.'

Still he did not answer. He walked beside me, perhaps half a pace ahead, with stiff, sharp steps, the heels of his shoes, as we moved from grass to gravel, digging in with a crisp and crunchy sound. My own softer-soled shoes compromised more with the surface.

'Did you know Hannay?' I asked. 'He was here in your time.'

'I don't remember him particularly well. I only heard about him afterwards. Good at cricket. Wasn't he head boy?'

'Yes.'

'Any good?' My brother's eyebrows were raised in an expression of cool detachment. I wondered, did he want to know at all? Was there not, in his attitude, a relentless disdain which was being forced to the forefront all the time as a counter to something that I represented in relation to the school?

'He was outstanding,' I said.

'And now?' The hint of indifference, even of anticipated pleasure in a reversal of that peak achieved by a boy younger

153

than Francis, who had barely impinged on him during his time at school, seemed to invade the question.

'I don't know,' I said. Then I added, with a smile, 'He may still be outstanding.'

'Hmm,' was all Francis said.

We lunched at the headmaster's table. He seemed genuinely pleased to have three old boys back at the one time, and kept up a jolly and provocative thread of conversation which imposed on the prefects an onus to join in, though with none of the forbidding pressures which I remembered from meals with Merchant. It was a different establishment now. They were self-assured, and genuinely curious. When one of them turned to me and said, 'What was it like in your day?' I laughed, and said, 'It's hard to remember, hard to know where to begin.'

'When were you here, sir?'

I smiled at him. 'You mustn't call me sir. I feel as though I were one of you. You're making me feel old.'

'But when did you come?'

'In the war.'

His blank stare distressed me. I was talking about a past which to him was almost history. Almost, not quite. There were still points of contact.

'And when did you leave?' He asked the question politely, and I told him.

'You wouldn't have been born then,' I said. 'Was Mr Merchant here still when you came? Or Mr Forrest?' I searched in my mind for other names, but could think of none.

The boy shook his head. 'I've only been at Coppinger five years.'

'And you're a prefect already?'

'I'm seventeen. I leave next month.'

'We stayed much longer in my day. Nearer ten years than five.' I wanted to ask him why, or how, he had come, but realised I could not. So instead we talked about work, and what he would do next.

Afterwards, over coffee, Francis and I discovered that Hannay was competent rather than outstanding. In engineering, in Birkenhead, he still played cricket, and seemed prosperous enough, if one was to judge by appearances, and by the fairly new Rover which he had outside. In his face I detected faint echoes of the aloofness and authority that had once been all-powerful over us. The charm was there, as well, that extraordinary capacity which all of us had admired at the time to draw forth an instinctive and universal willingness to turn his discipline, which had been strict, into a more positive force which I suppose we understood at the time as 'school spirit'. But it was tempered now, and over the eyes with which he looked from Francis to me, and back again, there were faint filters of doubt, even suspicion, about what we had made of things and how we stood in the order of whatever world we inhabited. It was too complicated to find out, of course, and Francis and I would have resisted any inquiry.

He had called in, on his way through, from a business trip to London.

'Do you do it regularly?' I asked.

'The trip? Or calling in?'

'Both.'

'I don't come this way. Not on business. But I do come back. Certainly every other year.'

'I don't see many names I know in the visitor's book. Where have our contemporaries vanished to? Do you see anything of Bates? Or Merriot? Do you ever meet Barnwell? Briggs?'

He shook his head. 'I never see any of them.' He frowned, with the effort of remembering.

'What about Lytton and Pritchett? Or Archer? Do you remember them?'

'Yes. Archer's done well. He took a degree at Leeds. He has his own business.'

'And does he come back?'

Hannay shook his head. I glanced at Francis, who had now finished his coffee, and was standing silent beside us. But his face, quite expressionless, did not respond to my look.

'Why is it that so few old boys from that time return here?'

In Hannay's face there was that softer, doubting quality again. 'Maybe they weren't happy,' he said. 'Maybe

155

Merchant gave them a hard time. It's really only those who liked it here who go on coming back.' He put down his coffee cup. 'Well, I must away,' he said. He put out his hand. 'Good to see you both. You ought to pay your subscription and get on the mailing list. Keep in touch. It's worth it.'

We said goodbye and watched him leave. He knew the new headmaster from previous visits and, apart from a warm handshake and more jubilant laughter, no time was lost in farewells. He climbed into his car, strapped over the seatbelt and drove away.

Later, Francis commented, a trifle bitterly I thought, on Hannay's apparent success in spite of no longer being the outstanding Head Boy. 'Why do people have such nice cars?' he said.

'But you always say you don't need one.'

'It's true. I don't. Absurd to have a car when you live and work in the centre of London.' He paused. 'It's just when you see one, like that, a nice powerful Rover, it reminds you of how much it once mattered.'

'He's done well, hasn't he?'

'Hannay? By all appearances.'

'Don't you think it's deeper than that?'

'In what way, deeper?'

'He seems well adjusted. It's not just appearances. It's down inside him.'

'Hm.'

It was later, walking in the sunshine, with Francis not altogether willing to spend even more time in a place that did not greatly affect him, but deferring to my curiosity, that I reverted to what Hannay had said.

'I never thought of coming back, or not coming back, in terms of how you felt in a place. That's what Hannay seemed to be saying. And it explains why there are so few from Merchant's time. He made people afraid. Why should anyone come back to re-live that?'

'He didn't make you afraid?'

'Not really.'

'And Hannay?'

'Hannay always seemed his equal.'

'Are you saying it's the only reason?'

'I don't know,' I said. 'You tell me. Tell me if you agree.'

'It's curiosity. That's the main reason.'

'You're wrong,' I said.

'No,' he said. 'I'm right. Overwhelmingly it is the reason. It's why I came with you today. Feelings are not involved. Not feelings, now. Nor then. Just curiosity.'

We had stopped in the roadway. In a sub-conscious response to what was almost a ritual, we had walked down into the familiar valley where the small tributary of the River Evenlode wound its way through meadows in which I had wandered so often in years gone by, to which I had come with Philpotts, at night with Lytton and Pritchett and Janet, and on one occasion with Francis, when he had returned to visit me. I stood facing him smiling and, knowingly provoking him to underline more firmly what I was convinced was an erroneous position, I said, 'You're totally wrong. You've misunderstood completely why Hannay comes back and others don't. Nostalgia doesn't work on curiosity.'

'Who says we're talking about nostalgia?'

'Of course we're talking about nostalgia. The great epidemic, touching everyone. It's associated with fear, and happiness, with our sense of failure or success, with what we have made of our lives.' I realised I was shouting at him, but I couldn't stop myself. All the curious disappointments of that week, Babette's failure to understand or to remember, Ursula's evasiveness, even Francis's own indifference, were suddenly falling into place in my mind. And behind them all was emerging a formula which was making sense of my father's attitude. I had to make Francis understand. He was the only one. 'Don't you see?' I shouted. 'Don't you see? It's as if everyone had a pointer on a scale which located some moment, some period in their lives when everything was right. And it's against that moment that the rest is judged. If you're lucky, if you're what is called "well-adjusted", then the point may lie roughly in the present or the near future, or just somewhere ahead of you. But I think that's rare. I think for most people the point is in the past: childhood, school, youth, university, challenge and opportunity in

157

early manhood, becoming what you become.' I stopped once again, a deliberate pause, and stared at him. I felt enormously exhilarated.

Along the narrow road came a tractor pulling a trailer piled high with hay. It moved slowly. The farm labourer driving it wore a grimy trilby and was smoking a cigarette. High up in the piled hay sat a young boy and two women in summer dresses. I felt suddenly foolish, shouting there in the road, though they could not possibly hear, behind the heavy thud of the diesel engine; all they could do was witness my gestures as I mutely harangued my brother.

We stepped back on either side to let them pass, waved up at them, and then once more faced each other. I could see in his eyes that it was no use. He would never agree, never accept. I had pre-empted that by the directness of my approach. Yet it did not matter since it was becoming clear to me even as I spoke. The diesel smell mingled with the afternoon scent from hedgerow and field. I waited for him to speak. But he just stared at me.

Then I said, 'Look at father. He is enslaved by the past. Do you think it's curiosity with him? It's not curiosity. It's fear. And it's a sense of failure. He's running away. Poor man. And he doesn't know where to go, except backwards in time. Even there, he's lost. He doesn't know where to stop.' I laughed at the thought of it, and then realised how cruelly painful it must be. I wanted Francis to respond, just to accept something of what I was saying. Please say something, I thought. Please agree. But he just stood, across the deserted road from me, staring back at me. 'So what does he do?' I asked, in the safety of a rhetorical flood of speculation. 'He falls back on nostalgic generalities: smoke from bonfires, the smell of tobacco plant at evening, Crimson Glory, the scent of privet just at this time in the year, old songs, old verses, old fragments of humour.'

'We're all susceptible to that,' Francis said.

I waited, but he said no more.

'But it's a matter of degree, of proportion. When he was a child, in Folkestone, at the beginning of the century, he would play in the garden, in summer, and he would stand under the privet hedge, and smell that smell of the yellowy

158

white flower, and think of deeds he could do in the world, of heroism, and pluck, of bandits and pirates and robbers. He's told me. So many times. Now, the thoughts have gone. All the detail has become trivial. And we say that only the smell remains. But in reality a faint, thin tidemark remains of the thought as well. It's indefinable, it cannot be captured. But it's there. And that's what we hunt for.'

'Is that why you come back here?'

'Yes,' I said. 'It is. Only it's different. It's experimental.'

Francis stared at me, his face set in sharp lines of disapproval. 'You're very cold-blooded,' he said. 'What do you do it for?'

'I'm afraid I don't know,' I said. 'I want to understand. I want to know where I'm going.'

'But why Father?'

'The same reason. He's always said we should learn by his mistakes. I'm trying to understand his failures, his fears, where it is he's running to, in his mind.'

'Running? He's come to rest, even in his mind.'

'Oh, no, Francis. He's afraid. He's running away, all the time.'

[VII]

I don't know why I did it. It was a peculiarly stubborn course to take, in the light of my experiences throughout that week in London. Having laid, as I thought, ghost after ghost from the past in a cold and calculating fashion, serving a purpose the full meaning of which was far from clear, I set out, just as deliberately on that Sunday morning, to attend church at All Souls, just as I had done so regularly as a boy home from school. I knew I would not meet Mr Porphyry. He had moved from London. Yet I was unprepared for the degree of change which I encountered in everything. The box pews had vanished, changing fundamentally the elegant interior; modern chairs accommodated the packed rows. The form of service was altered; the books were different; the pace of worship speeded up. It still *worked*.

I had no fault to find in that respect. But I had not come for spiritual comfort; I had come to assure myself that the past was firmly located here, as elsewhere, and that I could recover it for whatever purpose I might choose.

And the assurance was not there. The occasion throbbed relentlessly with present enthusiasms, firmly at odds with the enemies of the spiritual which can lurk within ritual and flow from psalms and hymns. There was none of that danger. So that I emerged, being almost carried out in the warmth of the Sunday morning, in the throng of excitement and voices, having tasted a present spirituality rather than re-absorbing a sense of divinity out of the distant past.

First on the steps, and afterwards crowded off them on to the pavement, I began to feel twinges of envy at not being part of this congregation.

'You're not one of our regular visitors?' a voice said. I turned. A woman in her fifties was beside me.

'I hope all are welcome?'

She laughed. 'There are always new faces, and of course everyone is welcome. We like to talk to strangers and I thought you looked a little lost.'

'Kind of you,' I said. 'No, I'm not lost. Bewildered, perhaps. I used to come here years ago. I wanted to renew acquaintance. But it's all so different.'

'When did you come before?' she asked. She was dressed in a grey summer suit with a pink blouse and straw hat. Unlike the majority of the congregation, she could have belonged as easily to the years when I had been regularly part of it as to the present.

I told her. 'I used to come with a Mr Porphyry.'

'I remember the name. A fine person. He's moved away.'

'He's living in the country now,' I said.

'Will you come and have some coffee? A few people always come back afterwards because we live near. In Wigmore Street.'

I hesitated. 'We?' I said, looking round.

'Do come.' She did not respond directly to my question.

I found myself agreeing to the invitation almost without thinking. A natural reluctance to become involved was

160

countered by a wish to learn about that to which I had once belonged; and belonged, it must be added, with a fervour which made my presence now more than just a fulfilment of curiosity.

'Where do you live?' she asked.

'At the moment, Paris,' I said. 'But I'm moving back to London.'

'And what do you do?' She smiled at the slight hint of surprise in my expression and went on: 'I mustn't ask so many questions. I'll find the others.'

She turned away. I watched the slow dispersal of the congregation and half-regretted that I could not move away as well. Of course, I could have done so; and there was, in this woman in her fifties whose name I had yet to learn, a certain militant Christian authority which was not entirely attractive. Yet something about the fortuitous nature of our encounter, coming as it did at the end of several days in which contrivance and deliberate reconstruction had dominated what was, after all, my summer holiday that year, kept me waiting for her; something, too, in her eyes, her manner, the persistence of her earlier questions, made me curious.

When she returned to me she was still more or less on her own. I could see others who by their gestures and attitudes were following, but she simply said to me that we would go on, and led the way towards the corner of Cavendish Place. She told me her name, Deborah Wilson, but otherwise concentrated on questions about me. It was a short distance to her flat. I was surprised, when we got there, at how large and comfortable it was, very much a family home; also, at the number of people, perhaps as many as twenty, several of them much younger than myself.

Reluctant again, I found myself drawn into conversation with a young man called Felix, who was tall and thin, with a long neck; he had lank flax-coloured hair and a deep voice. He was in his late twenties. Responding enthusiastically to the fact that I lived in Paris, he soon revealed that he had some knowledge of the city only to surprise me by asking where I went on Sundays.

I had anticipated an interest in art or cafés; not in churches. 'I usually have a rather lazy day on Sundays,' I said. 'I work quite hard the rest of the time.'

He asked me what I did, and I gave a description to him of my work.

'I say! Fascinating!' His eyes glowed. 'Do tell me more. I'm frightfully interested in art.'

I told him more.

'Do you know? I must tell Clare. Clare?' His deep voice arrested the attention of several people in the room, and a young woman who must have been about his age, attractive in a calm, unselfconscious way, though with the single striking feature of shoulder-length, ash-blonde hair, turned with what I thought was a faint hint of reluctance and came over.

'Clare,' he said. 'You just have to meet this chap! Absolutely fascinating! Lives in Paris and writes about art! What do you think about that?'

'It sounds exciting,' she said.

Felix said, 'I'll say!'

'It's not quite what it sounds,' I said. 'One city can be much like another when you're out pounding around after stories. And Paris is very expensive.'

I told her about my work. They spoke about what they did in London. Felix worked in insurance, Clare in the Great Ormond Street Hospital for Children, as a medical social worker.

'How do you decide on your stories?' she asked. 'Are you just sent out by your office?'

'It's a bit more complicated than that. One needs to know what's going on. You see, it's specialised in a way.' As I said it I seemed to hear my father's voice, and to see the words on that single sheet of paper: 'Don't boast of what you've done.' They seemed irrelevant; not to matter even. I was talking of facts, telling the simple truth.

'You're something of a sleuth, then?' she said. 'Digging out the dirt? Fakes, and all that? Art scandals?'

'Oh, Clare!' Felix said. 'I'm sure it's not as dramatic as that, is it?'

'I think Clare is teasing me, Felix,' I said. I noticed his adam's apple moving as he drank his coffee.

'Are you, Clare?' he said.

'Of course, Felix. I'm sure it's very boring work at times. Like mine. Or yours.'

'I'm not bored,' he said. He spoke manfully, as though endeavouring to take her in hand. At the same time the look he gave her was soulful and yearning.

Staring back at me she said, 'I am. Quite a lot of the time.' Then she smiled and shrugged her shoulders. 'But we can't all enjoy the romance of Paris. We can't all be investigating scandals, can we?'

'Would you prefer that?' I asked.

'Oh, God, yes I would.' She put her hand suddenly to her mouth, as though invoking the Almighty would meet with disapproval if noticed by present company. Then she glanced at Felix.

'Would you really, Clare?' he asked, his adam's apple moving vigorously up and down. 'I say, would you? Change what you're doing?'

'Of course I wouldn't, Felix. Don't be a complete ass. It's just the appeal of something different. I suppose you get fed up with it at times?'

'At times,' I said. 'But basically it's what I want to do.'

'You should be thankful for that.'

On an impulse, I said to her, 'Can I walk you home? Better still, can I give you lunch somewhere? Where do you live? Near?'

Felix frowned.

Clare laughed. 'Very near,' she said. 'I live here.'

'You mean—? Deborah, Mrs Wilson?'

'Yes. She's my mother.'

'I didn't know. How foolish of me.'

'How could you know?' She put her hand briefly on my arm. 'But thank you for asking me. There's so much more I want to know about your work.'

'I'll try and keep to the parts that aren't boring.'

'You mean, you'll tell me?'

'Of course, if you want—. Do you ever come to Paris?'

'I might. It's possible.'

163

'With Felix?'

She didn't answer.

'I'd love that, Clare,' he said. 'You know how much.' His look was appealing, and slightly pinched.

'If you come, contact me. But I'm only there until September. After that I'll be investigating nearer home.'

She nodded, thoughtfully. 'And what is the name of this agency?' she said.

I told her. 'I must go now. May I call again? When next I'm here?'

'We may meet before then,' she said. 'I'll show you out.'

Leaving the room I noticed Felix following us with his eyes, his long neck and somewhat untidy fair hair giving to his appearance an awkward, angular clumsiness, faintly forlorn. I wanted to ask about him, but could not phrase the appropriate question. And then, moving through the hall of the flat, in the sunlight, and watching the slight bounce of her ash-blonde hair at each calm, assured step, I dismissed Felix from my mind, and concentrated on her. Her equanimity disturbed me. Her faint interest in what I did was disturbing, too; and I was annoyed that I had to leave London so soon.

'Will you really come to Paris?' I asked.

'I might.'

'Do look me up. I'd like it if we met again.'

Chapter Eight

[I]

She did not come to Paris. The faint hope I had expressed at our parting remained unfulfilled. I was busy, first with the end of season sales, then with packing up and moving, and then, in the early autumn, settling down in London.

In the thinner, timeless light of mid-September, when the change of season from summer to autumn seemed to hang upon an ever-lengthening thread of palely radiant gossamer, I settled to the new responsibilities of my work, and the pleasures—combined with anxieties—of organising a flat in a city that had always been 'home' to me, though in such an odd and precarious way.

I found it changed, after my years abroad; and I realised how few friends I had there.

Briefly, just for two days, my father came up, ostensibly to help. The multitude of jobs he had had in his life meant that he could turn his hands virtually to anything, whereas my own practical skills were severely limited. But it was a complete disaster. Over-excited by the prospect, greatly relieved to be away from his women, he drank all the way from Somerset to London, and could hardly make it from the taxi to the front door. His vast reservoir of skills drained out as the drink soaked in, and he never got beyond making and re-making ever-lengthening lists of what needed to be done.

He slept off the drink; but was left in an almost invalid state the next morning, which he remedied in time-honoured fashion as lunch approached, and gathered sufficient strength to give me the only help I was to get from him, a long and ponderous dissertation about how I had 'come through life the right way up, sonny boy,' and that everything would be 'perfection.'

That second night was better. Going out together meant that his drinking was more restrained. But it also meant that the tide of melancholy flowed over him, bringing guilt about Alice, an almost fearful worry that Gladys should stay 'by my side to the end,' and the sudden determination to go back.

He left the next morning before I got up, a scribbled note of farewell being dropped on the carpet by the flat door. In it he apologised, and said he'd gone 'to face the music'. That was how he celebrated my 'homecoming.' He was no longer in a position, as he had once been, to humiliate me; he was just a potential embarrassment, and his action strengthened my resolve not to go down and see him for a while.

Francis was busy, and in bad humour. The political organisation he worked for was licking its wounds after electoral defeat. And he was always sensitive about revealing his own disappointment, a form of stoicism no doubt inherited from father. The same was not true of Melanie; she had descended on my brother, more or less as my father had on me, at the end of an unhappy love affair, and I heard at second hand his account of what had gone wrong, and why.

It overshadowed the early weeks back in London, and perhaps both consciously and sub-consciously created in me the genuine desire for that 'permanence' for which my father had so doggedly, and with so little success, hunted throughout the years of my growing up. If London was 'home,' then it needed to be a warmer, richer, more rewarding interpretation of the word. I wanted to be more fundamentally settled; I needed a wife.

It took time to acknowledge the need—so frequently alluded to by my father—to give it purpose, impose judgement and restraint. I had been vaguely annoyed at not seeing Clare in Paris. I had remembered, once or twice, our brief encounter, memory playing tricks, as it always does, jumbling together the lilting swing of her ash-blonde hair with the level, solemn gaze with which I had caught her watching me, just once or twice, on that first and only meeting. No more than the faintest hint of an attraction, the vaguest sensation of sympathy, could be descried from that meeting. Yet it was enough. On a warm, clear Sunday morning, late in the month, hesitantly, a trifle nervously, I went back to All Souls, with the intention of seeing her again.

I was nervous about her and her mother, worried that I should seem a stranger to them once again. I need not have been. It was a boyish concern of which I was half-ashamed afterwards, diffidently waiting in the fringes of the animated groups of people, peering hopefully in various directions, and faintly dismayed that I was the only one who seemed to know no one, since, contrary to my expectation, I recognised not a single face.

Then I saw Clare. She was already moving away, across Langham Place, on her own. Absurd to describe it as familiar, and yet the determined, almost defiant swing of her light-coloured hair was so instantly recognisable that it dispelled with certainty any lingering doubt I might have had about wanting to see her again.

I was glad she was alone. I crossed to the other side, catching up with her on the corner of Cavendish Place.

'Clare?'

She stopped and turned. 'Oh, it's you. Back, then?'

'You didn't come to Paris?'

She hesitated. 'We passed through. We weren't there long enough for me to—'

'It doesn't matter. I'd probably have been busy, anyway.'

We stood facing each other, not knowing what to say.

'Did you have—' I began.

'Are you settled into—' she said, at the same time.

We both laughed.

'You first,' she said.

'No, you.'

'Is your flat near?'

167

'It's not, actually. It's in Notting Hill.'

'What brings you here? No church nearer? Or old time's sake?

'There is nothing to equal this place,' I said, gesturing over my shoulder at the balustraded spire and the elegantly pillared entrance. 'It's more than old time's sake.'

'I suppose so,' she said. 'Having lived here always I don't think of the alternatives.'

'You're lucky. They're very different. But how are you? It's nice to see you again. How's your mother?'

'It's nice to see you.' She smiled, but at the same time there was a hint of puzzled restraint in her eyes. It checked me. I wondered if her apparent warmth and friendliness, the first time we had met, had been no more than politeness. Perhaps I had been mistaken in thinking that there was more to it than that. After all, I thought to myself, we only met once, part of a group of people drinking coffee after church.

'How's Felix?' I said, not really wanting to know the answer, but his somewhat unwelcome image persisted in intruding into the background of my thoughts. 'Where is he?'

She looked about her, as though he might materialise, and my heart sank, grasping from this that he was still potentially around.

'I—I don't know. I expected him to be here.'

'And your mother?'

'She's not well. I'm on my way back to her.'

'Is that why no one else is coming?'

She nodded. 'It's been a couple of weeks. Everyone's so helpful.'

'Can I do anything?'

She shook her head, and made as if to turn away and walk on.

'I suppose you have to go back? No time for walking?'

Her level gaze disturbed me; so did the deliberate tone of her reply. 'I do have time to walk. I would have gone with Felix to Regent's Park if he'd been here. That was what we had planned. But he must have overslept so I'll walk with you instead.'

We turned and retraced our steps up Portland Place. Relieved though I was that Felix had overslept, I was nevertheless a bit perturbed. And I asked her, 'How long have you known Felix?'

'Oh, for ever, it seems. We grew up together. His family lived near ours, in Scotland. I should, of course, put it differently. We lived near them. His father's the laird. We had no pretensions. Modesty's the badge of the Wilson tribe.'

'And is it big? Have you still a home in Scotland?'

'Yes. My uncle farms the land.' She talked about her home there, and holidays; moving to London; her father's work, then his death in the early sixties.

I answered, as directly as I could, the same kind of questions about myself. I laughingly called my father 'an old reprobate' and she said, 'What do you mean?'

'It's a long story, Clare. He's had several wives. What you might call a full life. And perhaps not altogether a good one. And he has a bit of a drink problem.' I shrugged my shoulders, half dismissing him, and hoping she might respond and give an indication of her reaction. But instead she remained silent, a disturbing characteristic of hers, in the face of any serious issue or piece of important information, that in time I was to come to know well. 'His health's not good,' I went on. 'He's settled in Somerset. Doesn't come up to London much.' I had a sudden image of my father and Clare's mother together, and was seized with momentary panic at the thought. Then it was dispelled. 'He's a lovable old man. But as I say, an old reprobate. Not a good father, in the accepted sense.'

'And your brother?'

'Francis? He works here in London. His flat's not far away. He works for the Conservative Party.'

'Do you support them too? Does your father?' She seemed seriously interested.

'I haven't really thought about politics,' I said. 'As for my father, he goes through every possible permutation. He admired Hitler, he had a grudge against Churchill for something he did when he was First Lord of the Admiralty—that was in the first world war, mind you. And

169

he thinks Clement Attlee was the greatest prime minister of the century. He might have a point there.'

'He sounds like a character. What's he up to in Somerset?'

I told her he mostly gardened.

'And he was in the navy?'

'It sounds ordinary enough,' I said, 'this retired naval officer, settled in Somerset with his fourth wife, tending roses, picking apples in the orchard, I suppose, just now. But it's quite a story.'

'And you have a sister, you say?'

I frowned. 'Yes. Melanie.'

'Why do you look like that?'

'I don't know, really. You see, we didn't grow up together. I don't see her much. When I do, it doesn't always go very well.'

Again, the silence, yet behind it the sense of sympathetic expectation.

Then I began to give her an outline of our fractured family childhood. 'You see,' I said, and paused, 'Melanie was adopted. That was after my mother died, and we were all small. I didn't see her again until she was grown up. When we met then it seemed as if it might be all right. But in reality we've never been able to recover that lost time. I suppose it sounds melodramatic. I don't mean it to. She goes from job to job, has different boyfriends. Sometimes we don't make contact for months.' After a brief pause, and looking ahead, I said, with a certain finality, 'We're not a *normal* family, I'm afraid.'

'Perhaps there isn't such a thing,' was all she said.

We walked in silence for a while. Then she said she needed to get back. We circled Queen Mary's garden, and I said, 'Can we meet again, Clare?'

She didn't answer straight away, nor look at me. Then, just walking along together, and without turning, so that it seemed she was answering an unspoken question posed within her own mind, she said, 'I can't see any reason why we shouldn't.'

'When are you free?'

'Not as often as I'd like to be. Hospitals never have enough staff. I really do work rather hard.'

'This coming week?'

'I can't manage that.' She paused. Then she said, 'I'd like to look at pictures with you. I know some people say one should do it alone. But I feel I don't understand what they're all about most of the time. I'm sure you could help.'

I felt an enormous sense of relief. 'I'd love to do that,' I said. 'I hope I'd be some good. When are you free?'

'I'm off on Wednesday the following week.'

I frowned. 'I'm afraid I'll be away then. You can't manage earlier?'

We eventually fixed a day.

'Will I pick you up?' I asked.

She shook her head. 'I'd rather meet in a gallery. It would give me the chance to be there early and prepare for my lesson.' She shook her head in an abrupt gesture of faint embarrassment, smiling up at me. 'Where will it be?'

Remembering Ursula's remarks, I said, 'Let's go to Apsley House. It's new for me as well. And it's recommended by someone whose judgment I admire. I'll tell you when we meet.'

[II]

I went to Apsley House with a clear sense of purpose. I had enjoyed every moment spent with her, so far. Being with her made me feel secure and confident. And I trusted her. I was faintly troubled by the prospect of having to tell her, at some time in the future, about Sarah and the child. And an uneasiness attended the prospect of actual encounters; I could not easily visualise her with Melanie or Francis, and even less so, later on, with my father. At the same time these were matters over which I had control, and the simple reality, which lightened my step as I approached Number One, London, was that Clare and I were living in the present.

She had said she would be early, in order to prepare for her 'lesson'. In fact it was I who was early, in order to prepare for her, to familiarise myself with a collection I had unaccountably missed out in the past, to allow myself to be absorbed, and calmed and animated by the unique forces which pulsate within the walls of art galleries. At least, they have always done so for me, from childhood on. As a lonely boy, then adolescent, the permanence of art, in London, was one of the few reassurances of growing up. And coming back, at holiday time, to English landscapes at the Tate, to the faces of English Kings and Queens in the National Portrait Gallery, to the heroism of battle in the Imperial War Museum, or to Old Masters in Trafalgar Square, was as comforting as a homecoming.

It puzzled me, now that I had to transmit something of all this to Clare. I had learnt enough of art jargon to despise it. Yet sitting and watching, almost with feelings of compassion, the motley crowds of people who look at pictures, it was impossible to escape a sense of there being some kind of wordless 'language' by which paintings convey their message, a way of 'reading' them that grants access as readily to the simple and the inarticulate as it does to those who have had what is called visual education. That paintings 'speak' to us is as obvious as the fact that poetry and music are two forms of communication which can be 'read' in two quite different ways by minds which could be indifferent to one, while besotted by the other.

Within the language, after the commitment, differences continue to abound. And I thought about them as I went up the steps of Apsley House, wondering how best to convey the impact without seeming pretentious. My step was light. I felt no hesitation, only the vital determination to see. Because it was Clare, she would see as well.

And so it was, in that elated mood of expectation and enthusiasm, during my first, cursory circuit of the rooms, that I came to be in front of that particular canvas, and to have, as it were, an object-lesson which could not have been better timed, in the particular 'language' of which I speak. It was a canvas which brought together and represented for me a world of conflicting forces and ideas. It gathered up both the profound and the personal. In one respect it could not have been more private, more directly related to me, as if the artist had reached forward a mere four hundred years with my circumstance in mind; in another respect it was a statuesque expression of the sombre passage of time, the silent beating of a message about the passing of generations of mankind. In paint and design, in light and colour, it delivered forth further 'statements;' and yet it was hard as well, holding back, retaining unto itself the impregnability of art; surviving each passing pair of eyes as an ode of Keats survives the temporary enmeshing of our individual and transitory emotions in the rocklike substance of its words. It was the first time I had seen it, and what struck me, with a further and fuller sense of the coiling and tangling relevance of art, its endless possibilities, its renewed and changing messages, was first of all the simple and obvious accident of a likeness. Standing in front of 'The Water Seller of Seville', I saw in the features of the old man those of my father as he had now become.

The likeness was not superficial, but exact: the close-cut hair, the high, wrinkled forehead, the long straight nose, the fallen cheek under the prominent cheekbone, the ear on which one focuses attention, the down-turned, patient mouth expressing that resignation which is a prelude to an ending of sorts; even the goatee, fashionable in the Spain of the period, but for grandees rather than water sellers, was identical with the one my father now wore. Perhaps this simple difference had prevented Ursula drawing the same conclusion; perhaps she had simply missed that visual connection. It did not matter. I was transfixed by the noble, resigned profile, and it was from that point that I moved on to discover in the painting the fundamental image that I had sought, consciously, before, forgotten about, let slip into the subconscious, only to have it presented to me now, a glorious revelation.

For I saw myself in the painting as well, twice over. I saw myself as the shadowy third figure in the background, looking on; and I saw myself as the youth who is sharing in what seems to be a profound ritual of purification, of giving and receiving, of supplication, and of thanksgiving. That solemn figure, a poor man by profession, yet in his mind an emperor come to grief, knowing his purpose, not pleased by it, not sorrowing over it, just fulfilling it. In what I saw

173

there was a message that transcended words, defied them by equalling them, even surpassing them. I had come nowhere near to that; and suddenly I felt anguish at what I was doing. Was it really enough? Was it a life? And would Clare mend it?

What of him? What of my personal prototype for this permanent image? What of my answer to Velasquez's question? For his art challenged my life. All the rubbish I seemed to write, glib, fatuous drivel about collections and periods and styles: what had it got to do with reality?

I came back again and again to the painting, tormented by its perfection, by the delicate balance in it between exact realism and the towering weight of symbol: the texture of the pottery, the shape, the feel of it; the splashed drops of water on the surface; the great goblet filled to the brim: the purifying fig—itself an endless symbol of fructification and ambivalence. It was the symbol, not for him, but for me. It ordained truth. It directed me upon the course of action I would have to take, in telling Clare all things concerning myself. I was not impatient that she had not arrived. I had myself come there ridiculously early; but time had vanished for me. I was released from distraction to invade with my eyes, again and again, the surface of the canvas. It was a form of siege. I wanted to find some further meaning, and I felt that perhaps it might come from a weakness, a chink in the painter's defences, his armour of colour and texture and design. Already, the evocation of my father had served to make something great into something special. But I was not satisfied with that. I wanted to fault it as well, and thereby come closer to the human being who had conceived this remarkable study of his own kind. For a while I felt the weakness lay in the third and shadowy figure, that middle-generation observer. But it was not so: his haunted and haunting uncertainty are as much part of the reality as the boy and the old man. They constitute two certainties between which is uncertainty: on the one side the clear, deliberate glow of innocence; on the other, the stern wisdom of old age. But it was in the fainter, shadowy figure in between that I saw myself, just as in the youth I perceived what I had once been, and in the old man, as well as defining so closely the physical characteristics of my father, saw also what I would one day become.

Clare found me standing in front of the painting. 'You look as though you have seen a ghost,' she said. 'Are you all right?'

I felt a sudden release of tension, turning towards her, and in as much as it is possible to pinpoint such occasions, I think it was then that affection resolved itself into love. It was certainly then that I knew, given time, I would be able to tell her everything.

'Yes, I'm all right. Whatever I told you before, about painting having an inner language, is true. Only more so. I can't get over this painting, Clare. And yet I don't know how to begin to explain what it is I feel about it. It's a silly way to begin, but do you see this figure, here? Well, it's the absolute, exact image of my father. You'll see. He even has the beard, just like that, on the end of his chin. And the lines, here—'

'Is this the first time you've seen the painting?' she asked.

'I've only seen it in photographs before.'

'But did you see the likeness before?'

'Never. Only now. Seeing it here. It's so different. The shape of the head, and the short hair. Even the ears, Clare.'

'Tell me about him,' she said.

And I did.

We seemed to stay there for hours. Exploring the paintings was a way of exploring ourselves. The oblique approach was part of it. The softness of Murillo, the boldness of Rubens, the sanctity of Ribera, the angry vitality of Turner, all evoked and evaded, at the same time, so that questions about art, like questions about ourselves, about each other, slanted in and out of one another like the very rays of light which gave form its meaning in the vessel of the eye.

[III]

Autumn turned into winter. The days shortened. The Christmas decorations went up in Oxford Street and Regent

175

Street. I declined an invitation from Gladys to go down to them for Christmas. It came with a letter from my father in which he said, 'Of course, you'll come,' and I felt almost afraid of him, as though I might provoke some awful, apoplectic rage by saying so. But instead, he wrote rather sadly, saying something to the effect that I was too high up for him now.

Of course it was not the reason, but it was close enough to hurt. The reality was, that in spite of much talk between Clare and myself about him as a character in my past, some kind of giant shadow over me that I still, metaphorically speaking, dodged about in, sometimes coming out into the sunlight of my own free self, then falling back into an idyllic recollection, through words, of past adventures always darkened by his eccentricities, I avoided bringing them together.

Circumstance was on my side. As he had found, on his visit in September, my father's health was no longer good enough for travel, even to London. I had the perfectly legitimate excuse of a new job and the busy autumn season of sales. And there was the additional distancing of mutual reproach: his, for my not going down; mine for his behaviour in September.

It allowed me to present to Clare a picture of him of my own shaping, and this inevitably led to a certain measure of mythologising. At first innocent and light-hearted, with time it took on a colouring which gave a drama to his personality no man could really be expected to live up to in the flesh. It was a deception of sorts, not serious, but faintly inhibiting. While it had been relatively easy to respond to her curiosity about my childhood with him, it had been less easy to tell her about later adventures. Notably, though Isobel and my father together had featured in our conversations, December came without my having mentioned either Sarah, or the child we had. It was a foolish evasion, made easier by the fact that she had married and, with the boy, now lived abroad, though this also should have made confession easy as well. But it led, by slow degrees, to the building up within me of certain tensions and reservations.

Why did I feel the way I did? Why, in the mid-seventies, when all around me among colleagues and friends there was an openness about such things that had changed fundamentally the old framework of guilt and secrecy which had been my own childhood experience, could I not also broach with Clare the facts which I knew would have to come out? There is no easy answer. The experience of many years had conditioned me to an over-cautious management of myself in my relationships with others. And now it was intensified by the feeling that some kind of natural and harmonious idyll was emerging out of my friendship with Clare that should not be threatened by too much confession.

Then came the announcement: Clare and her mother were going to Scotland for Christmas. I was not invited. I had somehow assumed they would remain in London, and had left myself free, treating Christmas at that time in a fairly cavalier fashion anyway. But it brought me up short; what exactly had I been at? Was it make-believe? A casual relationship, yet again? Something of which there had already been too much? With a sudden, decisive relevance for myself there came to me from the very past with which I had entertained Clare, the previously unremembered, passionate cry from my father, expressed in so many different and inevitably unfulfilled ways, yet best of all in the lines from a letter I had received before his love affair with Isobel, 'I must get cracking again, get dug in somewhere as soon as possible, always hoping it will be permanent.'

'Why don't you marry her?' Francis asked.

'Perhaps I will,' I said.

'She sounds all right. It's about time.' He sat in a deep armchair in the sitting room of his flat, a glass of scotch in his hand, his eyes fixed severely on me as I paced about in his room, staring at the curious collections of ornaments gathered in different parts of the world at a time when he travelled widely.

'And you?' I asked.

'We'll not discuss me,' he said. 'Not in that context. Not this Christmas.'

'It's an unfortunate time of year for bachelors. Shall we share the cooking?'

'I have all that under control,' he said. 'You can provide the drink.'

There were certain friends we had in common; relations as well, an aunt and two cousins. And there was Melanie. She arrived, emotionally dishevelled and unannounced, on Christmas Eve. Though far from satisfactory, her noisy advent brought a certain rough tension to the evening of Christmas Day, making it bearable enough. But the holiday as a whole was a gaunt affair. Melanie left as abruptly as she had come, three days later, and she managed, without saying anything specific, to deposit a residual sense of grievance about Francis and myself which left us in vaguely bad humour with each other. For parties we went our separate ways; and when we did meet and go out together I found it difficult to get rid of this curious distancing between us. We seemed to have less and less of present time in common.

I longed for Clare's return. The sense of emptiness had been made more acute by the abrupt way in which her departure for Scotland had been announced. Instead of accepting the pressures of her really quite strenuous job at the children's hospital, and the fact that her mother still made important decisions affecting both of them, I was tempted to reproach her in my heart for engineering a separation in order to emphasise, perhaps bring to a head, issues of need. Well, if intended, it certainly worked. I needed Clare. I wanted her and was impatient at the slow passage of the empty days immediately after Christmas and up to New Year's Day, after which she and her mother were due to return.

I resolved to tell her about Sarah and the child, and to bring her and my father together and see if the picture I had drawn of him in her mind was matched or destroyed by the reality.

[IV]

Clare had come with me to a morning sale at Christie's. It was a free day for her, and not a particularly onerous one for me. She made it exciting by the innocent enthusiasm with which she expressed her curiosity about the art world and its busy market place, so entirely different from the work she did. And I took a keen pleasure in explaining details, and pointing out the more important buyers, speculating on what they would go for, and how much they would spend.

It was an uncertain time for such speculation. Estimates were being wildly exceeded, new artists and trends being recognised and hotly pursued, and a general atmosphere of drama prevailed throughout many of the sales. It was a stimulating time to be writing about it, made even more so by her curiosity.

It was the March sale of modern British paintings and drawings. And there were good examples of work by Lavery, in whom I took an interest at that time. Though less dramatic than the Impressionist and Old Master sales, those of British art were of much greater personal interest. Moreover, the agency for which I worked had found a ready market for features on notable sales and prices, particularly where painters enjoyed any kind of local reputation, like Lowry for example. The manifestation of his standing, in a London saleroom, was noted in a more prolix way in northern newspapers. I had specialised a bit in producing features on such individual artists, and was now responsible for covering sales with this particular task in mind. At times it was possible to write four or five different feature articles based on a single sale, but directed geographically towards different points of the compass, depending on both artist and, to a lesser extent, subject matter as well. This was a good sale from that point of view, Lavery provided not only an Irish flavour, but a Scottish one as well which appealed to Clare.

It was a cold day in March. We came out of the King Street doorway and turned up towards Piccadilly. I had booked a table for lunch in a small Italian restaurant off Jermyn Street where we ordered saltimbocca, and a bottle of Barolo, and were progressing through a bowl of black olives while we waited.

'I've to write later this afternoon. Mustn't drink too much.'

'Will it be difficult?' Clare asked.

'Not really. The Munnings got a good price. What I can't understand is the interest in Russell Flint. His women are *awful*. They're like Vargas drawings.'

'They do have very silly faces, too. Almost oriental.'

'Are you free this evening?'

'It would mean leaving my mother alone.'

'How is she? Better?'

'Getting better.'

'She's ill quite often, Clare. Does it make it difficult for you, looking after her as well as working?'

'I manage all right. It was just a touch of bronchitis. It's almost gone now.'

We looked at each other for a moment or two. The restaurant was crowded and hot after the brisk March wind in Bury Street, the waiters busy. It was not uncomfortable, however; in spite of the numbers, and the closeness of the tables, I felt we were quite isolated and private.

'Would she like to come out with us? Is she well enough for that?'

She put her hand across the table and laid it on top of mine. 'It's kind of you to ask. Perhaps we could go back together tonight and see her. After we've been to a film?'

I let her hand rest on mine, not answering.

'I'd love you to tell her what you do. I've tried to explain it to her, but she seems sceptical, as though uncertain about my ability to explain. She's very interested in you.'

'Is she?'

Clare blushed slightly. 'She met that man you knew, Mr Porphyry. He was up at a meeting in All Souls. And of course mother asked all about you.'

I reversed the positions of our hands, holding hers now, and looking across, at first directly at her, and then down. 'And Mr Porphyry—?'

She held on to my hand. 'I never realised, from what you said. Coppinger was a kind of orphanage, wasn't it? And he was your guardian, really. It must have been very strange, your childhood in London. And what a man your father must have been!'

'It takes a lot of explaining, Clare—'

'I want to meet him. If he can't come up here, can we go down?'

'I suppose so.'

'I do want to. And Francis and Melanie as well.' She withdrew her hand to allow the waiter to serve us. 'I'm demanding too much?'

I shook my head. After the waiter had left, I said, 'There's something else I want to tell you, Clare. There was this girl, Sarah . . .' And I told her about Sarah, and then back beyond that to Mr Porphyry, and beyond that again to my early days at Coppinger; until the restaurant emptied, and the waiters stood around in bored detachment, wondering whether we had any place to go, and why we had no work to do.

Chapter Nine

[I]

He stood in the doorway, the early morning sun behind him, so that his face was in shadow. 'Remember me?' he said.

'Father!'

'As ever was.'

'Broken out?'

'I'm free,' he said. His voice trembled. 'Free from them both. I've escaped, old son. Couldn't stand it. Had to get away. Just had to get away.' He attenuated the last word, stretching it in a flat, nasal tone that was profoundly sad.

I felt caught in a sudden tide of panic. Of all the days, to pick this one and I looked at him in faint despair: this tired old man on my doorstep, dishevelled and defiant.

'Aren't you going to ask me in?' There was a flash of anger in the eyes.

Just for one moment, the sinking feeling inside my stomach, I actually considered whether I could refuse, and appoint somewhere nearby where we could meet. But I immediately dismissed the idea as preposterous. 'Of course,' I said. 'Have you had breakfast?'

'No. Not yet.' He stepped unsteadily across the threshold. 'We'll go off and have something in due course. Take a cab to the Connaught.' He spoke slowly, his voice slurred.

I frowned. 'Have you had *anything*?' I asked. I had caught the faint smell of alcohol as he had walked past me into the hall.

'Brandy. Just a half bottle. On the train. Had to have *something*.'

'No buffet?'

'On the milk train? Don't be a fool.'

'Where did you get the brandy?' I turned with a smile towards him, pausing deliberately outside the door.

He smiled back at me, slyly. 'Hidden away, old son. Hidden away. If those fiends had got it they'd have thrown it out.' He felt clumsily in his pocket, and eventually yanked out an almost empty flask.

'Isn't it a bit early for that?'

He shook his head from side to side. 'Day or night, all the same now. And the morning train was cold. I had to have something. Brandy's very good. Just the ticket. Like some?'

I suddenly laughed. 'It's good to see you. Come in. There's . . . there's someone I'd like you to meet.'

He marched in behind me, looking round expectantly. 'Someone here?' he said. 'Well, where are you hiding her?' Finding no one in the room, he gave me a stern look. 'Do I know her? Is she pretty?'

'Be patient, father.' I pointed round at the main room. 'Do you like it?' He seemed instinctively to recall his previous visit, when he had done so little to help, and a slightly pinched expression came over his face. 'You've made it very comfortable.'

'Take your coat off. I'll be back in a minute.' I went out and along the passage into the bedroom and closed the door.

'What is it?' Clare said. 'Who was it at the door? Is somebody here?'

I didn't answer her, but crossed to the bed and sat down on it. My faint amusement at his disastrously abrupt arrival was turning to anger and despair, and it must have shown in my face.

'You look terrible,' she said. 'Tell me what it is.'

'It's my father,' I said. 'He's just arrived.'

She sat up, holding the bedclothes in front of her. 'What's so awful about that?'

'He's drunk. He talks about having broken free.' I looked into her eyes, not quite knowing what to say. 'He's . . . he's always wrecked things for me. Not meaning to, but he adds such a huge dimension.'

I must have looked very miserable. She reached out towards me, letting fall the sheet, and suddenly we were in each other's arms. I heard her soft laughter, and held on to her more tightly.

'Darling,' she said, 'there's no way in which he's going to wreck this. You mustn't think it, even for a minute. What he does is his affair. You don't have to stand over it, or excuse it.'

'But always in the past, he—'

She interrupted me. 'We're not in the past.' Holding me close, and turning her lips towards my ear, she whispered, 'You can put your childhood away now. We'll do things differently.'

'Oh, Clare.'

She pushed me away. 'Go and make some coffee. Talk to him. I'll come very soon. It's time I met him, anyway.'

I went back, putting on the kettle on my way, and coming into the room to find him warming himself in front of the gas fire, which he had turned on. On the mantelpiece at his shoulder stood the now empty flask.

We stared at each other, he, it seemed, a bit defiantly. I felt calmed and relaxed.

'Who's the girl, then?' he said. 'Someone I know? Pretty? Is it serious, old son?'

'Her name's Clare,' I said. 'She'll come and have some coffee with us.'

'Are you in love with her?' He delivered the question sharply, not inviting a reply, but demanding one.

I didn't answer straight away, but smiled at him. 'Are you warmer now?' I asked.

'It's no business of mine, of course.'

'Yes, I am, as a matter of fact,' I said.

'And will you marry her?' The haughty, abrupt tone of his voice could have been that of a Victorian father, dealing with the man who had compromised his daughter and was being offered the limited options of marriage or a thrashing, or possibly both.

It made me laugh. 'You're rushing me,' I said. 'Since you're here I'll wait and see what you think. You mayn't like her.'

He sat down, staring into the fire. 'You're absolutely right, old son. Your father's an impatient old fool. Take your time, take your time, the world's before you—'

I think he would have gone on in this vein, only Clare came into the room, stopping by the door to look across at him. She was wearing my dressing gown. Her feet were bare.

'Hello,' she said. 'You're George. I've heard a great deal about you. I've been looking forward to meeting you.'

'Clare!' he said, getting unsteadily to his feet. 'But you're pretty as a picture! Far too good for him, I'll be bound! Come over here to the fire. Warm yourself.' He stepped back, making a place for her, and she approached, staring up at his face.

Then she turned and looked at me. 'He's exactly like the painting. It's quite extraordinary.'

'Painting?' he said. And then, thinking of Sarah perhaps, he asked her, 'Do you paint? Are you an artist?'

'I'm not,' she said. 'I'm a social worker in a children's hospital. It's just that we saw this Spanish painting in the Wellington museum. And the man in it is just like you. I didn't expect so close a likeness.'

'Handsome?' he asked.

'Which?'

'Why me, of course.'

'Both. He's at least four hundred years old.'

Clare sat down beside the fire. My father stood in front of her. I left them together and went to make coffee. It was the first time Clare had been to the flat, the first time we had made love. The first time, for her, with anyone. I could not get over my father's truly remarkable sense of timing; what an occasion to turn up as an uninvited guest for breakfast.

When I brought in the coffee my father was on his knees before Clare, holding her small, naked feet in his hands. He stared up at me, his eyes wide, his expression one of serious accusation. 'You didn't tell me!' he said. 'Clare has the most beautiful feet!'

She laughed. 'Put them down, George,' she said.

'Put them down?' he said. 'Put them down? I shall hold them forever! They are perfection. Perfection.'

I had a sudden, irrational, fear that he would remember Sarah's feet, and mention them, no doubt giving Clare the benefit of any comparison. But either he did not remember, or, for once, displayed tact as well as good judgment in concentrating only on the feet he was holding with such reverence.

'How much has your father drunk? He tells me just a little brandy. Is that true?'

'More than a little,' I said.

'Sober as a judge,' he said. 'Head clear as a bell.'

'But I need my feet back on the ground,' Clare said.

'I must kiss them first,' he said, his voice low and tender, almost reverent. Swiftly, his bearded head bowed down over them, and I watched his lips tenderly touch first one foot, then the other. When he looked up his face was serious. 'Perfection,' he said once more, softly, and gently lowered her feet to the carpet.

Clare was moved, and her laughter had a sweet sound. 'Oh, George,' she said.

'We must go out to breakfast, after we've had coffee,' he said. 'Won't bother with breakfast here. You're free, I take it?'

How he imagined this was a puzzle, but I knew I would have to spend some time with him, and I was relieved that I had an easy day before me, with no commitments that could not be put off.

It was different for Clare. 'I can't join you,' she said. 'I have to work. Indeed, I shall be late if I don't make a move now.'

'What are you up for?' I asked.

'Chelsea Flower Show, of course! I've got tickets some-where. One for you as well.' He felt for his wallet, but then let his hand drop without taking it out. 'I want to celebrate,' he said.

'I think the Cavendish is best for breakfast. What are you celebrating?'

'My freedom.'

'But you'll go back?' Under the stubborn determination his words lacked the familiar fire.

'You did ask me to come, you know. For the Flower Show. Remember?' He paused. 'You're right about the Cavendish. Appropriate place, though it's donkeys' years since last I was there. Now, ring for a cab. Haven't we all something to celebrate?'

[II]

'Reminds me of Calcutta,' he said. He walked slowly, his hand on my arm. In the room, which was on two levels, the almost defiant tone in his voice was a claim on the attention of the few residents there, whose muted voices were stilled as they stared for a moment at him.

'Calcutta?' I said.

'All Indians,' he said. 'Wasn't like this in Oscar Wilde's time. Nor in mine, neither.'

'You used to come here? With Laurie?'

'No. Not Laurie. Before that, old son. When I was a young man. Brought my first woman here.'

A dark-skinned waiter, young and with good teeth, indicated a table, and seemed inclined to move us into it, with a slight bow and a crab-like movement of his slim body.

But my father was having none of that. 'We'll sit up there,' he said, pointing towards a low-level balcony in a position three or four steps up from the main room. 'Keep an eye on things.'

'Yes, sir,' the waiter said, swivelling his body in the new direction. 'Absolutely as you wish, sir. The table right here, sir.' He went ahead, and pulled out the chairs, flipping the top clear of imaginary crumbs with a napkin. 'Residents?' he said, looking at me. I was about to shake my head, but my father said, in the same firm tones, 'Yes.'

He waited, like a ruined millionaire, for the waiter to push the chair in behind him, then he crooked his forefinger at him, and turning away from me whispered something which I did not catch into the man's ear. When he had taken our orders, and gone, my father turned to me and said, 'It's the only day to go. Get there early enough and it's not too crowded. No point if you can't see the flowers.'

We had left Clare off at the door of the hospital, protesting at the expense of going so far out of our way. My father had got out of the cab. When she put up her face to kiss him, he put his arms round her and kissed her full on the lips, and then raised his hand in salutation. 'You are perfection, Clare.'

She blushed, smiled at me, told me to ring her later, and then ran up the hospital steps.

Breakfast was elaborate, and took a long time. My father's appetite was unimpaired. He disposed of fruit and kidneys and bacon and toast. Then, on a signal to the waiter, a bottle of champagne appeared on the table in an ice bucket. 'I've always believed in a firm foundation for a heavy day,' he said.

'Do you mean the breakfast? Or the champagne?'

'Both. Champagne should always be drunk early. Early in a meal. Early in the day. There are better things later.' And he winked.

And there were better things later. Even before we left the breakfast table he ordered brandies, and when the waiter stared at him, the soft brown eyes opening wide in astonishment, my father's stern gaze fixed him, and he said, 'Doubles. No;' his voice went up a semitone: 'Trebles.'

It was as if he took me in hand that day in order to teach me how to drink. And for the first time in my life with him, and for the last time as it turned out, I was wholly on his side, without reservation, judgment or hesitation.

'Shall we go?' he said. He smiled at me mischievously.

'Mm,' I said. Neither of us showed the slightest inclination to move.

He looked round the by now deserted breakfast room of the Cavendish. 'Not the place it was. I like these darkies. 'But for all his dirty hide, he was white, clear white, inside, our good old, grinning, grunting Gunga Din.' They're good at their job. They want to do it well. Mostly. I suppose it'll change. Nothing works properly for long, does it? But we mustn't despair. Waiter?'

He had appeared across the room, and now hurried forward and up the steps. 'Sir!'

My father's eyes bulged at him a bit. He just said the one word, 'Bill.'

'I put it down to your room, sir. What's your room number?'

My father took a fat wallet from his pocket.

'I'll share in this,' I said.

He turned sternly towards me. 'You'll do no such thing. It's *my* freedom.' He looked back at the waiter. 'Run along and add it all up.'

The waiter frowned, but went away. He came back quite soon, not looking too happy, but with a reckoning in his hand which was swiftly paid, together with a generous tip. Then we left.

My father moved slowly on his way out of the hotel, and I held his arm as we moved out to the edge of the pavement. He looked frail; yet somehow charged up with drink and anticipation.

In the taxi he sat back quietly for a moment or two. Then, without turning towards me, he said, 'Well, is it to be Clare?'

I looked sideways at him. 'I hope so,' I said.

'Hope I haven't buggered things up.'

'I don't think so,' I said. 'I don't suppose anything like you has happened to her before.'

'Make sure it doesn't again, either.'

We both laughed.

He leaned back and closed his eyes. The stern profile sagged a little. Under the bone and flesh the fatigue showed through.

'Father?'

He opened his eyes and looked at me. In the moments of repose they had become suffused with the redness of uneasy sleep.

'Yes?'

'Do they know when you'll be back? Your women, I mean?'

He laughed, humourlessly. 'My women indeed! Of course not. I shall be back when I feel like it.'

'And Gladys?'

'Gladys had laid down the law to me too often. "If you get drunk don't bother to come back." That's her message. Had enough of it.'

'You'll take no notice?' I asked nervously.

'For two pins I'd finish with them both. They fuss over me all the time. I can't stand it.'

'But it is security, a home for you. It is permanent.'

He ignored that. 'And another thing I can't stand. Gladys has started inviting this clergyman around. I don't know if she thinks she's going to convert me, but I'm going to have to put a stop to it.'

'A clergyman? Is he Church of England?'

My father nodded, looking out of the window. 'The regular kind. Padre. You know. Name of Squarely. Pompous old fool. He and Gladys just talk gossip about people. I don't want her to go religious.'

'Would it be any harm? Might amuse you as well.'

He stared at me. 'Too late, old son. Too late.' After a pause, he said, 'Of course this padre looks at me a bit hungrily. He may get me in the end. Either that or I'll have to stop him coming.'

The taxi drew up at the entrance. There was already a crowd of members, but no queue. I helped him down and paid the fare. We went in.

He brightened visibly as we joined the bustle of movement, and became enveloped in the sweet and heavy mixture of scent. The great banked displays of colour represented, to him, an ideal of perfection. Never, now, to be attained, yet all his life there, as one of the beckoning beacons for our ambition, a measure of what can be done, what must be done, in order to triumph. I, who had seen him pitiful upon his knees in countless sour, suburban London gardens, wrestling with what he did not own, in the interest of an indifferent demand for mere order and stability, looked now at his aged, rheumy eyes as they watered in profound admiration before the displays of hollyhock and antirrhinum, phlox and zinnia, and great scented banks of sweet pea.

I was incidental to his enjoyment. And I was glad. I wanted to observe him more than the flowers. They were as incidental to me as I was to him, serving a function in the roundabout of action and response, a means to an end, which was some finer sense of him. Most of the time he would let pass through his lips murmurs of approbation, or envy, or disagreement with the award of prizes. But at times, silenced by excellence, he would for long moments stand with his eyes shut in front of flowers like stocks, breathing in their heavy scent and smiling at the memories coursing through his brain, perhaps searching, through remembered sensations, for something of himself that had existed in the time which I imagined he was now recapturing.

In their tall splendour, vivid colour and infinite variety of scents, flowers hold us to what is unchanging. In being so temporal, so freshly of today, they are eternal as well. No occasion on which I was with him quite compares, in its capacity for bringing together past and present, relieving pain, fulfilling desire, as that morning when, with my interest divided between the flowers and the changing expressions of pleasure which illuminated his eyes, we walked endlessly through the displays of colour and smell.

'We'll go and have a drink,' he said, eventually. Instinct or memory turned the proposal into a challenge, and he stood face on to me anticipating a lifetime's reaction: when had I not attempted to steer him away from drink?

'Perhaps more than one,' I said, with a smile. 'What's wrong with a few drinks?'

'That's the ticket,' he said. 'Chip off the old block.'

It was just after midday. The rather gaunt bar was not very full. He was relieved to find a seat, and sat down heavily, with a sigh. We drank several brandies without saying much.

'I hope this mean's you'll settle,' he said. 'Don't waste time.'

'I'll do the best I can.'

191

'I had my family, my children.' He made a sweeping gesture with his hand. 'I've always done my best. Always.' Then he took another drink from his glass. 'You have to be definite, decisive, certain,' he said. He clenched his fist. 'Passion should direct your course.' He made a little punching gesture in the air on the word 'passion.'

I questioned whether he had always done his best. In my mind I compared this form of defiance with so many previous confessions, just as sincere, of having failed. Perhaps it was possible to do one's best, and to fail; but the contradiction tempered and affected my reactions to him. In myself, in my perceptions about how to approach 'life,' I diverged from him, while at the same time indulging him as fully as I could on a day which I so wanted to be happy for us both.

'And if you're wrong?' I asked. 'If it doesn't go the way you want it?'

'All is for the best in this best of all possible worlds.'

'And you've no regrets?'

He looked away. 'Everything I've done I've tried to do fully, passionately, giving everything to it.'

With hesitation I said, 'I can't do things like that. I can't let go, the way you do. It's different. Perhaps I don't feel passionate like you, not about the same things. Perhaps not at all.'

He shrugged his shoulders. 'You'll do things your own way, anyway.' And he took another drink.

'We're celebrating your freedom, father. Not terminating mine.'

We drank a good deal. Eventually I said I would take him to lunch. I suggested Bentley's.

'Don't mind if I do,' he said. 'Must just go and see the last room of annuals. I love the smell of them. So nostalgic. All that colour, banked up. I think, in everyone's heart there is a garden, full to overflowing with flowers of every kind. Perhaps memory has made it out of many gardens. I've never been in a garden that matched the perfection I see in my mind. But here, it seems to be suggested all the time. Perfection.' He spoke the word with exaggerated feeling. Then he repeated it: 'Perfection. It's all absolute perfection.'

We ate oysters and drank champagne. Then we went back to the flat. When we got out of the taxi I had some difficulty getting him up the steps and into the house, but managed it, and then watched as he succumbed to sleep, sunk down in an armchair. I made one or two phone calls, then also slept.

It was during that evening that he broke most of the precepts. He did so with such untangled innocence that even now, when I look back, my eyes fill with tears. I 'came to' about a couple of hours later. But he was ahead of me. He had helped himself to a drink. It looked a fairly strong concoction, possibly brandy and a dash of lemon. My mind told me I should steer clear of it, and in fact remain in the slumped position I occupied in the armchair. But my body signalled a more positive message about the effect of the drink. Through this debate I heard him singing.

He seemed to be behind me. Not visible, anyway. And he was crooning softly, 'When skies are grey, dear, I don't mind the grey skies, you'll make 'em blue, Sunny Boy!' It was an intermittent recital, soulful, and subject to variation. He did not deviate from the few remembered phrases out of the Jolson 'spiritual,' but he delivered a variety of different versions de-ing and da-ing his way through the melody as an alternative to the words, to which, periodically, he came back.

I realised he was behind me, looking at books. He crossed once to take a large gulp from his glass. But he returned, and I heard pages hissing over in his hands, the humming of the song resumed.

When he stopped singing I said, 'Sing another one.'

'You awake, then?'

'For a few minutes. I was enjoying the recital.'

'Limited range, old son. Forgotten them all now. How do you feel?'

I leaned forward, rubbing my face. 'Better than I expected.'

'Need a drink? I helped myself. Was that OK?'

'Of course.' I looked round at him. 'When I was a child, living with you, you always used to sing. And I used to lie, in the mornings, pretending not to be awake because of the warm feeling it gave me. It was like a cushion.'

'We had a room not far from here, once. Do you remember?' He crossed over to his drink and took it up. 'Brandy,' he said. 'Restorative.' He looked at me seriously, then he laughed. 'Cheerio.' And he drank. 'You?' he said, pointing at my range of bottles.

'When I'm strong enough; I'll help myself, thanks.'

'Yes, a room in Parkham Villas. Wasn't bad. Just you and me, then. And Alice. You must have been young, about thirteen, perhaps only twelve.'

'Was it before you met Ursula?'

'Yes.'

'And was it only Alice, then?'

He didn't answer that, but stared at me, unseeing, as if remembering. 'She's stuck to me, like a limpet. I should have said no, long ago.'

'You needed her,' I said.

'I was weak. On my own two feet I'd have done better.'

I didn't answer.

'I worked then for Sir Geoffrey Manning. God, I worked hard! He was absolutely meticulous. Everything had to be right. Reminded me of it, today. He loved bedding plants. A passion for annuals and biennials. And he planned everything. 'Colour and smell,' he used to say to me, 'let's get it correct.' And I used to beaver away, watering in, measuring off individual plants so that they were all the right distance apart. He wanted it exact. He wanted results quickly. A bit mad, I suppose. Did you ever meet him?'

I tried to remember even some of the many gardens I had trailed my way to, an unwilling accomplice. 'Where was he?'

'Fine house he had. Swiss Cottage.'

'I must have come,' I said. 'I don't really remember.'

'Naval man, he was. Got on well, we did. Course, he knew about my career, what I'd done, ships I'd been in.' His old face looked pinched for a moment, a hint of indifference to what he had just recalled flitting through his eyes. 'When I got there, each day—I used to work a full day—we'd do this tour of the garden, and he'd rattle off what he wanted done. This here, and that, box of plants to go in, clear a bed ready for something else. He'd get quite involved, and his wife would have to call him away. "Bosun's call," he'd say. "Stick to the course, George." And off he'd go.'

'How long did it last?'

'Spring into summer. Then it went wrong.'

'What happened?' I expected him to prevaricate, as he so often did, since it was usually something going wrong with him rather than with them. But not so on this occasion.

'Extraordinary thing,' he said. 'He was having an affair with a woman half his age. Less. Someone he worked with. He was in Bond Street. A jewellery firm. Wealthy, of course. And the balloon went up. Divorce, the lot. It was in the papers. Of course I couldn't stay on after that. No interest. She didn't care. Broke her heart, I'll be bound. She cried once, asked me to help her. But what could I do? She was an old battle axe. Can't blame him, in a way. But I felt sorry for her. She didn't have much left, when it was over.' He got up, and poured himself more brandy. Then he turned and stood looking down at me. '"Bosun's call! Stick to the course, George!" I'll always remember that. Poor bugger.' He drank.

'Why do you say "poor bugger"? It seems that he had the best of it in every way.'

'He didn't last a year. Died of cancer. I only heard later, in Chelsea, when I was married to Laurie. Met the wife. She told me. *Mutatus mundi*, as they say. Or something like that.' He pointed at me, suddenly stern. 'Now don't you make the same mistake, do you understand? The love of a good woman. Settle for that. Nothing less.'

I smiled at him, and nodded, and said, 'Yes, father, I'll do my best. I'll do as you say. A good woman.'

'Clare loves you,' he said. 'That's the start of goodness.'

'I think I'll have a drink, now,' I said. 'And I think we'd better have some tea as well.' I heaved myself up out of the armchair and crossed to the table. I looked him in the eyes as I came close, and smiled. 'I don't feel at all bad, you know. Thought I'd have a head.'

He said, 'When we've gathered ourselves, old son, we'll go off again. What d'you say?'

I nodded. 'I can think of nothing better to do, father.'
I poured myself a scotch and found some soda. 'Do you
want any ice?' I said, taking my own drink through into
the kitchen, and putting the kettle on. He said that he
didn't, and when I came back he was sitting once again in
the armchair.

'It must have been then,' I said, 'that you met Ursula.'

'About then. Yes.'

'That autumn?'

'It must have been. Yes. It was in the autumn.'

'And Laurie? The same time?'

'I suppose it was. The same time. Roughly.'

I paused for a while, puzzled that, in so talkative a frame
of mind, he did not go on. He seemed hesitant, all of a
sudden. In my own mind I was trying to phrase the question
I wanted to ask him. If I did not ask it now I would probably
never know the answer.

Then he looked across at me, and in part he solved my
problem. 'You're going to ask me why I married Laurie,
aren't you?' He was pensive and restrained now, all of a
sudden serious and deliberative.

'Something like that,' I said. 'Not quite the way you put
it.'

'What, then?'

'I was going to ask you, why didn't you marry Ursula?
That's how I was going to put it.'

'It wouldn't have worked.'

'But Laurie didn't work, either.'

'For a while it did.' He shook his head slowly from side
to side. 'You didn't like it, did you? It made you unhappy,
didn't it?'

The kettle was beginning to boil, and its safety switch
clicked off. 'Yes,' I said. 'I'll never forget it. Do you want
anything to eat?'

He shook his head. I went into the kitchen. What he said
during that long day was all we ever said on the subject.
Memory and reflection were locked away, then, their value
and purpose unresolved.

[III]

'You must remember this about your life,' he said, 'the opportunities must be seized. You must take hold of them with passion, my son. Passion.' The word passion was uttered with an exaggerated fleshiness, as though it came from deep in his throat, and was delivered up with special thought and reflection. 'Don't let the people in your life slip away from you. Hold them all. Make them yours. Make them belong to you.' He raised his right hand in an uncertain gesture, as though with it he could steady his confused mind along the rather wobbly course of philosophic thought it was describing. 'Yes. Mark what I say. I speak with the voice of agony and of ecstasy.' He seemed also to like that particular conjunction, and repeated it as well, with a pause in between: 'Agony . . . and ecstasy.' The very extremes of feeling seemed to go through him, brief shivers of recollection. He was really very drunk; yet it did not matter. There was no immediate agony behind it. There may have been the general sense of his whole life, the churning seas of all that he had ever done tossing him now, a frail and ancient barque, on one last voyage of danger and discovery. But if that was so, then he was still in command, his hand on the wheel, that of an old and practised sailor who felt, through wood and sail and line, every pull and shift of wind and water, and was repeatedly compensating and making provision: 'I know,' he said. 'I know it all.' From the expression in his eyes I felt that perhaps he had temporarily lost the direction of his thought, and was gathering himself again to change course.

'What do you know, old man?' I said.

'I dunno what I know, but it won't stop me telling you.' He smiled, almost inanely.

In all my life with him, going over this sort of territory again and again and again, I had registered different degrees of condemnation, backed up by the frail but persistent outrage of a child first, then a youth, then a young man. I had stayed with him, caring; later I had been in the position of walking away, though still caring. Now, the condemnation was no longer there. It had evaporated. So had the sense of outrage, which derived from all sorts of things: embarrassment, shame, anger, pity, and an overwhelming feeling of waste. All that I wanted now was to see him through. I felt—I had never not felt—as a child; I was like the figure of the young Raleigh, in the painting by Millais, having the course that faced me pointed out. Though in my mid-thirties, and already confined by experience, by setbacks, by disappointments, by financial circumstance, by unfulfilled ambitions, I was, in his presence, still the child I had always been. And I knew I would remain so, as long as he had life and I was with him. Whatever I might establish with others—wife, children, friends, professional associates—with him there was a constant equation between us. All that had happened was that the equation had been almost worked out to an answer. Almost; not quite.

'What do you think has happened to Laurie?' At one point in the evening we had called round, a sudden and mad reaction to curiosity which mercifully had been met by an empty and darkened flat.

'Who knows?' he said. 'I don't. Nor shall I, my son. Not in this world.'

'And Ursula?' We had drawn a blank there as well.

'Oh, Ursula!' he said. 'Do we understand ourselves when we make decisions? Was it terrible, what I did? Should I have chosen differently?'

'It was terrible for me.'

'Was it? Tell me.'

I shrugged. My mind was invaded by memories of the event, crystal clear, and awful. 'It was not what I wanted,' I said. 'But it wasn't me getting married.' I looked into his eyes, wanting him to tell me to go on. The recollection was so vivid to me, so profoundly imbued with all the feelings of deprivation and emotional uncertainty that had been a permanent thread through my childhood, that I could not believe he would not recall the occasion in the same way. Even in his cups, surely he would remember? Yet his eyes looked back at me with indifference. 'Were you . . . were you . . .' His voice rose to a high pitch as he searched for the phrasing of his question. 'Were you . . . with me at the time? Did I tell you what I was doing?' Genuinely he could not recall, from memory, and his struggle to do so, through his befogged mind, gave intensity to his words; but then a deeper-seated instinct came into force; self-knowledge intervened, and, in much lower tones, he said, 'Or did I just do it, and then tell you?'

I nodded. 'That's how it was,' I said. 'You phoned me up at school.'

'And I suppose it came as a shock?'

I smiled. 'It did, rather.'

'Babette?'

I shrugged. 'And other things.'

He looked down. It seemed to me a matter of great curiosity that we could pursue so vast a conversation in a Chelsea bar, one of several we had visited that evening.

'I'll take you home now,' I said. 'We've had enough.'

'Yes,' he said, 'take me home.'

We still sat.

'Do you remember the precepts?' I said. 'The seven precepts?'

He looked up at me. Then he smiled, sweetly, mischievously, and once again raised his hand; he might have been a bishop blessing the world, a conductor embarking on a symphony. He shook his head from side to side: 'Broken. Every one.'

[IV]

Never before had I drunk my way through a whole day, from breakfast, through lunch and dinner, to nightfall. Yet, while I must have passed through many levels of inebriation, and cannot in any sense claim a particularly strong head where drink is concerned, I had ended the day no worse off than I might have been after a few drinks in the evening, or self-indulgence during and after a good dinner. Whatever it was, my sleep that night was deep and untroubled, and, when I did wake, my head uncannily clear. It was early, however, and after drawing the curtains to let the sunlight pour in, I returned to bed to think. There was no sound from the flat. If awake, he would have heard the curtains and come in to me. Instead, I would go soon and wake him. I was overwhelmed by a sense of wonder at the capacity he still had to engulf my life within his. It should have been otherwise; yet his presence now in the flat seemed already, in so brief a space of time, to have imbued the rooms with that ancient, elusive, penetrating middle ground between scent and sensation which betokens a human life. And, whether it was that, I drifted off into a brief moment of surface sleep, even as my eyes were tracing the lines of sunlight over carpet, bedclothes and wallpaper. I seemed to travel rapidly back in time to arrive again as a child at home from school with him. It was momentary; a forced and rapid perception, elliptical and therefore puzzling; but profoundly intense and troubling to the mind. It was as if I travelled back twenty years, had a brief and compelling recollection of how I had then felt, and was then as swiftly compelled into the present again. It had nothing to do with memory. Insofar as I could judge, then or since, it was not really a trick of sleep. Yet I have been unable to satisfy myself as to what it was, and unable to recreate the experience. What mattered about it was this: back to the 'present,' as it were, I perceived in clear and logical terms the two lives, his and mine, side by side within the same vague timespan. And the effect of this was equally intense; I was seized by a kind of terror that all those years, for him, had been grey and blank and deeply troubled, just as they had been for me reasonably rich in tone and diversity of experience, and in an overall sense of progression towards some kind of individuality. What redemption, I asked myself, could I pluck, for him, out of those twenty years? Was there anything at all? Or was I looking back on the blank wall of despair, covered and concealed by his rages and his love? Equally passionate, had they camouflaged a constant terror, sense of failure or defeat, of weakness, of the loss, long years before, of his pride, purpose and ambition?

Deeply moved by the beginning of what was to be a set of fears dominating that most wonderful summer, the very warmth and sunshine of which was to appear harsh and cruel in the end, I got up, and putting on a dressing gown went to him.

He was asleep, on his side, in the made-up bed. The curtains were drawn back, but the window faced the other side of the house so that the room was still shadowed, greenish in its overall colour. His clothing was littered about. At some time in the night he must have got up and knocked over the chair. It still lay on its side, and for the time being I left it where it was. For some reason, perhaps to check on how much money he had left, he had inspected his own wallet, and it now lay open on the floor, almost directly beneath his hand, which was hanging down over the side of the bed.

I sat down on the floor quite close to him, looking into his face, and waited. His breathing was heavy and even. It reminded me of my impatience as a child, sharing a room with him when he was drinking, and being frightened to get up and move about, to dress and begin the day, lest he should scold me for disturbing his drunken sleep. More rationally now I could remember this across the intervening years, and without the intense feelings induced by the sudden, imposed recollections. Almost in response to that recollection, I reached idly across and pulled towards me his wallet.

It was mild curiosity, no more. I was not interested in the kinds of secrets that might be gleaned from such sources, and in any case he had, for years now, pared down to a bare minimum the things he carried with him. In fact, so thin was it, when I placed my fingers on the leather surface, that I wondered if he had enough money left. He had spent generously at the beginning of the day and we had matched each other through substantial consumption of drink and food after that. He was essentially poor, often talked of his status as an old age pensioner and what it meant, frequently grumbled about his naval pension, and engaged from time to time, still, in small additional bits of employment. He 'kept by' a little for occasions like this, telling no one how much it was, or where. But it was so trivial a matter, almost laughable.

I think in my nervousness to know that he had enough, and ready to add something if he had overspent, I flipped open the wallet on the carpet, and looked at it where it lay. Perhaps recollecting past occasions of a very different kind when, as a child, I had rescued from his pocket the odd pound note, and secreted it away in reserve, not for myself, and not with dishonest intent, but simply to ensure that we had the wherewithal to survive, I looked up at his face. Then I had felt fear, though not guilt. Now I did not feel either, just compassion for him in the prison of finite things. Under the sun, the sky, the invisible stars which had so absorbed his attention and fuelled his imagination all his life, he seemed so little lying there, so tranquil in his deep breathing, so handsome in repose, so innocent.

The wallet was austerely flat. In one side was a 'lettercard' and a book of stamps. His return ticket was tucked into a smaller pocket. Behind, I could see the edges of three five-pound notes, and on the other side two single pound notes. That seemed to be all, and, moreover, was enough for his needs that day, or any other day. What did it matter, I thought. He was on his way back to Gladys and to Alice, and had really begun the journey, in his mind, the night before. His spree was over.

Idly, I lifted the edge of the final flap, and saw that there was something else there. I looked at him again, cautious this time, and reassured myself that he was still sound asleep. Then I pulled out what seemed to be an oddly-shaped envelope, clearly fashioned by his own hand to a particular size.

I took it out and opened the flap. Inside there was a photograph, though what I first saw was the back with a scrawled message which read: 'George, with all my love, I.' And then, along the bottom, 'June 1963.' I turned it over; it was Isobel. She was as I remembered her then, pretty and vaguely sad, the smile on her face gentle and slight, the expression reflective, and questioning and loving. It was a good likeness, capturing the essence of her, and bringing back to me most vividly those days spent with them together in doomed expectation of something wonderful that never happened, or at least never survived. Briefly it happened, of course; the photograph was evidence of that, so was the message faithfully stating their situation during a year or so.

A flood of pity and sadness overwhelmed me, so that the tears came into my eyes and began to run down my cheeks. I was afraid of the feeling welling up within me, and of being so exposed in front of him in this act of supreme intrusion which went far beyond the inspection of his wallet, and could only be excused on grounds of love. Crying quite freely, I put back the photograph in the envelope, and the envelope in the wallet, and then closed it over. I was about to push it back into the position in which it had been when I looked at him and saw that his eyes were open. He was watching me.

For a long time we just stared at each other. In order to do so, I had to blink away the tears, and I felt foolish, and wanted to smile at him, yet could not get my features into order. More than anything else, I wanted to put my arms around him, and hold him.

My fingers still resting on the folded wallet, I said to him, 'Isobel.' It wavered between being a statement and a question. In reality it came out of my swollen throat as little more than a whispered croak. I shrugged, said the name again, this time a little better, more adjusted to the impediments of speech. He briefly closed his eyes, and nodded into the pillow. Then, with his eyes still closed, his voice firm and calm, he said, 'The unity of all life, to which human beings aspire, can only be felt by two people in love.' He opened his eyes then, and looked at me. His face was without expression; drawn with fatigue, perhaps, and the effect of drink; but otherwise obscurely neutral. I could think of nothing to say, but it did not matter, because he went on: 'In my life I have loved many women, and loved them well. I have felt deep rapture, because I have given everything. And maybe I have made others happy, and maybe not.' He paused again, and closed his eyes this time, not opening them as he spoke, and it was slow and hesitant, his voice deeper now: 'But I have only ever been in love with two women, your mother, and Isobel. And both are swallowed up in the past. It might have been different, old son, but it's too late now. The life that I had, whatever

I did with it, it's gone.' For a moment he looked down, and pointed at the wallet; then, staring back at me though still pointing, he said, 'A happy married life is the sole human condition that can impart a sense of permanence to an impermanent state.'

I sensed the direction of his words. 'Don't philosophise:' I remembered the very formation of the words on the paper, read at dawn, that day in June. 'Don't say "why don't you do this or that".' Don't, don't, don't: I wanted to reach out my hand to him, and tell him it would be all right, that it was all right, that the waiting was over, that his unlisted precept for happiness, just enunciated, was the one I would follow with Clare. And that all would be well. But I was too troubled by his words to fashion any of my own.

'I tried very hard,' he said. 'Changing and moulding myself. I tried. I did. Oh, Isobel.' He paused. 'But it was too late in life.'

I could not argue, I could not contradict, I did not know the direction of his thought, how far he would go, what intrusion there would be into my own heart. I need not have worried. He was engaged in a spartan *confessio amantis*, the brevity of which made me look upon him with renewed respect. Two women, drawn from a lifetime, and that was all.

Now he smiled. 'It's over, sonny boy. The life that I had, old skin, whatever I did with it, it's gone now. I can't get it back. I can't get anything back. All of it, gone away. Isobel gone, your mother gone, Francis, Melanie, even you.' He began to cough. His face became quite red.

'Take it easy,' I said. 'I'm going to make breakfast. You just lie there.'

'I loved Isobel,' he said, pointing to the wallet on the floor. 'I awakened her, sexually. You know that? Her husband was nothing. He didn't know what to do! A fool! But she would cry out when I made love to her. Oh, Isobel!' He stared at me. 'I can't even do it now,' he said. 'It's pitiful.' He lay back and closed his eyes. After a moment or two he said, 'I'll have to be on my way. Party's over.'

'I know,' I said, my voice low. 'But take it easy. Tea? Or coffee?' Then, as an afterthought: 'Or champagne? I do have some.'

But he was coughing, his face red. And between coughs, staring hard at me, he said: 'Just tea.'

[V]

Decrepitude may be wisdom, as Yeats says, or not, as Eliot says, but it is still decrepitude. I had great difficulty with him. Heart, chest, bowels, bladder, legs, feet, blood, circulation. It was ironic that the only part of him that remained clear and witty as I tried to assemble him for his journey home was his head.

'I'm gone,' he said, 'in the wind,' and he wheezed at the effort of getting his body into the upright position on the edge of the bed.

'And no hangover?'

'No.' He laughed at the thought, but the laughter plunged him once again into a fit of coughing, and I stood helplessly in front of him watching his red, angry face distorted by the strain.

'It was a charmed day we had, old son,' he said, speaking quietly, as if not to wake the rumbling giant in his chest. 'But I'm afraid I'll pay for it now. I was saving up for it. Not the money, you understand. But the health. Being very good. Medicine, no drink, ephedrine, everything the doctor told me. I knew I couldn't come if I wasn't in tip-top form.'

'You'll be all right,' I said. I sounded more confident than I felt. His legs looked thin and wasted, hardly strong enough to hold up his massive trunk. And in the position he had reached, sitting on the edge of the bed, he looked very vulnerable, as though small forces could push him down again, while something quite massive would be needed to get him to his feet and moving towards home.

'I'll get it in the neck,' he said.

'From Gladys?'

'From both.'

'But why?' I paused. 'Didn't they know you were coming?'

He raised his eyebrows, and put on a strangely puckish expression, shaking his head from side to side. 'They didn't.'

'They didn't? You just walked out?'

He nodded. 'Georgie's been a bad boy.'

'So that's why . . .' I didn't finish.

'The morning intruder.'

'I can see how they won't be best pleased,' I said. 'But is it all that serious?'

'It depends on what shape I'm in,' he said. He looked up at me now, and there was a faint appeal in his eyes. 'I don't think it's going to be very good. Not by the time I get there.' He put his hand out, and held it very loosely in the air between us. 'You'll have to help me,' he said.

I took his hand and helped him to his feet.

'It's the circulation,' he said. 'Legs like dry timber. No flesh any more.' I steered him to the bathroom, and bit by bit he seemed to warm up his locomotive forces. There was a detached stoicism in the way he spoke about his body. It was a clumsy, run-down vehicle for his mind, which was increasingly critical of its inefficiencies.

'Do you need help dressing?'

He shook his head. 'If I take it easy, stage by stage, it'll be all right,' he said.

I left him, and went to prepare breakfast. When eventually he came in he looked better. The stern features, the tightly brushed hair, the touch of colour in his clothing, which, in men in their seventies, seems to become more incidental; all this restored a more normal pattern to his progress. After at first declining food, and drinking more tea, he looked at the things on the table, and helped himself to cereal. Then he had toast.

'You've an appetite,' I said, surprised. 'You never used to, after a binge.'

'That's because I never knew when it was over.'

'And you do now?'

'It's over. That was the last time.'

'But you've said that before.'

'I won't again, though.'

'When Chekhov—' I hesitated, suddenly doubtful of the wisdom of what I intended. But I noticed he had stopped with a piece of toast in the air, and was waiting for me to go on. 'When Chekhov was dying at Yalta he had champagne at his bedside, and it was the last thing he tasted. Not a bad way to go, is it?'

He put the toast in, and then spoke through the crunching. 'Not bad at all. Will you do it for me, old son?'

'I'll do my best,' I said.

'But then I'll know,' he said. He looked faintly bewildered.

'You'll know anyway.'

We drove in a taxi to Paddington. I told the driver the route I wanted him to take, marginally different from the one he would have chosen, but traversing certain streets we had known together and even lived in together. And I told him we had plenty of time, which we did, and asked him to drive slowly. 'Royal Progress, eh?' he said, with a laugh. And I laughed, too. 'You could say that.' I did it out of love; but I was aware also of a thin element of cruelty which is contained in love, and which in this instance was submitting him to a tapestry of recollections which I could not wholly predict, since my participation had been so different from his own. All I was doing, in reality, was to present to him the whitish-yellow flower cone from the privet hedge, and let him do the rest.

His was an incurable disease. I was deliberately bringing on another bout of it in order to take his mind away from physical ailment, and concentrate it once again on a flickering sequence of ancient, familiar images. If he knew what I was doing, he said nothing. The wonderful May sunshine, flooding trees along the edge of the park with citron green and lemon yellow, was somehow too cruel, it was so magnificent. Yet his stern profile, turning from side to side, expressed no feeling at all as he drank in details of a theatre he had quitted long before and, after this visit, would not see again.

'Is that where you ran?' I asked. 'That morning? The first time you came to Coppinger?' I pointed across the park, northwards.

He nodded, but said nothing.

'Do you remember the toyshop that used to be there? Pringles, wasn't it?'

He nodded again. Deep in his throat I heard a hum of agreement, but no more than that. I let pass the allusion in my words to an affair he had once had with a woman working there. She had gone; the shop had gone; only the memory bobbed before my mind in the vivid guise of my own recollection of standing on that pavement, with him, either waiting for her, or about to go to her. What his recollection might be I would never know. I could not bring myself to test it out.

After that I became silent, and watched him as his eyes turned from side to side, drinking in the changed detail of habitual territory. This had been ours; was still, in memory; and all I was doing was recharging the bank of sustenance on which he might feed his incurable nostalgia.

Just briefly, I was reminded of similar journeys the two of us had made, to the same railway station, only with me as the potential voyager, a child or youth on my way back to school. And I was caught and held by the phenomenon of our reversed roles: he was returning to discipline; I, once he had gone, would take up work, and move freely about among friends, visiting Clare, having a discretion over my actions which was increasingly being taken from him. It was a passing thought, but a sad one, and it lingered in the back of my mind during that morning drive, and even after his train had left.

We still had time at Paddington for a drink, on which he insisted.

'Pick me up for the journey, it will.'

'You won't drink on the way down though, will you?'

'No,' he said, with exaggerated repugnance. 'I just need a pick-me-up, now. That's all. A little brandy.'

He walked fairly steadily through the door of the buffet, his travelling bag looking ludicrously small in his large hand, and I followed him, taking his arm as we approached the bar. 'A little brandy' turned out to be a large one, and though now we had limited time in hand, he managed to order a second.

'It's changed, hasn't it?' I said, looking round.

'Everything has.' He drank. 'God, that's better. Strength to face the music.'

'Will it be warlike?'

'Of a martial character, old son, you can be sure of that.'

'You'll be all right,' I said.

He took another drink and stared back at me. Then he winked. 'Indestructible,' he said.

I smiled at his power of recovery. I was conditioned to believe him. In a jocular manner, over a pint of beer, in a truculent way when dead drunk, in sickness, in health, his claims to indestructibility were written now so firmly on my own memory that it was the easiest thing to believe him.

'You'll live for ever,' I said.

'Yes,' he said. 'George'll live for ever!'

He walked ahead of me down the platform. His step much slower now, there still remained in the flexing of his knees, his left giving in a slightly more pronounced way than his right, that nautical appearance that was infinitely memorable, infinitely dear to me.

I got him on to the train and into a seat. He insisted, then, on coming back along the corridor to the window. He followed me, moving slowly, until eventually the two of us had assumed positions the exact reverse of what I remembered, in that same place, on so many previous occasions when I had been setting off back to school leaving him in London. But if that occurred to him, as it certainly did to me, there were other, more important feelings dominating his mind. As swiftly as the mood of confidence in his indestructibility had developed, it now began rapidly to evaporate again. In a voice that did not seem to me to rise much above a whisper, he said, 'It won't be long now, my son.'

I laughed, and put my hand over one of his where it grasped the window ledge. 'Don't say that.'

He looked back at me, and shook his head. 'Give Clare my love. She is perfection. You realise that much, don't you?'

I nodded. 'Take it easy,' I said. 'We'll do this next year. Perhaps I'll be married by then.'

'Oh, I *do* hope so,' he said. 'I do hope so.'

Barely trusting my own face, I said, 'It was a wonderful day. I felt such a release, being in London with you. It's years and years, isn't it?'

He didn't seem to hear what I was saying to him. 'Those were wonderful days, my son. You were my staff and compass.' He gave a slight shake to his head. 'You didn't know it, but you were. Whether things went badly, or whether . . .' He petered out, realising, I suppose, that nothing had ever gone well. 'Whatever the state of play, you forced me to a semblance of order, a need to do things, to deliver up an account of myself.' Momentarily, he seemed to stand up straighter. 'Well, there's only one account, now.' He pointed upwards. 'Remember Agnes? When Jip lies dead on the floor?' He put his forefinger to his lips, and then he winked.

'You're being melodramatic,' I said, and smiled back at him. 'You will live for ever!'

Chapter Ten

I

Gladys's voice was essentially reassuring. It was much else, besides, carrying among other things a note of severe censure. But at the heart of her complicated message there was a quiet note of control backed by confidence. Her training as a nurse was becoming a genuine asset. 'He's had an accident,' she said. 'I tried again and again to phone you yesterday, but you were always out.'

'Is it serious?'

'It could have been. But it wasn't, luckily.'

'What happened?'

'He fell. I hope you weren't as drunk as he was. He got off the train, fell over a porter's trolley, dropped a bottle he was carrying and broke it, then fell on the glass and cut his leg open and his arm. Very foolish indeed. Why I should go on with him I often wonder. He's a reprobate and he'll never change.'

I felt a sudden surge of guilt. The day before, getting back to the flat from Paddington, I had found an opened bottle of gin missing, and in its place a five pound note, tucked behind other bottles, but hidden only superficially. He must have had it in his small travelling bag throughout the taxi drive. Old reprobate indeed!

I debated whether to tell Gladys, and decided not. She was still talking: 'It's been an awful strain, you know that. Not just now, but all the time. And going off to London like that was just foolish. You should never have invited him. I know he rang me. But that's not really what matters. It's just not fair of him, he can't treat me like this. Well he won't be able to, any more.'

'Shall I come down?'

'He's a very silly old man. Come down? Do you mean is he going to die or something? He's a long way from that. But you're always welcome. You know that. He always likes to see you.'

'Can I speak to him?'

'He's in hospital. Just for the night. Bit of a shock, you see, the fall. And then all the drink. Why did you let him?'

'You know the answer, Gladys. Who's ever been able to stop him?' I paused. 'I'm sorry it's happened. I'll come at the weekend. How serious is it?'

'It's a nasty cut,' she said. 'Jagged piece of glass. But clean. That's the only good thing you can say about alcohol. With luck it'll heal.'

'Why do you say "with luck", Gladys?'

'You know the state of his health. Your father's an old man. There's not much blood gets down into his legs, because of poor circulation. So it may take time. I've talked with the doctor at the hospital. He must give up that sort of thing. That's what they say. As if they needed to,' she went on, a dry laugh in her throat.

'At least he's in good hands,' I said. 'If I can help, Gladys . . .'

We both knew there was nothing practical I could do, and I sensed anyway that she was not altogether unhappy about the new situation. There had been a shift in power. She was moving more towards the centre of the action.

'Once I get him back, today, we'll see how things are.'

She rang off, then. The old fool, I thought. Why had he to get himself plastered? Yet I could not really be angry. My own carefully calculated farewell journey to Paddington with him must have left a grey shadow over his journey, shrouding it in an invisible mist of regret.

Two days later a letter arrived from Alice. It was full of what she did not know, delivered in tones which hinted at a certain measure of rivalry between herself and Gladys in the new situation which was developing.

212

'My dearest, You will have heard of your father's accident, since Gladys assured me she was trying to get through to you on the telephone all this evening. For what it is worth, and that it's much, I've decided to add my own two-pence halfpenny-worth. But I'm sure you will come down soon, in any case, and piece together everything that occurred.

'The first thing to be said is that he's a very naughty boy. Should never have gone off like that without telling one of us, at least. And I hope he'll never do it again. It may well be that he won't be able to, in any case. But while that would be a form of justice, it's far from my thoughts to wish that on anyone, least of all your father.

'I heard about the accident first of all from Gladys. She said he was drunk. Well we all know about that. I'm sure he left you sober. You would hardly put him on a long train journey with drink inside him. Where he got it from is the puzzle. Anyway, it was hardly surprising that he fell over, although I'm always telling them at the station not to leave those trolleys out in the middle of crowded platforms. It's all right when there aren't any people about, but when it's crowded it's so easy to be jostled and then fall. And the train was crowded. There was a great deal of blood. And I think he behaved quite badly, threshing about and shouting. Somebody even fainted. They got him to hospital, stitched him up, and kept him for the night. And that was almost that. The only problem, according to my friend down there, the almoner, whom I alerted about him as soon as I could, was that he gave some trouble in the night, saying he wanted to be let out, and no one was going to keep him in hospital against his will. But they managed to hold on to him. And he didn't come out until this morning.

'I saw him briefly, and he's very sorry for himself, poor dear. Nurse's orders are that I can visit him this afternoon again. I shall then hear all about his trip, and how you were.

'He'll be very chastened, for a while, and it will put an end to his gallivanting. But it seems it won't be more serious than that. Gladys says the cut may take some time to heal. We'll have to see.

'I will do everything I can. You know that. But I hope it won't be too long before you come down.

'My love to you, Alice.'

Her letter was followed, two days later, by another.

'My dearest,' she said, 'I had a long talk with your father. He said you had telephoned him. That you were busy this weekend, but coming down to see him next weekend. I'm very glad about that. He's rather glum. Down in himself. It's not being able to move about that really upsets him. And he sees it as a matter of months before the cut properly heals up. I think he may be right. Gladys is more cheerful about it, but she doesn't think it will be altogether easy getting him back on his feet. He's very irritable, of course. No one can blame him for that. But I suspect it's all a bit more complicated than it might be with someone younger.

'It's made worse by the weather. Such sun as we've never seen. And so warm. I puff my way into town, feeling so sticky. I'm sure I look a fright. Then out again, even worse. He's issuing instructions about watering, and I had to buy a new fixture for the hose today. Of course, all such expenses are mine, since the garden is my responsibility, but I don't mind at all. He watches from the window, and I'm sure he laughs at my own feeble efforts.

'We look forward to seeing you in a week's time. Love from Alice.'

[II]

The prisons of old age are worse than the prisons of youth; there is nothing to look forward to, there is only the past. My thoughts about the reversal of our roles took on a darker, more intense colouring after the accident. Coming out of Paddington Station, after seeing him off, I had thought to myself, he's lucky enough. Protected, guarded, watched over, nursed, humoured, scolded, he was as I had been. He would be looking out from the train window, just as I had done, perhaps with tears in his eyes, for often that had been my condition. Only for him, as the thinning, attenuated suburbs of the city which had been his home throughout his nomadic life, passed by him where he sat

214

in his window seat, it was the last time. He was seeing it on a final journey home. 'Home'? Well, had not Coppinger been that to me? Why should not the finality of his present situation rate the interpretation of warmth, comfort and rest?

It was only instinct, at that stage, which told me he had made his last journey. Now the accident, little by little, was to confirm the fact.

I told Clare about the accident Her training made her echo Gladys's warning, that healing might be a problem, and she explained the difficulties to me. She was appalled by the idea of him absorbing so much neat drink and then falling about among the pieces of broken glass on a crowded platform. Yet the firmest image she retained of him was of his bearded head bowed low over her feet.

'No one ever kissed my feet before, I'm happy to say,' she said to me. 'The fact that your father has done so means I can talk about it to you. Perhaps to others as well.'

'We had a wonderful day together. It was sad, his last visit to London, I suppose. I've never drunk so much in my life. Nor felt so well after it.'

'And never will again, I hope,' she said with some intensity.

'It's not hereditary.'

'So they say.'

The urgency of going to see him was tempered by my preoccupation with Clare, and by the flow of information and reassurance coming from both Gladys and Alice. It was also a busy time, with end-of-season sales as usual, and in the event I did not get down for several weeks.

It was almost by accident, coming out of Christie's and passing one of the galleries which then flourished upon the outpourings of American art, that I noticed Sarah's name listed among eight or so contributors to a group show. I went in. It was some days after the opening, and several canvases were sold, including two of hers. From prices generally, I realised that she was doing remarkably well. It was the first unqualified pleasure I had ever derived from Sarah. Her undoubted success, detached entirely from me now, filled

me with a sense of relief at her obvious fulfilment. Even
within the paintings themselves I saw enough, stylistically,
to feel reassured that she had continued some kind of
evolution that had integrity. Echoes of her words came
back to me, inducing neither regret nor longing. It was
as though I now looked back upon myself then as another
person, less easy to live with, less mature, but at the
same time less the object of the shame that periodically
in the past had assailed me. Not all I felt was relief. For
Clare my feelings were a quite different set of emotions,
more measured, more diverse. At the same time, they were
demanding. We saw much of each other, and wanted to see
more.

He did not reproach me for not coming sooner. He
was just withdrawn inside himself. It was as if he looked
out at me from the encompassing mass of his own flesh,
immobilised now, in one chair or another, his wounded
leg on a footstool, the dressing on it quite loose, so that
from time to time the air could be allowed to get to it.
He was absorbed by the situation. It would preoccupy
him in all sorts of different ways. He would rage at his
own foolishness. He would report medical opinion on it.
He would relate it to his general state of health. He would
make it a counter in his curious scale of judgments about
the level of attention he was getting from Gladys. He
would use it as a factor in deploying the ready services of
Alice.

Yet he was also, in a most odd way, detached from it. It
was a fact, and a factor; there on his leg, propped up on
a stool, dressed and re-dressed, talked about, manoeuvred
both physically and psychologically, the wound was a disembodied thing which seemed quite remote from his mind, as
though it were a handicap in golf or an endorsement on
his driving licence preventing him from driving. It was
not *him*. One was witnessing one of the later, if not
ultimate, stages in the process of growing old in which
rational mind compensates for declining physical power.
The disbelief with which, in middle age, we dismiss as
a passing irritation what is a permanent set of bodily
changes—greater girth, stiffness in the shoulders, failures

of sight and hearing, shortage of breath, fatigue—is still there in old age, performing a function as real as chemistry in the human body. And part of what it does is to distance the mind from the disability.

It did not heal. It did not bleed, it did not suppurate; it ran. A slow stream of colourless liquid flowed from it, as if from the very slightest of springs on a bare mountainside, creating no more than a limpid wetness in a tiny area. It was relentless, just like a spring of water. Nothing could stem it. Powerful as well, not with physical force, but in that pervasive way in which liquid spreads and is absorbed, bit by bit raising the level of saturation of everything with which it comes into contact.

Gladys explained it to me. 'There's no blood there, you see. His circulation has gone.'

'But there was blood when it happened.'

'It was deep enough, the cut. It reached a vein. That's healed over. But there's nothing near the surface. No good tissue, no blood vessels.'

I frowned at her. We were in the garden. 'What does that mean?'

'It means it will take a long time. It may not heal.'

'Not heal?'

She deliberated for a moment, staring at me. Then she said, 'He isn't well. He doesn't have the strength to fight this.'

'What are you saying?'

'I'm saying that it may be a matter of months. Perhaps the autumn, perhaps earlier. The summer's a very trying time.' She paused. 'Ultimately,' she said, 'there is the risk of gangrene. It has to be watched.'

'He's dying, then?'

'We're all doing that. But he's ahead of us. It's a matter of making it easy for him, both physically and mentally.'

'That won't be a simple task, will it?'

She looked at me for a while, then she said, 'It depends what time you can give to him.'

Alice said, 'Tell me your end of the story.'

At first I was puzzled. Although I had known her many years, and on many occasions had given her exhaustive detail on my own and my father's actions, I had not anticipated going back over the details of what happened on the fatal day. It was enough that he had got drunk, and fallen, and brought on a crisis. I thought that Alice, like Gladys, would be concerned about coping with the future, and of discussing more immediate issues.

'His arrival was a complete surprise,' I said. 'I didn't even know there was a train that early.'

'He must have been up at the crack of dawn, you might say. Left with the larks.'

'How would he have got into town?'

'A lift, probably. A milk lorry. Perhaps a tractor. It was market day, and there's always traffic very early.' She paused. We looked at each other. Her stare was one of blank inquiry. 'So how did the day go? And tell me about Clare,' she said with a slightly indulgent smile.

She listened silently as I told her, first, how I had met Clare. The fullness of detail indicated to Alice its importance to me, yet she had few questions to put to me, and after a brief interval reverted to her inquiry about my father's day in London.

'When did he start drinking?' she asked.

'On the train.'

'And went on all day?' She seemed to be reconstructing in her mind comparable occasions, if I was to judge by her wistful expression.

'More or less.'

'He must have been very drunk.'

I shook my head. 'It wasn't like that, Alice,' I said. 'It wasn't really what you'd call a binge. It was a very happy day. I'm sorry it ended the way it did. But I'm not sorry about the rest of it.'

'I'm not reproaching you, my dear,' she said. 'We're at fault more than you. It was what he was coming back to made him get drunk.'

'What do you mean?'

Her steady gaze was faintly unnerving. 'I can't pretend, my dear, that I have ever been able to offer him more than the merest fraction of what he wants. You mean far more to him. It's the same with Gladys. She cares for him, gives him affection. But his cravings, perhaps for something inexpressible, go far beyond us.'

'Somewhere out among his stars, Alice?'

She nodded several times. 'Yes, perhaps.'

'So why—' I began to ask, and could not satisfactorily conclude a sentence which might well have implied the wastage of many years.

'I felt I could compensate for all the frustration of his squandered abilities.'

'And you looked after him because of that? All the years, and all the money you've spent on him, getting him out of scrapes?'

She smiled, almost secretively, and then said, 'I added it up, once.'

Stifling my incredulity, I said, 'You did what?'

'I added up all the money I spent on him, since first we met. I kept details of course. All along.'

'For thirty years?'

'Yes.'

I could not bring myself to ask her the exact sum. I just waited, expectantly.

She volunteered the sum. It ran to several thousand pounds. 'I gave it gladly,' she said. 'With all my heart. And would do so again.'

'And what has he given you?'

She sighed. 'Not enough, my dear.' She looked at me so calmly, her hands folded in her lap, everything about her appearance carefully cared-for and complete. 'I don't expect you to understand. But I would not have it otherwise than what it has been, except—'

'Except now? Would you like it now to be just the two of you?'

'Always, I wanted more of him to myself. That's my only regret.' She paused. 'It was a happy day, then, that you spent together?' She seemed serene and calm. 'Tell

219

me again about the flowers. I went with him occasionally, when we were both in London. It was such a treat.' She almost blushed at the recollection.

I went over again for her the middle part of our day together, describing as best I could the banked array of flowers, the people, the scented atmosphere.

'And in the evening, you went to Chelsea? Was that wise? You didn't see *her*?'

'Laurie? No.'

'I meant Ursula.'

'No.'

'You saw no one?'

I shook my head. She reminded me of Hercule Poirot.

'And the bottle of gin? Where did that come from?'

'It's impossible to think of everything, Alice. I had it in the flat, with other drink.'

'But did he ask you for it?'

'Lord, no. He just took it. But he left money for it, tucked under a glass. If he'd asked I'd have . . . well, I'd have tried to stop him, but I suppose I would have let him have it in the end. I could hardly refuse.'

'Well, you see what it's led to.' She stared at me. 'Of course I'm not saying it's your fault.'

'Gladys thinks he doesn't have very long.'

She nodded. 'It won't heal, the cut.'

'He won't be easy to look after, will he?'

She gave a little shrug. 'We'll rally round,' she said. 'There's the district nurse. And of course Gladys knows what she's doing. I can lend a helping hand. We'll muddle through, my dear.'

'I'll come down when I can.'

'You're very important to him. You realise that, don't you? He'll need you.'

'Yes, I know.'

How was it that she was still here, I thought, still with him, still prepared to give all that she had for him, still prepared to face the permanence of rejection, almost as though she fed on it? On countless occasions, going back to my childhood, I had placed before him, in the role of surrogate suitor, her undying and unquenchable love for

220

him. And his response, varying in detail, and intensity, had been rejection. The tokens of that love, measured out in sums of money, were an amazing detail; confirming its stubborn, abiding nature. I could only marvel at it. It was as intractable a story as his whole life had been. Yet it cast shadows, both back in time, and forward, over the months and possibly years that lay ahead. For if my father did not love her, what did he feel for her? He was not an indifferent man; that could never be said of him. Whether it was about carrots in the garden of our childhood home, or rosebeds and apple blossom in the cottage garden on which he now fixed his impotent gaze, the intensity of his feelings was a passionate reality. Suppose, to balance her love for him, there was hate? Deep-seated, abiding, as yet unspoken? What would she do with that, if it surfaced? I trembled at the thought of its presence, and dreaded its possible manifestation. It was unthinkable; and yet, knowing my father, I could not be entirely sure as decrepitude increased, and as he looked back over the blank years of his past, that one day within him there would not break out some fire of retribution, or final recrimination.

Suppressing the dark thoughts, I reassured myself by the undeniable resilience in Alice's disposition. She was worried about immediate things, like his drinking, and his other women. This was curious. I had not, up until then, told her about the photograph in my father's wallet, though my memory of it was still vivid. She had lived her life vicariously through and around him for so long, still felt threatened by the figures of Ursula and of Laurie, and yet did not mention Isobel, when it was Isobel, rather than the other two, who had most nearly of all threatened the very purpose of her existence. Perhaps it reflects badly on my sensitivity towards her, that I should have mentioned her at all. Worse still, I deliberated over it, conscious of the effect which might ensue, but hesitating over phrasing the question in such a way as to gain access to Alice's real feelings. The demon of curiosity takes many forms; for me, it is not so much knowledge of facts as reactions to them which satisfy the relentless, stain-like spread of the desire to know.

'Has he ever mentioned Isobel to you?'

She looked at me quite sharply. 'Is she in London now?'

I shook my head. 'I don't know where she is.'

She thought for a moment before speaking again. It was as if she were recollecting another unsavoury episode out of the past, and doing so with distaste, yet forced into it by jealously or suspicion.

And all the time, as I sat there in the stillness of that small room, remote from the world, with these three lives pulsing relentlessly away, and with the shadows over them of other more distant lives entangled in their network of passions and feelings, I was aware of the manipulative instinct in me, cruelly dispassionate. Why had I mentioned Isobel? Because Alice had not? Why had she not? Possibly because—like him not wishing to talk of his naval career since it represented the unattainable grail of his life, and therefore failure—Isobel stood to Alice as an emblem of perfection in his heart, and was therefore the most dismissive of all elements to her.

'Why did you mention Isobel?' She did not ask the question easily. It seemed to stick in her throat.

'Because you did not.'

She turned aside from looking at me, and put her hand on the table. 'But my dear, there are many women I do not mention.'

'She is important in his life.'

'Still?'

We looked at each other. I weighed up in my mind whether or not to tell her about the photograph. It was so vivid, my recollection of his eyes on me, as I intruded so directly into his heart, pulling from his wallet that tiny, fragile, boyish secret. Would it matter? What would it do, either to her or to him? The fact, and its impact, was just a speck of dust caught in a sunbeam; and yet it seemed to me that an understanding of women revolved around that weightless, untouchable fragment of light, to be deployed if I saw fit, either then or at a later date. Just then, I decided against. Without offering the evidence, I nodded.

Alice knew to accept it as true, knew at the same time that she could not ask me to tell her more about my reasoning.

She was slow to speak again. 'Did he . . .?' she said, hesitating. 'Did he contact Isobel?'

I shook my head. 'No, Alice, nor any of the others. He won't ever see them again. Not any of them.' I tried to laugh at the spectre of so many. 'You'd think there were crowds of witnesses who had participated, and were now called to account. Gladys is right, he's an old reprobate, isn't he?'

'No longer.'

'Is it a relief?' I asked it, conscious I suppose that it was in questionable taste, and yet fairly sure, having known Alice through most of my life, that she would not resent it.

She looked at me and smiled. 'The honest answer to that is, I really don't know. After all, I didn't get him in the end, did I? Only part of him.'

She spoke as if he had gone from us already. I was seized with a sudden fear that this might be so, and felt within me a strange resolve to try and disentangle at least something of his mind, his character, his story, before he passed from us. All the ingredients were gathered there, in that tiny little space of garden and cottage, in that curious conjunction of himself, his women, and me. Only the true direction of ultimate curiosity was lacking.

[IV]

And so began the strange last series of pilgrimages westward, through the long summer, to learn wisdom from that recalcitrant hermit. I went in a mood of humility. I had faltered in the very area in which he was strong. I could not command, from within myself, the kind of passion that drove him on. I could not bring forth in others that equally intense feeling for him, that love which had dominated Alice's life for almost thirty years, and had swept up others along the way. I did not feel in myself anything like the bitter rage that flooded through him when he was blocked or frustrated in his desires, when he was crossed or angered. I could not compare myself with him.

His very faults took on a virtue as they became confined within the straitjacket of his dying body. That virtue was wisdom. It was not benign. That would have been too

223

...n to expect after so turbulent a life. He fretted; and
. too easily this turned to intense rage, indiscriminately
directed against all of us.

Gladys bore the brunt of it. Nothing she did for him was
right for long. And she did everything for him. She even
tried to protect him from Alice, whose intrusions were of a
proprietorial nature, irritating both her and him, persistent,
ill-timed, and often culminating in bathos.

June passed into July, and it was wonderfully warm. I was
down for the weekend and by coming had allowed Gladys to
leave for two nights with her sister. This, of course, was like
Christmas Eve on the Western Front in 1914. Alice crossed
over with a frequency that I thought would drive my father
quite off his head. I even felt superfluous in the practical
sense, as she produced laboriously prepared dishes of food
to add to the groaning provisions already left by Gladys, and
insisted on helping with the dressings on his leg.

Thus it was, that hot July Saturday afternoon, that the
three of us were together in the room. We had lunched
there, and I had cleared away, bringing in the tea he always
took at that time, and sitting down myself near the window,
a little way from them. His leg was up on the footstool, and I
could see that the dressing had become damp. There was the
faint odour of lavender in the room, from the toilet water he
occasionally rubbed into his neck and hair and shoulders.

'I'll change the dressing when you've had your tea,' I said.

He nodded.

'No, my dear. I'll do it,' Alice said. 'I'd better practice
again, given the opportunity. In an emergency I'll be able
to cope then, won't I?'

He nodded again. He seemed indifferent.

'Gladys may not always be able to manage,' she went on.
'The more the rest of us know the ropes, the better.'

He took his time drinking his tea, and looked across at
me, his eyes showing a certain measure of fatigue. At that
point he was in one of his benign moods, and his usually
hawk-like, tense features were relaxed. I noticed that Alice,
who was sideways on to him, had her eyes fixed patiently
on the middle distance, and I thought to myself she was
vaguely nervous about starting on his leg too early. I raised

224

my eyebrows in an unspoken question: was he content that she should take over? And he read and responded with a slight nod.

I took out the tea things, came back to my chair under the window, and began on my book again. I was reading *The Return of the Native*, and had just made that second, subconscious but deeper entry into the book which comes after the first four chapters or so, when the great landscape's entanglement of one's stabilities gives way, as always in Hardy, to the even more formidable territory occupied by the minds of his characters. I was content to read on, hearing only as a low background hum the noise of their voices, mainly hers, though interrupted with directions from him 'You can throw that.' 'Use a fresh piece.' 'It's looking much better.' 'Loose? Or a bit tighter?' 'Leave it loose.' These and other phrases punctured the prolonged activity which Alice was pleased to take her time over.

'You can go into town if you want,' he called across at me.

I looked up. 'Do we need anything?' I knew we had all we needed.

'Time off,' he said.

It seemed like an invitation to Alice to sit with him. I was surprised, but agreed to go if I could get her anything. 'There are a few things,' she said, still dealing with the dressing on his leg. 'I'll have to go and see.'

She had fussed at it long enough, I thought. Yet I could appreciate the pleasant feel, for a short while, of the dry lint and gauze resting on the fresh towel, until the liquid from his wound once more saturated everything. Perhaps because of this he let her go on, and, having stopped my reading I watched in a kind of vaguely horrified fascination as she fussed and fiddled, prolonging each detailed action of winding, tying, folding and patting.

At last she stood up, her hands clasped in front of her, her eyes turned, first towards her own handiwork, then down towards his head. He also was looking down at his hands, and my own interpretation, perhaps unfair, of what he was thinking, included impatience.

Then, as I watched, she leaned forward and down, letting her arms go backward behind her body. They were a nterbalance to her plump, serious face, which descended further still, and, with eyes now closed, planted upon an ill-defined area somewhere between his labouring brow and the sparse hair on the top of his head, a noisy, awkward, self-conscious kiss. For a moment she was frozen in the attitude of a fairy out of pantomime; she could have been grasping, in one of those outstretched hands a wand with a star on the end of it. In my imagination I briefly dressed her plump and shapeless form in satin and tinsel and gauze, and it brought me close to laughter in the silent, pregnant atmosphere of the room. But her face, in that brief progress down to the surface of his skull, during the obvious kiss, and immediately afterwards as it paused, perhaps scenting the smell of him underneath the odour of lavender, was suffused with an expression almost of holy and righteous love. It had about it a sacramental quality. Nevertheless, I was nervous about how it might be received, and stared across at him.

Even as her plump cheeks hesitated above his head, the eyes closed, the nostrils quivering slightly, he stared at me, his face drained of expression, his eyes tired, strained, his jaw slack: and he winked. Then he raised the hand nearest to her, and as she stood upright and brought her arms down to her side, he reached out and took and squeezed her hand, an expression on his face of vague gratitude which produced in his throat an even more vague sound, something like a groan, indicating reception of her tribute. I was content to leave them after that.

Chapter Eleven

[I]

I rode up the hill slowly, towards the ridge which overlooked the town from the northwest. The bicycle had a slight fault in the pedal mechanism and clicked on each revolution. It was irritating, particularly on the steep bits, when I feared a more substantial slip that might pitch me off balance. It was some years since I had cycled, and with all the traffic on the more important roads down in the Vale I had felt quite nervous. But now, winding my way uphill along narrow roads that threaded their way from one village to the next, all was deserted. It was the beginning of September. The afternoon sunlight was warm. No breath of wind disturbed the leaves or grasses in the hedgerow. And the scattered gatherings of cloud, high up, far away, had the settled look of a summer landscape by Ruysdael.

I passed through a village, and out beyond it, climbing still. The apple trees in the cottage gardens were laden with fruit. Though there was neither mist nor haze in the air, the curious paleness of the late afternoon sunlight, which out across the Vale could be seen in intermittent sunbeams falling on the ordered pattern of fields and hedges stretching for many miles, fell close at hand on the still detail with a sharpness that clearly etched each leaf, tree trunk, clump of bushes, gate-post or building. Only birdsong disturbed the air.

Eventually I stopped, quite out of breath at the unfamiliar exercise, and pushed the bicycle in off the road to a gateway

227

field which looked down over the countryside to the
th east. I climbed over the gate, and lay down in the thick
rass.

I would have liked to have slept, I was so tired. But I
could not. I had gone riding out of desperation, to get away
from the cottage and from the three of them. But now, far
above the town, and alone, all I could think of was his angry,
silent face, his fearful eyes, his great belly and feeble arms,
his slack hands hanging down with nothing to do, his leg laid
out across the stool still weeping springlike from its wound.

One could hear the liquid in his lungs, the water in which,
so Gladys told me, he would eventually drown. 'Was it to
here, or here?' I had said to Gladys, hitting my own chest
with my hand stuck out straight across it, as though one
could measure him like a vessel marked off in inches up to
the point which would prove fatal.

I hated the indignity of it all. The last rites, for him,
seemed to have begun with a great engine brought into the
room to lift his gross form from chair to commode, back to
chair or into bed. And he hated it too. He looked so helpless,
and at the same time so bitten into by fury. When, Gladys,
when? Please tell me, I used to say to myself, under my
breath. You're a nurse, you know, you have answers, I have
never been through this, you have, many times; how does it
end, how soon, does one know, can one be sure? But all she
could say, in response to my pleading, was that it would be
soon.

Soon! It had been soon for so long. Now I wanted it to be
now. I sat up and looked out across the grass. I desperately
wanted the strands from which might be drawn some dignity
to hold together. And yet all the time I felt that he was falling
apart, and that, on the brink of physical corruption, some
wild gathering of instincts with him seeking to upbraid the
world, would flail out at us all, destructive, vindictive, a
wild expression of his permanent terror. There had been
indications. His temper had become short, and he was
often most demanding. Difficulties seemed to arise on little
more than a whim or trivial accident or gesture. Yet all
the time all of us were drawn back to that room he now
inhabited day and night, to sit and watch and wait and

occasionally talk, pervaded by the now nauseous scent of lavender.

I was very tired. To come down from a busy week and engage in night-time vigils at his bedside was wearing. All the time I was aware of the fact that we were getting him through a prolonged struggle between his will and the body's relentless decline.

I had been down several times through the summer, usually at weekends, and once or twice with Clare as well. But as his strength declined and the difficulties of nursing him increased, I came alone, to some extent with her approval, in spite of the fact that she got on well with him. It was, she said, a form of farewell, and good for us to be alone together. It was frustrating as well, going on through the summer months, like a foredoomed campaign in which relentless commanders refuse to capitulate. I wanted it to be over, and to go back to her. And one of my reliefs, which gave pleasure to him during our long vigils together, was to reassure him about Clare, and about our intention to be married. He asked often about her. He demanded that we should have children. And in the strange atmosphere of the room to which he was confined, with his unreal and ominous expectations, these exchanges constituted a welcome allusion to a more normal life beckoning me from far away.

The padre, Mr Squarely, whom once he had ordered out of the house, jealous I suppose about the conversations he had with Gladys, now paid occasional visits and sat with my father, whom he called 'Commander', talking of politics and of the second world war. And it was during one of these visits that I had slipped away to ride out into the afternoon sun.

For a time I lay in the grass close to the road. Then I got up and walked forward through the uncropped grass a little way until the field began to curve down, and there came into view more of the foreground landscape of smooth hillocks descending through rich farmland to the meadows below. All this that I loved, this heart-of-England magic of red apples and blackberries and small bricks making up high walls, shadowed by trees or glowing in sunlight, failed to

229

make its usual impact on my senses, refusing to admit me into an atmosphere for which I yearned, sunk as I was in desperation at the unhappy, unfolding death in the town below.

The best that could be hoped for was that it would now come swiftly, and that the disintegration of feeling into abuse and retribution against those who surrounded him, and of which there had been some caustic evidence already, would not drift into areas of agony or terror such as I knew to be possible. The fear was there, the rage, the anguish, the intense perception of life-long hurt, most of it self-inflicted, but no easier to bear because of that, and from these it was by no means difficult to imagine arising against us all a charge of indifference or neglect or lack of love which would turn to gall his final hours.

The doctor had said quite firmly he should be moved. Gladys had resisted, on his behalf, but also on her own. She found no great difficulty taking his abuse. She was much more resistant than Alice, whose yearning for his affection had remained unsatisfied for so long that any crumb was welcome. In addition, as a nurse, Gladys was familiar with how things would be at the end, and wanted to put off for as long as possible the drugged farewell, the somnolent departure.

And so, on the hillside, I was obsessed with the questions which filled our minds in the cottage, and the peace I sought was as evasive as ever. I cycled back, letting the bicycle freewheel down and down through the still air which parted with a rushing sound in my ears as I gathered speed.

[II]

Putting him to bed was a major tussle. So much had to be just so. Because of the strange contraption needed to hoist him about, his whole life was concentrated in the one room round which the rest of the cottage now revolved. His bed, quite high, was in one corner. And I took it in turns with Gladys to be with him. A low light was on all the time, so that, in his fitful sleeping he would wake to familiar things.

I sat with him that night, and because he asked I told him about the bicycle ride, retaining for him only the idyllic qualities. Perhaps he sensed that I was not telling him everything, or perhaps he just felt regret anyway at a set of experiences towards which he could reach out only an unavailing hand. Whatever the reason, he lay back against the pillows, his expression benign, his eyes closed, his head nodding from time to time as I associated for him the apples on the trees, the honeysuckle and blackberries in the hedgerows, with places we had shared together in the past.

He drifted into sleep. It must have been about eleven. I should have done the same, since his pattern at night was to wake in the early hours when the effect of the various medicines wore off, and make a succession of demands upon whoever was with him. But instead I went on reading for more than an hour, until after midnight, and then, under an increasing if sub-conscious pressure, set aside my book and began to write down some of the feelings and thoughts of that day.

I keep no journal. Like him, I suppose, I treat diaries as functional things, to signpost one forward, and, in retrospect, constitute an awkward and not always accurate assembly of facts. I had, at that stage, published one book, was at work on another, and was dissatisfied with both, just as I was dissatisfied with the generally forgettable quality of much else that I wrote. Subject to the heart-disease of my generation, which was indifference, I had tried and failed a number of times to find my way forward into what is called the 'creative' field of fiction or poetry. I knew that in him there was a 'story'; but I considered it unwriteable. Nevertheless, responsive to some deep unsatisfied yearning, I felt the need that night not to let slip away the feelings that had run through my mind on the hillside about getting him safely through those days that were left, and bringing him to some kind of peaceful end. There was within me a vague yearning for some form of redemption, and though I could not perceive it at all clearly, it seemed to me, sitting there in the silent room, listening to his breathing which was so peaceful, just at that time, that the redemptive force, if it existed at all, lay between us. I had sought to get expression of it over a period not of days or months even, but of years, in the form of wisdom from him, in the form of recollection and memory, in the form of helpful advice about women (which had done me little or no good!), in the form of encouragement in what I did. And, of course, this was no use. What had I got but 'Seven Precepts', all worded negatively, all relevant, unarguable, but leaving me unsatisfied as to the deeper redemptive force I believed was there.

He had turned sideways, on the pillows, and I could see his face, hawklike yet relaxed, his hand resting out across the covers. Suddenly his eyes opened, he rolled onto his back, and cried out, 'Up! Up! Up!'

I crossed over to him. 'What is it?' I said. 'You can't get up.'

He stared harshly at me, his eyes wide. Then he repeated himself: 'Up! Up! Up!'

I still stood in vague bewilderment before him, not knowing what to do. In spite of the urgency with which he addressed me, he had not really raised his voice sufficiently to wake anyone else.

Having stared back at my uncomprehending face for many seconds, he said, 'Sit me up, you blithering fool! Can't you understand? It's the pain! Pain! Pain!' His voice was high with anguish.

I hauled him forward, pushing pillows behind his back, fixing him into a vertical position on the bed.

'Where's the pain?' I asked.

He looked directly in front of him, ignoring me. 'Everywhere! Everywhere! Everywhere!' The triple agony was expressed in a high falsetto voice on the brink of becoming a scream. He was rigidly upright in the bed, tense with what seemed to me a form of hysteria. It most closely paralleled a child's tantrum; if he had possessed the strength and movement, he would have kicked and fought. As it was, the eyes averted from me and staring down the bed represented a threat of some unspecified act of rebellion if I did not do exactly what was right. And I did not know what to do.

232

I could see he was having difficulty with his breathing, the signals of distress bubbling up from within his lungs. And when he reached out his hand in a sudden and peremptory gesture, I put into it his asthma breathing aid. His great hand closed gently around the small balloon-shaped rubber base, and he swung it to his lips, puffing the contents down his throat as though the mixture was an elixir of life. It brought little, if any, relief. Momentarily, a shadow was lifted from his eyes, but in psychological response to the familiar medicine for past distress which had long since been outstripped by more fundamental faults in his system. His great trunk began to sway backward and forward in the bed, and each time he reached the forward pitch a little groan escaped his lips. His hand holding the breathing contraption in it had fallen to his side, and, not knowing what else to do, I reached out and tried to take it. He let it fall, and I put it on the table. But when I then tried to take his hand he jerked it away.

'Do you want anything?' I asked. 'Something to drink?'

He just went on rocking forward and back, but into the slight groans which escaped his lips in time with his movement there now was introduced a tone of a peculiar, childlike quality. Like a two-year-old who has been left in a cot to recover from a tantrum or fit of weeping, or has cried before going to sleep, he crooned now a monotonous, high treble song of eternal reproach from which I and all the world were excluded. 'Oh, oh, oh,' he went, 'oh, oh, oh.' Then from his lips, still in the triple form which had so eerie a quality, like a ritual appeal to nameless gods, he began to conduct some very private inquiry within his own mind. 'I can't, I can't, I can't,' he sang out, in a high tremulous, plaintive wail. Then, 'You must, you must, you must!' Then groans again, 'oh, oh, oh.' Then more muted groans, in the form of humming.

I sat in a state of numbed bewilderment. I had no grasp of what this meant. Was it a stage downward? Was he on the brink of death? What should be done? I would have called Gladys. But he was clearly in sufficient command of himself to be able to indicate whether that was what he wanted or not, and in the circumstances no action was better than action which might run counter to his wishes.

The sounds lessened. Like a child, he seemed to be hypnotising himself back towards sleep, and I sat silent beside the bed hoping this was so. But a sudden upward slide in the register which so widely covered the musical range of his doleful complaint took his sleepy, middle C groaning up an octave to a sudden new expression of distress which frightened me momentarily. 'No! No! No!' He wailed, and his face was screwed up against some imagined terror. With his teeth out, his bearded chin came up towards his nose making a hideous mask. And rocking again in little, weak, but still quite furious thrusts of his body, he went on, eliding closely each phrase: 'I won't go! I won't go! I won't go!'

As with a child, though infinitely more puzzled, I agreed, and soothingly voiced my confirmation that he need not go. 'Please rest, Father. Lie back on the pillows. Relax.'

He seemed to hear me for the first time. The screwed-up face straightened out into an expression of awful tiredness. He turned his head, and his eyes met mine. They were cold and angry, and haunted by fear.

In a low voice, quite gentle, he said, 'Get Gladys.'

I began, very quietly, to protest. 'She's very tired, Father. It's the middle of the night. She needs to sleep a bit. Won't I do? If there's anything at all—'

He went rigid, began again his terrible rocking, and in an intense wail which had suddenly sailed up again into a high falsetto, he cried out, 'Get Gladys! Get Gladys! Get Gladys!'

I got up and crossed the room, turning on another table lamp. He was rocking. As soon as I looked back he repeated his demand. Then I went out.

Conditioned to him, or to years of professional training; perhaps responding as women do; she took little enough time to register and react. 'I won't be a moment,' she said.

I returned and told him. He nodded, and went on rocking. She came in after that, and went straight over to him. 'What are you fussing about at this time of night? What's the matter?' She ignored his silence and plumped the pillows behind him, though I had already attended to them, and he showed no inclination whatever to fall back into them.

234

He sat rigidly upright, staring ahead, and looking for all the world as though he were gathering strength.

When she could think of nothing more to do, she said, 'Well, what is it? Aren't you going to tell me?'

He began again to rock. 'Pain! Pain! Pain!' he wailed.

'Where?' she asked. 'Where's the pain?'

'Everywhere! Everywhere! Everywhere!'

So awful was it that I wanted to cry. So comical, that I could barely suppress laughter. Unfamiliar with each and every stage in his illness and expecting death too often before it came, I had developed a form of incipient hysteria which tended to bubble to the surface at any untoward development in his state of health. In contrast, Gladys, whose experience of death was wide, including two husbands, had a quite different approach to him, playing down in importance the crises which he so loved to provoke.

'It can't be everywhere, George. It can be in your leg, or your chest. But not everywhere. Where is it?'

'It's everywhere, you stupid woman.' He spoke in a fierce whisper. 'When I say it's everywhere, that's exactly what I mean. Stop being so patronising. I'm not a child. Your fussing is driving me out of my mind. Do you understand? Out of my mind.'

His energy was quite extraordinary. Before his stern gaze she looked down, and I felt her appearance was one of crumpled defeat. But he was not finished. Looking haughtily at her he said, 'You are an incompetent fool. Do you hear me? An incompetent fool!'

The effort of raising his voice to a shout brought on a violent fit of coughing. He reached out his hand, as he had done to me. Though it was an irrelevant aid, she dutifully handed to him the small bakelite contraption. He puffed and coughed and spluttered for a while, still sitting bolt upright. When it was over he lifted the edge of the sheet and wiped his lips.

Trying to take in breaths, and keep calm, and prepare for further words, he sat upright still, his haughty gaze turned towards her. For a long time he stared at her. It was not hate in his eyes, but indifference. 'I will go into hospital in the morning. First thing, do you understand?'

She nodded, without looking at him. He stared at her with a kind of solemn dignity. 'I have lost faith in you,' he said. He repeated the words, the second time more firmly, and slower. They were those of a child of five. It was as if he had picked up the phrase from adult conversation without understanding it, but impressed by the tone of judgment in which he had heard it used; and now, feeling that the time demanded the dropping of some solemn epithet irrespective of the more serious implications, he was uttering a final verdict on her performance.

She stopped all movement, and looked up at him. I was surprised at the calmness in her face. Like a mother, she absorbed this new evidence of wilful antagonism between them, judged it swiftly enough, and set it aside. If, deep down within her there was surprise, or wonder or disbelief, or even the postponed intention of retribution, they were concealed behind the flat lack of expression as she absorbed this new spectre of imitative wisdom. So faith was lost in her, was it?

He sat upright still, and quite stiff, though no longer rigid as he had been when rocking and groaning earlier on. He looked straight in front of him, down the bed, and with dignity seemed to be contemplating, just as a child might, the words he had uttered, not with any improved grasp of their meaning, but merely in self-satisfied realisation that they had struck home. And I admired in Gladys, and loved her for it, that calm indifference in her attitude to his most grievous insult.

[III]

The ambulance came in the early morning. Though he had eventually reclined among the pillows, fitfully sleeping again, it had been a very disturbed night, with both Gladys and myself staying with him, for the sake of each other as much as anything. I thought at dawn she might ask him again about the decision he had made in the night. But nothing was said. In any case he was exhausted and frail, his eyes old and indifferent to our ministrations. And it was almost with relief, and a look that amounted to a welcome, that he stared up into the faces of the two young ambulance men who cheerfully greeted him as 'guv'ner', and trolleyed him out on their stretcher through the morning sunlight where it fell on the dew-laden grass and on the panoply of rose blooms which he would never see again.

The initial adjustment was by no means easy. His first night was bad. He cried, screamed even, and disturbed the sleep of the other patients. The night sister had to give him an additional sedative, and he seemed even weaker when I went in to see him the next morning. I must have sat for half an hour at least beside his bed before I was sure he knew it was me. Even then, the first acknowledgement of the fact was an embarrassing wail from close at hand: 'Take me out! Take me out! Take me out!'

The faces of the other patients around the ward would have been hostile if they had cared enough. I looked at them nervously. Then I reached out my hand to take hold of his where it lay on the bedcovers. Without looking at me, he pushed it away.

There were two nurses in the ward going round together, one carrying a tray of medicines, the other distributing them with cheerful and friendly greetings to the predominantly geriatric inmates. Though he was not yet on their schedule, they stopped and greeted him as well. I thought he would react either frostily or with anger. But instead he smiled at them and made a small gesture of the hand which, for all his weakness, had a good deal of charm.

'You're looking better,' the nurse said, swiftly smoothing bedclothes and putting her hand to the pillow behind his head in a passing, efficient gesture.

'Am I?' he replied, with feeling.

'Oh, yes,' she said, enthusiastically. 'Much.'

'That's good.'

'And you don't want to leave us?' She said it with a smile, teasing him.

'No,' he said, and shook his head. 'No. I'll stay if you'll have me. And if they'—he waved his hand sternly towards where I sat—'If they give you any trouble, fire them out! Take no nonsense.'

'They're very welcome. You'll be glad of visitors until we get you right.'

They moved on and left us. I wanted to laugh at the extraordinary way he had of charming strangers while antagonising those closest to him. Ambulance drivers and nurses benefited from the full force of his friendship, little realising what turbulence lay beneath. He still seemed to be in a rather stony, sulking mood, but I sat on, my hand still close to his, and eventually, when I tried again, he allowed me to take and hold the warm, slack fingers and palm.

And so began the shared vigil, the quiet, hypnotic bicycle rides through the laneways on the outskirts of the town, between the cottage and the hospital. The warm, still days were parcelled out between us. And the hospital, being small, accommodated our desire to spend as much time as possible with him.

My brother, Francis, came down and stayed. My sister as well. Others, too, were drawn into the pattern of visits which were extended leave-takings. And, after the emotional hiatus of his transfer from home to hospital for the last time, the anguish both before and after, those occasions when he still demanded to be brought back, and reminded us that we had promised he would not go into hospital, I was eventually lulled into a false anticipation of peaceful decline.

In any case, he had now to rise above the drugs which were given, partly to ease his pain, partly to restrain the intense fury with which he was still able to rend the night air. That he managed to go on making his mark, as it were, could be gauged in the mornings from the looks and comments of other patients, and from the reports on his condition briefly given by sister, nurse, or occasionally doctor.

August ended. In just one night, early in September, it became appreciably colder, and the next morning, before the sun had gathered strength, there was a refreshing feeling of autumn in the still, clear air, an indefinable prickle in the nostrils, heralding the chemistry of change. I felt it could not be long now; and my feelings were echoed by Gladys, who was almost cheerful about it, and by Alice, who was busy preparing to go into town, planning to come on to the hospital and relieve me at about noon.

[IV]

I could see from the expression on the ward sister's face that it had been another bad night. He was always impatient in the mornings to see one of us, and I was early enough to catch her before she went off duty. It was really several expressions mixed, rather than one. And she paused to let them register, while I stood politely waiting for some kind of report before going on into the ward. Vexed, she gave me, first an angry look, then a scolding one, and then composed her features to indicate resignation shifting to despair.

Rather inadequately, I said, 'Is anything wrong?'

She shook her head. In a low voice she said, 'He's going down like an ox.' A brief wintry smile flitted across her lips. 'He kept the ward awake for hours with his groaning and shouting. And such language! You wouldn't—' she stopped herself. 'I was going to say, you wouldn't believe it. But of course you would. He seems to survive all normal drugs and sedatives; he's like Rasputin. Eventually I had to give him a shot. And now he's *very* sorry for himself. I'm afraid you'll get little out of him for the next couple of hours.'

I felt an inclination to apologise to her, but instead raised my eyebrows, and turned to go into the ward. 'I'm afraid you'll get some queer looks in there,' she called after me.

And so I did. The severe faces of those whose sleep he had disturbed transferred blame on to me as I walked towards his bed. Propped against pillows, his lined face was slumped forward on his chest, the eyes closed. It was drawn downwards, the jaws not together though the lips were closed, and this gave a strange look of sombre, death mask dignity to his features.

I sat down beside the bed, and began to read *The Return of the Native*, ignoring the other patients and hoping that in an hour or so the frosty looks would soften.

The superhuman strength he seemed to command, during all those final days, woke him earlier than I had expected. I noticed his hand move slightly on the bedclothes, and looking up saw that his eyes were open. He had not otherwise moved, and I leaned forward in case he should speak.

'George is in the doghouse,' he said, his voice very low. 'Bad behaviour last night. Kept everyone awake.'

'I know.'

'You've seen the sister?'

'I have.'

'Mm.' He closed his eyes and raised his eyebrows so that his forehead wrinkled into furrows. 'Bad show, I'm afraid. I'm not popular around here.'

'Did you abuse anyone?'

He thought for a moment, then gently nodded his head and glanced at me. 'Everyone,' he said, his voice a low whisper. 'Just about everyone, anyway.'

'Oh,' I said. 'Do you want me to go round and apologise?'

He shook his head. 'It doesn't matter. Nothing matters. All be the same in a thousand years, old son. What is it to you, or to me?' His expression was sad and resigned. With the sun out it was warmer, a cloudless day. The sun fell on the shrubs outside the window, and the scented September air mingled with the vaporous smells of the ward in unequal conflict.

'Why?' I asked. 'What were you shouting about?'

He pressed his lips together. Under the goatee beard his mouth puckered at the painful recollections. 'I was afraid,' he said, turning his head towards me. 'I am afraid. Oh, my son, I shouldn't say it to you, but I wish it was over.'

I squeezed his hand, and looked away. He seemed then to slip downward into a drowsy slumber and I read for a while, tempted by the smells and the birdsong outside to go and walk in the hospital grounds, yet fearful that he might wake —that in any case he was not fully asleep—and find me gone, a situation that could provoke further anger.

It was after eleven that Mr Squarely came into the ward. On his healthy, smooth features under the carefully brushed, silvery hair, was an expression of calculated concern and reverence. Though he glanced across at my father, whom

240

he liked to spend time with, he deliberately circled the other patients first, and even spoke certain brief phrases of comfort to the elderly man between my father's bed and the door, before turning back to us, so that the full and final weight of his presence should be directed down, like a dove from the clouds, on his aged skull.

'I want to say a prayer for you, Commander. Give you God's strength on your journey through this troublesome illness.'

My father looked up at him with a wonderfully sincere expression of belief in his eyes. 'Thank you, padre,' he said. 'Frightfully good of you.'

Emboldened by his warm reception, the Reverend Squarely raised his voice, both in volume and pitch. He wanted the ward to join with us, though in attention or admiration rather than prayer. 'We must pray for strength,' he said. 'It is what we all need, the inner strength that derives from prayer.'

'Will it do any good?' my father asked. His face had an innocent expression on it. The inquiry was heartfelt. He seemed to be reaching out, within his mind, for some new level of comfort, some truly spiritual relief that would lift him clear of the physical anguish.

'God's hand, Commander, is reaching out to you, as it reaches towards all sinners.' Though with one hand Mr Squarely was clutching a fat bible to his large stomach, the other was free, and he made a small, uncertain gesture with it in the air, imitative of God's hand, but by no means as confident as his words were.

'Well, I'm certainly an old sinner,' my father said.

'No more than all the rest of us,' said Mr Squarely. 'God's redemption is there for everyone.' He stared briefly but sternly round the rest of the ward, recollecting no doubt the indifference he met with, together with the lack of social compatibility which was all too clearly his silent complaint against the world, something to which he could not take exception in the case of my father.

'That's good,' my father said. 'Do you think I'll make it?'

Mr Squarely frowned. 'Make it?' he repeated.

My father pointed his finger upward. 'In? Do you think I'll get in, padre?' He paused. The expression on his face was one of sincere anguish, and I wondered what had happened. Was it the over-use of drugs? Or was this a deathbed conversion?

'"If we acknowledge our sins, He is faithful and just to forgive us our sins, and to cleanse us from all unrighteousness."'

My father continued to stare intently into Mr Squarely's face. 'But will that be enough?' he asked. 'Will that get me in?'

'My son,' said Mr Squarely, 'we must pray.' He reached out his plump hand and rested it on the top of my father's head. He, in his turn, seemed to respond physically by lifting the top of his head slightly towards the pressure of the warm palm, closing his eyes and concentrating with his anguished features a supreme effort of commitment to this new avenue of spiritual salvation.

'I so want to,' my father said. 'I so want to. I so want to.'

Mr Squarely paused again at this. In the silence my father opened his eyes again and looked at him.

'Want to?' the clergyman said, puzzled.

My father again pointed up. 'Get in!' he whispered, his voice quite loud.

There was a suppressed snigger down the ward. I sat and stared in embarrassment at the page of the book open in front of me, still undecided as to the seriousness of my father's mental capacity for absorbing this great mystery of the Christian faith.

But Mr Squarely had a more practical grasp of his duties, and he went on in a rather too penetrating voice: 'O God, forgive this son his sins. Redeem him to thyself, and grant him the salvation promised to each repentant sinner. Amen.'

I thought my father would join him with an 'Amen' of his own, but instead he just nodded his head, and, when the padre's hand was removed, opened his eyes and looked up at him.

'Do any good, d'you think, padre? Get me in?'

'You must trust in the power of prayer, Commander. That's what I always say.' We were firmly back in this world. 'I'll pop in and see you tomorrow.' He glanced round the ward as he turned to the door. 'Goodbye, everyone. God bless you all.'

After he had left I sat still, watching my father's unmoving face, his closed eyes. I thought perhaps the strain, or some residual force of medication, was making him doze off. But after a while he opened his eyes and looked sleepily down the bed. 'He's all right, old Squarely. Top drawer type. Out of fashion, these days. Can't find his own sort among the patients. Like me, he belongs to the past.'

'What did you think? About what he said?'

He shrugged his shoulders. 'Won't do any good, old son. It won't do any good. You have to believe, you see.' He closed his eyes. 'You have to believe.'

It was just before noon that Alice came into the ward. He had been heaved up by two nurses and propped more firmly with pillows, in preparation for his early lunch. He had been tidied a bit, as well. It only served to make him more forbidding.

As soon as he saw her, his eyes, deep in their sockets now, and fiery with a most terrible mixture of fear and rage and impotence, glared at her. She moved towards him slowly, encumbered with stick and handbag and shopping, which included small gifts for him. I stood up equally slowly at her approach; the changeover in our vigil had become, like all such repeated acts, a form of ritual involving almost numb responses. She looked hot and tired and distressed, and stopped once on the measured way she made towards her first target, which was always the corner of his hospital bed, and from which she generally carried out a mute survey of the ward and its occupants, starting with an inspection of him, and coming back to him again with a tardy smile and a shy greeting.

But he gave her no time for that on this occasion. 'You!' he said. 'What do you want? Can't you see I'm dying?' He spoke with measured, deep solemnity. The ward went silent. Everybody stared. The nurses stopped in their distribution of trays and food.

Alice advanced two steps towards the bed.

'Stop!' he said. 'Answer me!' This time his voice had risen to a shrill cry. He was quite oblivious to his surroundings,

243

concentrating only on her. 'Hello, George dear,' she said, her voice calm still, her face ignoring the virulence in him. But she was then silent, unable to reply truthfully to a question the answer to which was self-evident. She moved forward another step, and reached out her hand towards the rail at the foot of the bed.

From his throat there came sounds, half sobbing, half incoherent beginnings of words. Then he got out another question. 'Can't you . . . can't you see it's over?' His face was crumpled up with the agony of whatever it was he felt. 'It's finished! I don't want any more of it! I don't want to see you any more!' His mouth was spread in an awful grimace, a ghoulish grin of despair and crumpled capitulation to the tide rising within him.

'Father,' I said. 'Please!' I reached out a hand towards him.

'No!' he wailed. 'No! Keep away from me!' He hunched away his shoulder, withdrawing his hand, leaving me suspended in a futile gesture. But I was not the object of his present fury. Looking back at her, his stern, wildly animated countenance filled with anguish, he spoke again with extraordinary violence. 'It's you! You! You!' The third time he pointed his finger.

Alice was trembling. She had reached out and was gripping the bar of the bed tightly. Her face had gone quite pale. Her lips looked puffed up, and her tongue came out and licked them once or twice as though she was trying to speak. But she could phrase no words together, and just stood her ground under the fury of his eyes.

'Squarely's blessed me for Heaven, the old fool! But I'm on the way down! Do you understand, you stupid woman?'

'You can't,' I said. 'Father, you—'

'Shut up,' he said, sideways to me, his voice almost normal.

Throughout this, movement in the ward had remained completely frozen, including the two nurses. They were young, and probably more frightened than the patients, who at least had come to terms with some of my father's eccentricities. Everybody listened in silence. Seeming to gather himself upward in a kind of regal fury, though in fact it was only his patriarchal head he raised, together with his hand which he pointed towards the door of the ward behind her, he spoke now in a low clear, controlled monotone: 'Go away. I do not want to see you again. You have betrayed me. I don't need you any more.'

I was as frozen as everyone else. I looked at her, but her eyes, wide now with terror and disbelief, were fixed on him. She still trembled, and her small beautifully kept hand gripped tightly on the bar. Then I turned towards him, and his equally fixed gaze and gesture.

Suddenly, outraged at her refusal to obey him, and summoning still further reserves of an energy I could not credit, he emitted in his high-pitched shriek, 'Go! Go! Go!'

Just as she had come, with her handbag, her shopping bag, and her stick, she turned in front of everyone and walked slowly to the door. Before going through it she paused and looked over her shoulder. He was still staring and still pointing. Her eyes were filled with tears, and I thought to myself, quite casually, she must be seeing him all blurred. Then she turned away and went out.

I immediately followed her, and heard behind me as I went the slow, nervous resumption of conversation and movement from the nurses. What could they do, except pretend it had not quite happened? Surely, I must do the same?

'Oh, Alice,' I said, catching up with her, 'how dreadful! He's been terrible all night. They're all heartily sick of him. He's too strong for the morphine or heroin they give him. And it's making him go dotty.' I took her arm and walked with her out into the sunlight.

Her voice was troubled, but she had it more or less under control. 'It's all right, my dear. He didn't know what he was saying. He didn't mean it. You're quite right. It is the drugs. Poor George. He's so frightened. I'll go back in the morning. I brought this for him.' She took out of her bag a bottle of lavender-scented toilet water. 'I saw he'd run out yesterday. Give it to him. With my love.'

I looked at her tearful face and did not know what to say. Attempting to smile at me, and putting her hand on my arm,

245

she said, 'Go back to him. He needs you. And I want to be alone. Go on.'

With little wish to see him just then, I went back. But though I felt he was not asleep, he resolutely refused to open his eyes, and lay back against the pillows with his hands down the bed, motionless, forbidding. He had declined lunch, and when Gladys arrived an hour or more later, he was in exactly the same position. Touching his hand briefly I said to him, 'Goodbye, father. I'll be here tomorrow.'

Only then did he open his eyes. He stared at me, consciously softened his gaze, nodded almost imperceptibly, and then closed them again.

That was the last time I saw him. Gladys went in early the next morning, and I was to follow. But she found him quite frail, though peaceful, and within an hour, his hand resting in hers, his breath weak but tranquil, he died.

I was standing among his roses when the news was phoned through, and Alice came out to tell me. And I have given an account of that. It was the perfectly ordinary, almost idyllic point of departure, when I first considered the nature and substance of my father's life, and came to the conclusion that it had been profoundly and consistently unhappy. But if it was the point of departure, it was not quite the end of the story. One further, fragile exercise in reconstruction awaited me.

Chapter Twelve

[I]

I expected no more surprises. His stoic life had a spartan end, though perhaps more in the austere than the noble sense. Apart from Gladys and Alice, Francis and Melanie, and one or two other relations, no one else turned up at the house for his funeral, and we easily fitted into two cars. We were no more awkward a crew than is usually brought together by such occasions, and my most intense feelings were concerned with the tiny trivialities which I saw as belittling his life. I could not keep my eyes off the pale, plain sides of the coffin on its mobile plinth which, in response to some hidden, electronic message, would shortly grind into action, carrying his mortal remains into the furnace. It was all so logically simple and spiritually empty. It was not here that I would find any symbol to explain his death, or his life; only an embracing ritual, tired, mechanical, to be hurried through. The Reverend Squarely did his best. Perhaps, of all of us, he believed most in my father's spiritual redemption. Yet in my encounters with him I had quite swiftly dismissed any prospect of working out what he did believe, or regarding it as having much importance anyway. The whole business was to be got through as quickly as possible, and from that point of view Mr Squarely performed well.

It was only at the end of the service that I noticed a figure at the back of the crematorium chapel, a woman whom I presumed to be waiting for another, later service. There was an additional exit to the right of the altar, by which mourners would usually leave, so that they need not pass back through the chapel. It was towards this that our group began to make its way. Some instinct, however, held me back, some vague sense of familiarity gleaned from the half-glance over my shoulder. And a more direct look led to recognition: it was Isobel.

I side-stepped, told Mr Squarely I would follow in a moment or two, and went back to where she was still sitting. She turned her calm, level gaze towards me.

'It is Isobel, isn't it? Of course! I'm pleased you came. You must have seen the notice in the paper. Will you come back? For tea?'

She looked at me, smiled, then shook her head. 'I'll just sit here for a while, then go home. I didn't mean to be noticed. I'm surprised you recognised me. It seems a long time.'

'Thirteen years,' I said. 'No one forgets that date, do they?'

'I suppose not. Was it all right at the end? Peaceful? No pain?'

I nodded. 'He was frightened, and he got angry once or twice. His last years were settled. That was Alice in the black straw hat. And it was his wife wearing the headscarf. Her name's Gladys.'

Isobel nodded her comprehension of a whole sweep of events which came down to certain very simple facts as far as she was concerned. There was no need for me to explain more.

She indicated this when she said, 'I had to come, more to say goodbye than anything else.' After a pause, and looking up at me she went on, 'You know, he loved you the best. More than any woman. He loved you in a way that many women long for, as well as wanting the passion. It's a rounding, enfolding love, that takes account of the whole of your life, not just the moments of desire—' she faltered. 'I'm not expressing myself well, but you know what I mean, don't you? You, of all people, can forgive him much for that.'

She spoke so calmly; yet her words had brought me closer to tears than the service, and it was only with difficulty that I said to her in reply, 'I don't need to forgive him, Isobel.'

'Nevertheless, it is probably of his sins that people are thinking.' She said it gently enough. It was the nearest she came to any reference to the others, only one of whom, Alice, had come anywhere near her, and even then, no meeting had taken place. 'You'd better go,' she said. 'The others will be looking for you. I'll sit here for a bit.'

'Isobel,' I said; then paused before going on. 'He always carried a photograph of you in his wallet. Right to the end. You'd written a message on it, with love, and the date.'

'Did he show it to you?'

'No.' I shook my head. 'Never. I found it once beside him, when he was sleeping, and he woke while I was looking at it. I thought he'd be angry. But he spoke of you with great feeling.'

'Perhaps, when you think of it, you would send me a photo of him. A snapshot would do.' She gave me her address which I wrote down.

'Of all the women he ever knew, Isobel, he loved you the best.' I paused, putting away my pen, and the piece of paper with her address on it. 'He told me once you were the most wonderful woman in the world. That was before I met you. He meant it.'

She heard this tribute in silence, and did not respond. I could think of nothing more to add.

'Goodbye,' I said. She made no answer, and I turned and walked back towards the curtained orifice through which my father's body had trundled on its last journey, and out past it, into the September sunlight. I met with no impatience. Mr Squarely was speaking noisily, and to everyone, and it proved difficult, even after I had arrived, to get everyone into cars, our padre included, and back to the house.

Melanie got on well with Gladys and sat with her. Francis organised tea and drinks and sandwiches, and then talked with Gladys's relations, and her few other friends who had come back. It was perhaps right that her comforters should have been more numerous than his mourners; yet, detecting in them something which was hinted at not for the first time, relief at Gladys's liberation, and seeing also the not unnatural degree to which they stuck together as a group, I resented it. But it did emphasise another way of looking at this part of his strange story: Gladys and my father had met in their sixties through a marriage bureau, they had spent a few turbulent but companionable years together, and now it was over. She was being reclaimed by her own. Perhaps even she felt relief as well as pain.

I sat with Alice. We had spoken little since his death, but this was no occasion to discuss either it or her future plans. In fact, she commented on the food and drink, more than on anything else, and seemed studiously to avoid any remarks about Gladys's friends and relations, or about Gladys herself.

'A pity Francis has to rush off,' I said. 'And Melanie's going with him.'

'Probably better that way,' she said. 'And you go tomorrow?'

'I must.'

'Will you come and talk to me this evening?'

I said I would.

Francis joined us. I had described to him, the night before, that last scene in the hospital ward. I wondered now, looking at him, whether he had been right in calling it a form of poetic justice. He said to me, 'What are your plans? Going back tonight?'

I shook my head. 'I'm staying the night. Then I'll go back. Have you work to do?'

'Frantic,' he said. 'Absolutely frantic. Party conference coming up, and chaos seems to reign wherever I look. A firm grip clearly needed, so I must hurry back.'

I left him with Alice, and went to talk to Melanie. She was travelling to London with Francis, and then on the next day to Norwich where she was working in an infant school. Both of them had agreed that I should go through my father's things, though in any case there was virtually nothing to settle, in any conventional sense. It was warm enough to go into the garden, which we did, and I told her about pushing him out in his chair, on its castors, to prune the roses, or at least trim them, as he did, during those final days.

'He was a fine old chap, all told,' Melanie said. 'But I'm not sorry he's dead. It was miserable at the end, wasn't it?'

I hesitated before replying. 'He was in some pain, but drugged of course. I think it was being afraid that made it most difficult.'

'Is that why he sent Alice away?'

'Did Francis tell you?'

She nodded.

'I don't know, Melanie.'

'What happened? He just said he was angry and in pain, and didn't want to see her?'

'That's true. That's what happened.'

A faint, inquisitive smile was on Melanie's lips. 'There must have been more to it than that,' she said. 'Wasn't it a terrible thing to do?'

'I suppose it was.'

'Francis thinks it was just.'

I wondered how much Francis had said. I did not know what to tell my sister. I had no perception, really, of how she viewed 'the fine old chap' as she described him, but the disturbing thought was gathering dimension in my mind that her feelings, whatever they were, must almost certainly be very different from my own. For what was he to her, looking back over thirty years? What residual, stored-up love could she recover? And from where? She had no need to make amendments or adjustments in her recollections of him. Indifference did the task for her; his indifference to start with, in letting her pass from him as a child and become adopted; her indifference later, when there seemed to be no particular use or purpose in resuming the family tie in other than a relaxed and easy, off-hand way as familiar friends. While, superficially, we were there for a common purpose, and with shared feelings, perhaps there existed a whole set of differences between us, unexplored, and beyond the range, now, of exploration. Between Melanie and myself, over the years, a subtle barrier had been built; between Francis and myself a barrier as well, though different. And being together, at these final obsequies, confirmed rather than softened the lines of demarcation between us all.

251

Not telling Melanie the truth, as I thought it to be, was a trivial evasion in itself. Yet when I reasoned it out in my own mind I realised that it defined him as a different character for each of us, and was therefore more profound in what it meant than in what was said. When I then considered Gladys and Alice, the same rule applied. Little nuances of difference emerged between us in how we interpreted his actions and feelings. He was not half-crazed with heroin when he rejected Alice; he rejected her because he had no further use for her, did not love her, and had always been bored by her. And no matter what I might feel for her, and against him for his attitude towards her; and no matter what I might have done about it in all the long years in which she had been involved with us both, long enough to give her most special status; and no matter how much regret and pity about the past might swirl around us like a confusing river mist; the simple and quite pitiless truth stared forth from his savage disposition and his savage final acts as an inescapable argument setting forth exactly how it was.

Her tears tried to mend this, but could not. Thirty years, half an adult lifetime, had been dismissed in a moment of petulant anger. And if I did not love him, I would have hated him for that. After all, Alice was the only woman to have played a lasting part in my own growing up, from early childhood into my twenties. Though the mature mind, judging from outside, might condemn his savagery deriving from thoughtless cruelty and selfishness, there was an animal justice in his act, breathtaking in its severity, yet driving home the message of human isolation.

With Gladys, nature prevailed in a mundane way. She had married an old man for company, and out of very contained affection. She had known he was sick; her professional skill had led her to recognise, within him, that the time clock of his dissolution had started already when they met, and had been accelerated by bouts of drinking in old age which annoyed her almost to the point of breaking up their marriage. She had stuck it out, for company, for affection, for love. And his response to that had not been bad. But her essential reaction to his death was relief. She was free to rejoin her own family. They certainly viewed it that way, and had always looked on him as both a physical and a moral burden. Perhaps rightly.

So his death did not reconcile and draw together. It did the opposite. It dispersed: Gladys to her own kind; Alice to a permanent loneliness, a self-imposed isolation conditioned by years of setting aside her normal friends and gregarious pursuits in order to devote her life to him. Metaphorically, Melanie left with a shrug of her shoulders, ultimately dismissive of him. And Francis went back to his work with renewed energy amid the pressures which permanently controlled his frantic activity.

We went for a walk together before the taxi came to take himself and Melanie to the train. She remained in the cottage, helping to clear up. Out in the evening sun, on the country road, stepping along together and discussing what Alice and Gladys would do, what father's life added up to, what Melanie had felt, and in the end coming round to ourselves, I voiced the feeling that had been going through me about everyone being dispersed by his death.

He nodded. 'It's a relief, really.'

'I don't mean that,' I said. 'It is a relief. But you know how people say, it'll bring us together, or we must stick together. What I feel is the opposite. It pushes us apart.'

He thought about that, then he said, 'It does neither. He was there. He's gone. We go on as before.'

'Is there no redemption?'

'What do you want to redeem?'

I paused. 'His life, I suppose.'

'Do you mean in the religious sense?' He smiled his amazement. 'Do you want to *save* him? Are you thinking of more permanent, eternal fires than those at the crematorium?' He had stopped and was staring at me. A slight smile hovered around his lips.

I shook my head. 'Not in the religious sense. No. That's not what I mean. I mean in the sense of something being passed on. To us. To you. To me.'

He shrugged his shoulders, and set off again along the road.

I wondered if there was something I could tell him that would make him see the point on which my own grasp seemed uncertain.

'Did you notice the woman sitting at the back of the chapel?'

'Yes. Who was she? I took her to be a stranger, curious in the way people can be about death.'

'It was Isobel. Father lived with her in the early sixties. They were very much in love.'

'Mm. Seem to remember something about her. Children, weren't there? Is that what went wrong?'

'Not exactly,' I said. I paused. 'Funny, her turning up, though.'

'Must have seen it in the *Telegraph*.'

In the words I had exchanged with her there had seemed to be, even if clumsily expressed, a crystalline quality about the understanding which she and I had shared. Yet the idea of getting this across to Francis had to be dismissed, even as I contemplated it. It would take eternity. I remembered that sense of danger I had felt, the previous summer, when he and I had gone back to Coppinger. He had viewed things differently then. He had viewed everything differently. And now this would be different. It would foment conflict between us in interpreting what he was, and why. It would upset the delicate balance within me of judgments and reconstructions, of siftings and accumulations.

I turned back along the road. 'I don't really know what I mean,' I said. 'You see, the funeral wasn't upsetting *enough*. I was glad when he died. I was glad when his body was burnt. I was glad to think of his ashes scattered over the grass in Somerset. And after all that, what is there to be sorry about, or sad about, except his whole life? What's the sense of it?'

He walked along beside me, stiff and silent.

'I want to talk to him,' I said. 'I want to ring him up and tell him how it went. I can see him, with a smile on his lips, winking at me. Can't you? Don't you want to do the same?'

Francis stared ahead of him. He nodded his head in general agreement, but did not speak.

'I want to believe that something is good in him, and fine and noble.'

'Difficult,' Francis said.

There was nothing more I could say, and we left it at that. The taxi came, and he and Melanie departed. With Francis, the tussle within his heart to reconcile his instincts with his judgments was deeper and more prolonged. I do not know whether it is over yet. Apart from the conversation we had on the afternoon of the funeral, we never really talked about it again. We talked about him, of course. We talked about ourselves. But never once did we bring together the two, and make what would amount to a confession of failure, or inadequacy, in the mutual feelings that run like an unbroken thread through one's life, all of one's life, long after the death of a parent. The cord is there, always. It is woven from many strands; the silk of love is mixed with the hempen strength of kind; strands of duty, respect, jealousy, fear, even hate, may play a part. And for each person it is different. And the difference barricades us within our collective perceptions, so that they weave together undisturbed by intrusion or challenge.

The departure of Francis with Melanie was a relief. Alice went back to her part of the house, and Gladys and I sat for a while, tired and empty. Sitting there in the stillness, with nothing left to say, and staring at each other, the sense of his presence was suddenly overwhelming, all over again. I could smell the lavender water pervading the air. I was about to repeat the words I had said to Francis, about wanting to tell him how his own funeral had gone, when I noticed that tears were running down Gladys's cheeks.

'It's a relief it's over,' I said. 'You mustn't cry.'

'It is a relief,' she said. 'It's just I shall miss him so much. He was an awful bully. He led me such a dance. I don't know what I got out of it, him heaving and bubbling and gasping away. Then shouting at me. Years since he was any good in bed. And he could be so angry. You wouldn't believe the things he said and did. But I shall miss him. I'd rather have all that, and worse, than the emptiness. He was the best I ever had.' Suddenly, through her tears, she laughed. 'I shouldn't compare him with the others, should I? Not to

255

you, anyway. But I seem to pick casualties. It's my problem. My first husband, Reginald, was much older than me, and he was an invalid. Then there was Arthur. He was a nervy one. More my own age, and full of humour. Very different from Fred. A dark one, Fred was.' She had already begun the process of folding away and putting into store, beside the memories of other men, the admittedly rather special feelings she had about George. It was an advantage she had over Alice. In both cases Time was being encouraged to amend, even to heal, Truth.

She wiped her eyes. 'I'll see about supper,' she said.

'I'm not hungry,' I said.

'It'll give me something to do.' She blew her nose and got to her feet. 'You won't forget the case? I don't want to have to sort it,' she added.

'I'll do it tonight. I have to go and see Alice. She asked me.'

Since his death Alice had behaved in a trance-like manner. She had seemed frozen by it, moving, if anything, more stiffly about the house, her little bouts of weeping shaken off and dismissed as weakness, since his death had been 'a merciful release'. I had not spoken about the final episode in the hospital at any stage, and now thought that it would not come up, but be folded away by us both. I was therefore surprised when she raised it with me.

'I don't want you to think badly of him,' she said. 'Shouting at me, the way he did, and sending me away.' She looked at me, calm now, though evidence of her tears was still to be seen in her eyes and slightly puffed cheeks.

'He shouldn't have done it, Alice.'

'He didn't mean it,' she said. 'He still loved me, in his own way. It was just the drugs they were giving him. Heroin, morphine, they made him unbalanced, and it was that. It tipped his mind against me, because I have been with him the longest.' She said this with a note of pride in her voice.

'You're right, of course,' I said. 'That does explain it.' I paused. 'It was cruel of him, even so.'

'He was a cruel man.'

'And you never minded that enough to break with him?'

'I could not have done it. Deep down, I believed he loved me. He needed me, all along.'

'Yes. He did. He needed you.'

'You must retain your respect for him.'

'There's no question of that.'

'I don't know how I shall cope with the garden.'

'You're quite good at coping, Alice,' I said, and I was conscious of the irony in my words. Already, she had woven for herself the material of necessary deception on which her life might now depend. In this she differed, fundamentally, from Gladys, and I could see no future in them staying together. They could not agree on, nor ever share, the memory they had, since it contained more of dispute and bitterness between them than it did goodness deriving from him. But I wanted to change the subject. 'Will you stay here?' I asked.

'It is my home. Why should I move?'

'And Gladys?'

'I won't put her out. If she wants to stay, she can.'

'Will you go away? For a break?'

She shook her head. 'If you ever need to get away from London,' she said. 'If you want to come down here, there'll always be room. I'd love to see you, from time to time. In fact, as often as you want. And Clare as well.' She paused. 'I hope she understands.'

'It's not a problem,' I said.

[III]

I left the sorting of his papers until they had gone to bed, and the cottage was quiet. And it was then that I came across the diary. Almost by accident, for the little volume, when I found it, was not really a diary at all, but a small blue notebook which had cost ninepence, and looked as though it might have been bought to list groceries. The price, in pencil, was still written on the back page. It was not with the other diaries, which had been bundled together with thick rubber bands and put into an old leather case, but on its own, or at least, with a curious assembly of what at first appeared no more than rubbish, including used Christmas wrappings, greetings cards, labels from gifts and newspaper cuttings, including one about an inquest held at Coppinger twenty-five years earlier. I had sorted almost everything else, including the main bundle of diaries, and I had been disappointed by the messiness of it all. Generally speaking, he was a diarist of the worst kind, as far as posterity went. No flavour of his days emerged from the lists and reminders, the bald facts about letters written and received, the meetings with potential employers or with women, the changes of address which recorded his nomadic existence.

I am talking of diaries covering more than a quarter of a century, kept for I know not what reason, deposited so carefully in this case, and probably not looked at for years before his death, if, indeed, he had ever gone back to them at all.

If I understand him only a little, they represented frail order in the midst of widespread chaos. And they were looked upon by him in just that light. Carefully kept, never scrutinised, they were 'the record', like the log of a ship, in which time and position were paramount. Their existence, their survival, provided the evidence of one man's disposition in time, within the universe. But as I had turned the pages of first one, and then another, jumping back as far as the end of the war, the occasional flashes of insight that came to me from brief phrases like 'Finished with Ursula. *No Use*' or 'I have lost Isobel. I have let her down. Same as ever' or 'Row with the Wains. My fault. *Exeunt Omnes*', I realised that for him to have the logbooks safely filed away was one thing, but for him to consult them with anything but anguish and regret would have been virtually impossible.

So that when I opened the blue notebook, and saw written across the top line the words 'The Perfect Weekend', carefully underlined, I hesitated over something quite different from anything else in his 'effects', as they are most properly called.

I give what he wrote:

Easter, 1944
April 8th Saturday

258

'3.³⁰ a.m. Dressed and after a cup of tea caught the 4.²³ from Kent House Station arriving Victoria 4.⁴⁵. Walked to Paddington and arrived 10 minutes before the train started at 5.³⁰. I ran a certain amount of the way through Hyde Park as I thought I should be late. Changed at Didcot about 7 o'clock into a slow train to Oxford, stopping at Radley. The train from Oxford arrived at Coppinger at 9 o'clock. Walked from station through village to school, about two miles, signposted. Pleasant morning, stepped it out and arrived before 10 o'clock. The two boys came running out to meet me from their house. They must have been watching from a window. They look fit and healthy and happy.'

I read on through a factual description of the school, then of the village and of finding a place to stay, and then of the rest of that, his first day at Coppinger, in which we went by local train to the nearest town to do shopping and have tea. 'I had a pint of beer at the Blue Lion and then we walked back across the fields—the weather was warm and the walk was quiet, ideal and happy.'

He wrote details about the old village house in which he was staying and the family, 'Faith' who had a pony, 'David' who was mad about tennis, 'Jill' who was the youngest.

April 9th Sunday
Heard the cuckoo at 7.⁴⁵ a.m.
Dressed by 8 o'clock.
When David and his father came back from early service we had breakfast:

> Porridge cream and plenty of sugar
> 2 fried eggs, fried bread
> 4 rashers bacon (own pig)
> Toast
> Home made marmalade

Arrived at school at 10.³⁰ when the two boys and I slowly walked to Chapel which lasted from 11.⁰⁰ to 11.⁵⁵. We all three sang the hymns and Psalms and I thoroughly enjoyed it—they sing up well, both of

them. Happy atmosphere. Weather showery, but not
depressing.

Both that day and the next were spent in walking, and from
his brief outline of routes taken I could recall the precise
topography of that weekend. At eight years old I must have
been exhausted by it all, and I smiled when he referred to
giving me rides on his back 'as he occasionally thought he
was tired—perhaps he liked the rides!' He also mentioned
Francis and me singing for him. We must have given a brief
recital of campfire songs, and he recorded a few lines of one
of them, a disembodied quotation, without comment:

> *Seven for the seven stars in the sky,*
> *And six for the six proud walkers;*
> *Five for the cymbals at your door*
> *And four for the gospel makers;*
> *Three, three the rivals,*
> *Two, two the lily-white boys, clothed all in gree-en-oh,*
> *One is one and all alone, and*
> *ever more shall be so*

That last day, he recorded, 'was sunny and bright'. There
was no reference to the job he was then doing, but it was
necessary to depart after lunch, and he recorded the fact of
the three of us walking as far as the village and then saying
goodbye.

'So ended a perfect weekend,' he wrote, 'one of the
happiest times of my life—The boys are so wonderful and
loyal to me that they deserve a better father and I pray
that they will get on in life and have many happy days and
years—Francis is on my mind as he worries greatly about
his work. He seems to miss his mother.' (Here the word
'He' had been crossed out.) 'They both have fine voices,
and sing well.'

I turned over the pages which followed. They covered two
further visits he paid to Coppinger that year, in July and
October. They covered visits at Easter, in June, in August,
in September and in December of the following year. He
spent Christmas that year near the school, in which we two

boys stayed. There was no indication of why we could not go home, but it was not an unusual occurrence, and in fact it was clear from what he wrote that there were many other boys at Coppinger then, something I vaguely recalled anyway and related now to his more precise detail.

In mid-1946 the entries stopped, abruptly, at the conclusion of a visit which was certainly not his last. The remaining pages were blank. I read my father's last entry. 'This will very likely be the last time together, as Francis leaves Coppinger in the autumn. This is the tenth visit I have made. Every time they have been the happiest days of my life. And now I can only hope for a better future for all of us, with God's help. God help us all and guide us in our future actions. Goodbye, my dear sons. Life is a series of heartbreaks. May we all be happy together some day. Please God you both make good.'

I read the whole journal through, not without feelings of the most acute anguish. Many times through it he used the word 'happy', and wrote of happiness. It seemed to obsess him and at the same time elude him. It was as if this small, stubby blue notebook was in fact a passport which he had repeatedly used to travel into a realm where people lived happily together and where he could join in for given periods of time, the details of which were recorded on the pages like endorsements or visas. He came out of unknown darkness, in London or other cities. He came from unspecified, probably boring employment, to which he had to get back. He came from 'relationships' which were touched upon, obliquely, in brief references like 'Wrote to C' or 'Sent card to Dorothy'. But throughout the logbook covering those visits to Coppinger it was as if he firmly cut the lines between his ordinary life and the brief idyllic weekends he spent with us.

The writing had a consciously positive ring to it. Obviously entered up in the evening or in the morning, within the confines of his skill it was both vivid and fluent. And in addition deeply felt. Yet it was the isolation that fixed itself in my mind. Austere as the little book was, it was special to Coppinger, and its *Leitmotif* was happiness. It was his passport to the territory where happiness is found, and it was valid for just two years. Within those two years it covered, in days, only slightly more than a month. On each occasion some reference, no matter how fleeting, indicated the sharp, keen sense of the time passing when he was with us and of it being of a special, benign character. At the latter end, in the entry for September, 1945, he wrote on the last day of one visit how I had been 'a little tearful' at the coming departure. It was again when we had gone out walking, this time along the river valley below the school which I loved best of all, and which even then he identified, in those pages, as mine. He wrote then: 'On the way we ate the cake which Miss Brooks had bought at the Sale of Work. It was very good. She looks after me well. Had a pleasant afternoon talking about old times. And I wonder to myself, will it come right, and will we all be happy together some day?'

By that stage in my reading I had a clear image of him as he then had been. It derived forcefully from that first page, him running through the trees of Hyde Park on his way from Victoria to Paddington. He had told me many times about it, so that it was in no sense new. Yet the way it was written had a spartan quality which fitted in with the essential journey he was making, the first of so many, from different places, to a place he was turning into his own enforced heartland. And in each of them, and in his faithful record, there remained this stripped quality of spartan austerity and clear direction.

Now, a second image was beginning to emerge: of us. I could visualise, where he wrote of us 'talking of old times', Francis and myself with him, on the banks of the stream, under the willows, watching the slow twisting waters which fed the Evenlode and then the Thames, talking about life as it had been before the death of my mother, and back in time even earlier. I would have been nine years old, Francis fourteen, and my father in his mid-forties. I would soon be as old as he had been, and he was now only scattered ash.

Francis had departed, so had Melanie. And here was I, being transported back by means of strange, remote images, unanswered and unanswerable questions, and small touches of penetrating reality.

All the time it forced me down a road that I would rather not have taken, to a conclusion about him at which I would

262

rather not have arrived. It was contained in this Greek view of happiness, quite different, I think, from our own twentieth-century view, which is that we can snatch it in fragments or sections or periods of life. The Greeks saw happiness austerely, as a lifetime's achievement, a crown that could only be awarded after death. We treat it too much as he did, as though it were some kind of idyllic island territory in the endless grey sea of indifferent existence. He travelled to it each time with his passport in his hand, and checked in through severe controls where everything was scrutinised to ensure that he qualified. Obviously, for a time, he did. And with a stabbing, painful humility I saw myself in the page of that notebook, a frail eight-year-old, sickly, homesick, missing him, greeting his visits with unrestrained joy, and investing them with incorruptible qualities which he called happiness. I question his definition, holding to the Greek view. They saw it as a sum of experience, lifelong. 'Call no man happy till he dies; he is at best but fortunate.' And that did make sense. But the sense it made was hard and painful. If it went wrong, and stayed wrong, what was left? An unhappy man? An unhappy life? Was it a bearable conclusion?

He was dead, of course, now; so did it matter? Should not I fold away all the papers and diaries, and burn them? I could then remember him for the good side of his character, the handsome, passionate man whose indelible mark had been left on so many people; the towering father who had lavished love on me in his eccentric, uneven way; I would be free to imagine the wistful boy, in Folkestone, under the privet hedge, preparing for life; the young naval officer whose career, traced in meticulous detail in one of the papers before me from ship to ship between 1914 and 1926, ending with an abrupt axe-cut of fate; the lost years of the Great Depression and the thirties, the struggle to hold together with my mother, as first Francis and then myself, and then Melanie were brought into the world; and that was only half his life! Yet if I did that, if I destroyed it all, would it not be a lie? Ingrained within his features, now vanquished by fire, yet for me as permanent as those of the water seller of Seville, was a sum of conclusions which made painful sense.

263

With his hand on the pitcher, and his fingers grasping the goblet brimful of water, the ripe fig floating within it, was that old man any wiser or better? Had he detected a greater, more profound truth?

Puzzle and epiphany, decay and strength, the refinement, through time, of both good and bad; it was my sense of this, of the fairness of it to him, that salvaged the documents. That, of course, was a trivial matter. A long-since retired naval officer, living in a Somerset cottage with his fourth wife, with a ribbon of mistakes and failures behind him, and death waiting ahead of him, how could this record have more than a transient relevance, even to those who loved him? No, it was not the documents; it was the decision to recover and explore by unlocking the secret of his unhappiness that mattered, for in my mind the conscious act set in motion a subconscious force, the final fruits of which are set before you in these pages. I was tired, and sad. I went out into the garden.

Orion flamed in the sky. Set in the panoply of Heaven it should have belittled all thoughts of him and his unhappy life. It did the reverse. He assumed in my mind the fixed proportions of a star. His finite life was over. No further act could change the disposition of all the things he had done. Yet, like some mythic hero, shaking off mortal coils, and stepping away from the surface of the world to join himself to the great frieze of legend nightly spread before us across the skies, my father had already assembled the chosen garb, and clutched in his hand the club with which he would defend his acts and go roaring on through eternity. He was Orion, mighty hunter, of great beauty and gigantic strength.

Images streamed across the star-studded firmament, his stars, his life, his quest for happiness. And though they contained anguish and terror and pain, and though the quest had faltered and failed many, many years before, and though all the other people who were casualties seemed to litter the past, I nevertheless felt a warm protective shield surrounding me and lifting me up above the torrents. I was still protected, as I had been throughout my childhood, by the shield of his love. It would go on protecting me until my death. Like a deposit of gold that cannot be touched, unchanging and incorruptible, it would be set against the debt of other weaknesses: he had enriched me for life by it. Whatever partial measurement I could make of its deployment towards others, I was firmly assured of the overwhelming part love had played in shaping my own existence. In that it was redemptive.

[IV]

I was left, in the end, only with him. I was isolated within my recollection of his life, and therefore my sense of his character. Standing out under the stars, that September night, with the scent of roses around me, and the stillness of the countryside disturbed only by the distant barking of a dog, I felt tired but at peace. All the impulses deriving from him, from my memory of him, and from the painful exercise of comparing it with the experience of others close to me, were reconciled or at least at rest. And the sorting out of his diaries and other papers had resulted in just a few tidy piles of things inside the cottage, ready for me to take with me when I left the next morning. Among the discoveries there had been a certain number of photographs. And among these photographs there had been one of him beside a pond as a child caught in the moment of launching a model boat. In his lifetime I had never seen it. He had hidden it away for nameless reasons, and only after his death was it there, with the diaries and other papers. There were photographs, too, of him as a young lieutenant in the navy, on board ship, in tropical kit, with a pipe in his hand, with a smile on his handsome face. Why were all of these put away, hidden from his and the world's gaze?

Gathered together inside the house, neatly sorted, preserved from the fire, they presented him to me in a multitude of guises within which there still seemed to be contained that immense vigour, that passion which was his most abiding characteristic and the justification for his perpetual claim that he would live forever. His unhappiness has become for me a symbol of the perpetual possibility hanging over everyone. It remains as real to me now as when first it emerged, dimly, bit by bit, during that final summer. It will remain with me till I die. Yet though it seared his heart, all his life long, it is nevertheless redeemed by the erratic love which gave me certainty amid the confusion of being his son. So that the certainty he could never give to his own life he passed on to me. And in doing so he achieved one of those strange portions of immortality of which every parent can be sure. And he knew. Of that I feel certain. When I placed the privet flower upon his dying breast, encouraging his mind to reach back, through memory, to his own childhood, and then forward again to the present, mine and his, about which there was nothing more to say, I had closed with him in a disembodied embrace for the last time.

I have tried to put it higher than that. I have tried to give him more. I have tried, in my own fashion, to ennoble him. But perhaps it was neither necessary, nor ever possible. Declaring all his life that he would never grow old, that he was immortal, he nevertheless did grow old, and die. And his body was burned, and the ashes scattered, so that nothing was left. Only in my own mind was I able to respond to the wish that had inspired him once, yet humbled him in the end, the wish for immortality in which he had believed with such natural, blind passion, the wish to which I could reply, one last time, by whispering to the vacant, star-studded September night what he had so often declared, 'George, live for ever!'